MWD

Hell Is Coming Home

BRIAN DAVID JOHNSON

and

JAN EGLESON

illustrated by

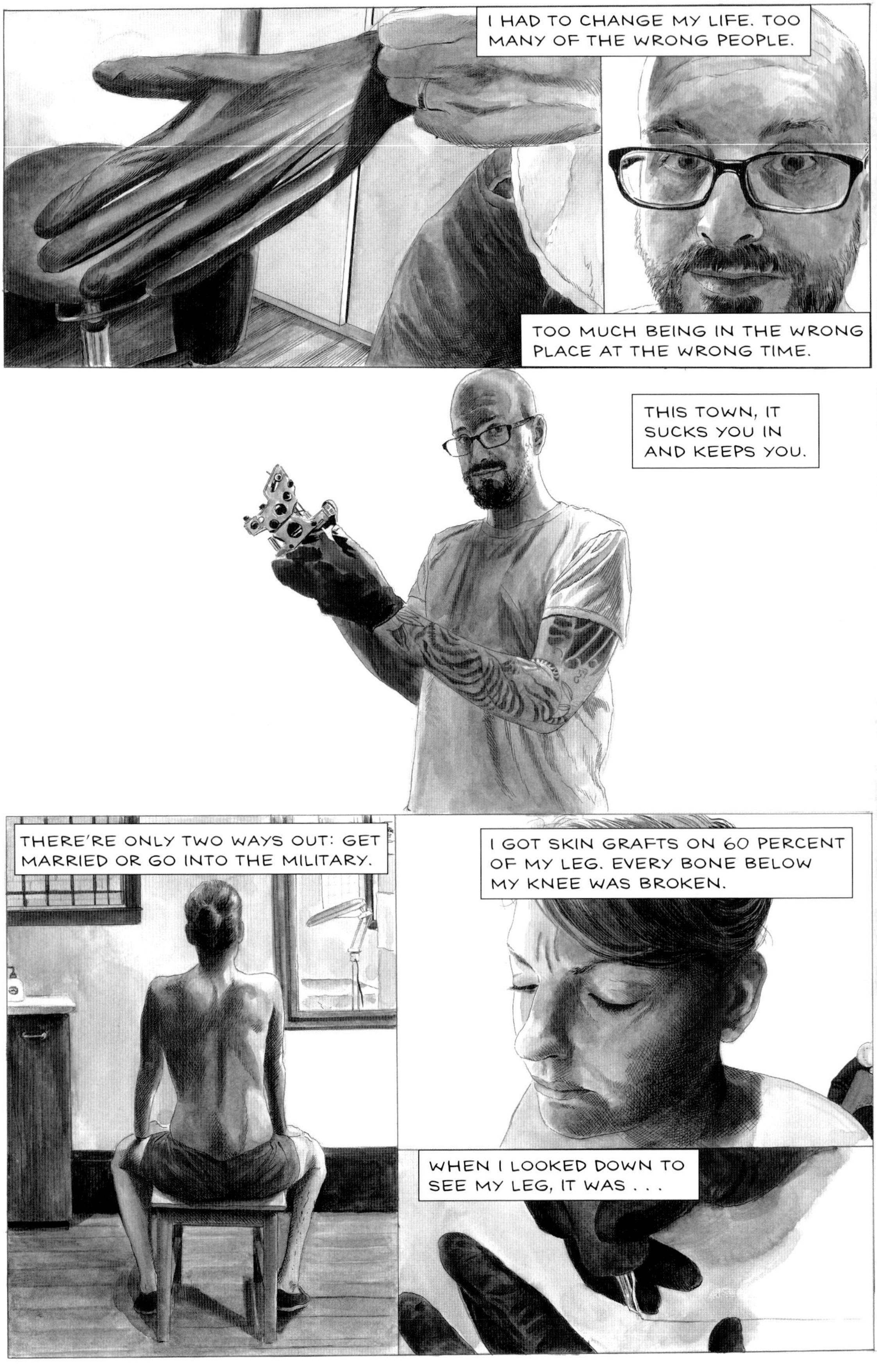
I HAD TO CHANGE MY LIFE. TOO MANY OF THE WRONG PEOPLE.
TOO MUCH BEING IN THE WRONG PLACE AT THE WRONG TIME.
THIS TOWN, IT SUCKS YOU IN AND KEEPS YOU.
THERE'RE ONLY TWO WAYS OUT: GET MARRIED OR GO INTO THE MILITARY.
I GOT SKIN GRAFTS ON 60 PERCENT OF MY LEG. EVERY BONE BELOW MY KNEE WAS BROKEN.
WHEN I LOOKED DOWN TO SEE MY LEG, IT WAS . . .

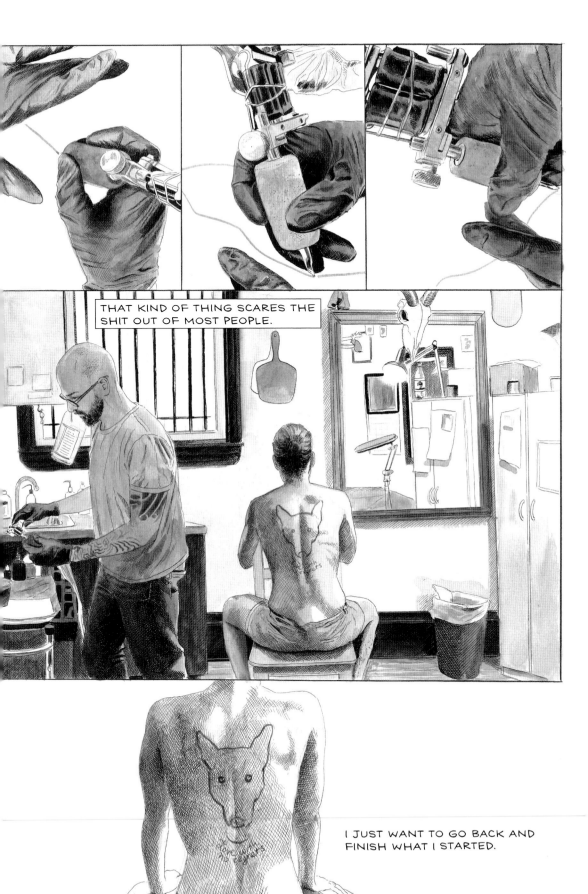

THAT KIND OF THING SCARES THE SHIT OUT OF MOST PEOPLE.

I JUST WANT TO GO BACK AND FINISH WHAT I STARTED.

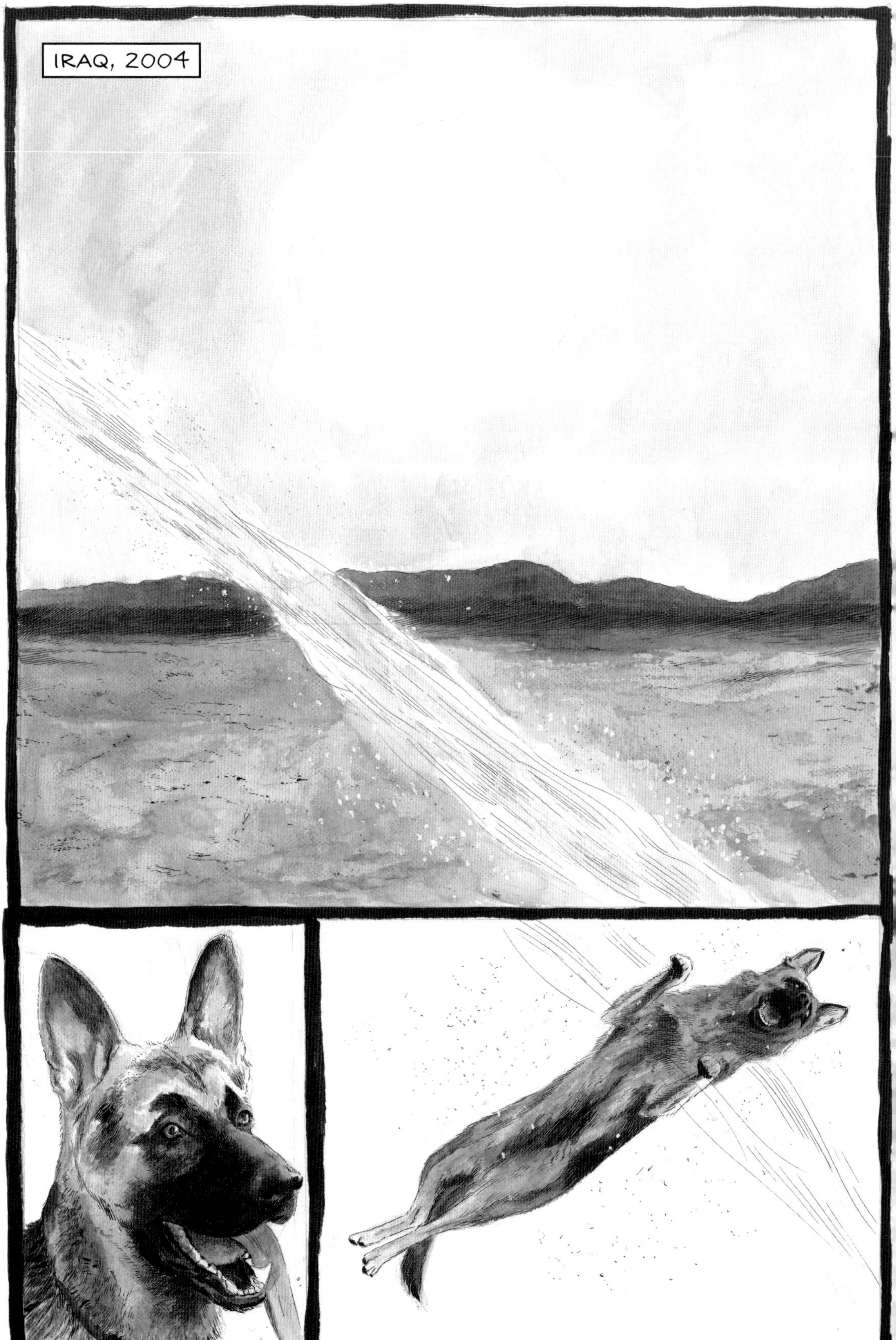
IRAQ, 2004

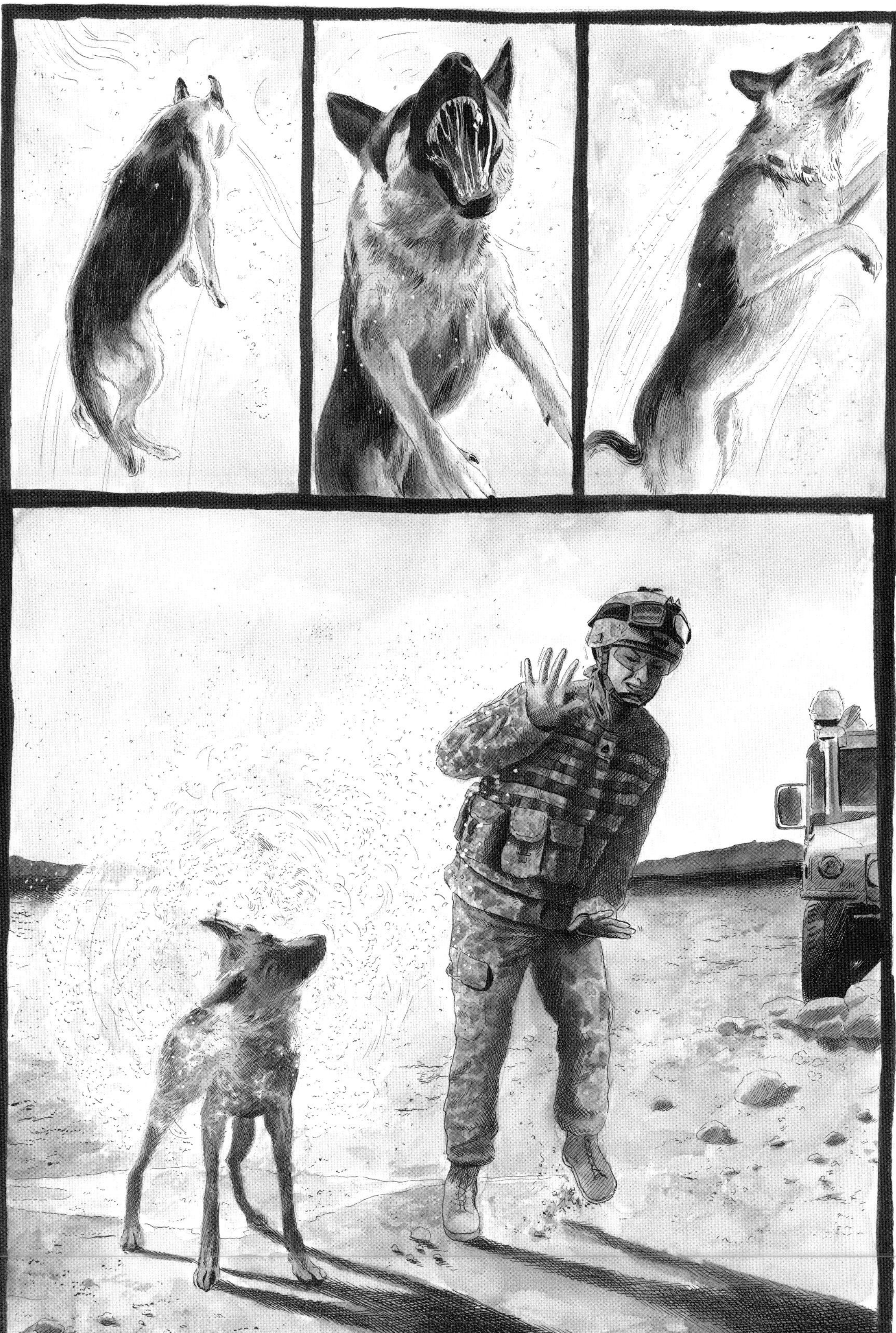

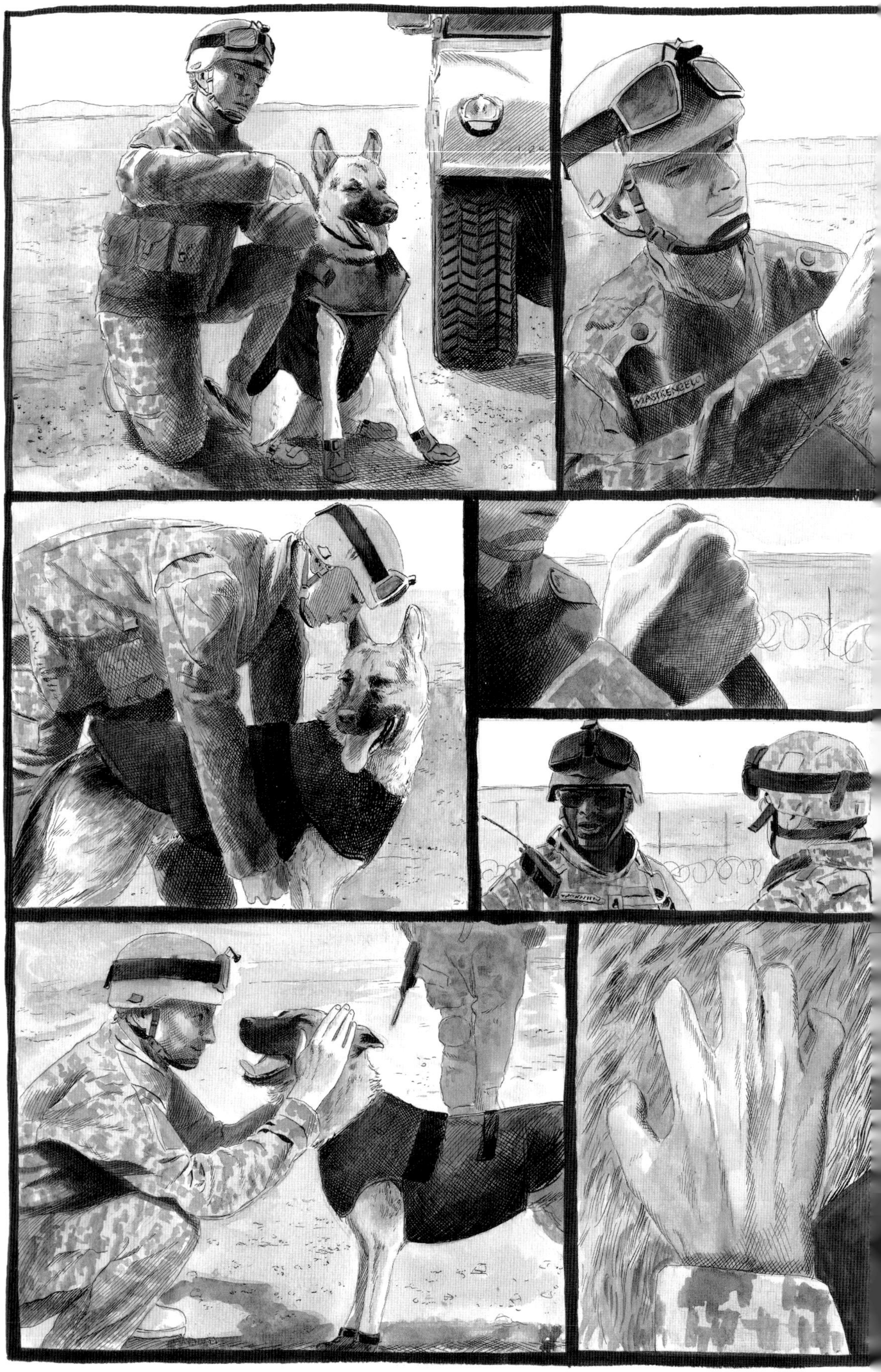
MASTRENGELO

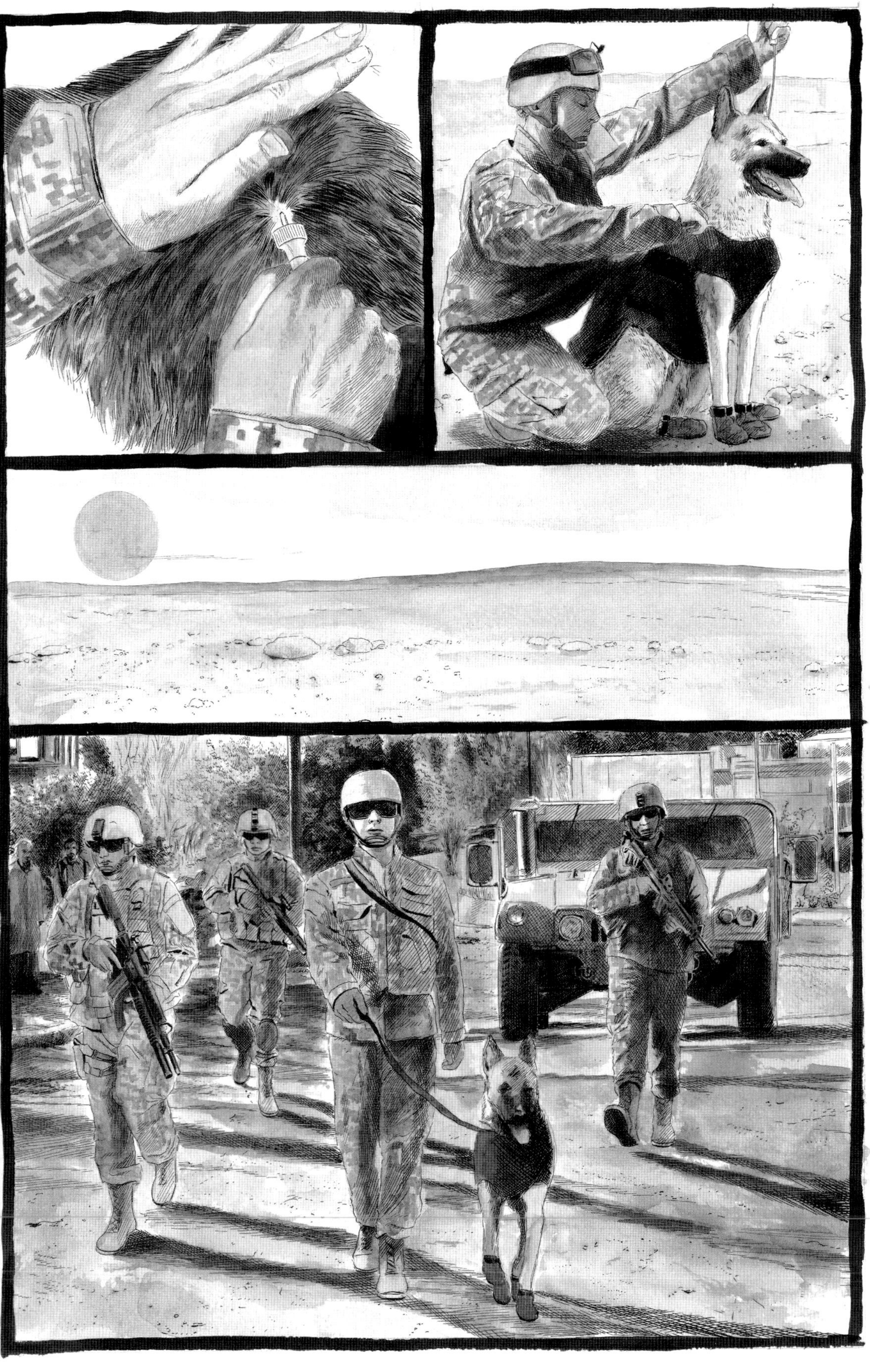

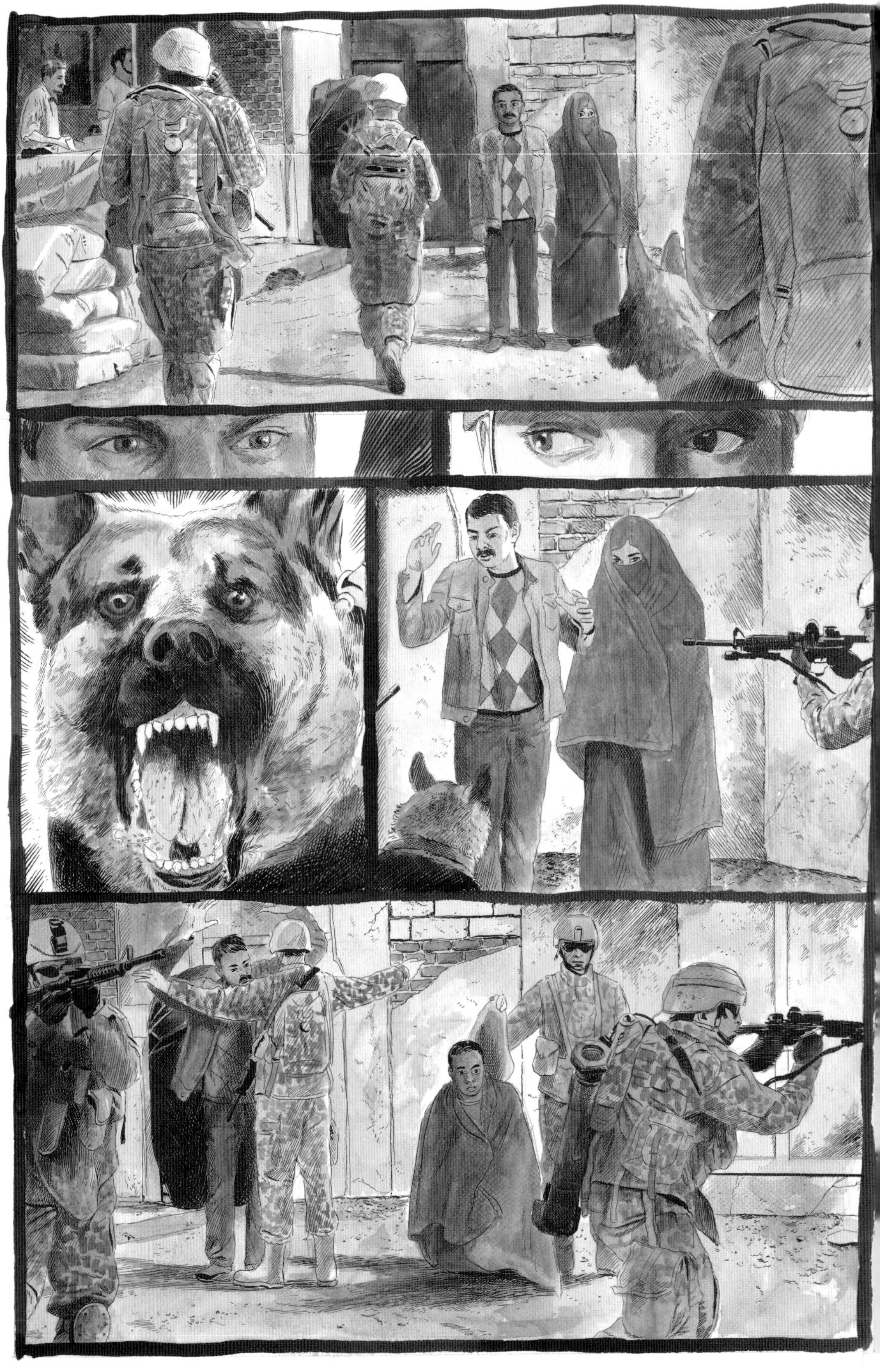

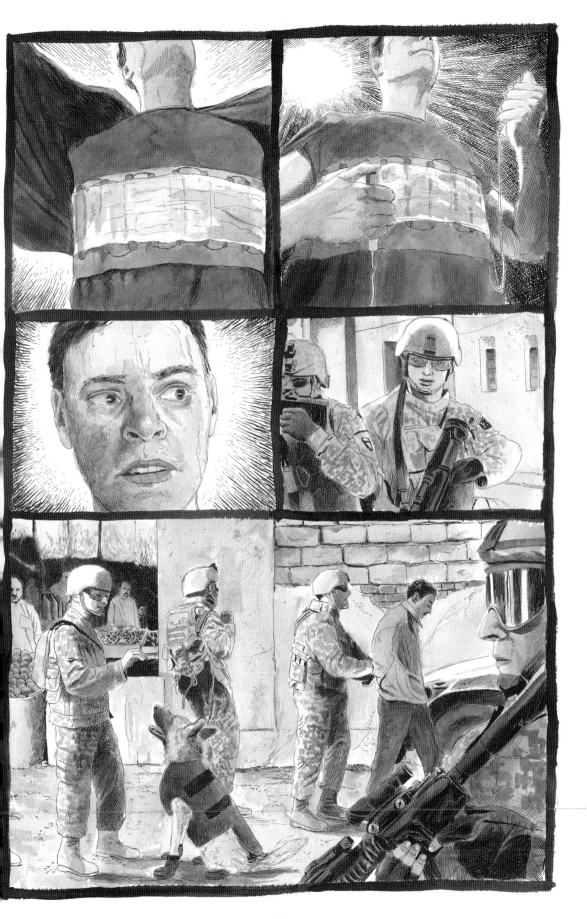

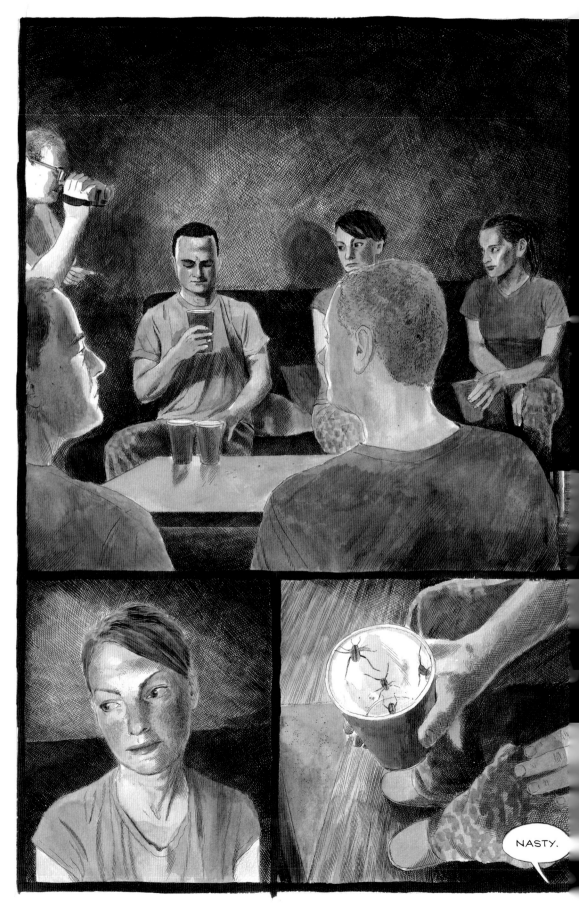

NASTY.

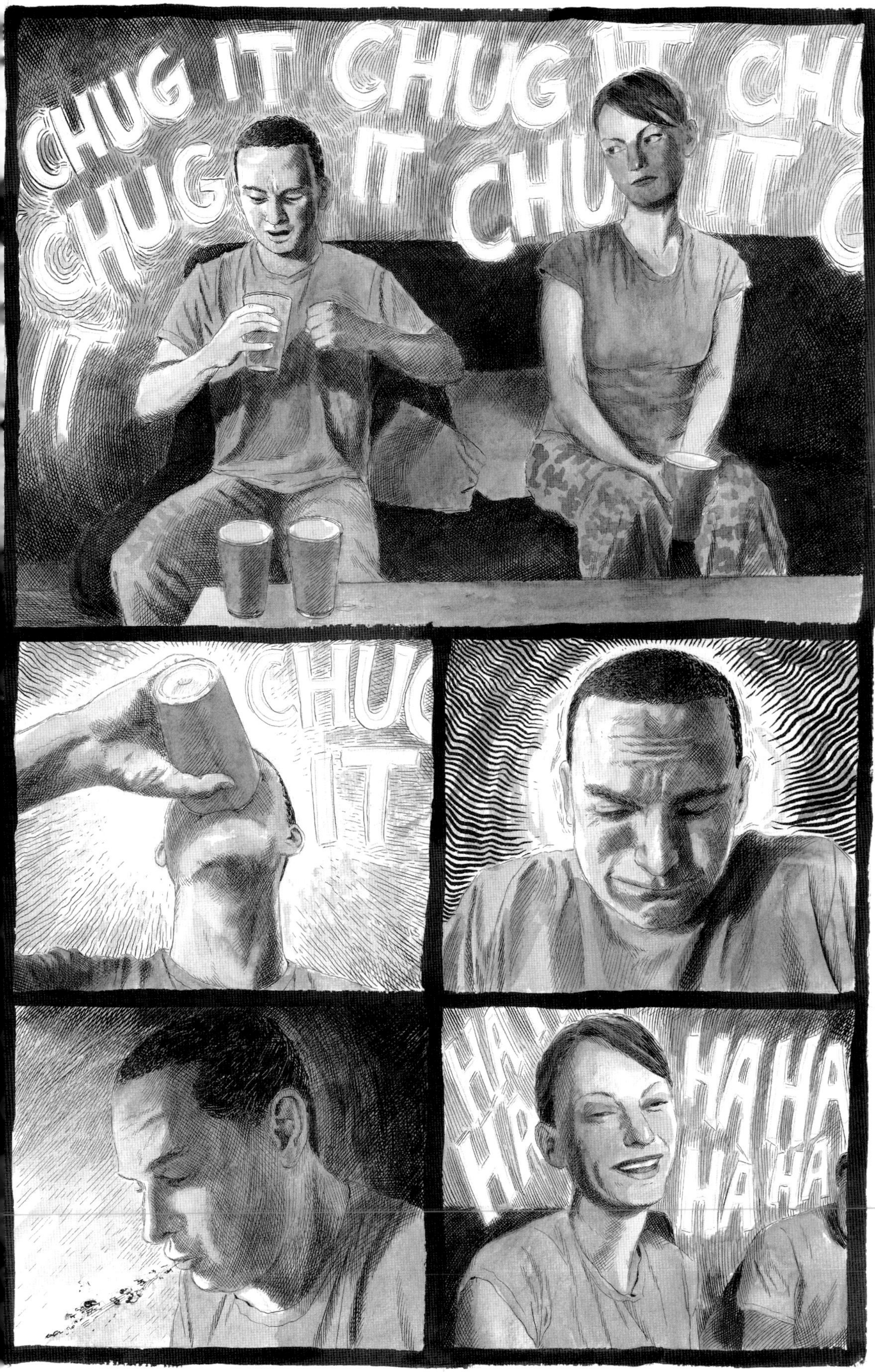
CHUG IT CHUG IT CHUG IT CHUG IT CHUG IT CHU
CHUG IT
HAHAHAHAHAHA

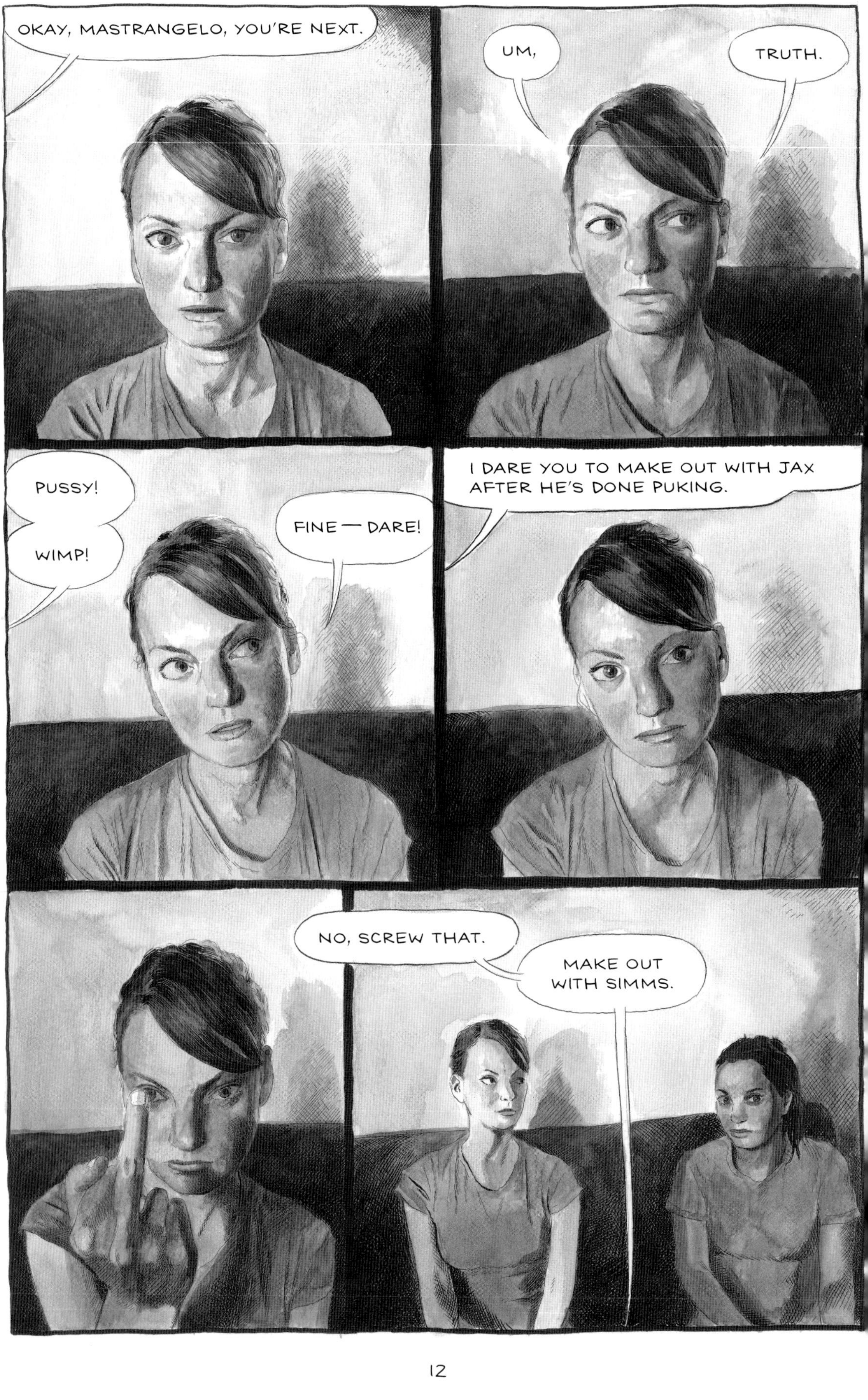
OKAY, MASTRANGELO, YOU'RE NEXT.
UM,
TRUTH.
PUSSY!
WIMP!
FINE — DARE!
I DARE YOU TO MAKE OUT WITH JAX AFTER HE'S DONE PUKING.
NO, SCREW THAT.
MAKE OUT WITH SIMMS.

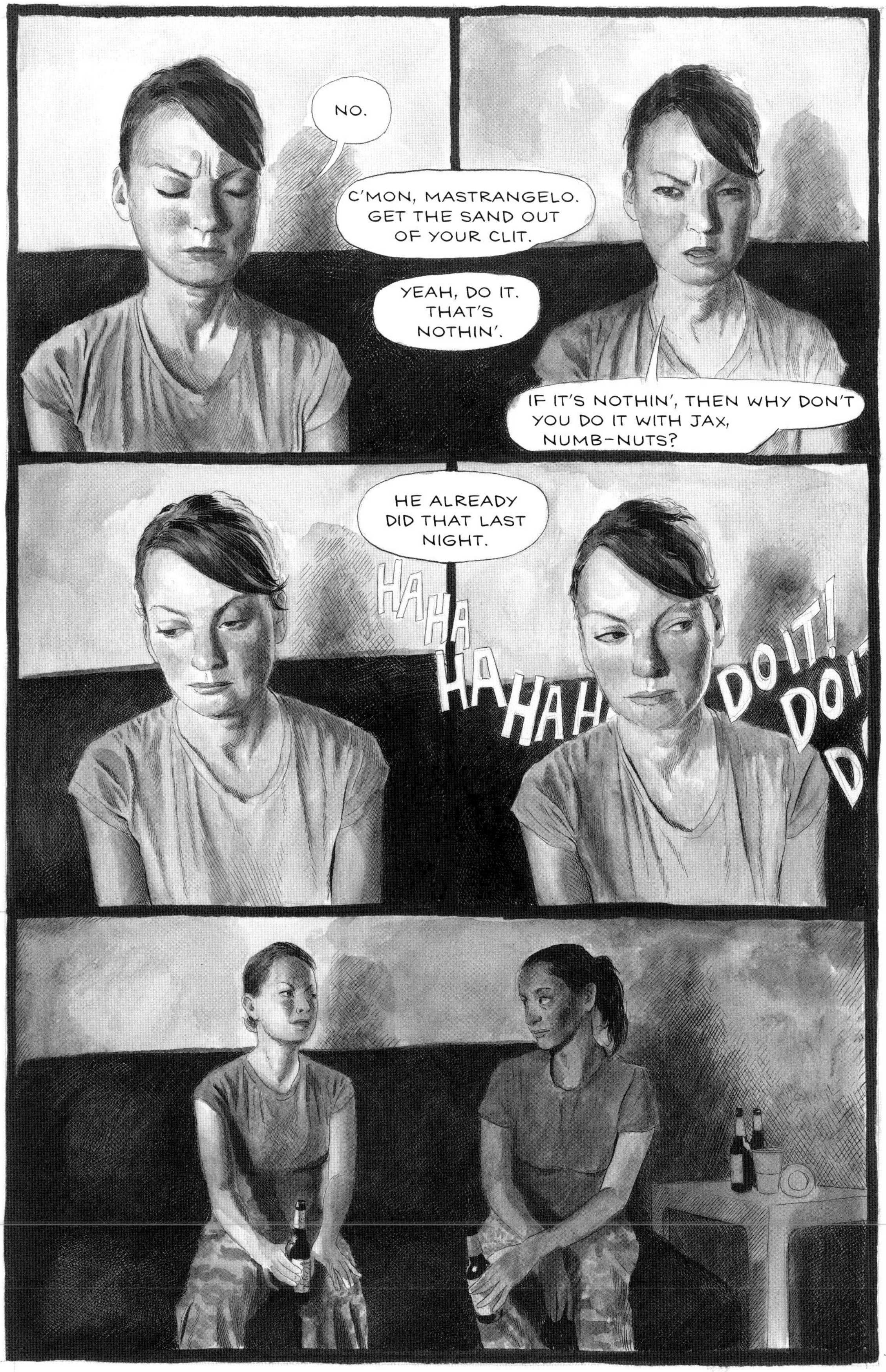
NO.
C'MON, MASTRANGELO. GET THE SAND OUT OF YOUR CLIT.
YEAH, DO IT. THAT'S NOTHIN'.
IF IT'S NOTHIN', THEN WHY DON'T YOU DO IT WITH JAX, NUMB-NUTS?
HE ALREADY DID THAT LAST NIGHT.
HAHA
HAHAHA
DO IT!

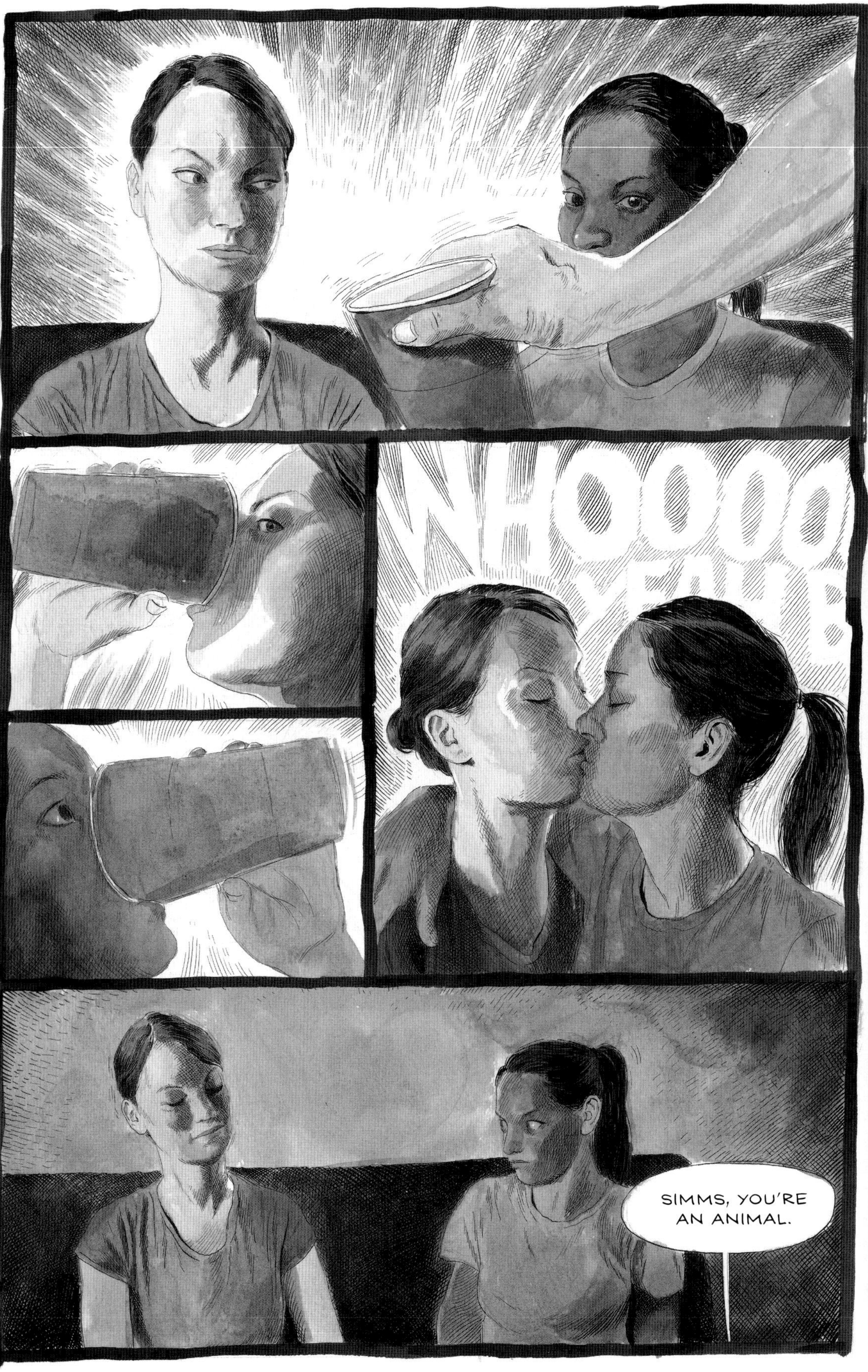
WHOOOO
SIMMS, YOU'RE AN ANIMAL.

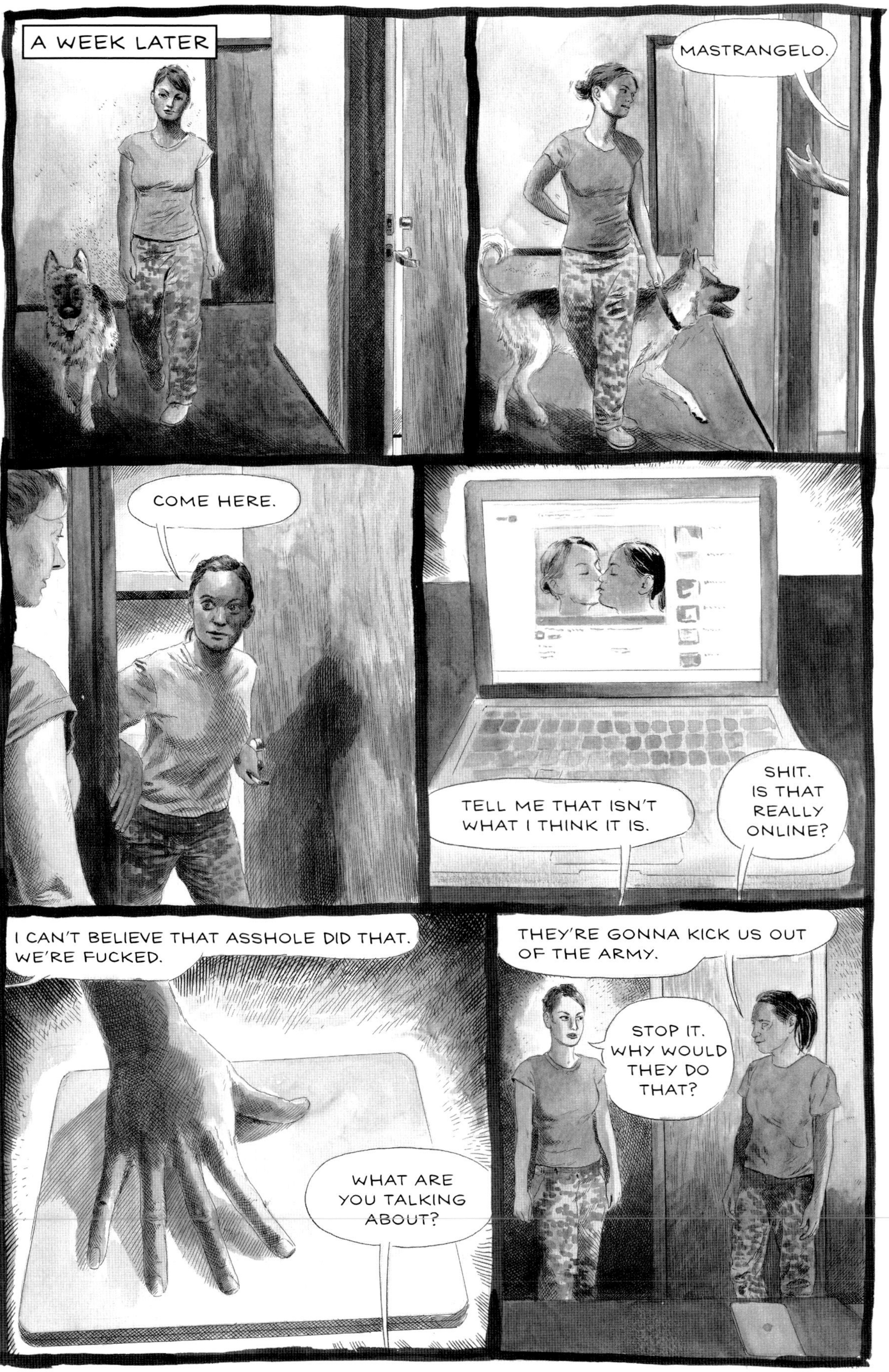
A WEEK LATER
MASTRANGELO.
COME HERE.
TELL ME THAT ISN'T WHAT I THINK IT IS.
SHIT. IS THAT REALLY ONLINE?
I CAN'T BELIEVE THAT ASSHOLE DID THAT. WE'RE FUCKED.
WHAT ARE YOU TALKING ABOUT?
THEY'RE GONNA KICK US OUT OF THE ARMY.
STOP IT. WHY WOULD THEY DO THAT?

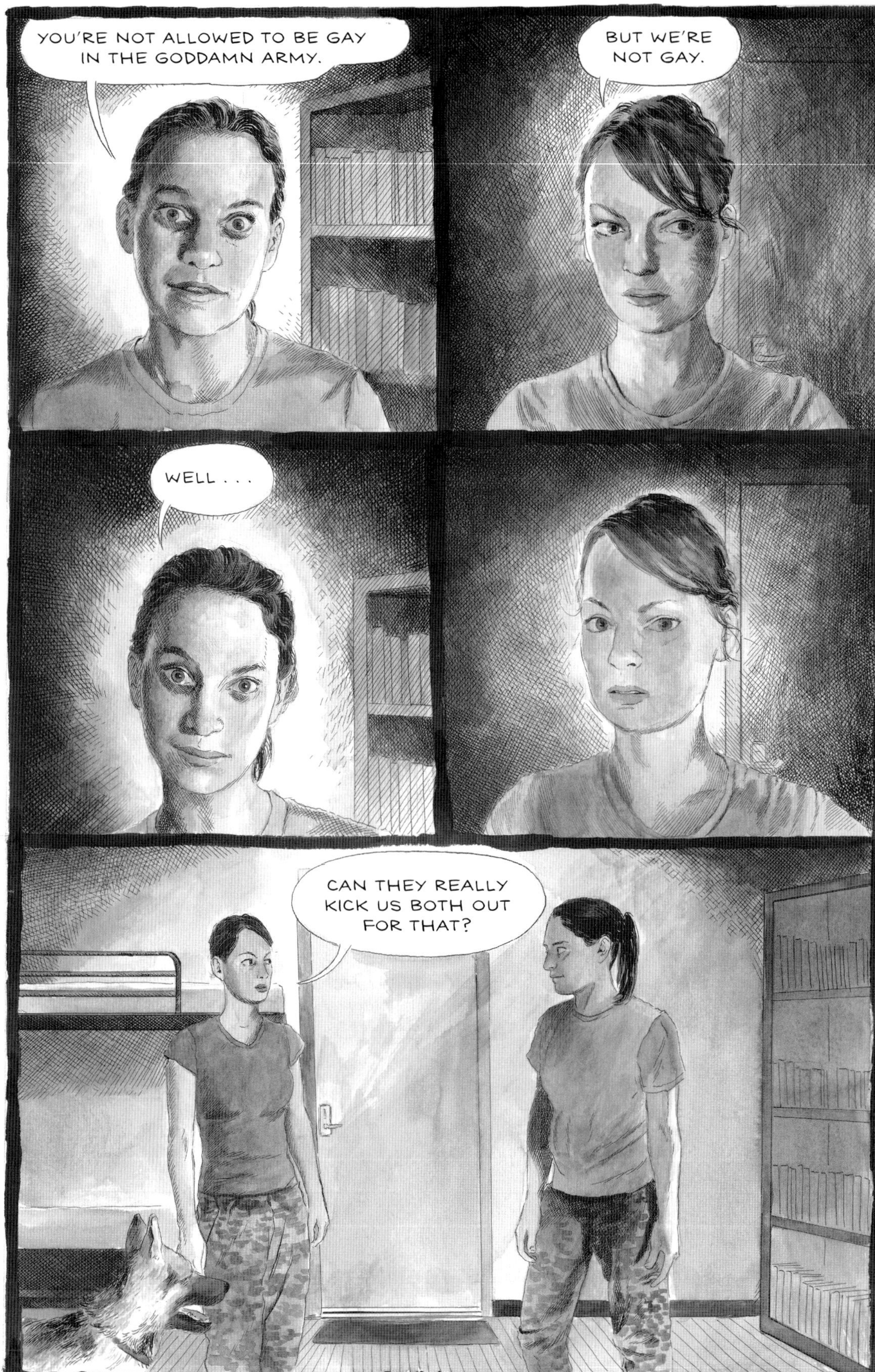
YOU'RE NOT ALLOWED TO BE GAY IN THE GODDAMN ARMY.
BUT WE'RE NOT GAY.
WELL . . .
CAN THEY REALLY KICK US BOTH OUT FOR THAT?

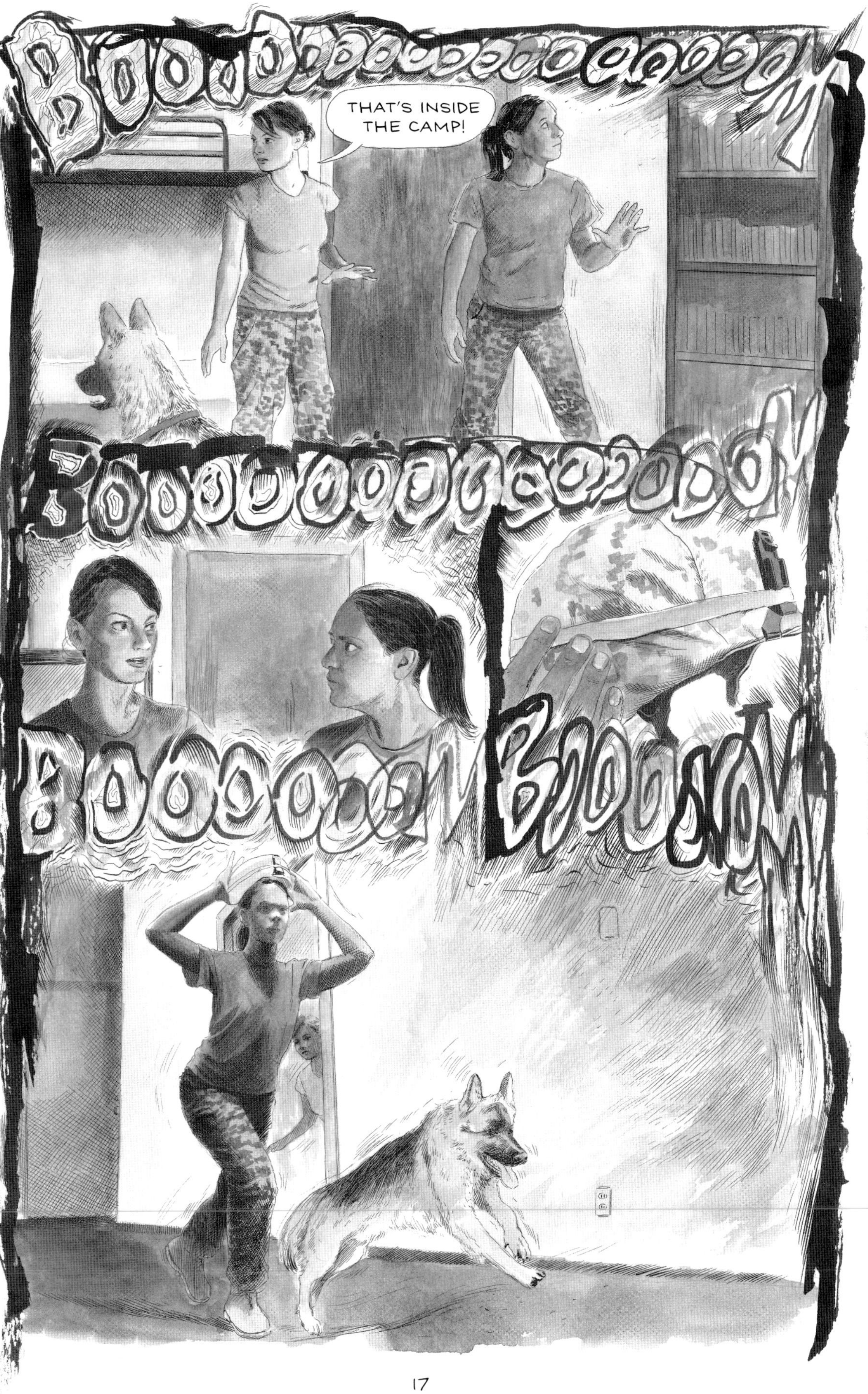
BOOOOOOOOOOOOOOOOM
THAT'S INSIDE THE CAMP!
BOOOOOOOOOOOOOOOM
BOOOOOOM
BOOOOM

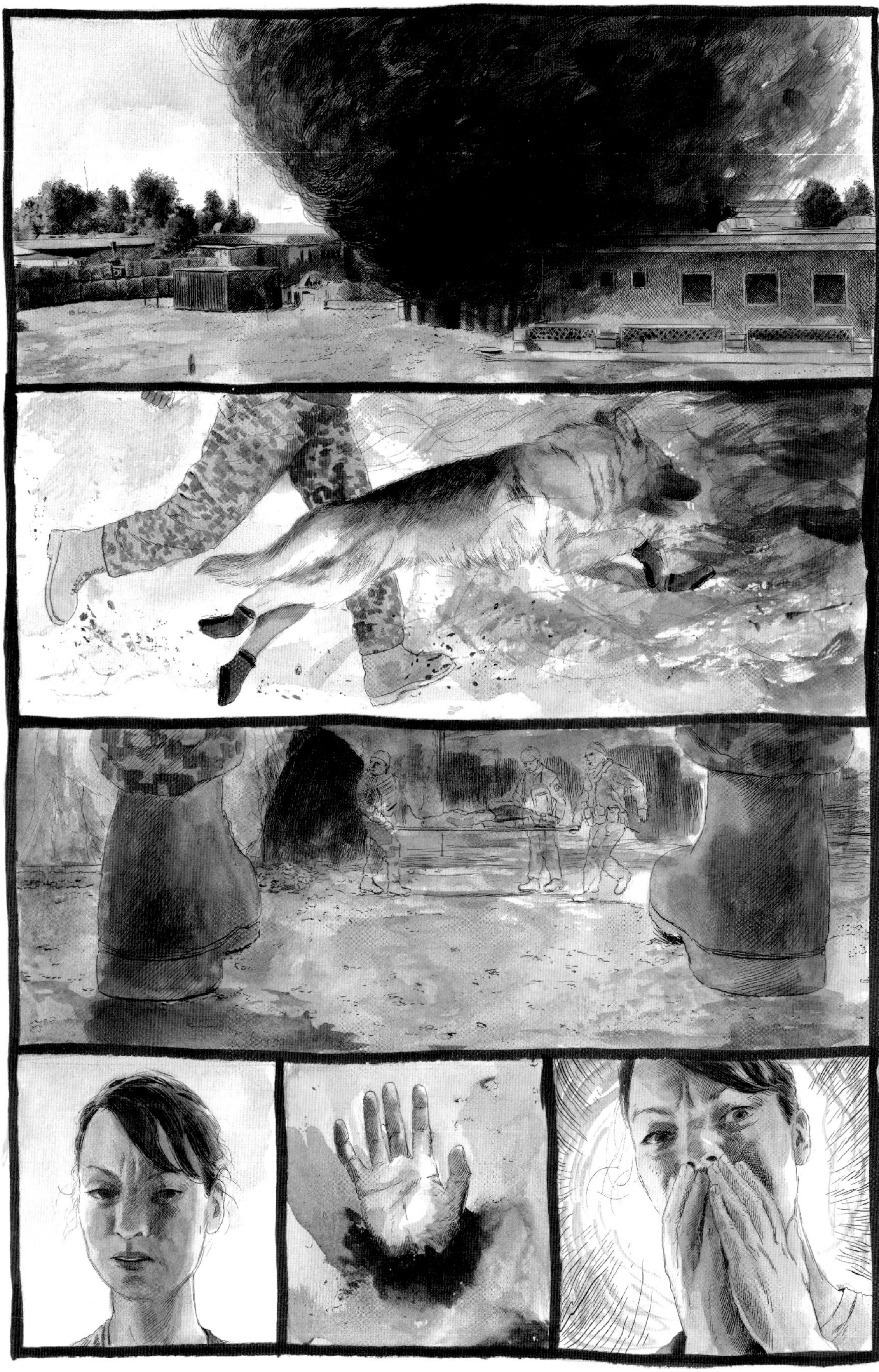

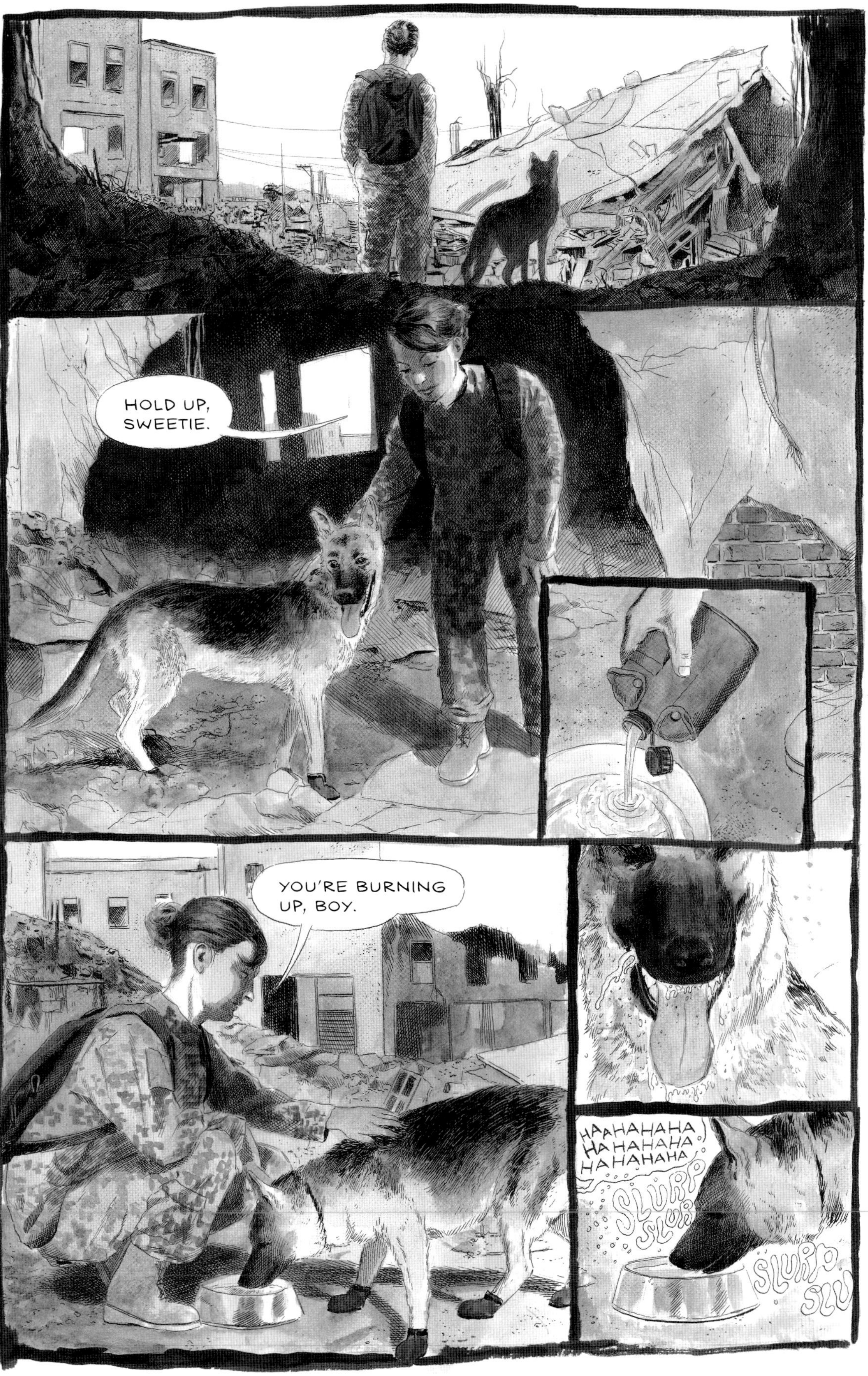
HOLD UP, SWEETIE.
YOU'RE BURNING UP, BOY.
HAHAHAHA HAHAHAHA HAHAHAHA
SLURP SLUR
SLURP SLU

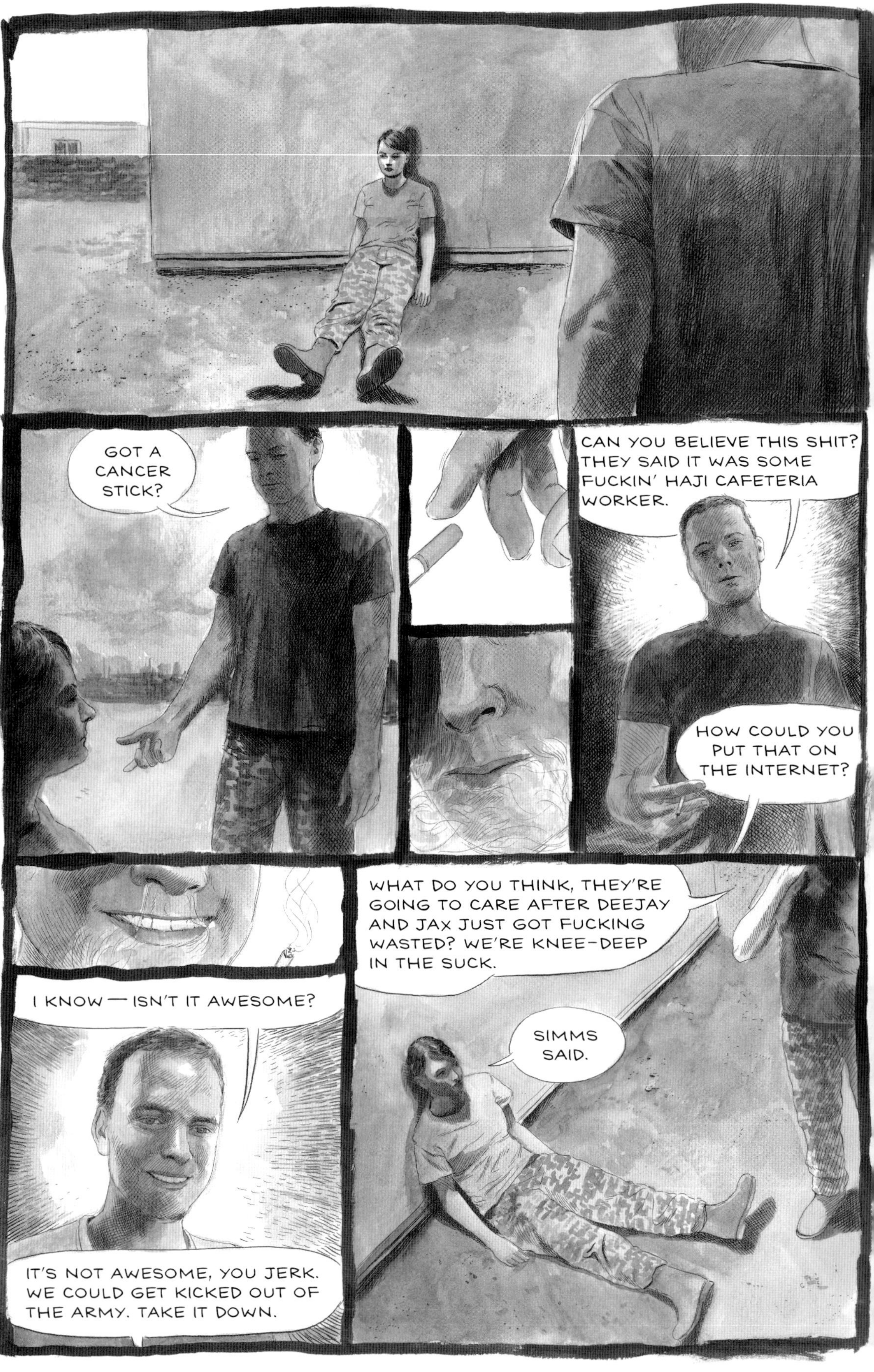
GOT A CANCER STICK?
CAN YOU BELIEVE THIS SHIT? THEY SAID IT WAS SOME FUCKIN' HAJI CAFETERIA WORKER.
HOW COULD YOU PUT THAT ON THE INTERNET?
I KNOW — ISN'T IT AWESOME?
IT'S NOT AWESOME, YOU JERK. WE COULD GET KICKED OUT OF THE ARMY. TAKE IT DOWN.
WHAT DO YOU THINK, THEY'RE GOING TO CARE AFTER DEEJAY AND JAX JUST GOT FUCKING WASTED? WE'RE KNEE-DEEP IN THE SUCK.
SIMMS SAID.

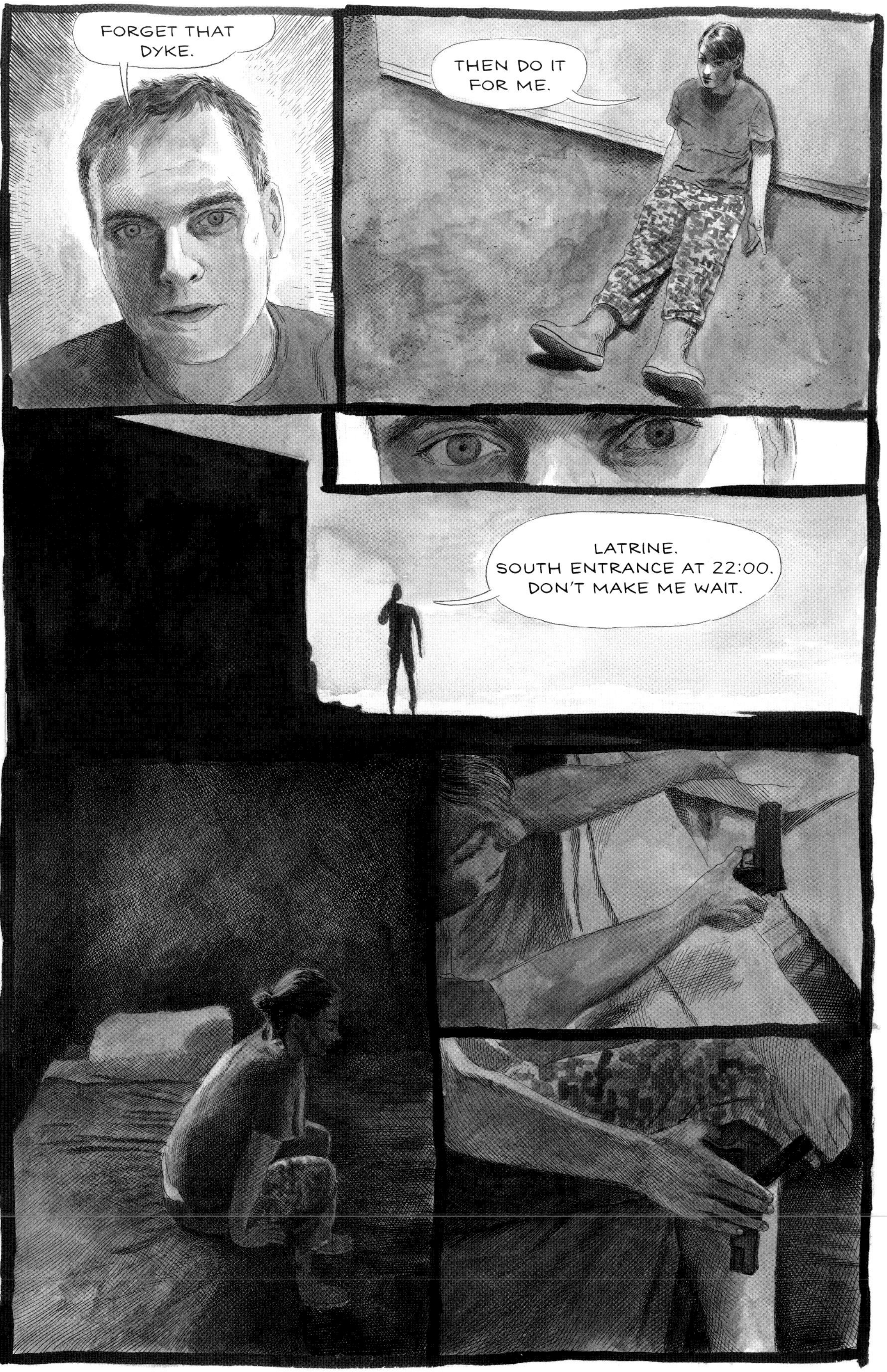
FORGET THAT DYKE.
THEN DO IT FOR ME.
LATRINE. SOUTH ENTRANCE AT 22:00. DON'T MAKE ME WAIT.

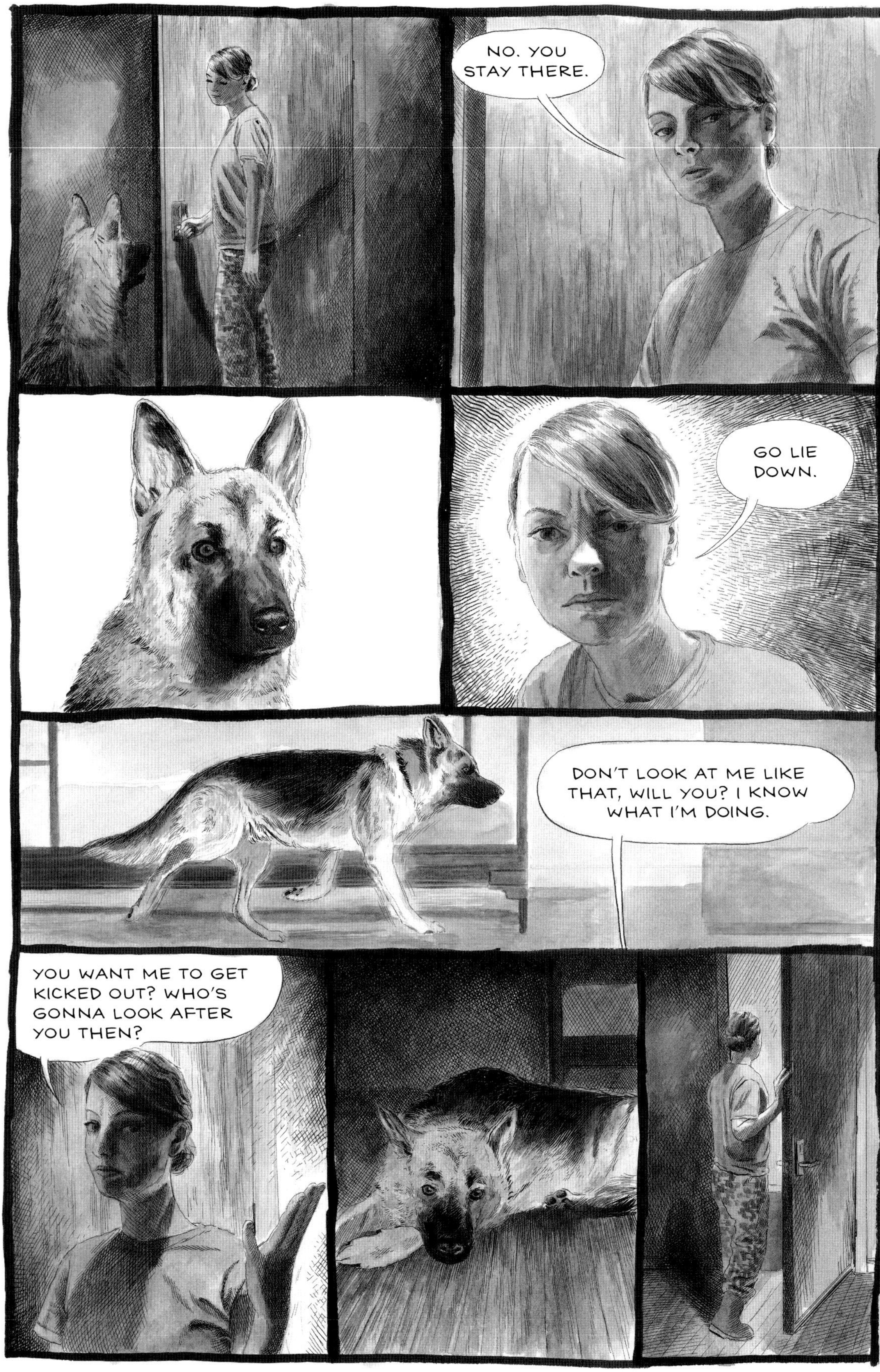
NO. YOU STAY THERE.
GO LIE DOWN.
DON'T LOOK AT ME LIKE THAT, WILL YOU? I KNOW WHAT I'M DOING.
YOU WANT ME TO GET KICKED OUT? WHO'S GONNA LOOK AFTER YOU THEN?

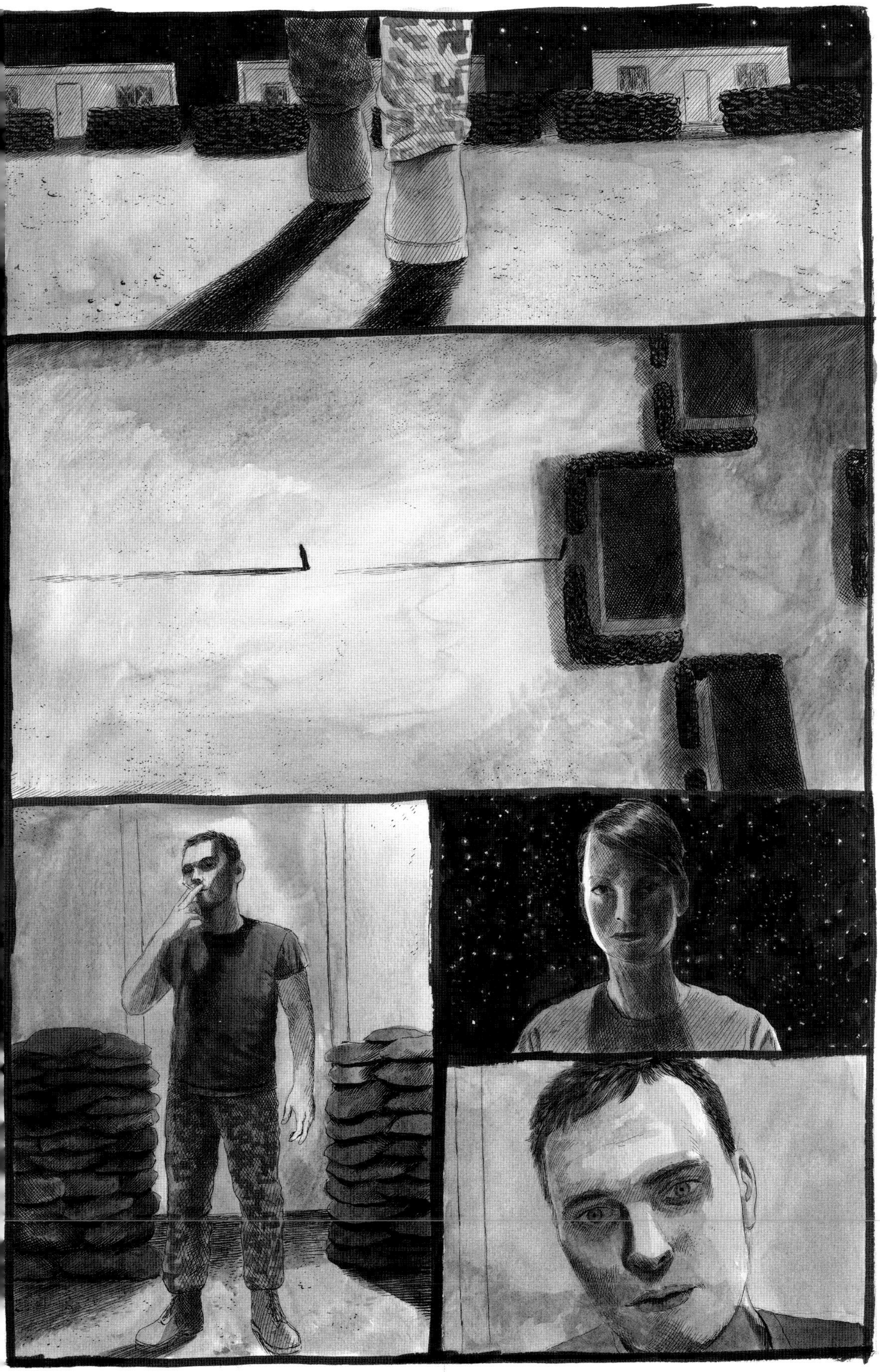

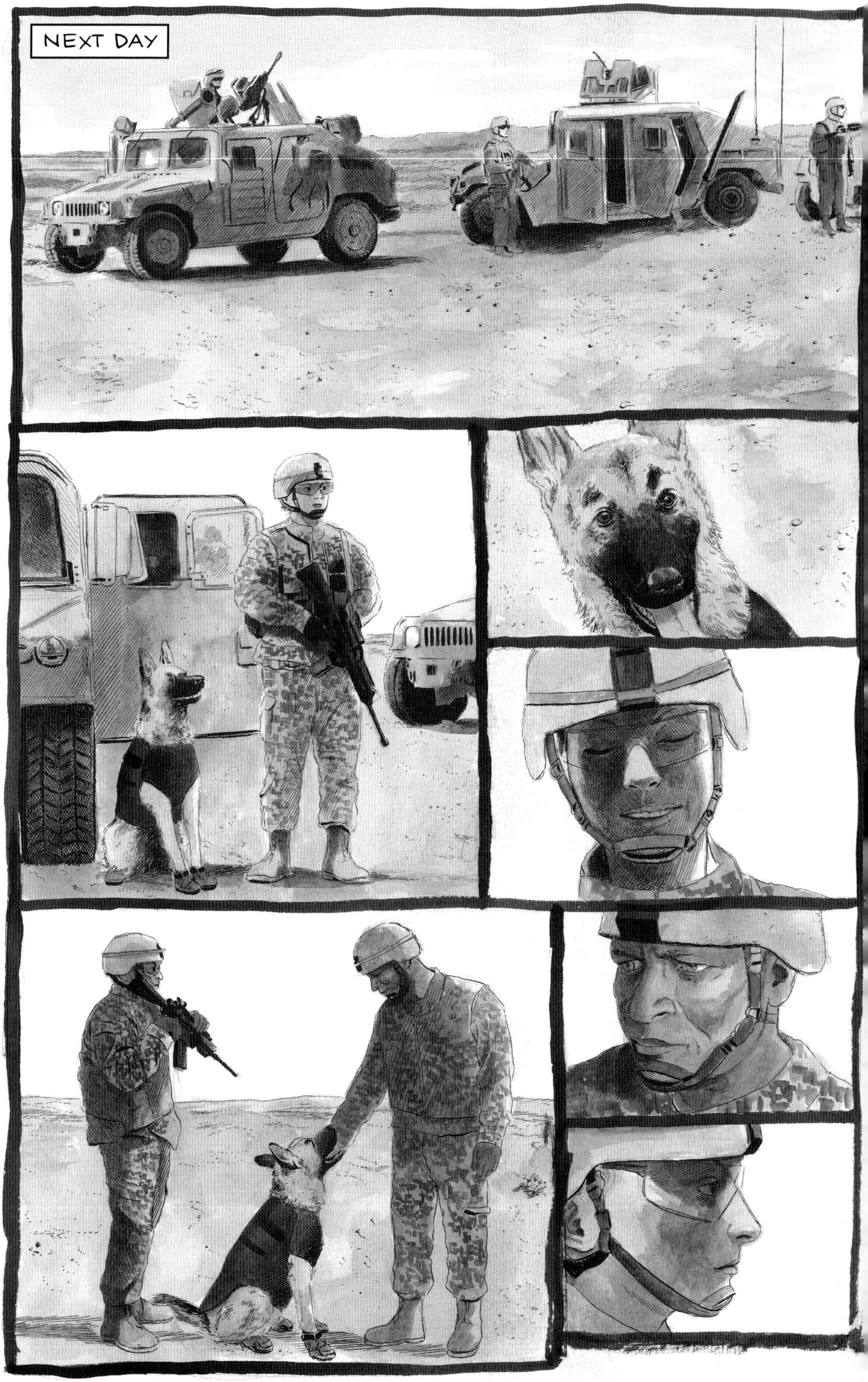
NEXT DAY

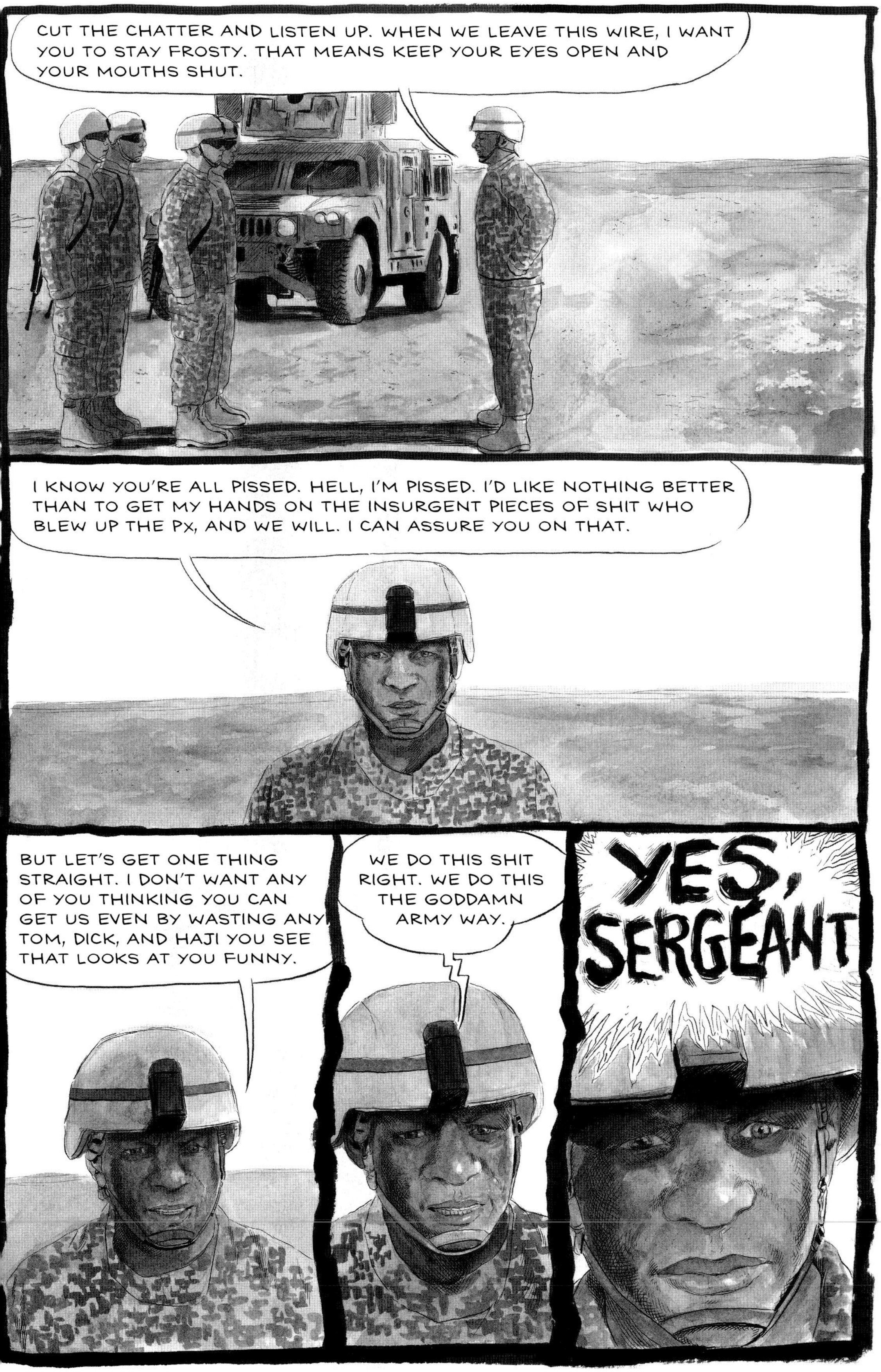
CUT THE CHATTER AND LISTEN UP. WHEN WE LEAVE THIS WIRE, I WANT YOU TO STAY FROSTY. THAT MEANS KEEP YOUR EYES OPEN AND YOUR MOUTHS SHUT.
I KNOW YOU'RE ALL PISSED. HELL, I'M PISSED. I'D LIKE NOTHING BETTER THAN TO GET MY HANDS ON THE INSURGENT PIECES OF SHIT WHO BLEW UP THE PX, AND WE WILL. I CAN ASSURE YOU ON THAT.
BUT LET'S GET ONE THING STRAIGHT. I DON'T WANT ANY OF YOU THINKING YOU CAN GET US EVEN BY WASTING ANY TOM, DICK, AND HAJI YOU SEE THAT LOOKS AT YOU FUNNY.
WE DO THIS SHIT RIGHT. WE DO THIS THE GODDAMN ARMY WAY.
YES, SERGEANT

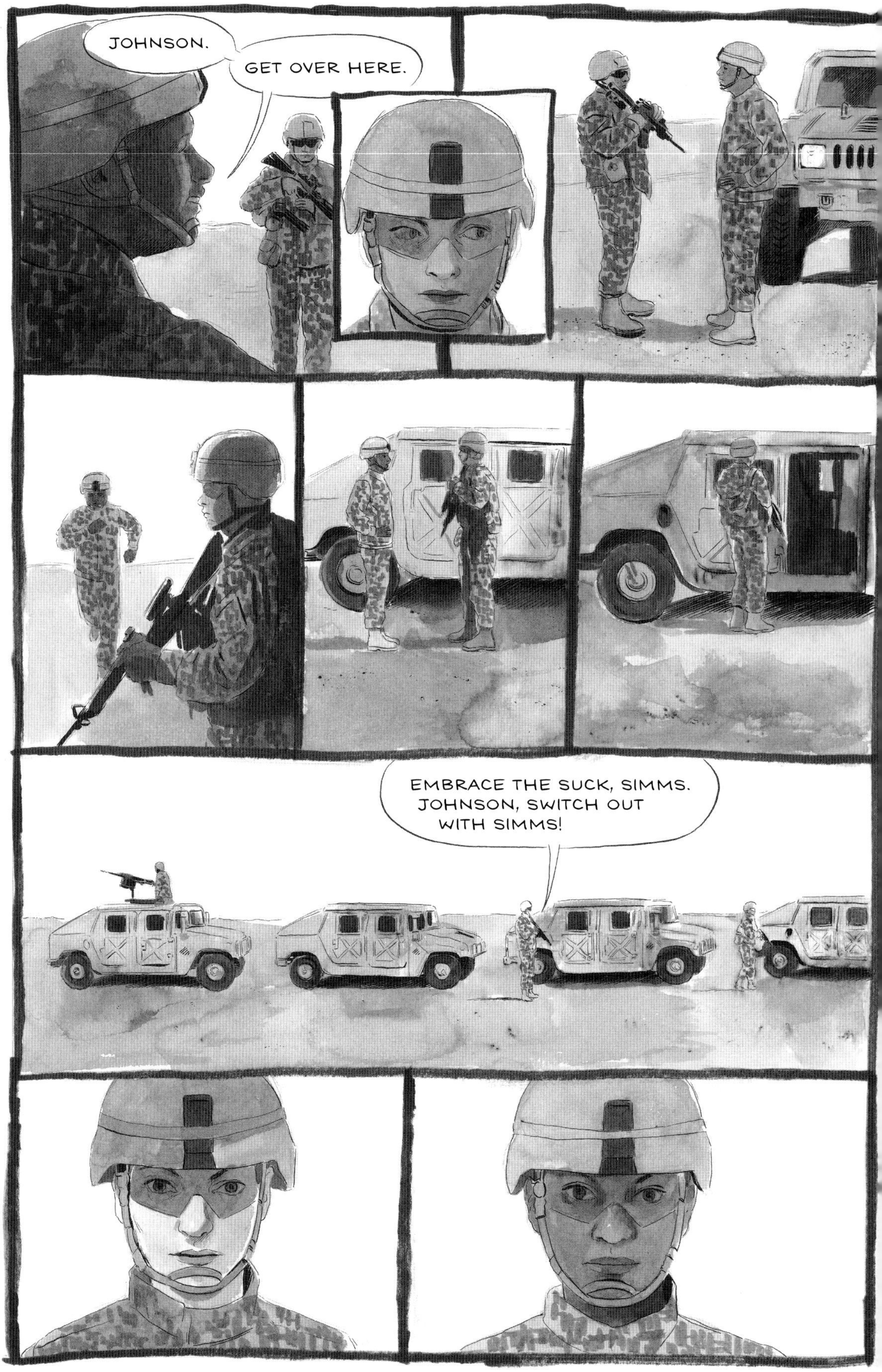
JOHNSON.
GET OVER HERE.
EMBRACE THE SUCK, SIMMS. JOHNSON, SWITCH OUT WITH SIMMS!

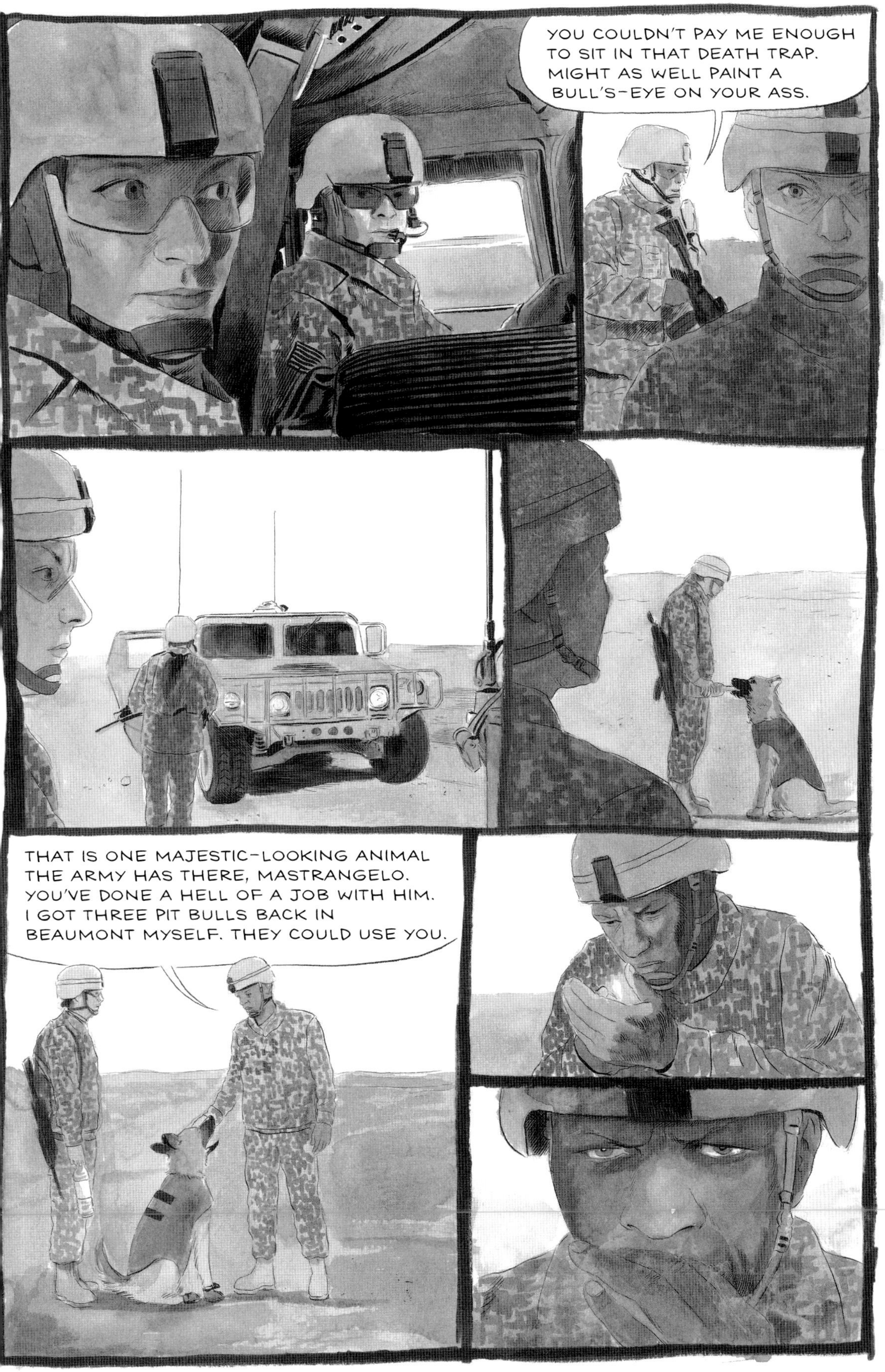
YOU COULDN'T PAY ME ENOUGH TO SIT IN THAT DEATH TRAP. MIGHT AS WELL PAINT A BULL'S-EYE ON YOUR ASS.
THAT IS ONE MAJESTIC-LOOKING ANIMAL THE ARMY HAS THERE, MASTRANGELO. YOU'VE DONE A HELL OF A JOB WITH HIM. I GOT THREE PIT BULLS BACK IN BEAUMONT MYSELF. THEY COULD USE YOU.

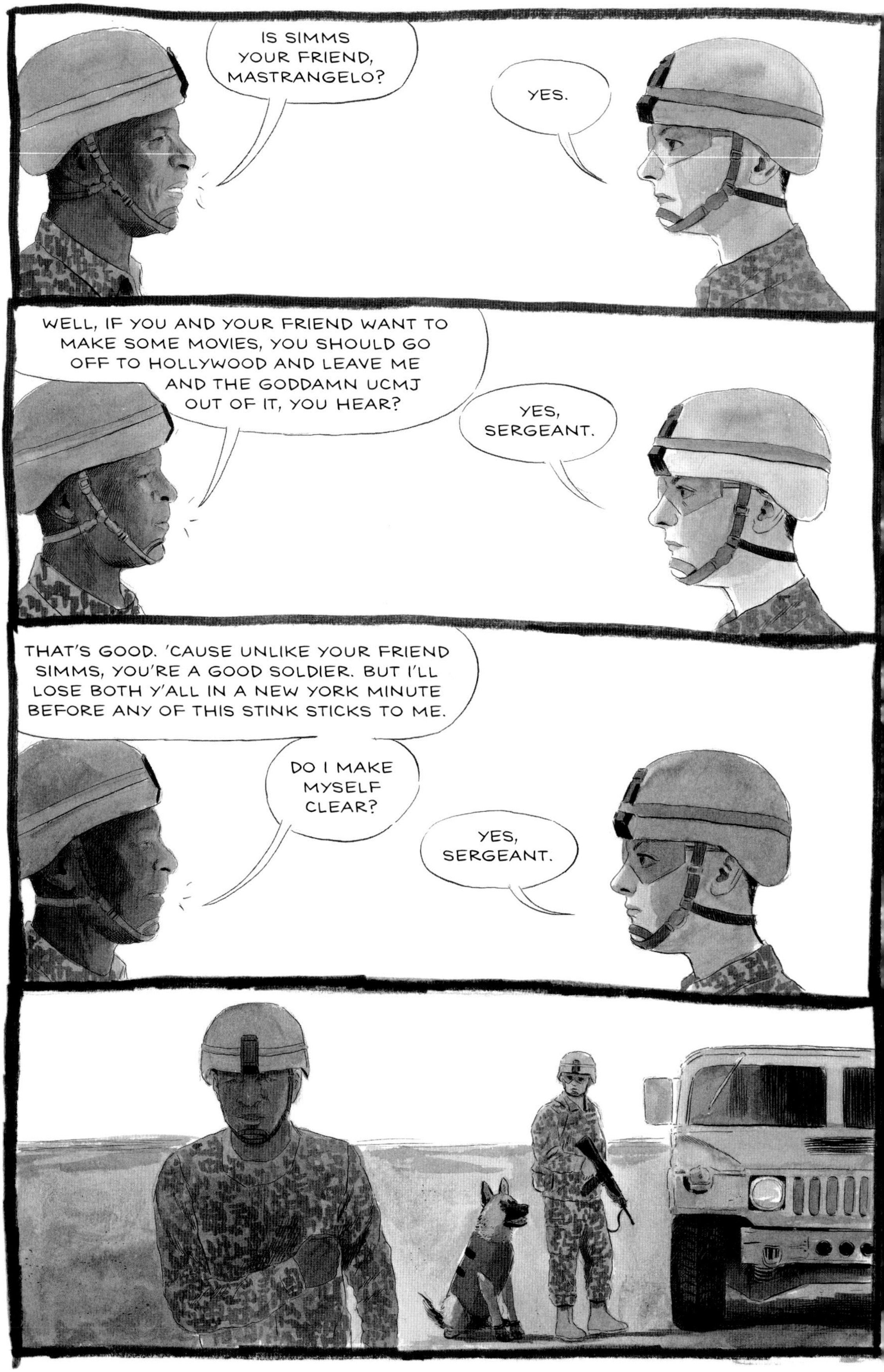
IS SIMMS YOUR FRIEND, MASTRANGELO?
YES.
WELL, IF YOU AND YOUR FRIEND WANT TO MAKE SOME MOVIES, YOU SHOULD GO OFF TO HOLLYWOOD AND LEAVE ME AND THE GODDAMN UCMJ OUT OF IT, YOU HEAR?
YES, SERGEANT.
THAT'S GOOD. 'CAUSE UNLIKE YOUR FRIEND SIMMS, YOU'RE A GOOD SOLDIER. BUT I'LL LOSE BOTH Y'ALL IN A NEW YORK MINUTE BEFORE ANY OF THIS STINK STICKS TO ME.
DO I MAKE MYSELF CLEAR?
YES, SERGEANT.

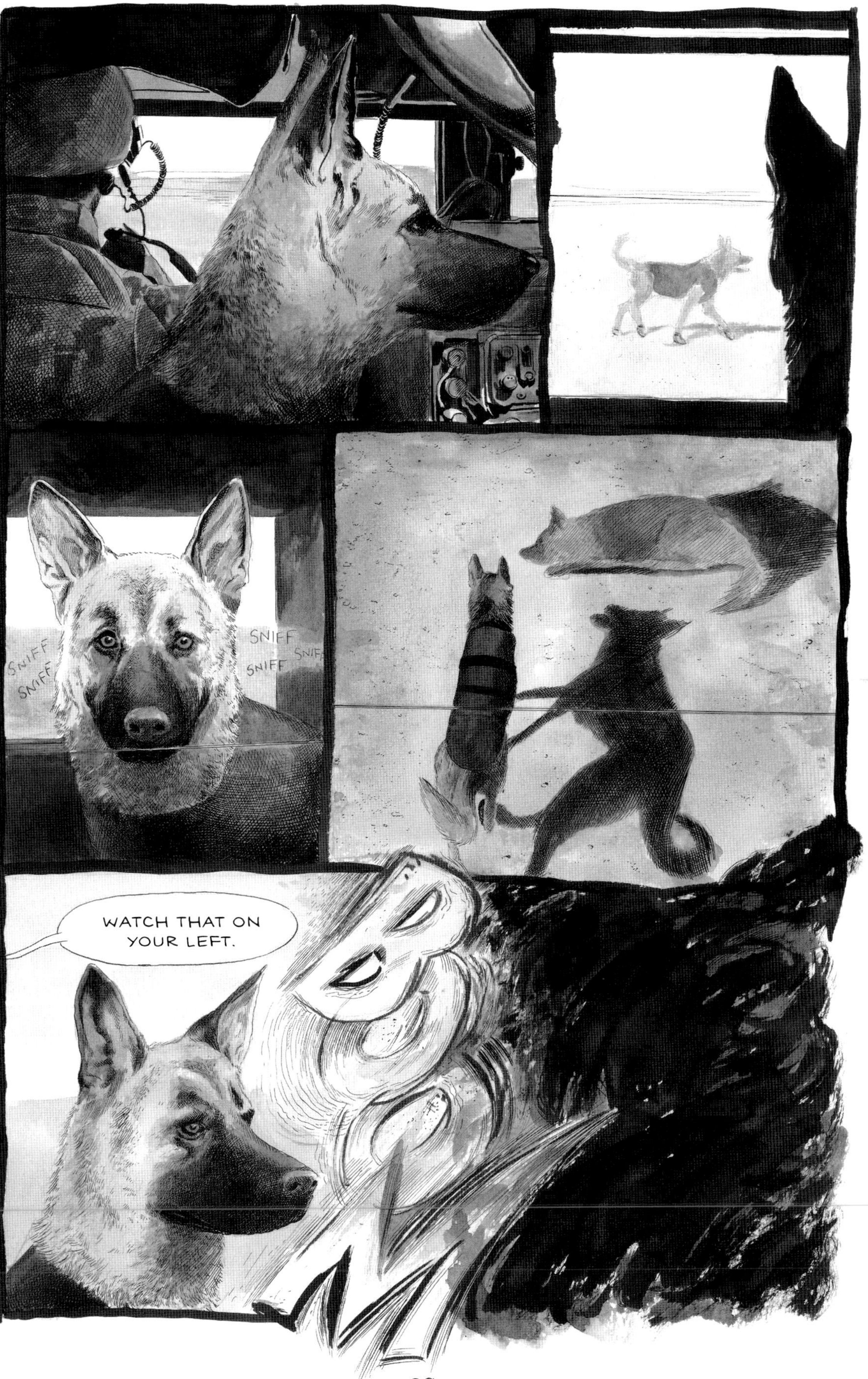
SNIFF
SNIFF
SNIFF
SNIFF
SNIFF
WATCH THAT ON YOUR LEFT.

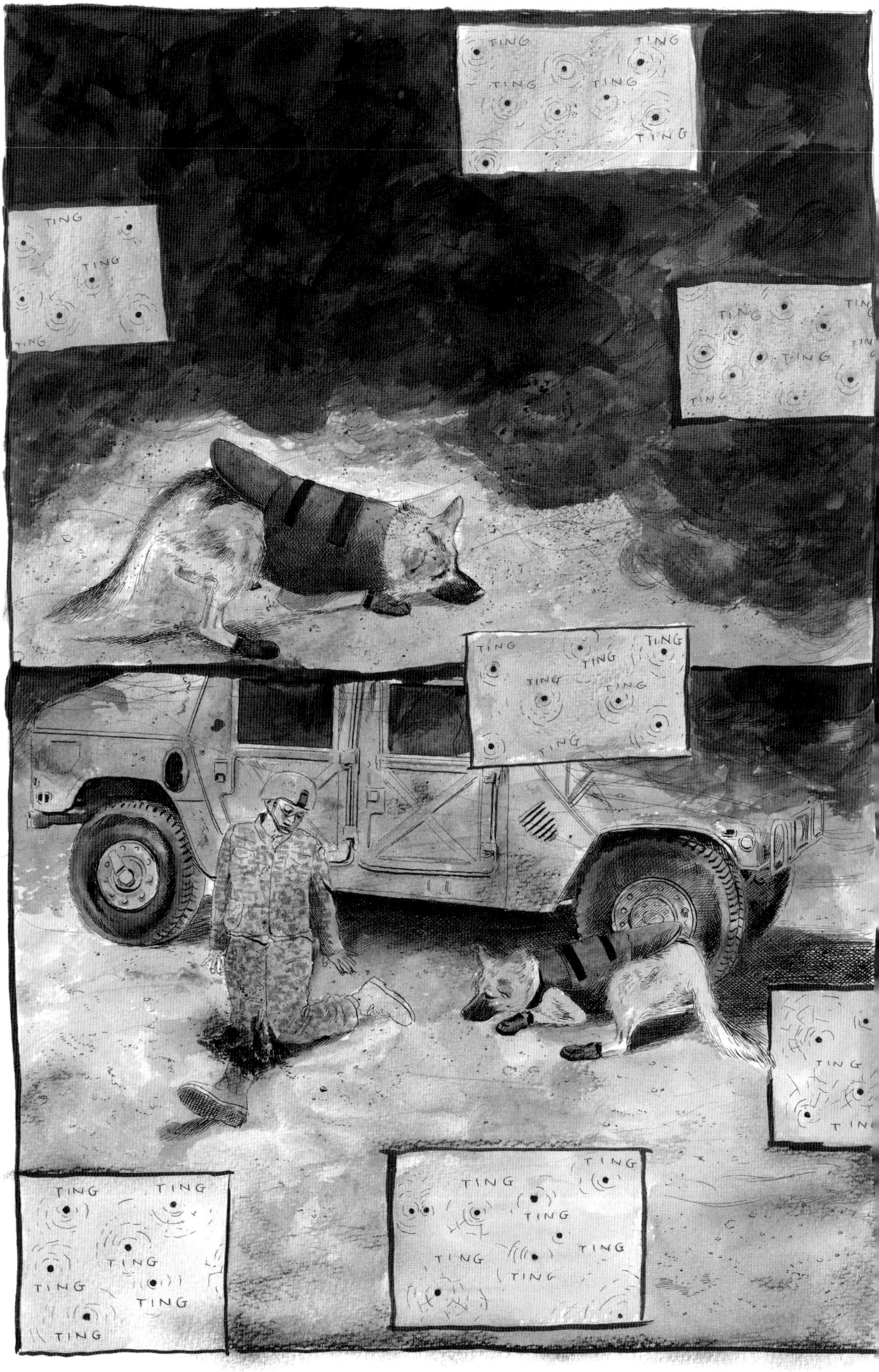
TING
TING
TING
TING
TING
TING
TING
TING
TING
TING
TING
TING
TING
TING
TING
TING
TING
TING
TING
TING
TING
TING
TING
TING
TING
TING
TING
TING
TING
TING
TING

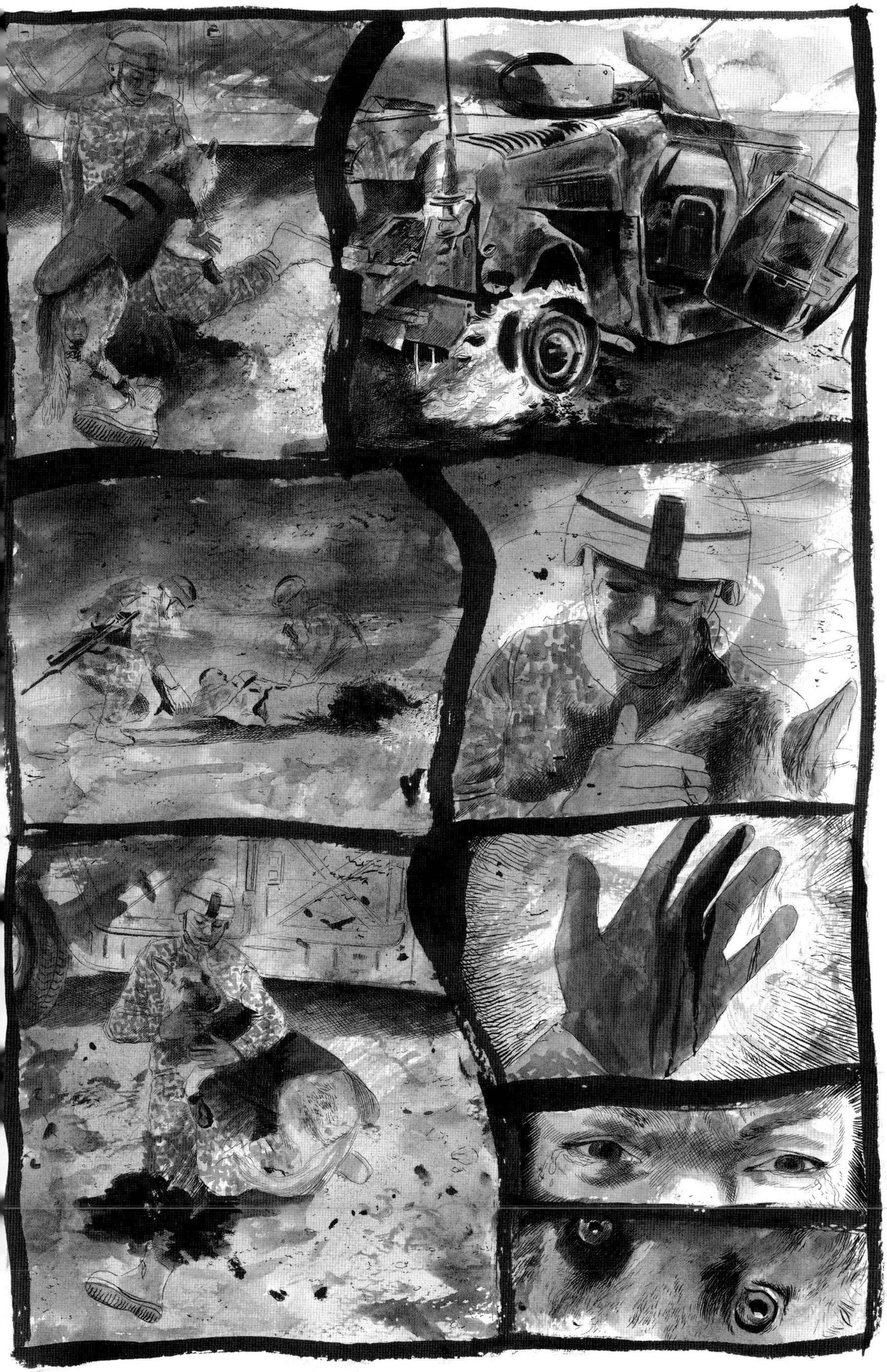

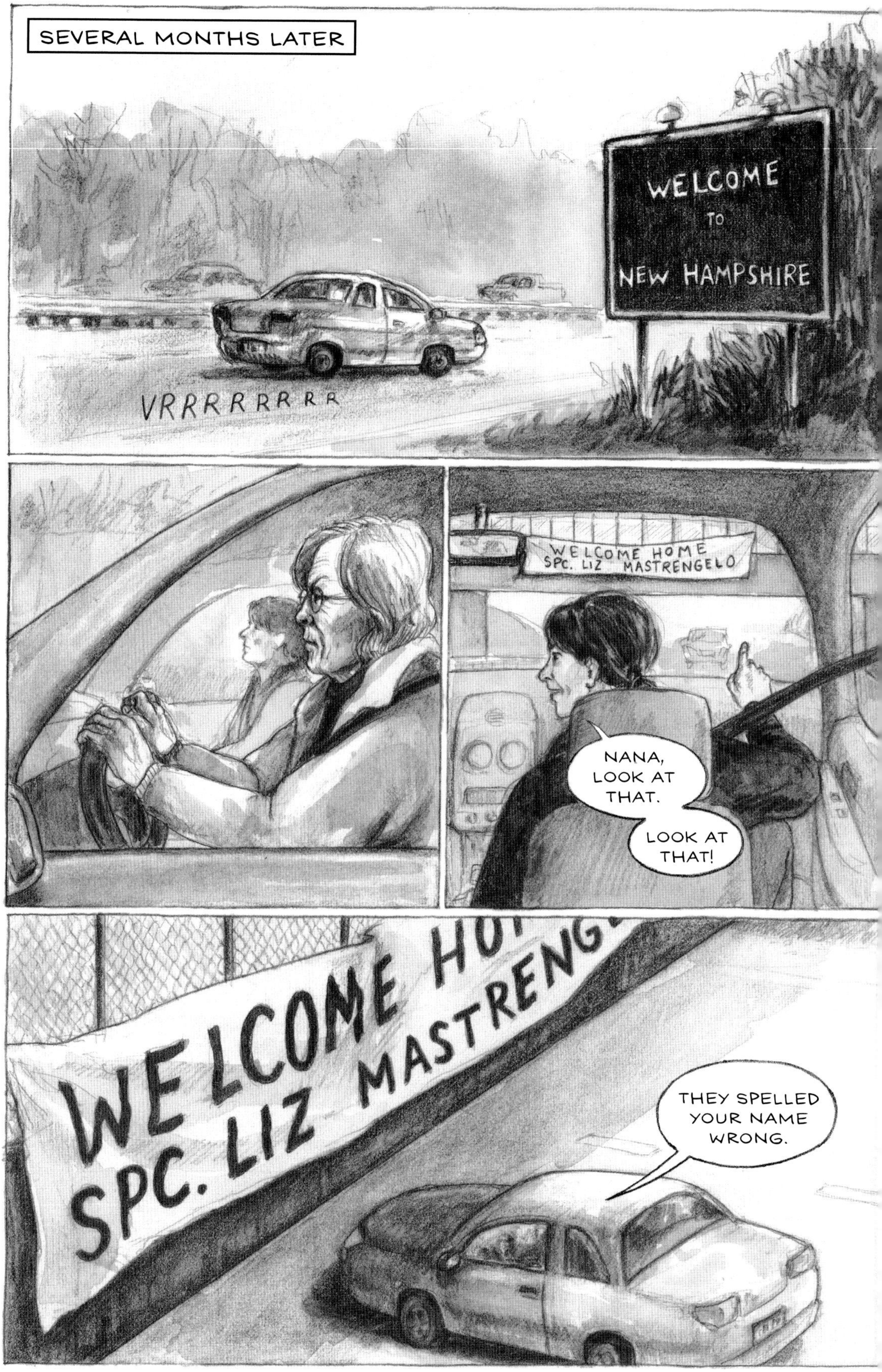
SEVERAL MONTHS LATER
WELCOME TO NEW HAMPSHIRE
VRRRRRRRRR
WELCOME HOME SPC. LIZ MASTRENGELO
NANA, LOOK AT THAT.
LOOK AT THAT!
WELCOME HO
SPC. LIZ MASTRENG
THEY SPELLED YOUR NAME WRONG.

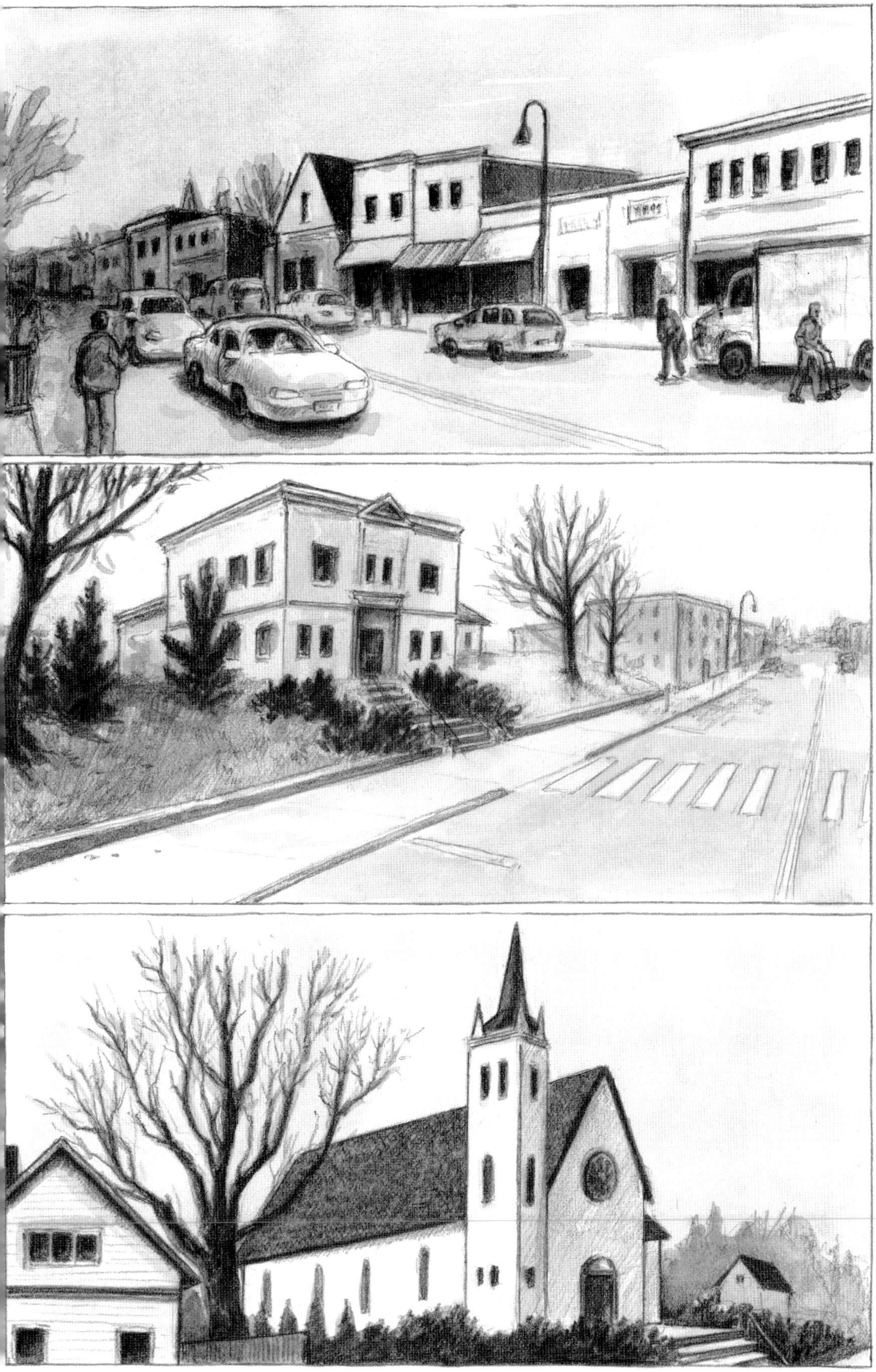

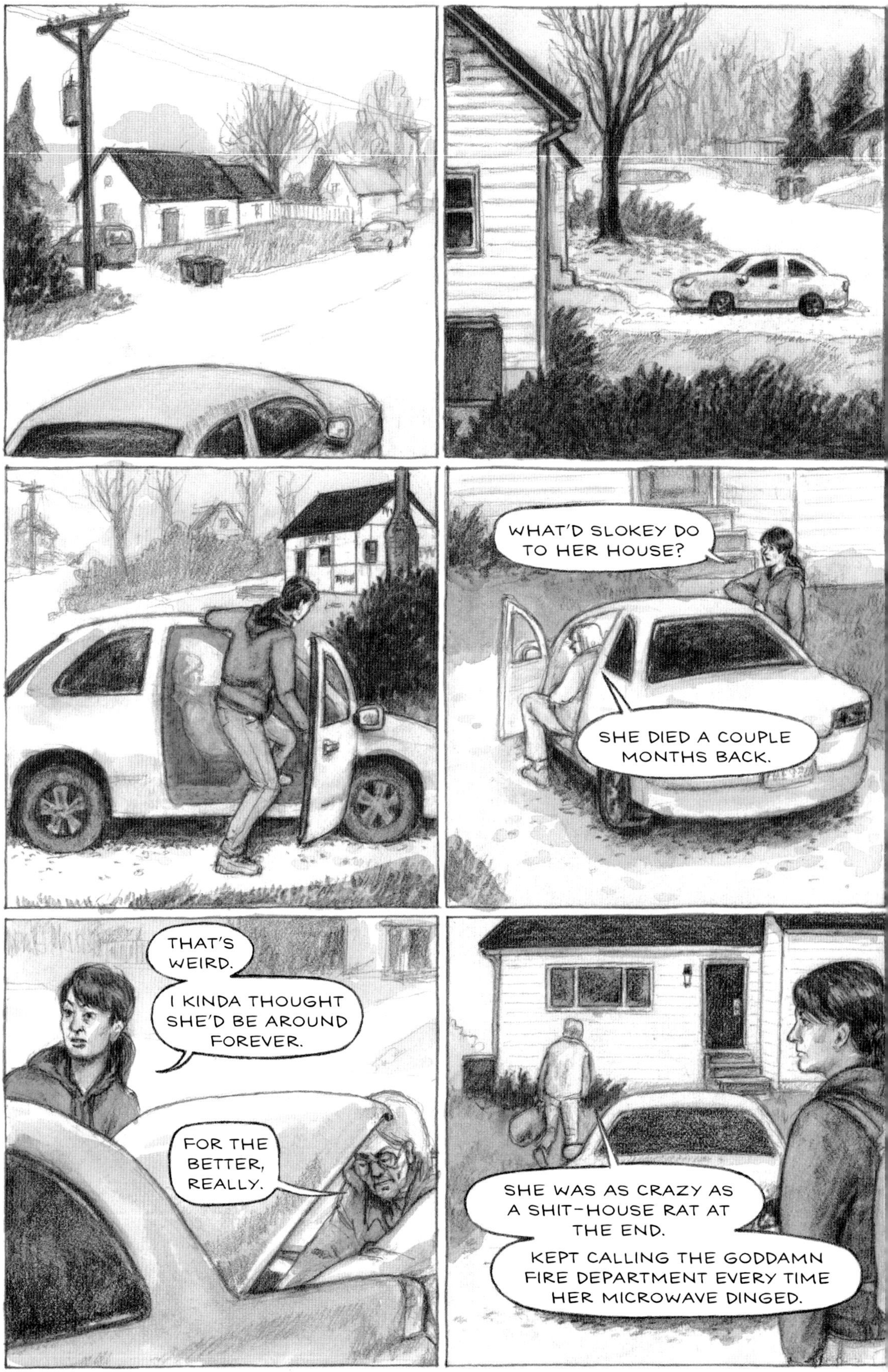
WHAT'D SLOKEY DO TO HER HOUSE?
SHE DIED A COUPLE MONTHS BACK.
THAT'S WEIRD.
I KINDA THOUGHT SHE'D BE AROUND FOREVER.
FOR THE BETTER, REALLY.
SHE WAS AS CRAZY AS A SHIT-HOUSE RAT AT THE END.
KEPT CALLING THE GODDAMN FIRE DEPARTMENT EVERY TIME HER MICROWAVE DINGED.

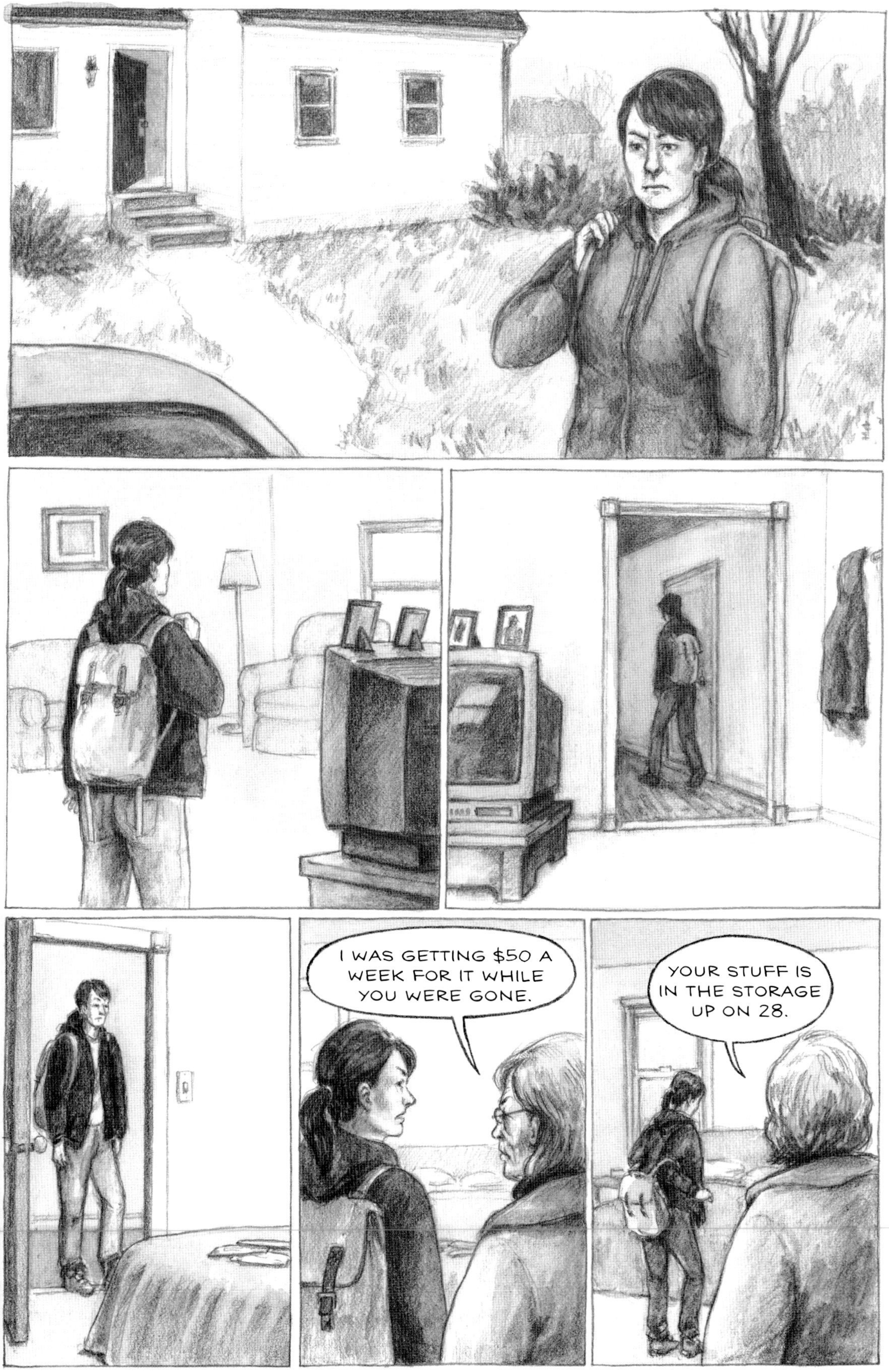
I WAS GETTING $50 A WEEK FOR IT WHILE YOU WERE GONE.
YOUR STUFF IS IN THE STORAGE UP ON 28.

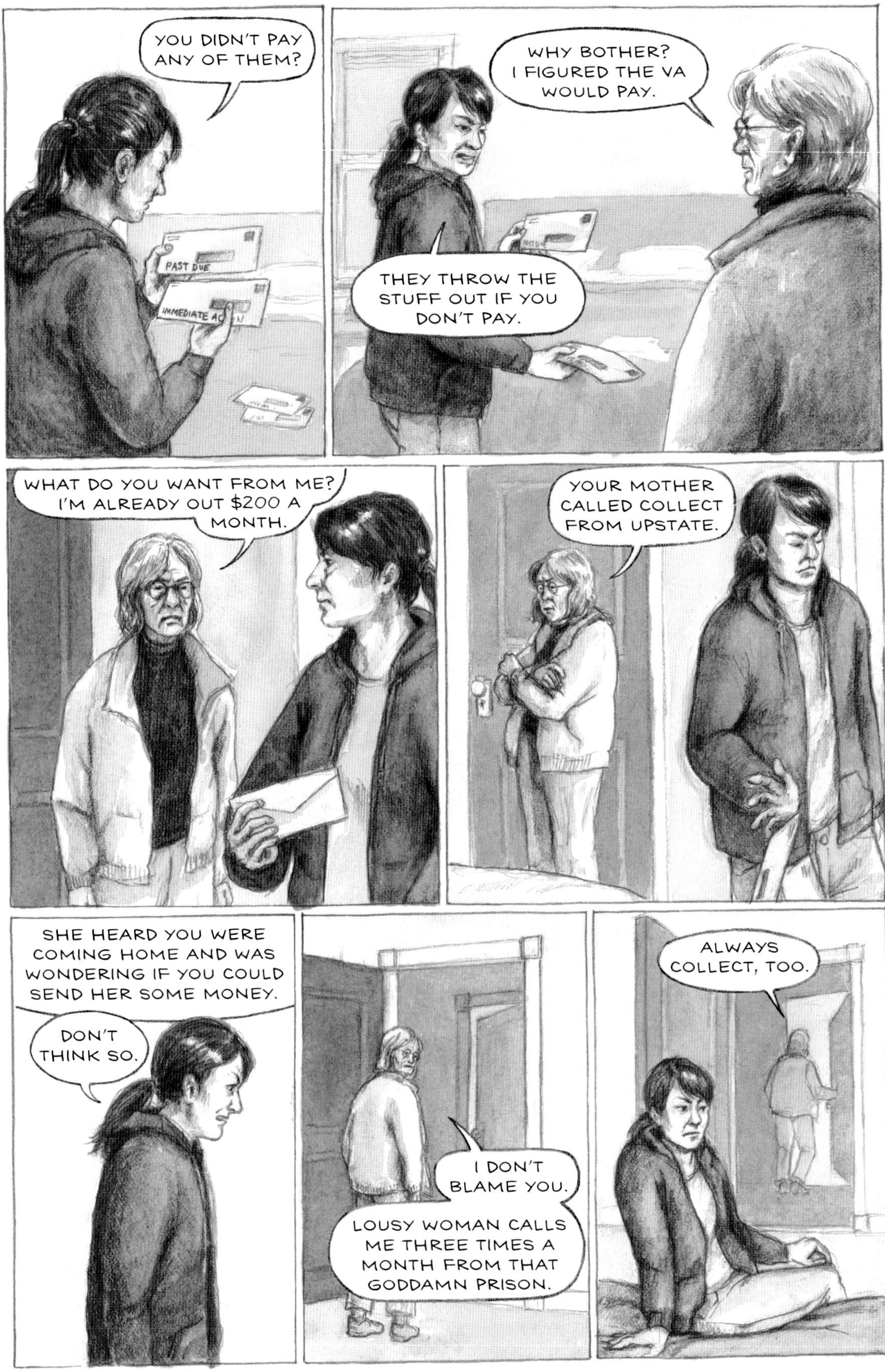
YOU DIDN'T PAY ANY OF THEM?
PAST DUE
IMMEDIATE AC
WHY BOTHER? I FIGURED THE VA WOULD PAY.
THEY THROW THE STUFF OUT IF YOU DON'T PAY.
WHAT DO YOU WANT FROM ME? I'M ALREADY OUT $200 A MONTH.
YOUR MOTHER CALLED COLLECT FROM UPSTATE.
SHE HEARD YOU WERE COMING HOME AND WAS WONDERING IF YOU COULD SEND HER SOME MONEY.
DON'T THINK SO.
I DON'T BLAME YOU.
LOUSY WOMAN CALLS ME THREE TIMES A MONTH FROM THAT GODDAMN PRISON.
ALWAYS COLLECT, TOO.

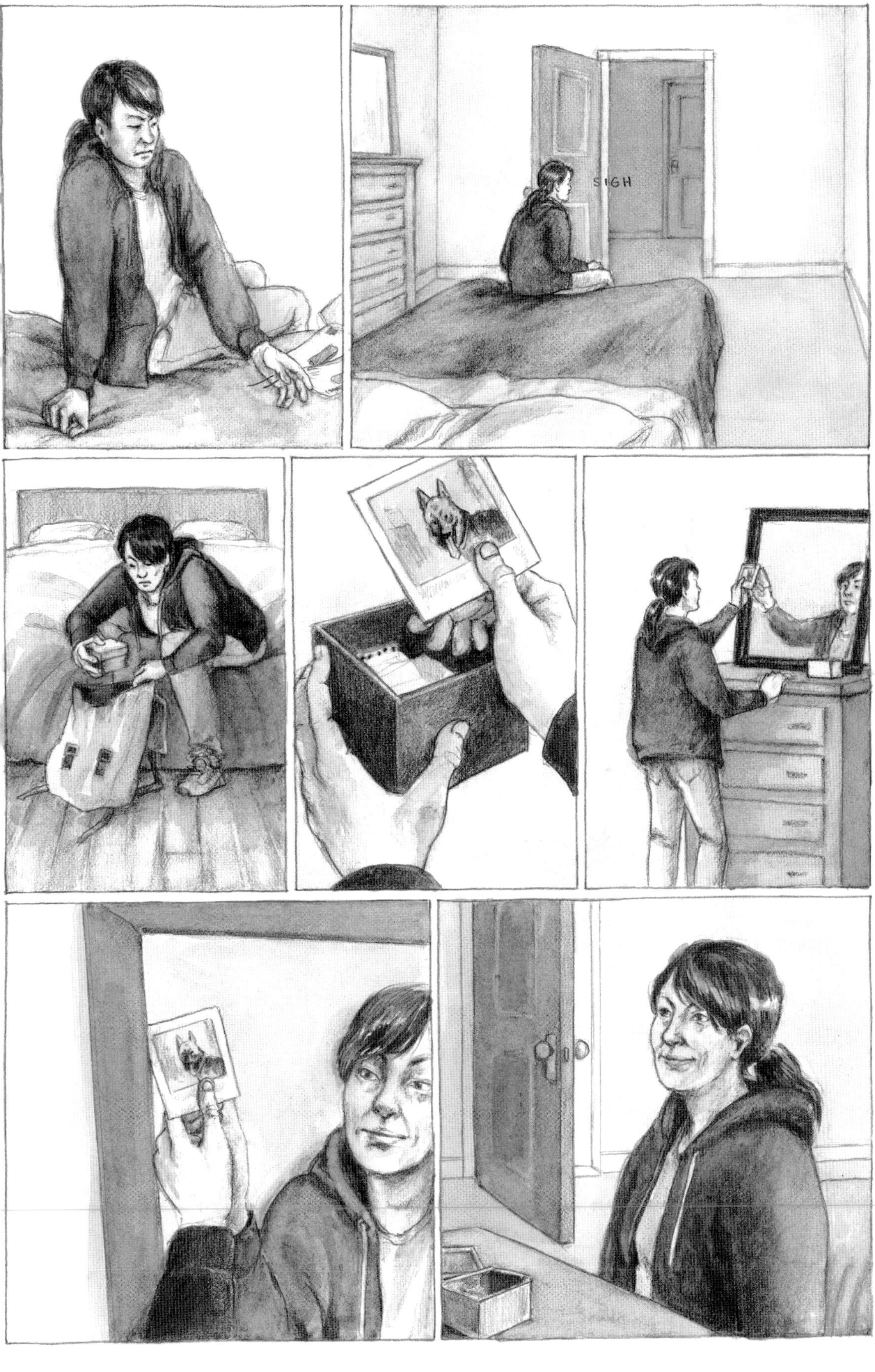
SIGH

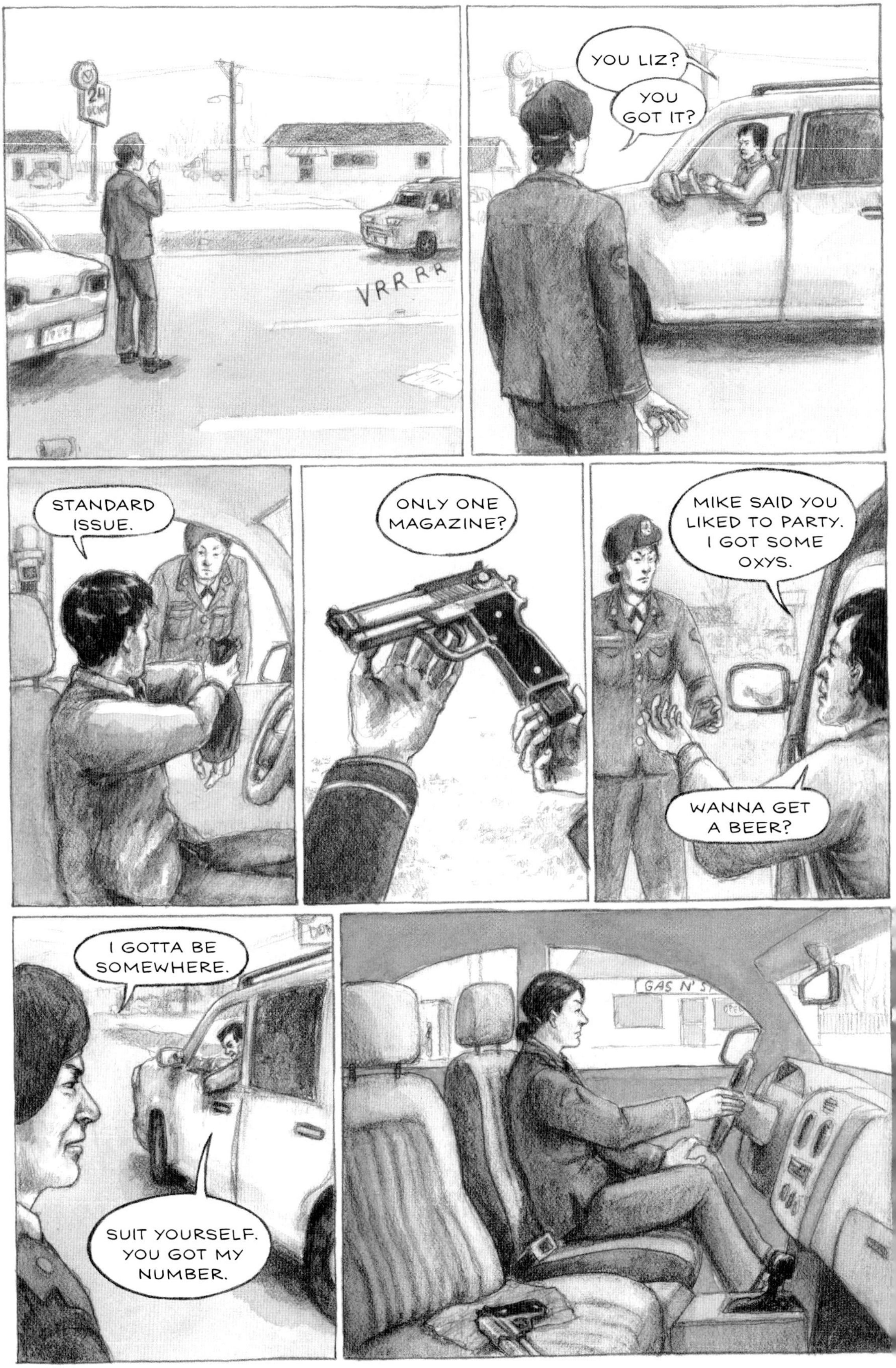
VRRRR
YOU LIZ?
YOU GOT IT?
STANDARD ISSUE.
ONLY ONE MAGAZINE?
MIKE SAID YOU LIKED TO PARTY. I GOT SOME OXYS.
WANNA GET A BEER?
I GOTTA BE SOMEWHERE.
SUIT YOURSELF. YOU GOT MY NUMBER.
GAS N' S

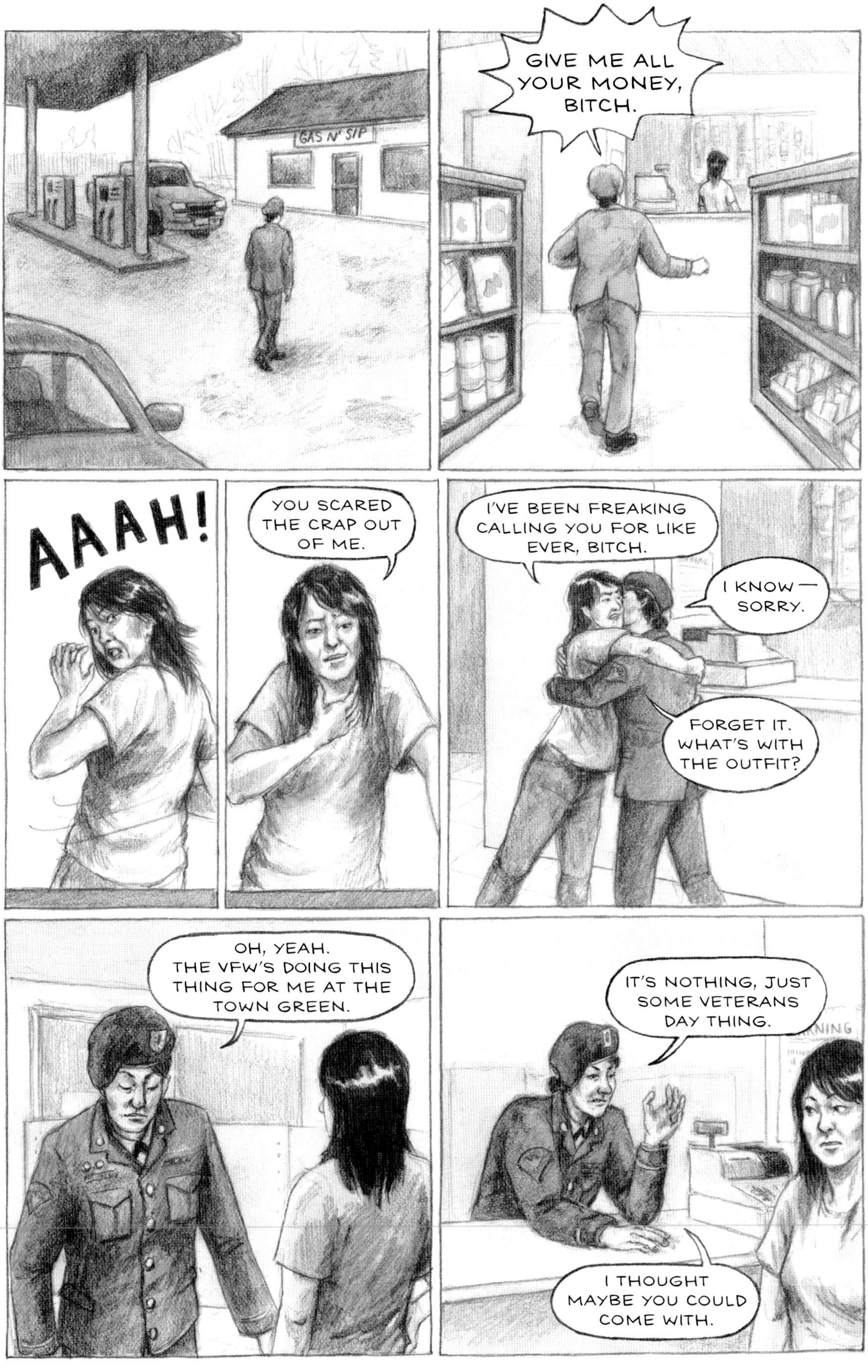
GAS N' SIP
GIVE ME ALL YOUR MONEY, BITCH.
AAAH!
YOU SCARED THE CRAP OUT OF ME.
I'VE BEEN FREAKING CALLING YOU FOR LIKE EVER, BITCH.
I KNOW — SORRY.
FORGET IT. WHAT'S WITH THE OUTFIT?
OH, YEAH. THE VFW'S DOING THIS THING FOR ME AT THE TOWN GREEN.
IT'S NOTHING, JUST SOME VETERANS DAY THING.
I THOUGHT MAYBE YOU COULD COME WITH.

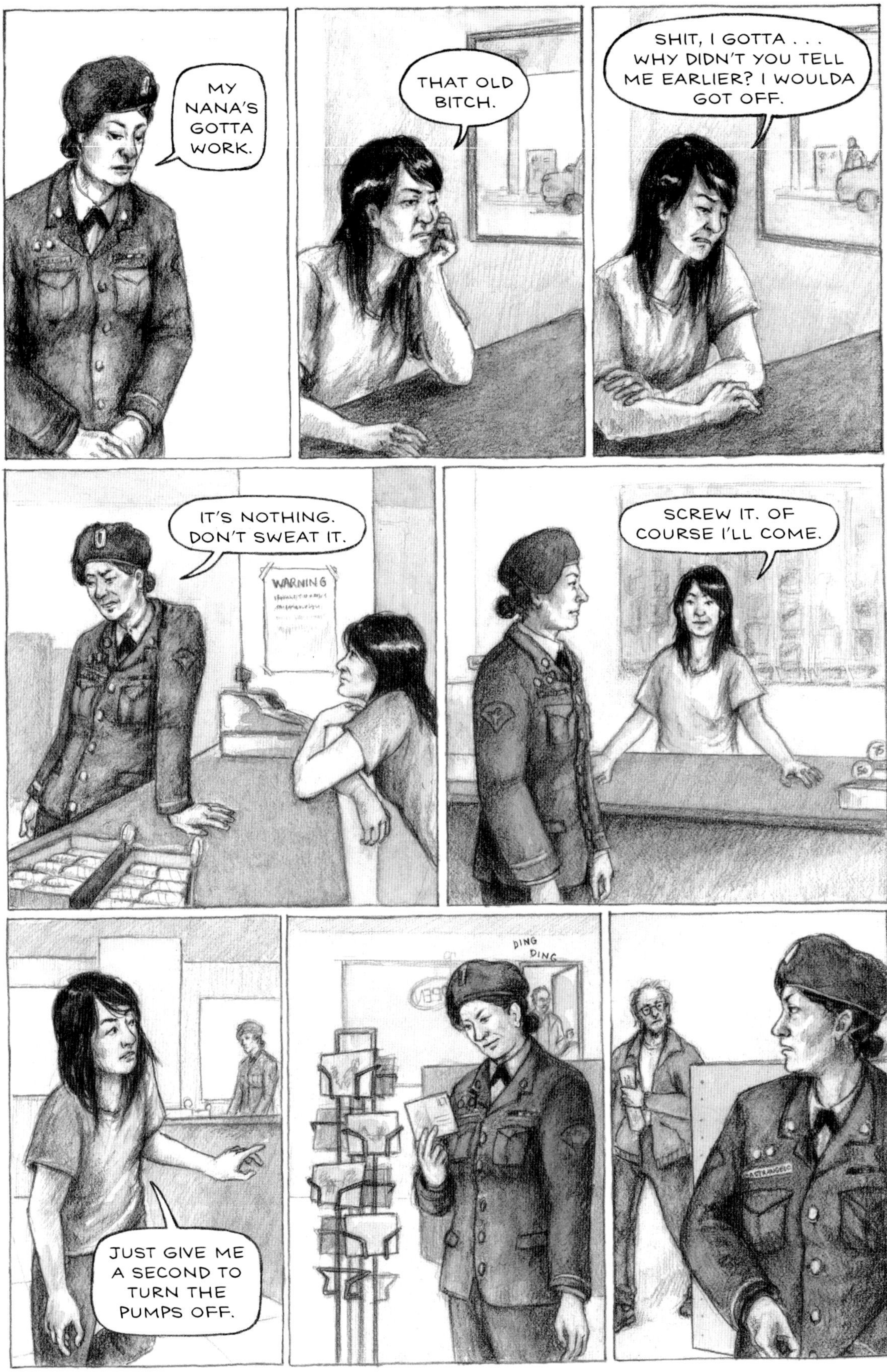
MY NANA'S GOTTA WORK.
THAT OLD BITCH.
SHIT, I GOTTA . . . WHY DIDN'T YOU TELL ME EARLIER? I WOULDA GOT OFF.
IT'S NOTHING. DON'T SWEAT IT.
WARNING
SCREW IT. OF COURSE I'LL COME.
JUST GIVE ME A SECOND TO TURN THE PUMPS OFF.
DING DING

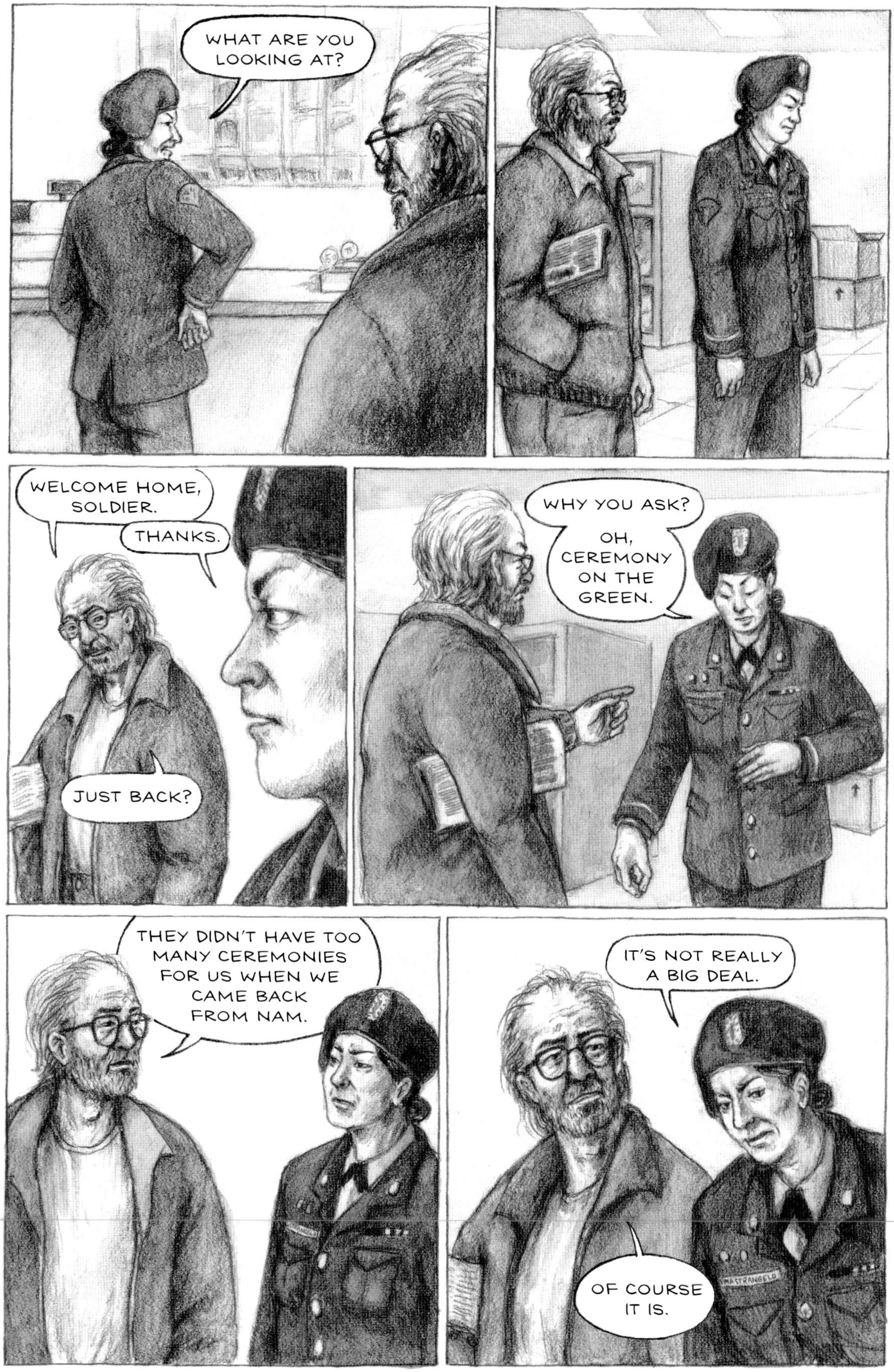
WHAT ARE YOU LOOKING AT?
WELCOME HOME, SOLDIER.
THANKS.
JUST BACK?
WHY YOU ASK?
OH, CEREMONY ON THE GREEN.
THEY DIDN'T HAVE TOO MANY CEREMONIES FOR US WHEN WE CAME BACK FROM NAM.
IT'S NOT REALLY A BIG DEAL.
OF COURSE IT IS.

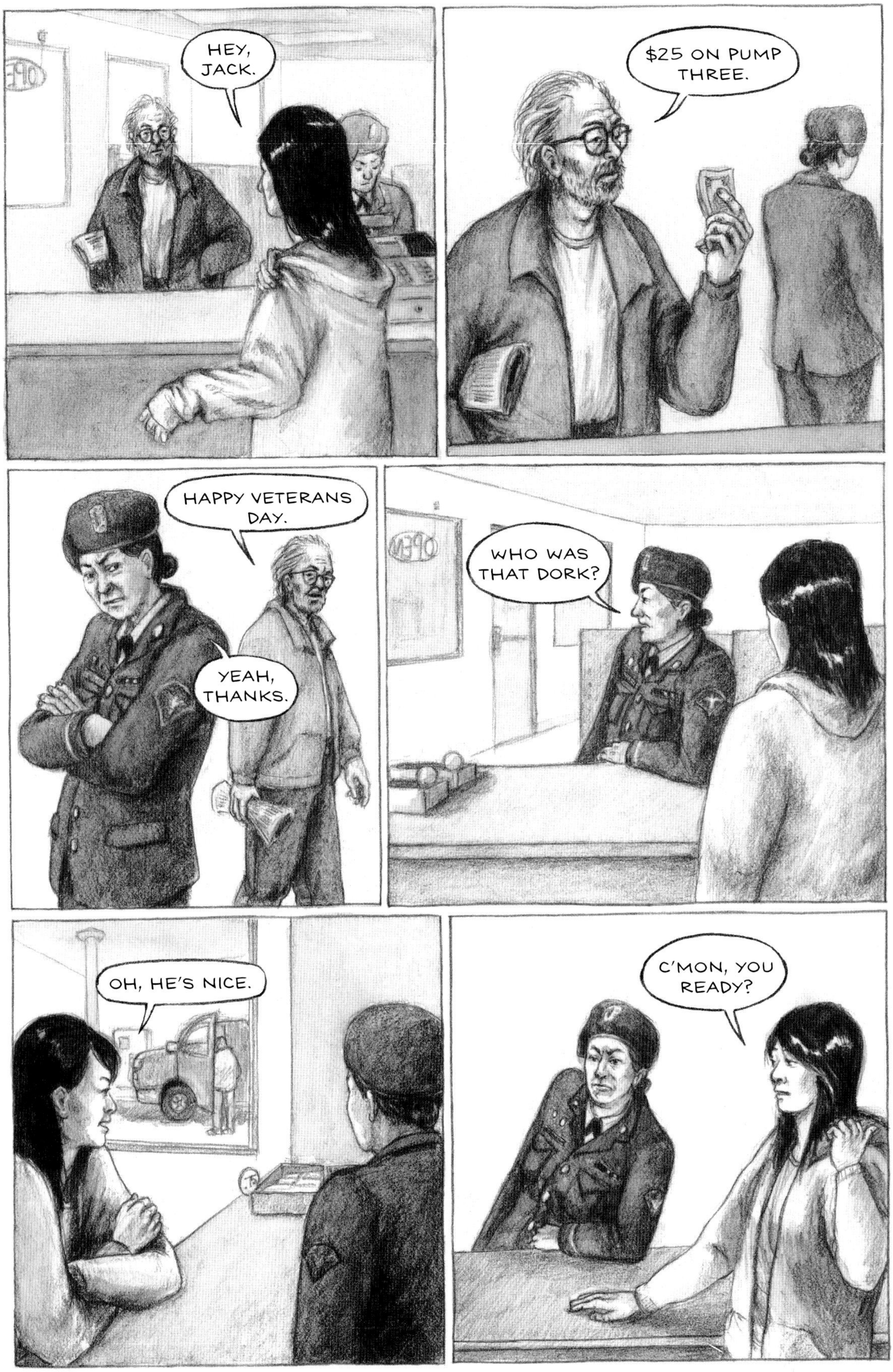
HEY, JACK.
$25 ON PUMP THREE.
HAPPY VETERANS DAY.
YEAH, THANKS.
WHO WAS THAT DORK?
OH, HE'S NICE.
C'MON, YOU READY?

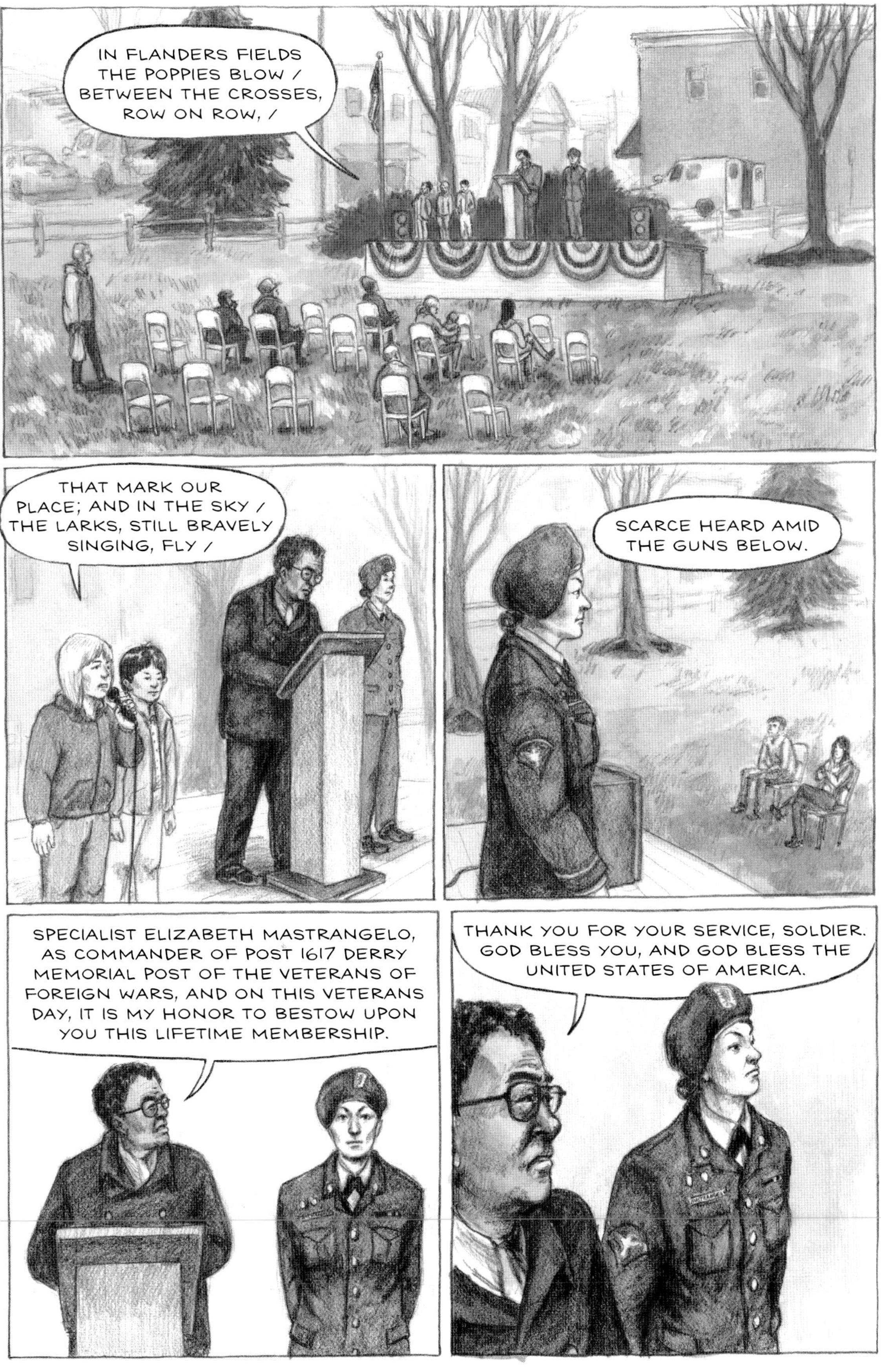
IN FLANDERS FIELDS THE POPPIES BLOW / BETWEEN THE CROSSES, ROW ON ROW, /
THAT MARK OUR PLACE; AND IN THE SKY / THE LARKS, STILL BRAVELY SINGING, FLY /
SCARCE HEARD AMID THE GUNS BELOW.
SPECIALIST ELIZABETH MASTRANGELO, AS COMMANDER OF POST 1617 DERRY MEMORIAL POST OF THE VETERANS OF FOREIGN WARS, AND ON THIS VETERANS DAY, IT IS MY HONOR TO BESTOW UPON YOU THIS LIFETIME MEMBERSHIP.
THANK YOU FOR YOUR SERVICE, SOLDIER. GOD BLESS YOU, AND GOD BLESS THE UNITED STATES OF AMERICA.

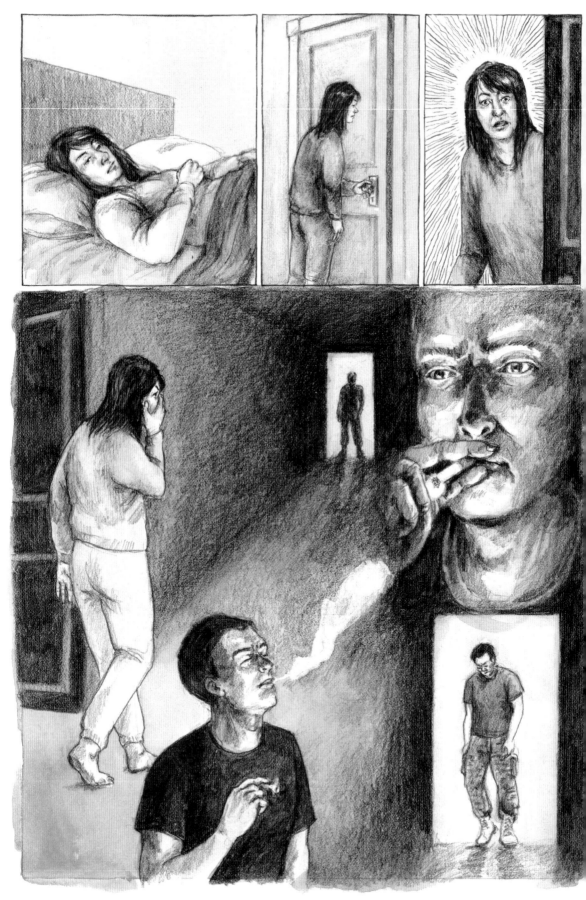

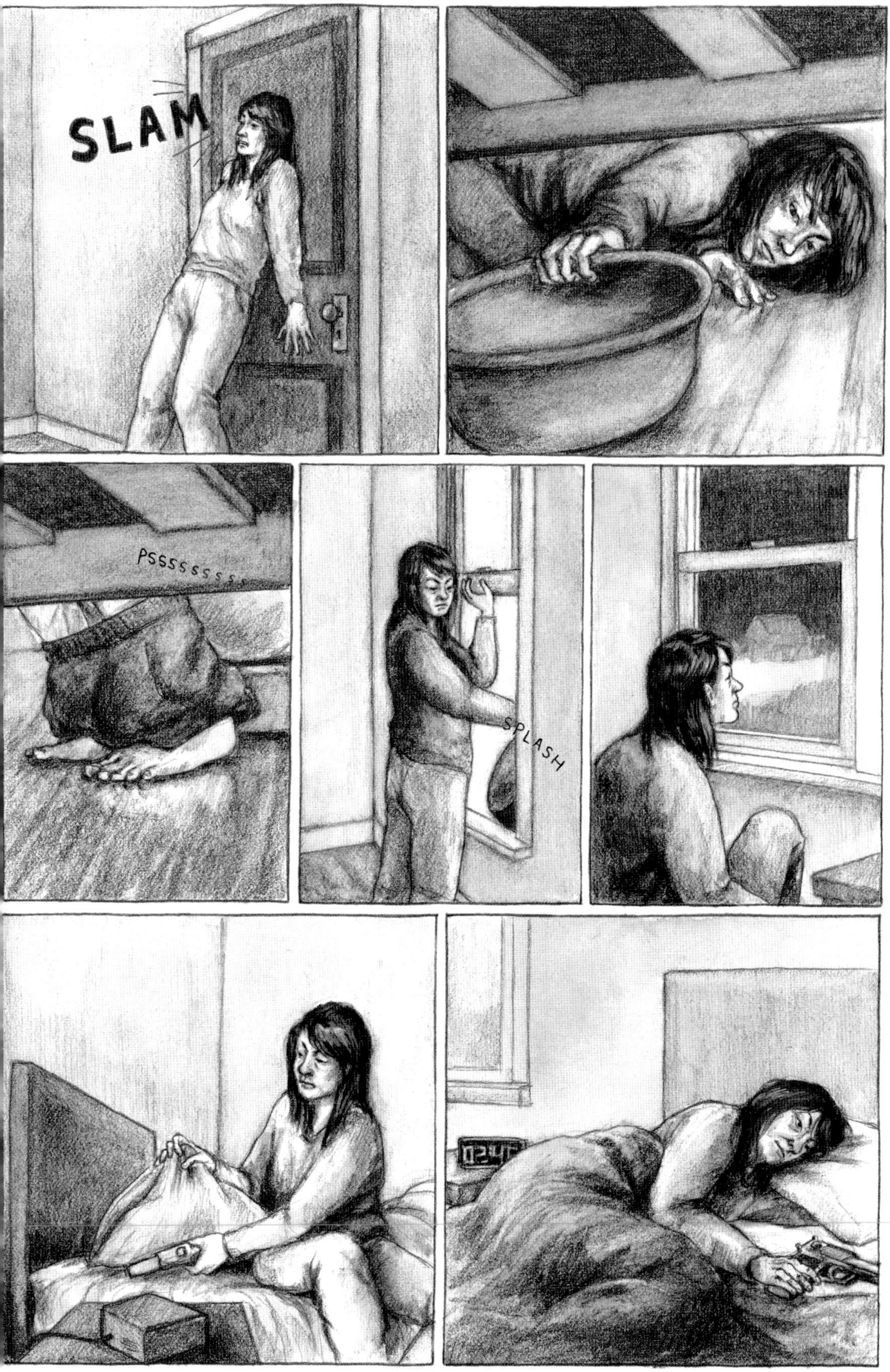

SLAM
PSSSSSSSSSS
SPLASH
0240

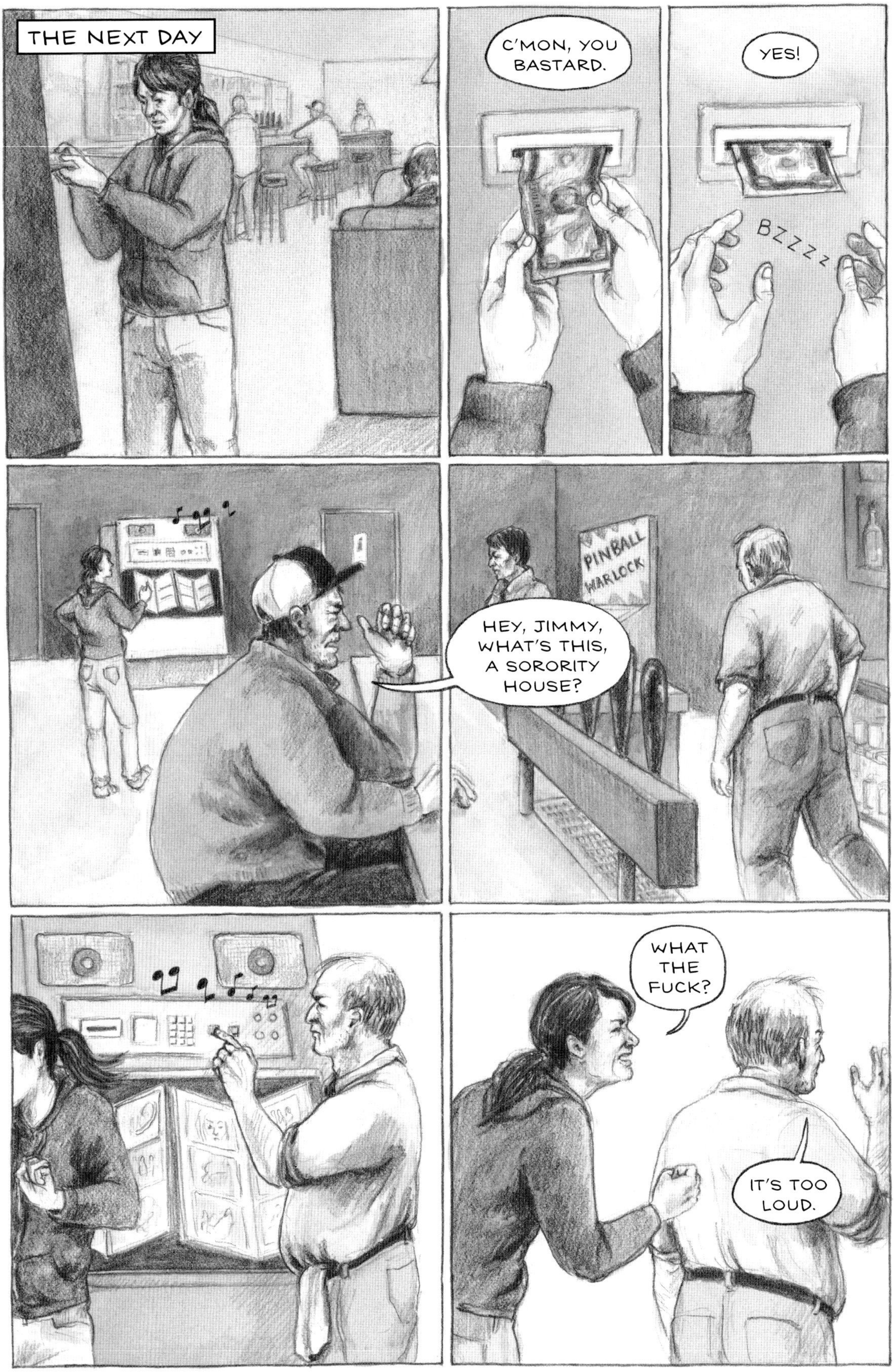
THE NEXT DAY
C'MON, YOU BASTARD.
YES!
BZZZZZ
HEY, JIMMY, WHAT'S THIS, A SORORITY HOUSE?
PINBALL WARLOCK
WHAT THE FUCK?
IT'S TOO LOUD.

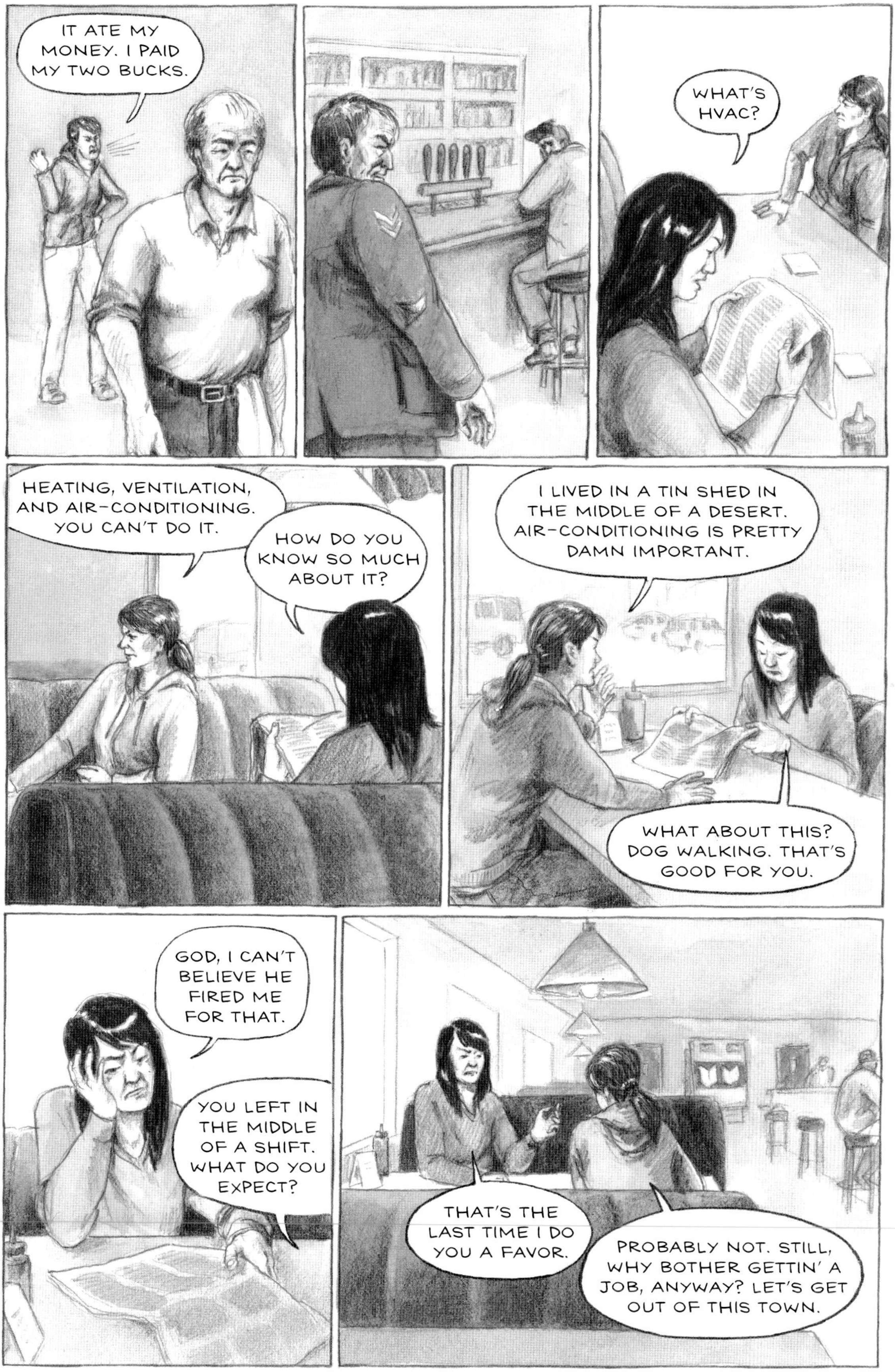
IT ATE MY MONEY. I PAID MY TWO BUCKS.
WHAT'S HVAC?
HEATING, VENTILATION, AND AIR-CONDITIONING. YOU CAN'T DO IT.
HOW DO YOU KNOW SO MUCH ABOUT IT?
I LIVED IN A TIN SHED IN THE MIDDLE OF A DESERT. AIR-CONDITIONING IS PRETTY DAMN IMPORTANT.
WHAT ABOUT THIS? DOG WALKING. THAT'S GOOD FOR YOU.
GOD, I CAN'T BELIEVE HE FIRED ME FOR THAT.
YOU LEFT IN THE MIDDLE OF A SHIFT. WHAT DO YOU EXPECT?
THAT'S THE LAST TIME I DO YOU A FAVOR.
PROBABLY NOT. STILL, WHY BOTHER GETTIN' A JOB, ANYWAY? LET'S GET OUT OF THIS TOWN.

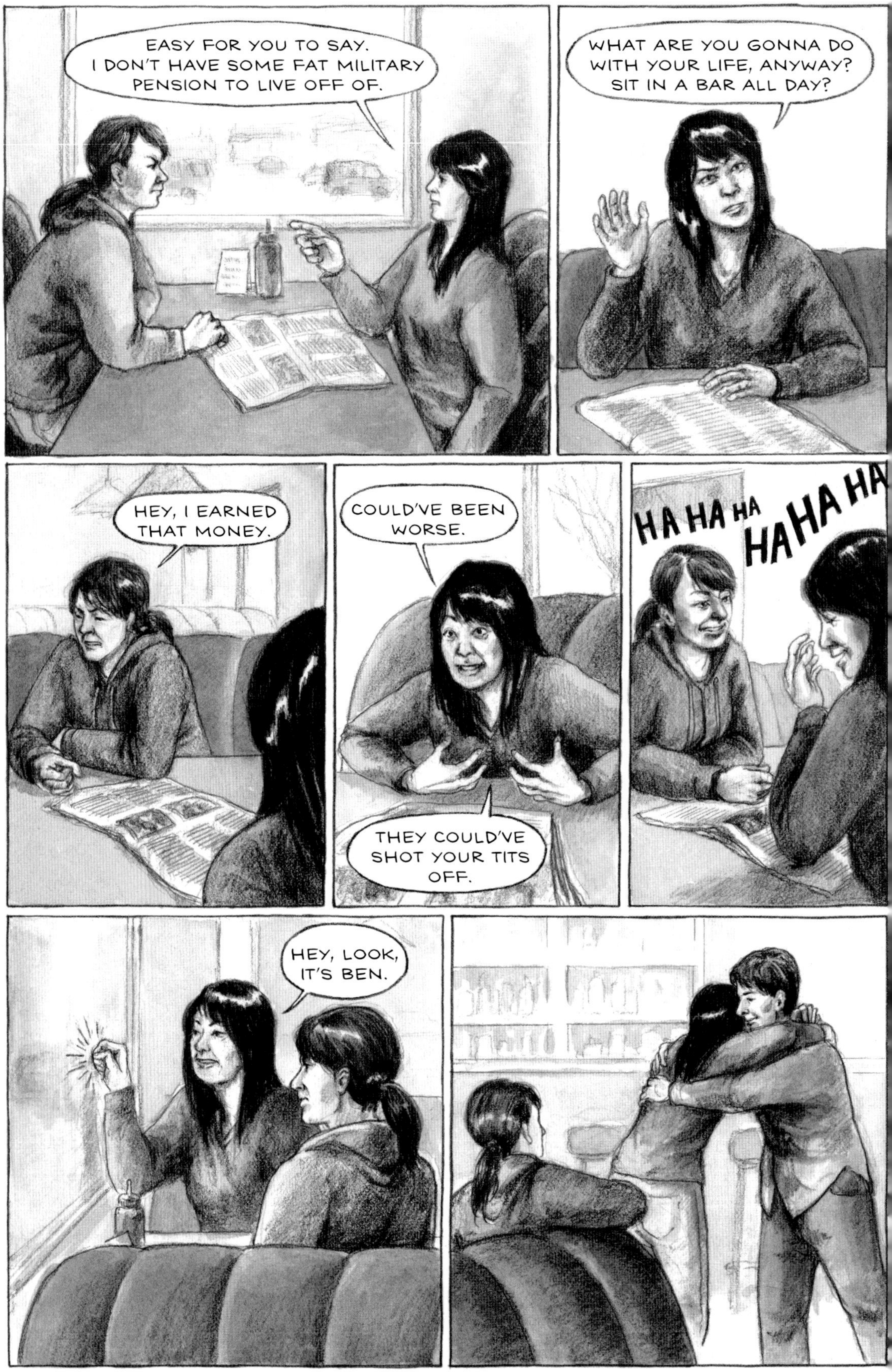
EASY FOR YOU TO SAY. I DON'T HAVE SOME FAT MILITARY PENSION TO LIVE OFF OF.
WHAT ARE YOU GONNA DO WITH YOUR LIFE, ANYWAY? SIT IN A BAR ALL DAY?
HEY, I EARNED THAT MONEY.
COULD'VE BEEN WORSE.
THEY COULD'VE SHOT YOUR TITS OFF.
HA HA HA
HA HA HA
HEY, LOOK, IT'S BEN.

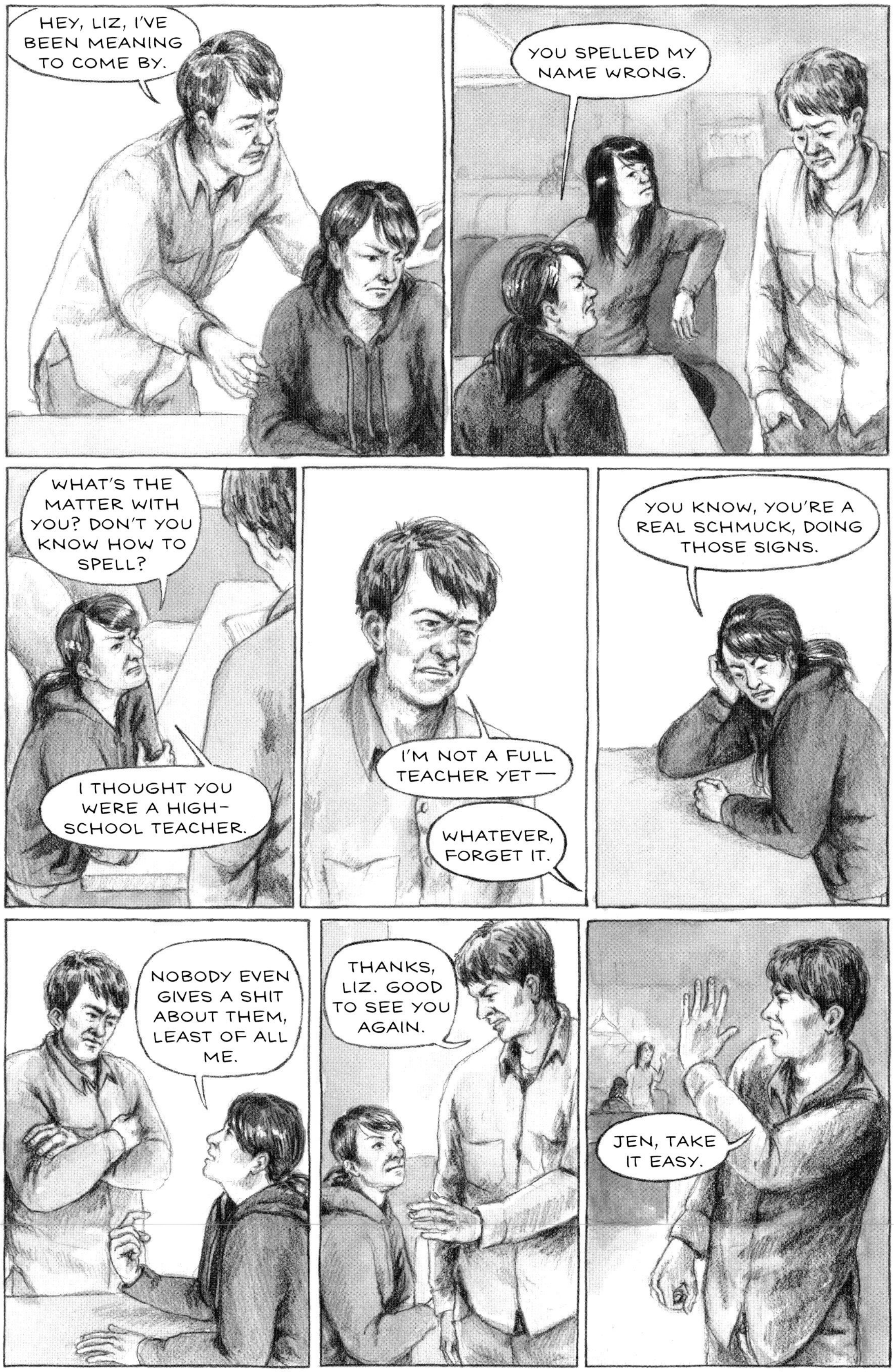
HEY, LIZ, I'VE BEEN MEANING TO COME BY.
YOU SPELLED MY NAME WRONG.
WHAT'S THE MATTER WITH YOU? DON'T YOU KNOW HOW TO SPELL?
I THOUGHT YOU WERE A HIGH-SCHOOL TEACHER.
I'M NOT A FULL TEACHER YET—
WHATEVER, FORGET IT.
YOU KNOW, YOU'RE A REAL SCHMUCK, DOING THOSE SIGNS.
NOBODY EVEN GIVES A SHIT ABOUT THEM, LEAST OF ALL ME.
THANKS, LIZ. GOOD TO SEE YOU AGAIN.
JEN, TAKE IT EASY.

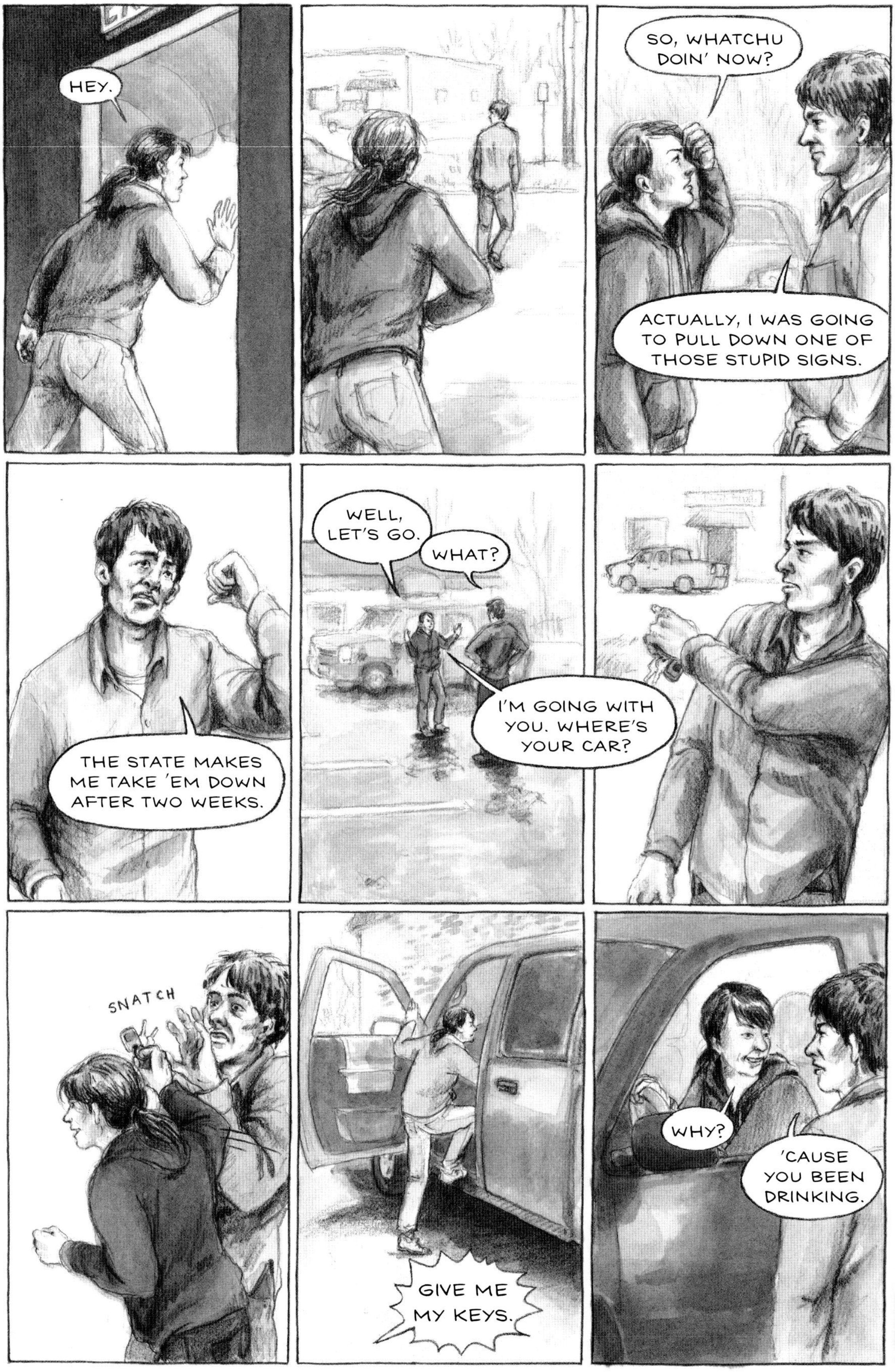
HEY.
SO, WHATCHU DOIN' NOW?
ACTUALLY, I WAS GOING TO PULL DOWN ONE OF THOSE STUPID SIGNS.
THE STATE MAKES ME TAKE 'EM DOWN AFTER TWO WEEKS.
WELL, LET'S GO.
WHAT?
I'M GOING WITH YOU. WHERE'S YOUR CAR?
SNATCH
GIVE ME MY KEYS.
WHY?
'CAUSE YOU BEEN DRINKING.

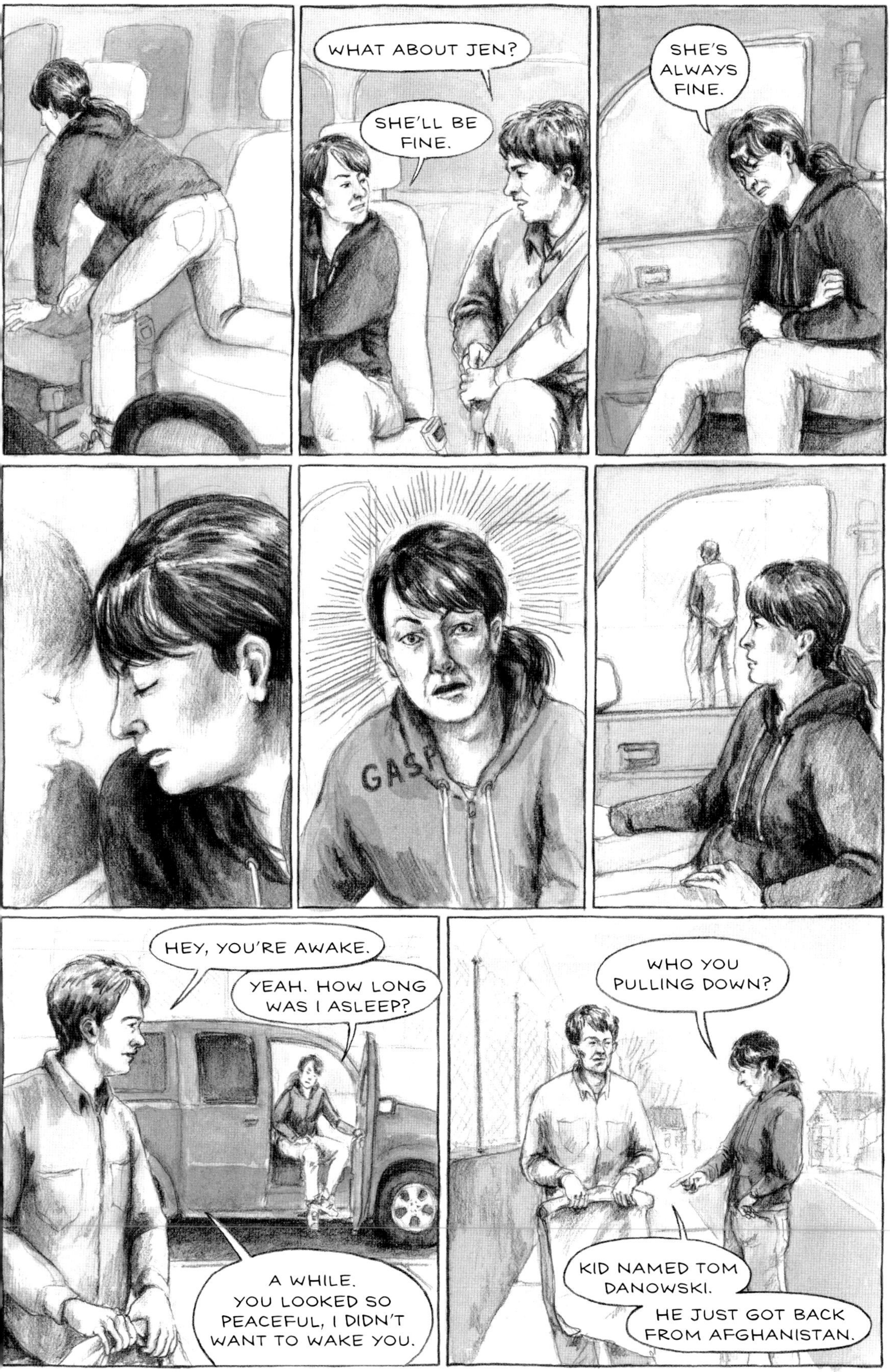

WHAT ABOUT JEN?
SHE'LL BE FINE.
SHE'S ALWAYS FINE.
GASP
HEY, YOU'RE AWAKE.
YEAH. HOW LONG WAS I ASLEEP?
A WHILE. YOU LOOKED SO PEACEFUL, I DIDN'T WANT TO WAKE YOU.
WHO YOU PULLING DOWN?
KID NAMED TOM DANOWSKI.
HE JUST GOT BACK FROM AFGHANISTAN.

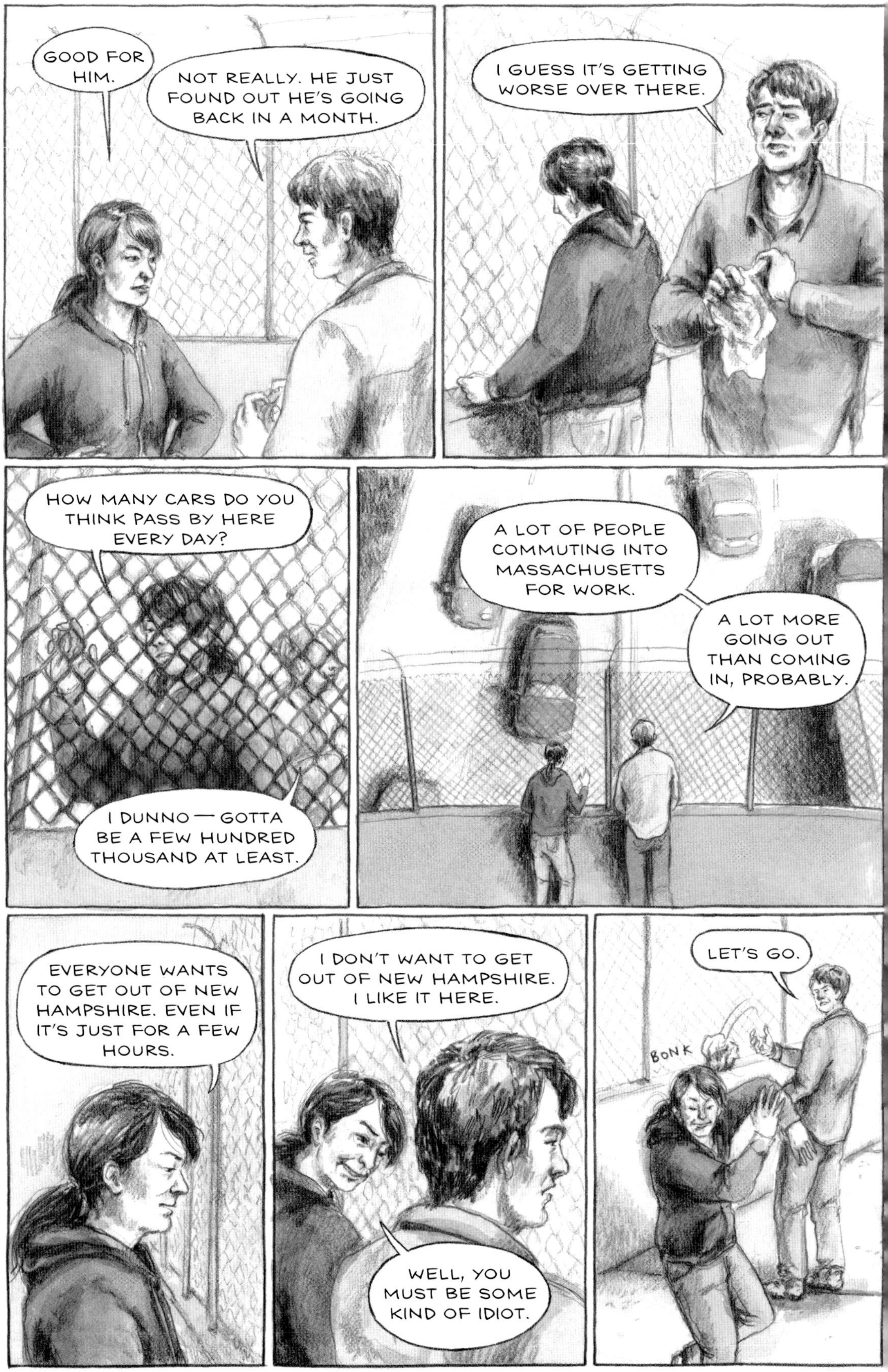
GOOD FOR HIM.
NOT REALLY. HE JUST FOUND OUT HE'S GOING BACK IN A MONTH.
I GUESS IT'S GETTING WORSE OVER THERE.
HOW MANY CARS DO YOU THINK PASS BY HERE EVERY DAY?
I DUNNO — GOTTA BE A FEW HUNDRED THOUSAND AT LEAST.
A LOT OF PEOPLE COMMUTING INTO MASSACHUSETTS FOR WORK.
A LOT MORE GOING OUT THAN COMING IN, PROBABLY.
EVERYONE WANTS TO GET OUT OF NEW HAMPSHIRE. EVEN IF IT'S JUST FOR A FEW HOURS.
I DON'T WANT TO GET OUT OF NEW HAMPSHIRE. I LIKE IT HERE.
WELL, YOU MUST BE SOME KIND OF IDIOT.
LET'S GO.
BONK

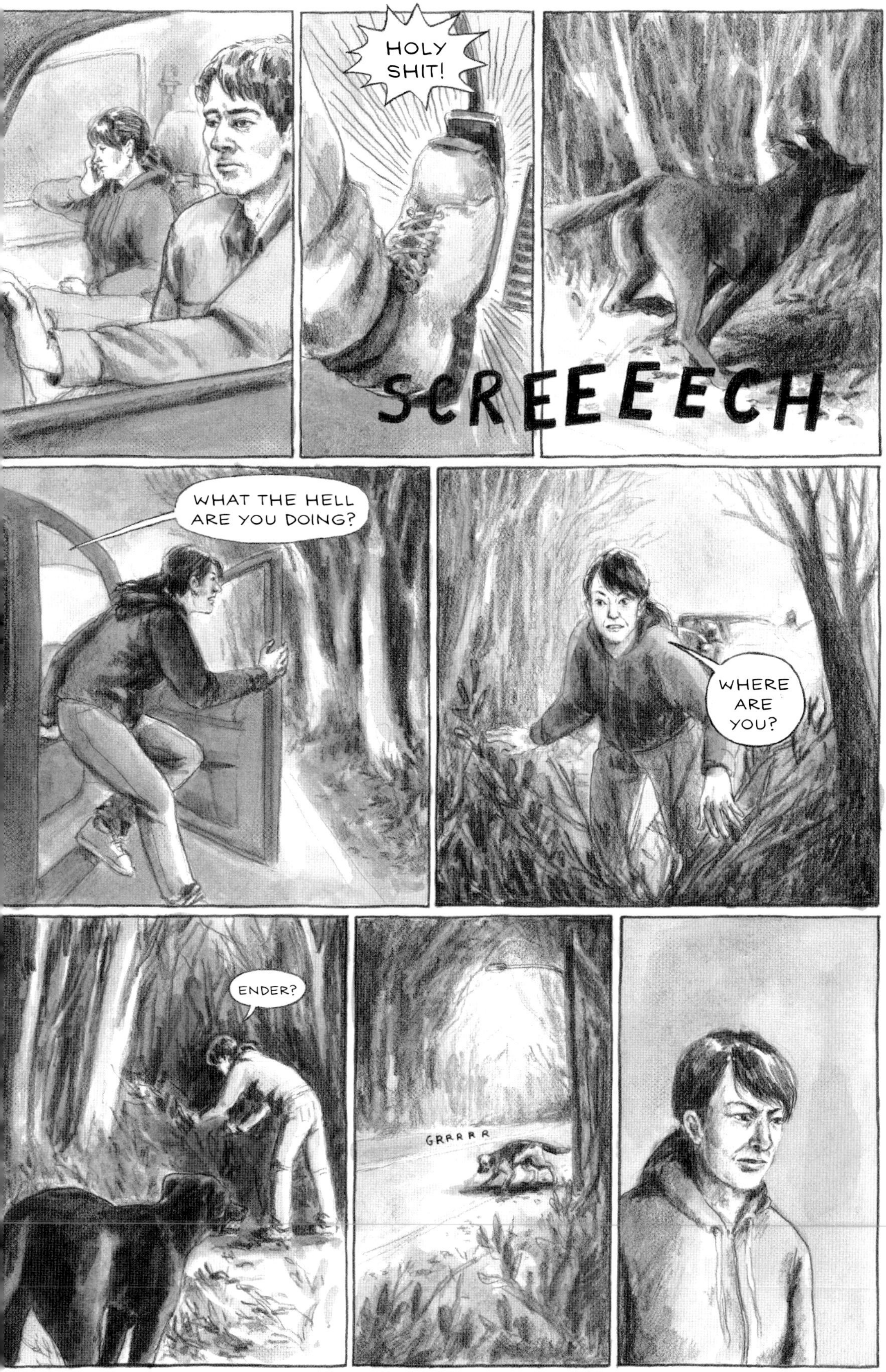
HOLY SHIT!
SCREEEECH
WHAT THE HELL ARE YOU DOING?
WHERE ARE YOU?
ENDER?
GRRRRR

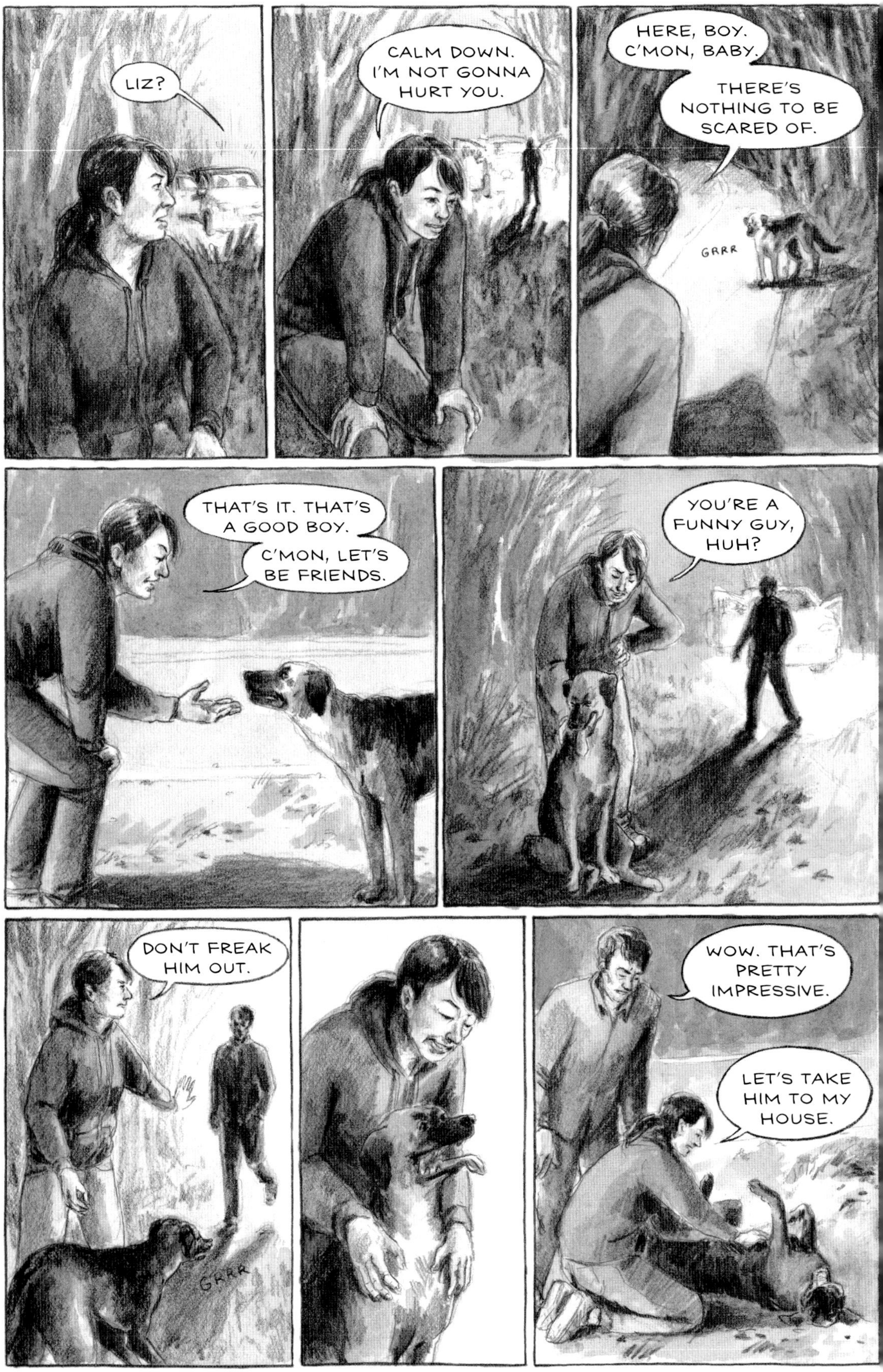
LIZ?
CALM DOWN. I'M NOT GONNA HURT YOU.
HERE, BOY. C'MON, BABY.
THERE'S NOTHING TO BE SCARED OF.
GRRR
THAT'S IT. THAT'S A GOOD BOY.
C'MON, LET'S BE FRIENDS.
YOU'RE A FUNNY GUY, HUH?
DON'T FREAK HIM OUT.
GRRR
WOW. THAT'S PRETTY IMPRESSIVE.
LET'S TAKE HIM TO MY HOUSE.

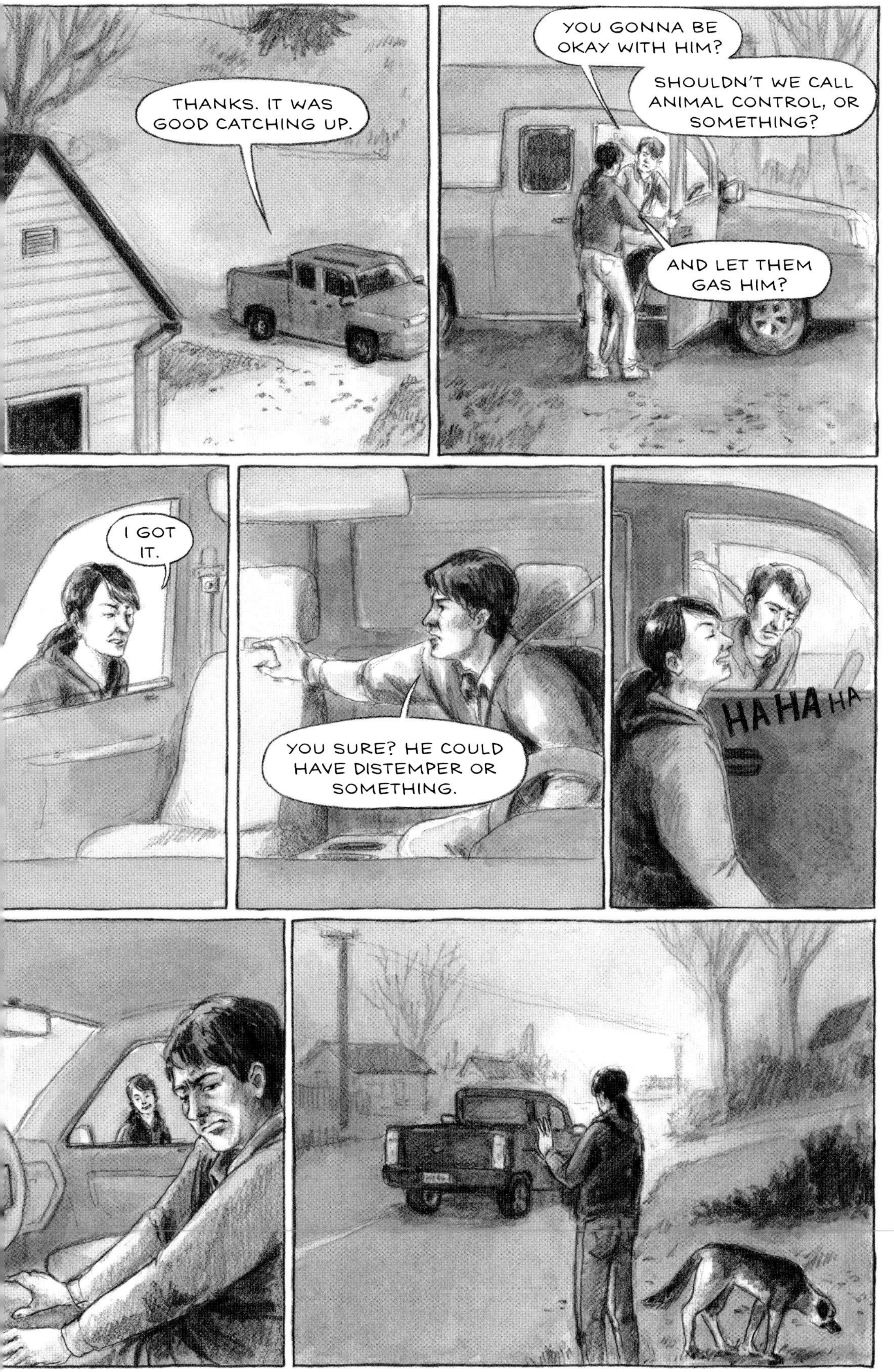
THANKS. IT WAS GOOD CATCHING UP.
YOU GONNA BE OKAY WITH HIM?
SHOULDN'T WE CALL ANIMAL CONTROL, OR SOMETHING?
AND LET THEM GAS HIM?
I GOT IT.
YOU SURE? HE COULD HAVE DISTEMPER OR SOMETHING.
HAHAHA

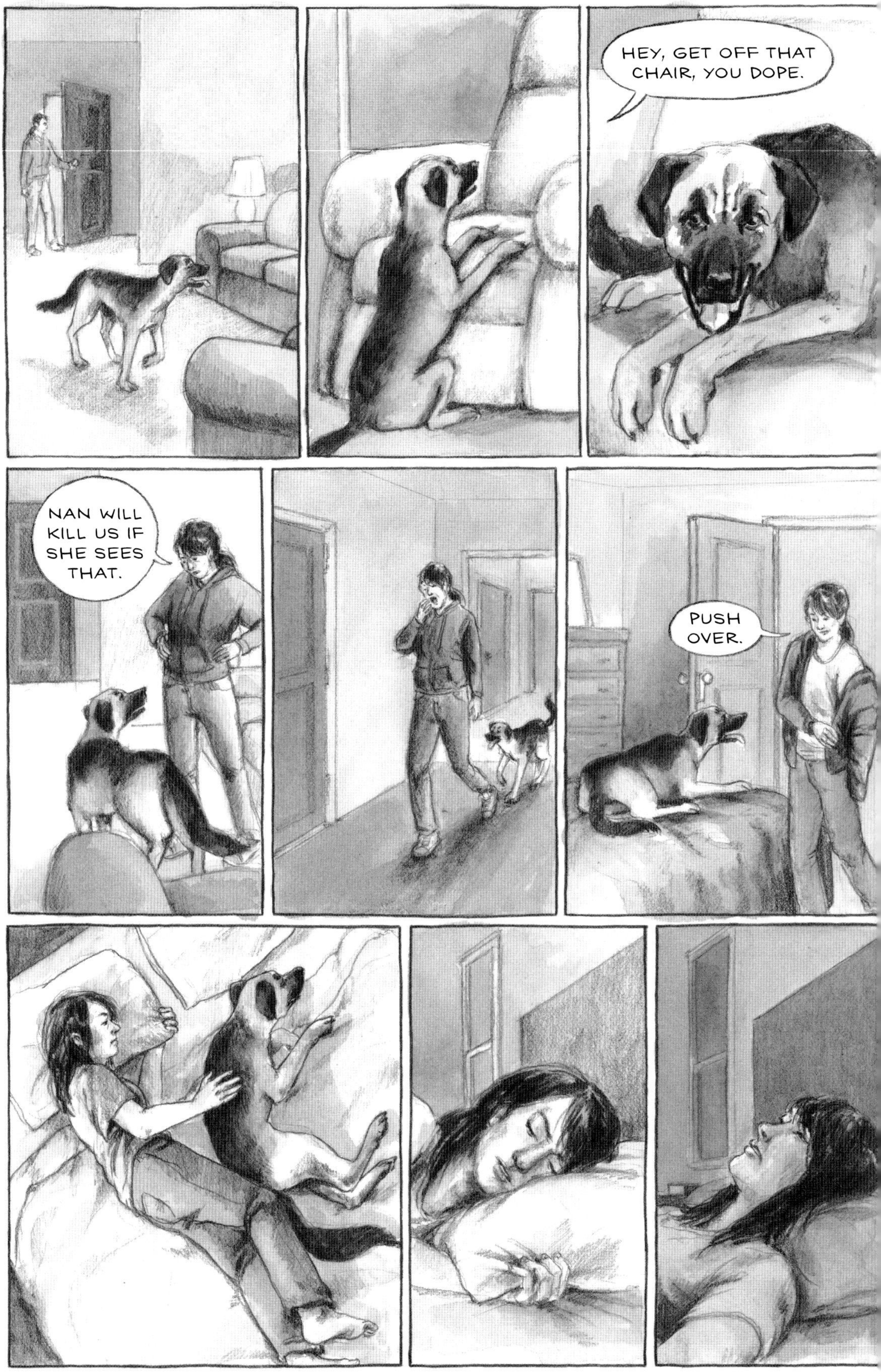
HEY, GET OFF THAT CHAIR, YOU DOPE.
NAN WILL KILL US IF SHE SEES THAT.
PUSH OVER.

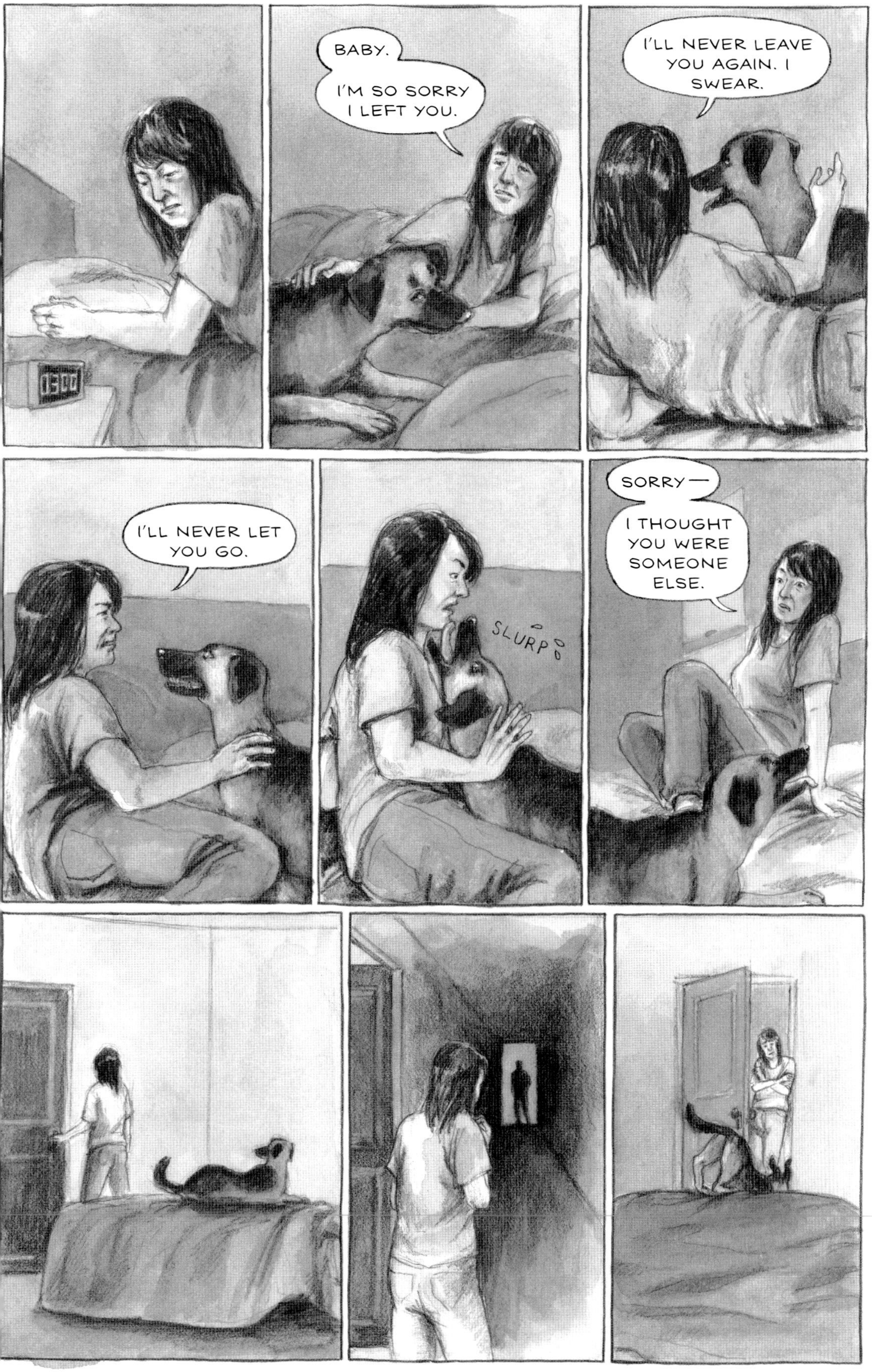
BABY.
I'M SO SORRY I LEFT YOU.
I'LL NEVER LEAVE YOU AGAIN. I SWEAR.
I'LL NEVER LET YOU GO.
SLURP
SORRY—
I THOUGHT YOU WERE SOMEONE ELSE.

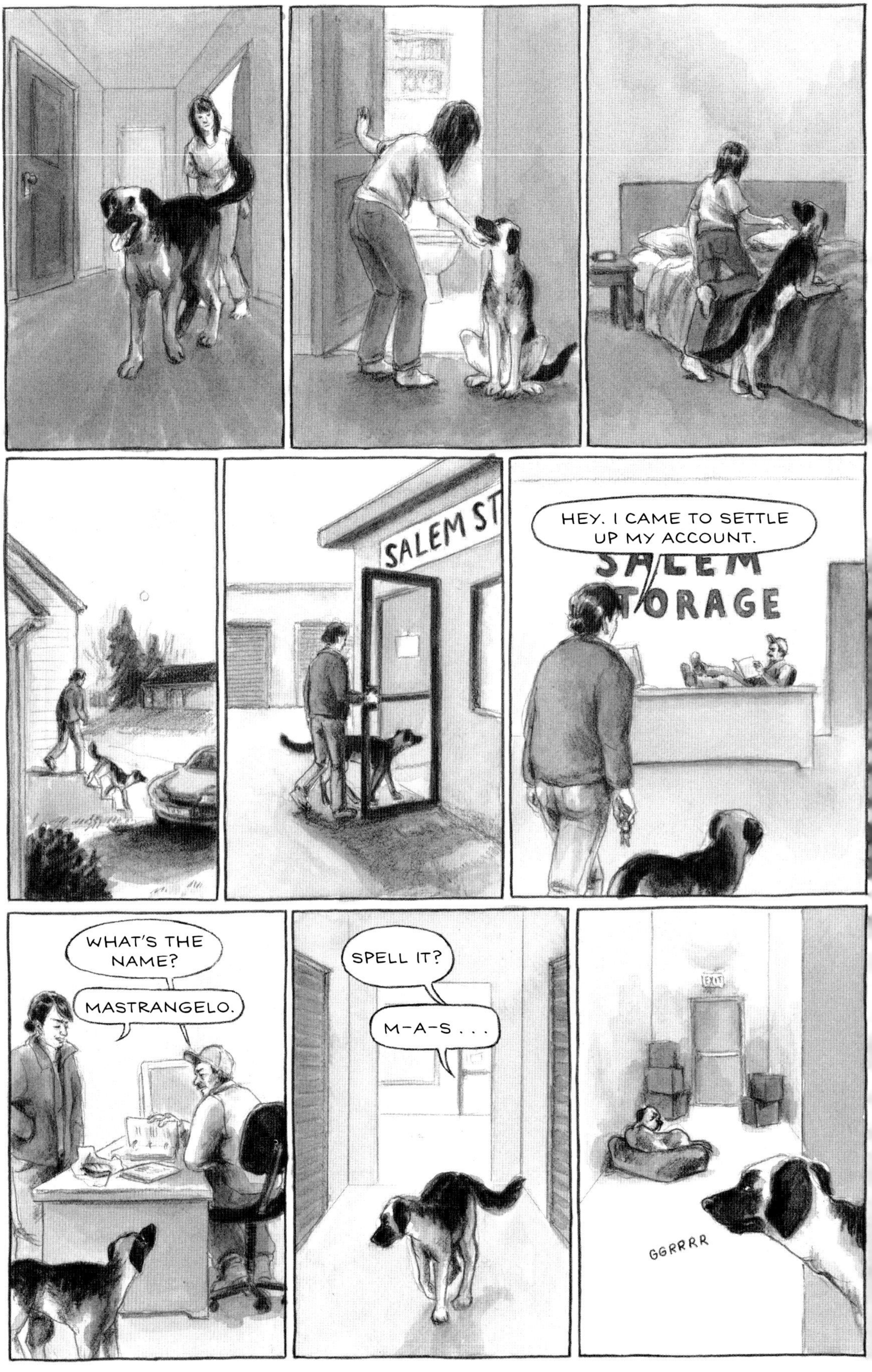
SALEM ST
HEY. I CAME TO SETTLE UP MY ACCOUNT.
SALEM STORAGE
WHAT'S THE NAME?
MASTRANGELO.
SPELL IT?
M-A-S . . .
EXIT
GGRRRR

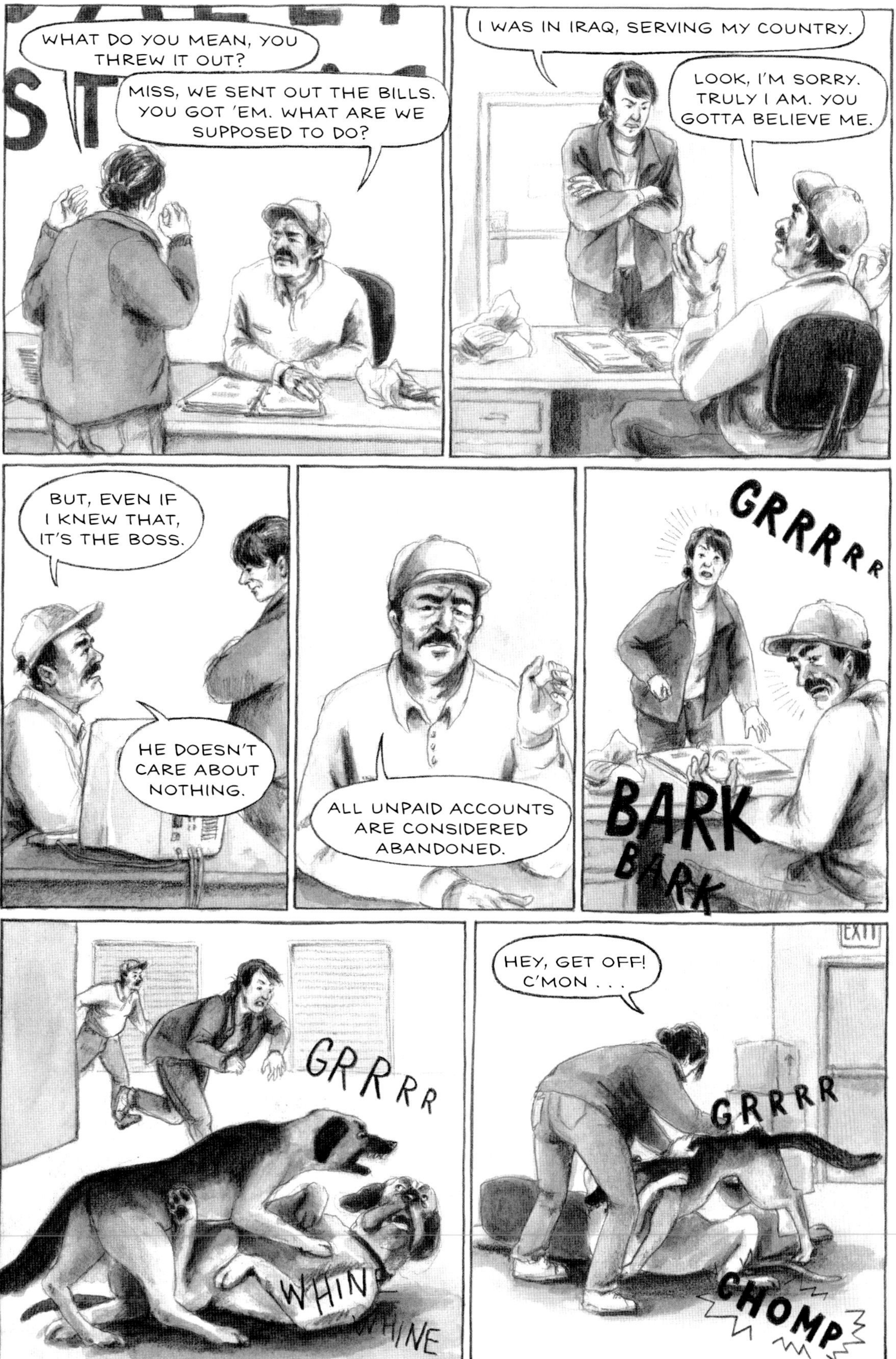
WHAT DO YOU MEAN, YOU THREW IT OUT?
MISS, WE SENT OUT THE BILLS. YOU GOT 'EM. WHAT ARE WE SUPPOSED TO DO?
I WAS IN IRAQ, SERVING MY COUNTRY.
LOOK, I'M SORRY. TRULY I AM. YOU GOTTA BELIEVE ME.
BUT, EVEN IF I KNEW THAT, IT'S THE BOSS.
HE DOESN'T CARE ABOUT NOTHING.
ALL UNPAID ACCOUNTS ARE CONSIDERED ABANDONED.
GRRRRR
BARK
BARK
GRRRR
WHINE
WHINE
HEY, GET OFF! C'MON . . .
GRRRR
CHOMP

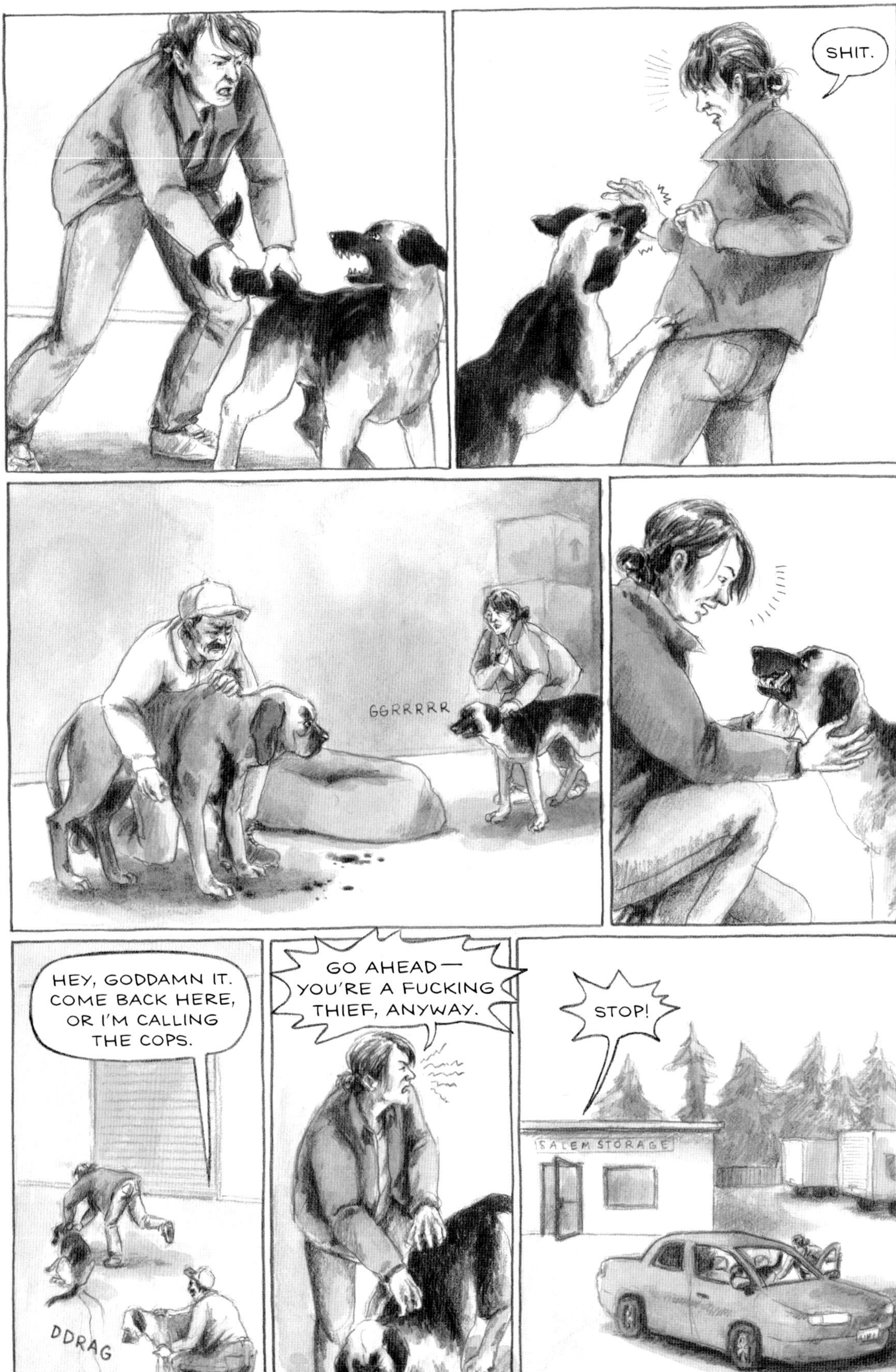
SHIT.
GGRRRRR
HEY, GODDAMN IT. COME BACK HERE, OR I'M CALLING THE COPS.
DDRAG
GO AHEAD— YOU'RE A FUCKING THIEF, ANYWAY.
STOP!
SALEM STORAGE

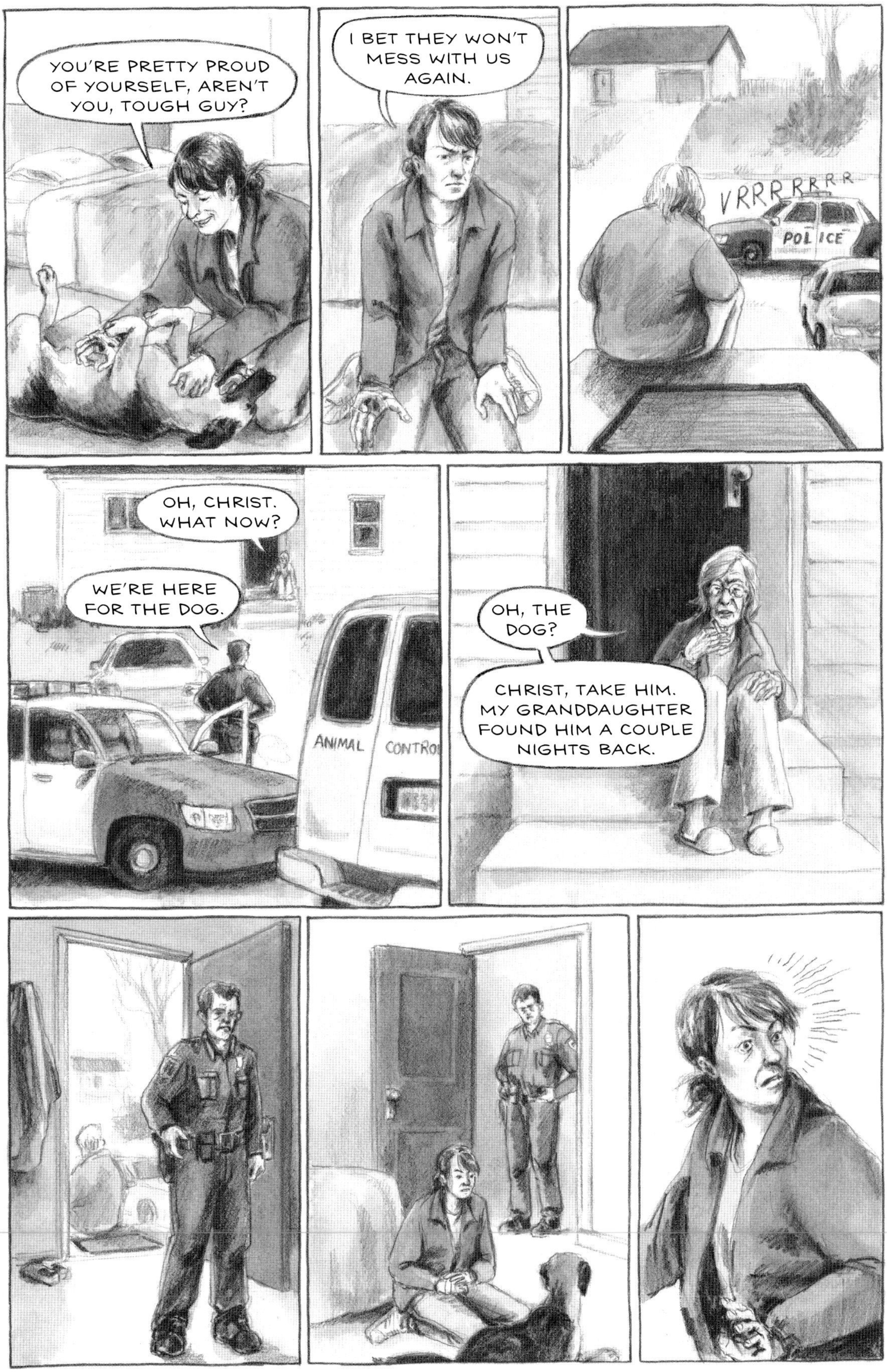
YOU'RE PRETTY PROUD OF YOURSELF, AREN'T YOU, TOUGH GUY?
I BET THEY WON'T MESS WITH US AGAIN.
VRRRRRRR
POLICE
OH, CHRIST. WHAT NOW?
WE'RE HERE FOR THE DOG.
ANIMAL CONTRO
OH, THE DOG?
CHRIST, TAKE HIM. MY GRANDDAUGHTER FOUND HIM A COUPLE NIGHTS BACK.

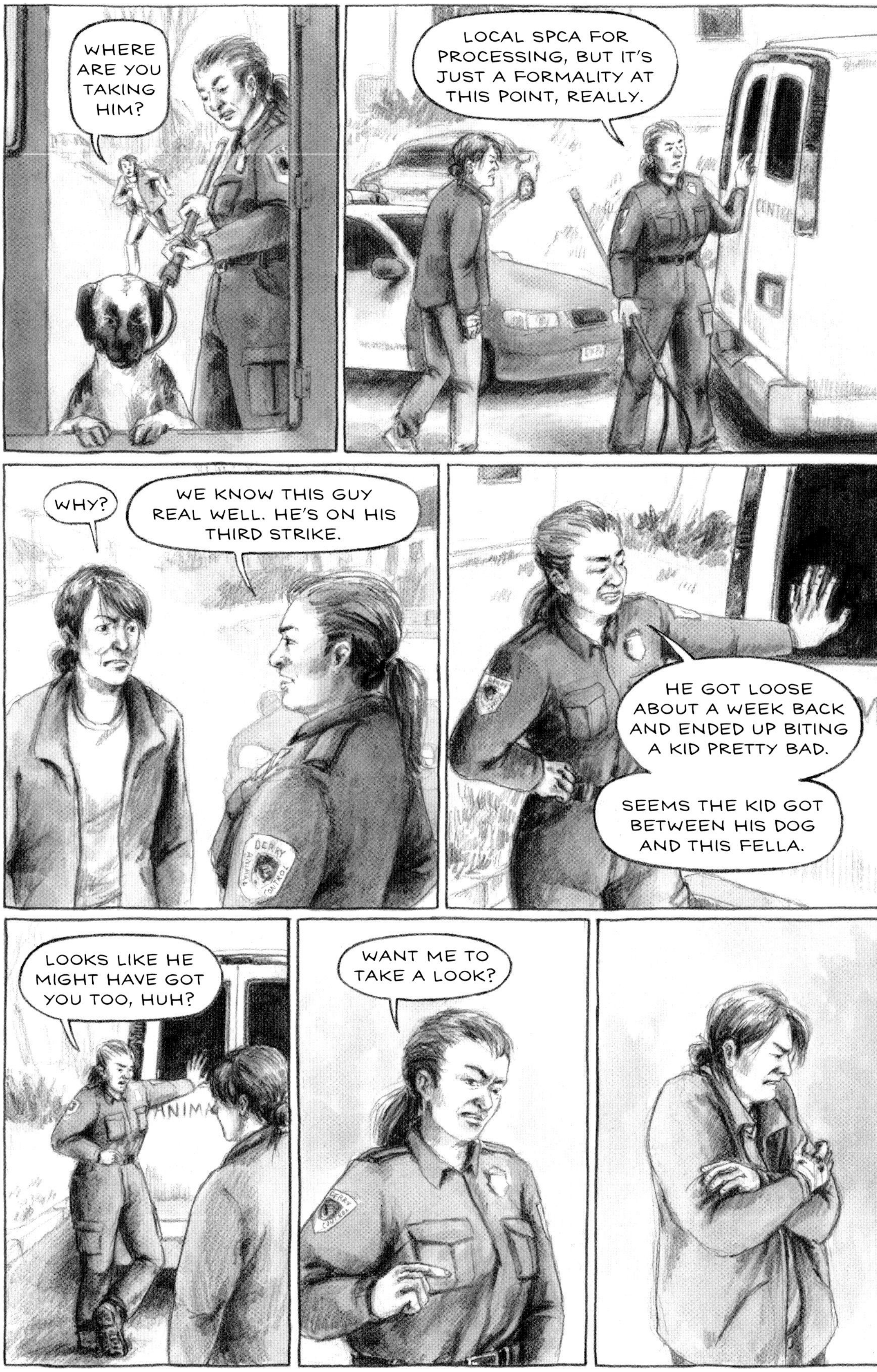
WHERE ARE YOU TAKING HIM?
LOCAL SPCA FOR PROCESSING, BUT IT'S JUST A FORMALITY AT THIS POINT, REALLY.
WHY?
WE KNOW THIS GUY REAL WELL. HE'S ON HIS THIRD STRIKE.
DERRY ANIMAL CONTROL
HE GOT LOOSE ABOUT A WEEK BACK AND ENDED UP BITING A KID PRETTY BAD.
SEEMS THE KID GOT BETWEEN HIS DOG AND THIS FELLA.
LOOKS LIKE HE MIGHT HAVE GOT YOU TOO, HUH?
WANT ME TO TAKE A LOOK?

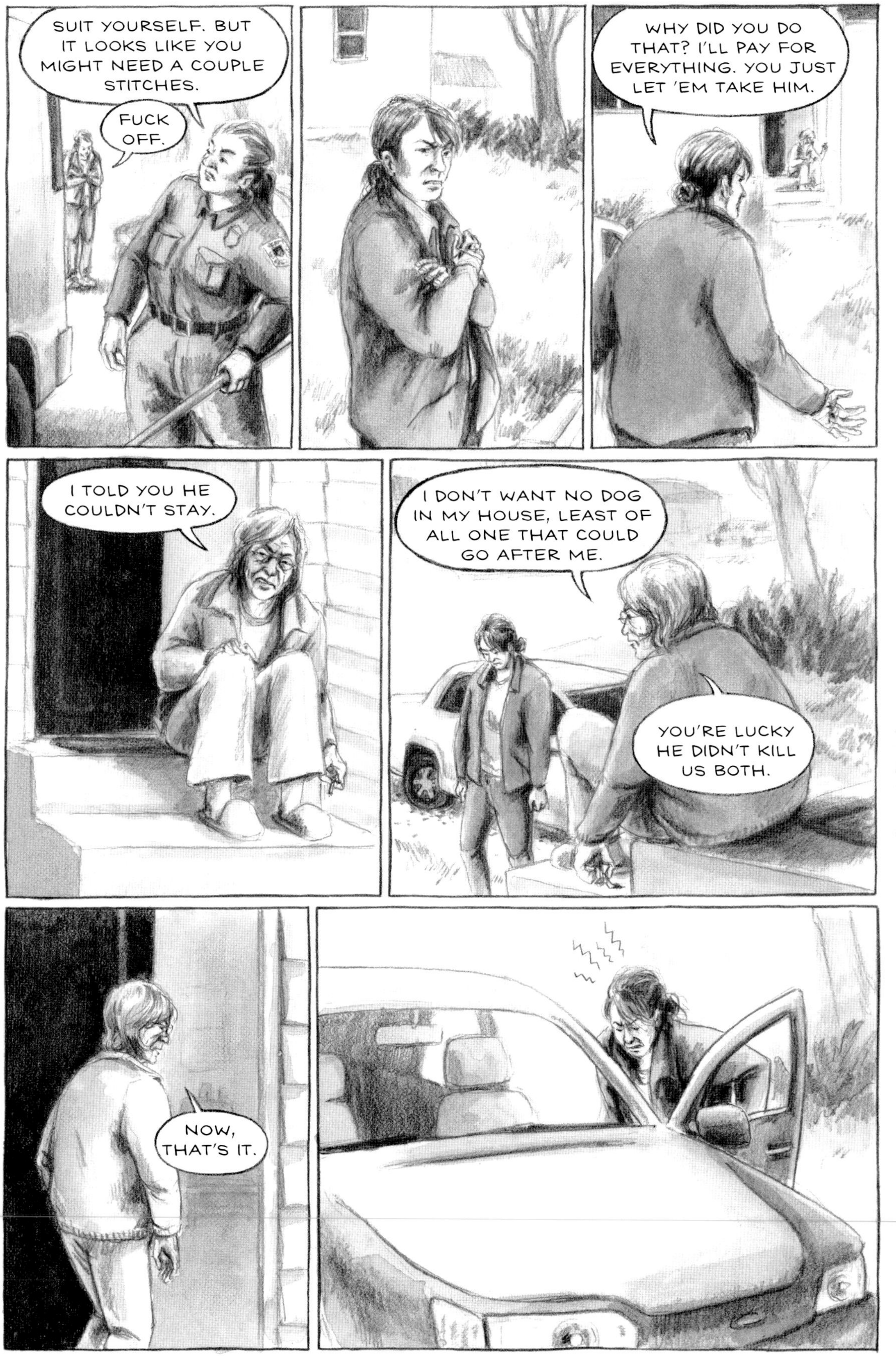
SUIT YOURSELF. BUT IT LOOKS LIKE YOU MIGHT NEED A COUPLE STITCHES.
FUCK OFF.
WHY DID YOU DO THAT? I'LL PAY FOR EVERYTHING. YOU JUST LET 'EM TAKE HIM.
I TOLD YOU HE COULDN'T STAY.
I DON'T WANT NO DOG IN MY HOUSE, LEAST OF ALL ONE THAT COULD GO AFTER ME.
YOU'RE LUCKY HE DIDN'T KILL US BOTH.
NOW, THAT'S IT.

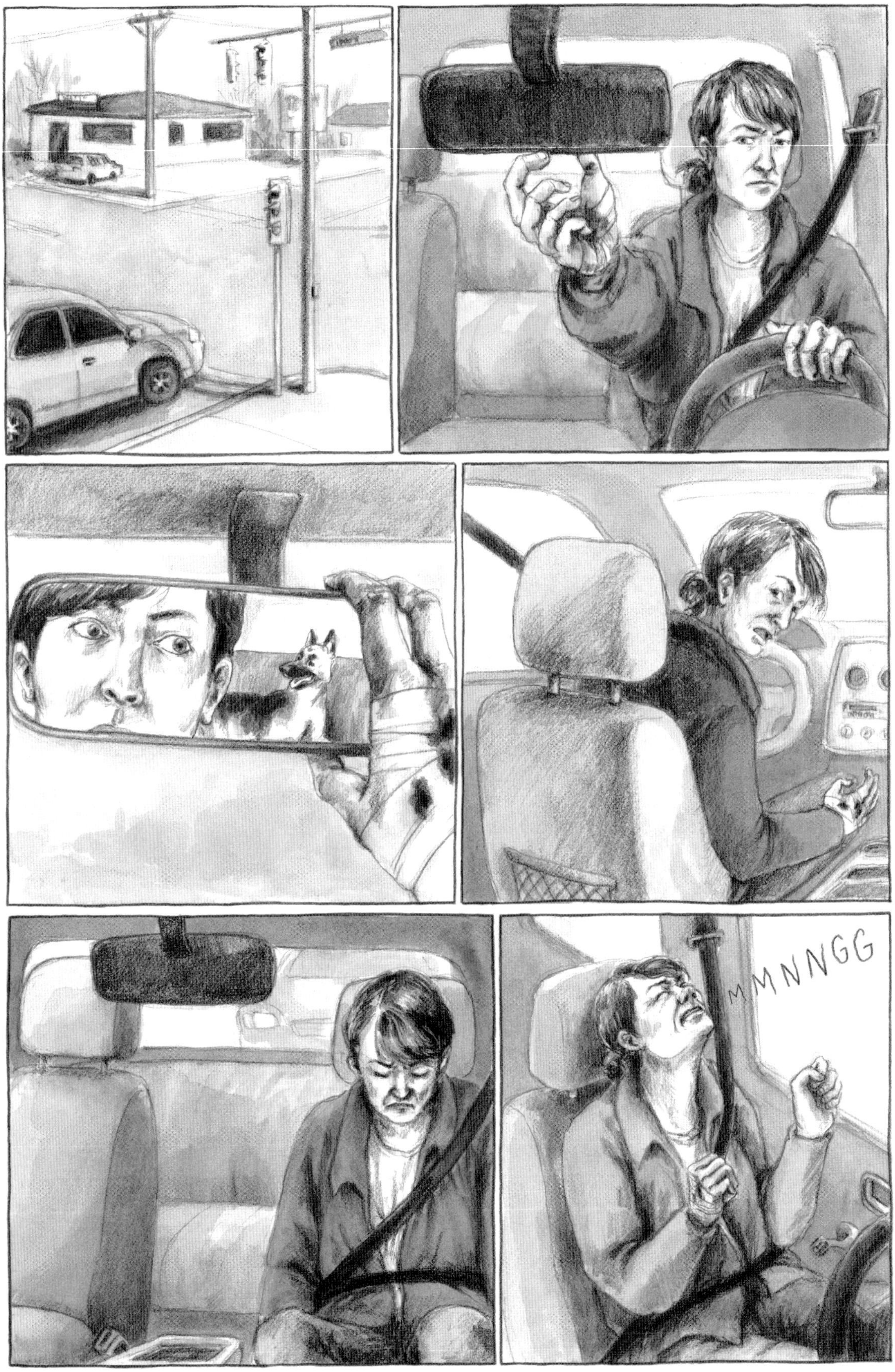
MMNNGG

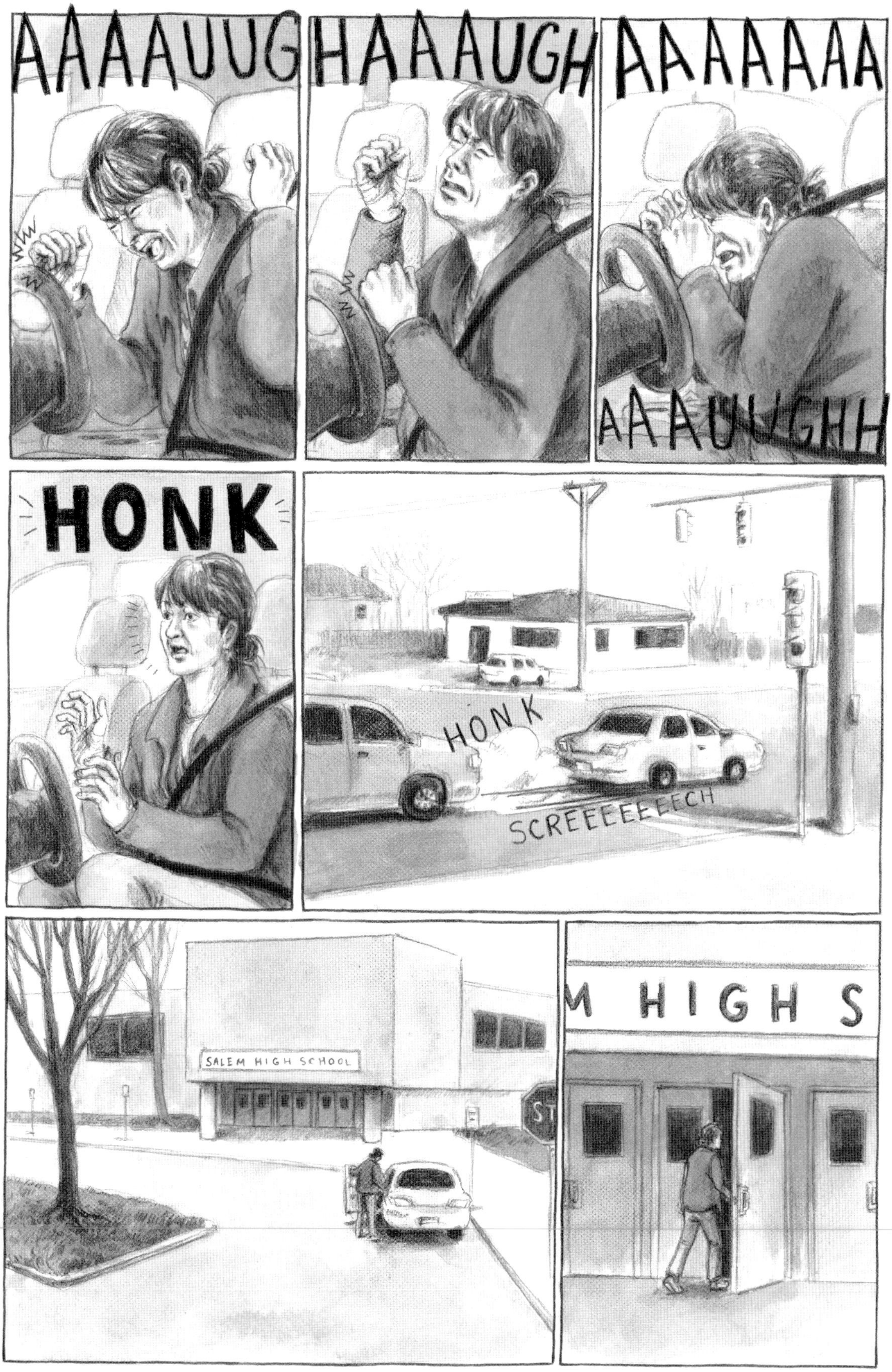
AAAAUUG
HAAAAUGH
AAAAAAA
AAAAUUGHH
HONK
HONK
SCREEEEEEECH
SALEM HIGH SCHOOL
M HIGH S

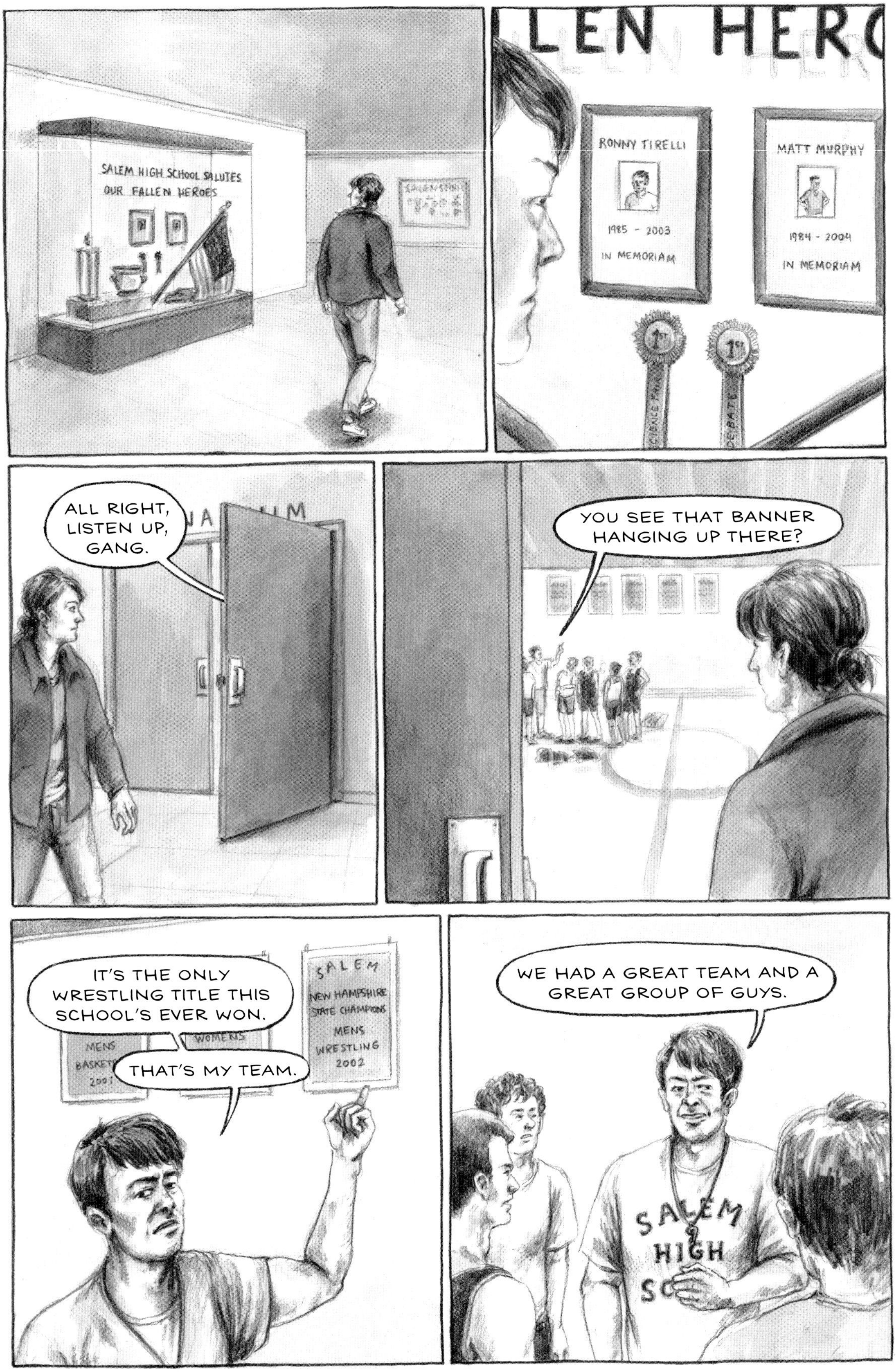
SALEM HIGH SCHOOL SALUTES OUR FALLEN HEROES
RONNY TIRELLI
1985 - 2003
IN MEMORIAM
MATT MURPHY
1984 - 2004
IN MEMORIAM
ALL RIGHT, LISTEN UP, GANG.
YOU SEE THAT BANNER HANGING UP THERE?
IT'S THE ONLY WRESTLING TITLE THIS SCHOOL'S EVER WON.
SALEM
NEW HAMPSHIRE STATE CHAMPIONS
MENS WRESTLING
2002
THAT'S MY TEAM.
WE HAD A GREAT TEAM AND A GREAT GROUP OF GUYS.

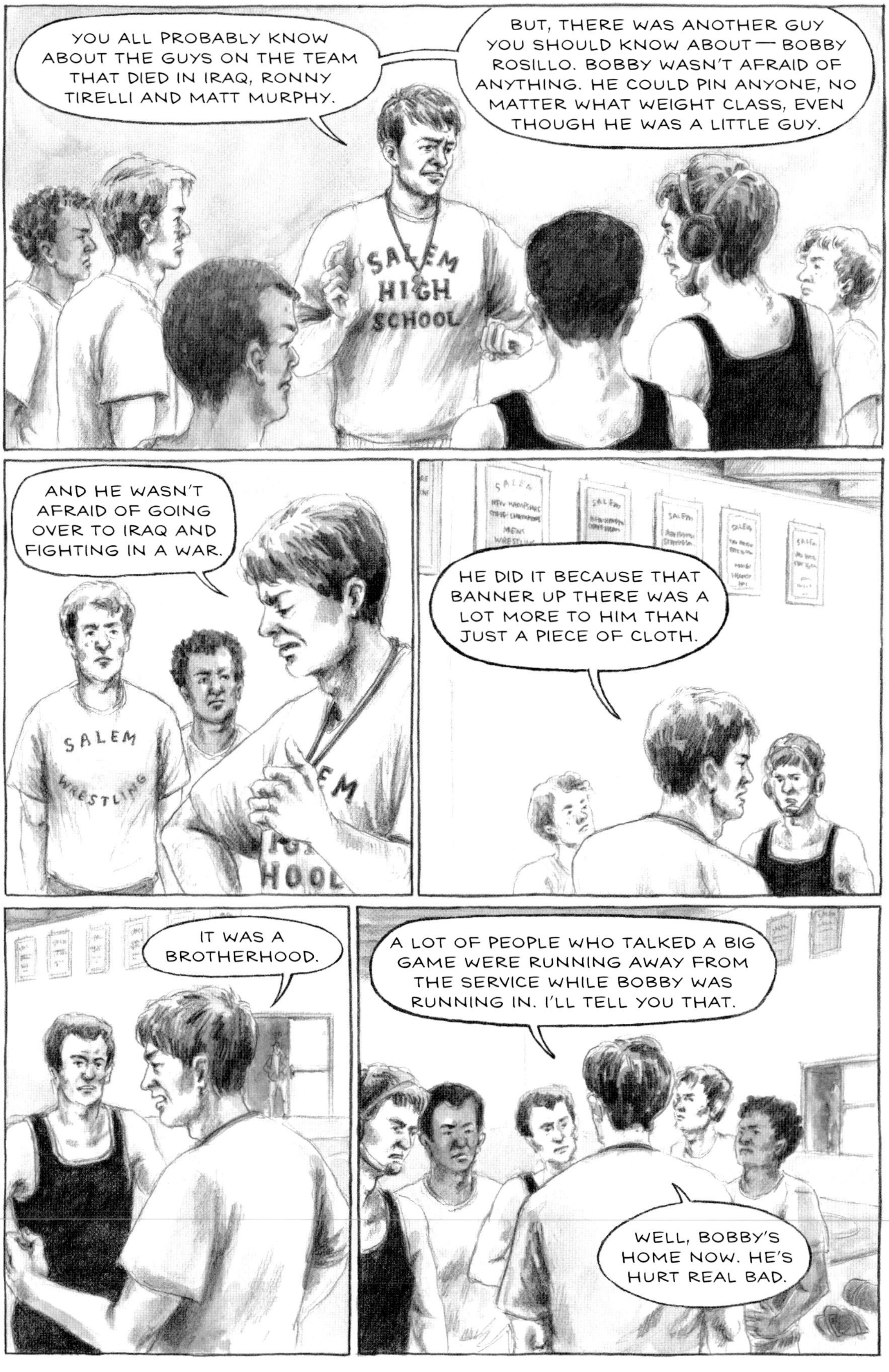
YOU ALL PROBABLY KNOW ABOUT THE GUYS ON THE TEAM THAT DIED IN IRAQ, RONNY TIRELLI AND MATT MURPHY.
BUT, THERE WAS ANOTHER GUY YOU SHOULD KNOW ABOUT — BOBBY ROSILLO. BOBBY WASN'T AFRAID OF ANYTHING. HE COULD PIN ANYONE, NO MATTER WHAT WEIGHT CLASS, EVEN THOUGH HE WAS A LITTLE GUY.
SALEM HIGH SCHOOL
AND HE WASN'T AFRAID OF GOING OVER TO IRAQ AND FIGHTING IN A WAR.
SALEM WRESTLING
HE DID IT BECAUSE THAT BANNER UP THERE WAS A LOT MORE TO HIM THAN JUST A PIECE OF CLOTH.
IT WAS A BROTHERHOOD.
A LOT OF PEOPLE WHO TALKED A BIG GAME WERE RUNNING AWAY FROM THE SERVICE WHILE BOBBY WAS RUNNING IN. I'LL TELL YOU THAT.
WELL, BOBBY'S HOME NOW. HE'S HURT REAL BAD.

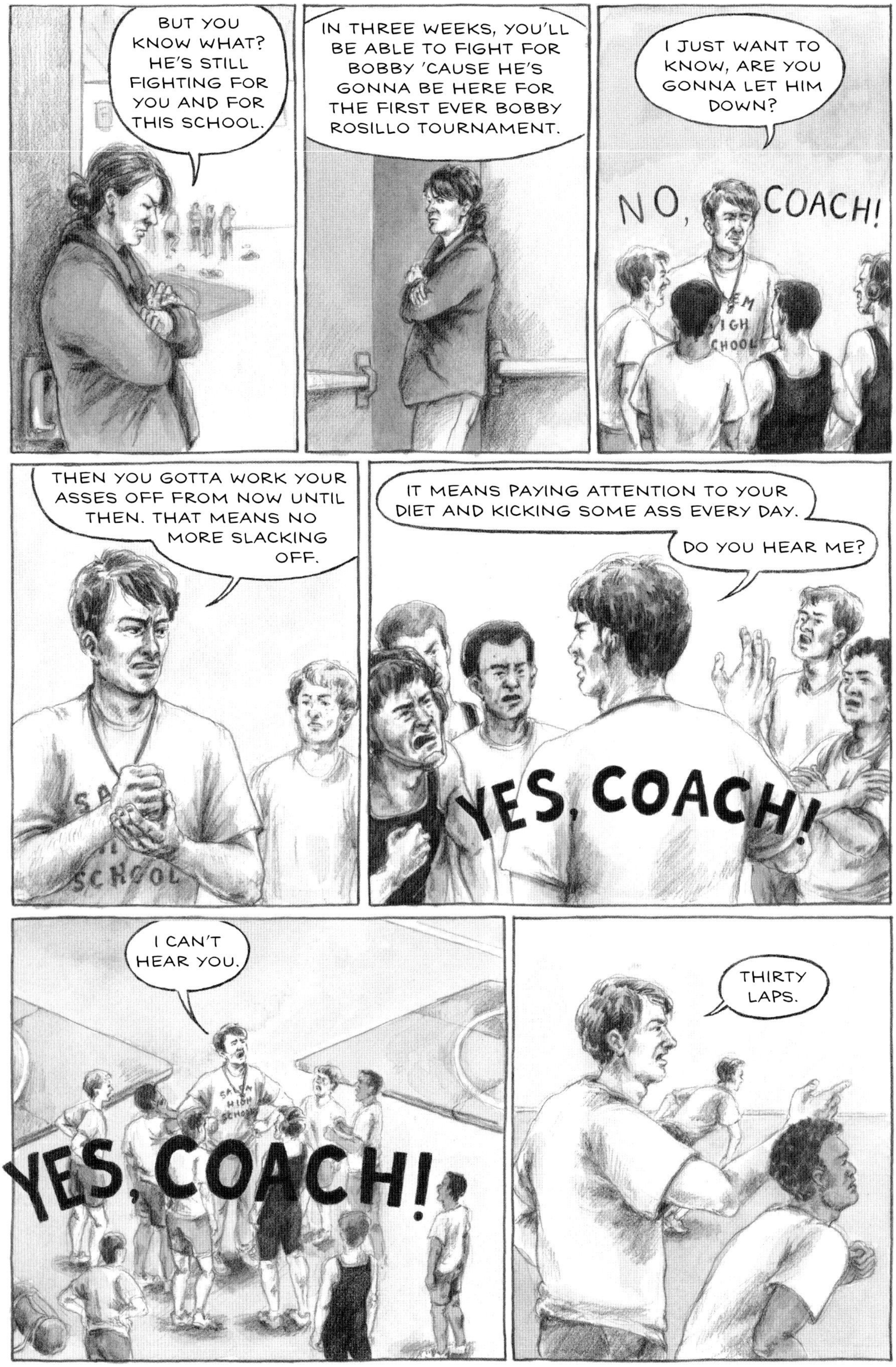
BUT YOU KNOW WHAT? HE'S STILL FIGHTING FOR YOU AND FOR THIS SCHOOL.
IN THREE WEEKS, YOU'LL BE ABLE TO FIGHT FOR BOBBY 'CAUSE HE'S GONNA BE HERE FOR THE FIRST EVER BOBBY ROSILLO TOURNAMENT.
I JUST WANT TO KNOW, ARE YOU GONNA LET HIM DOWN?
NO, COACH!
THEN YOU GOTTA WORK YOUR ASSES OFF FROM NOW UNTIL THEN. THAT MEANS NO MORE SLACKING OFF.
IT MEANS PAYING ATTENTION TO YOUR DIET AND KICKING SOME ASS EVERY DAY.
DO YOU HEAR ME?
YES, COACH!
I CAN'T HEAR YOU.
YES, COACH!
THIRTY LAPS.

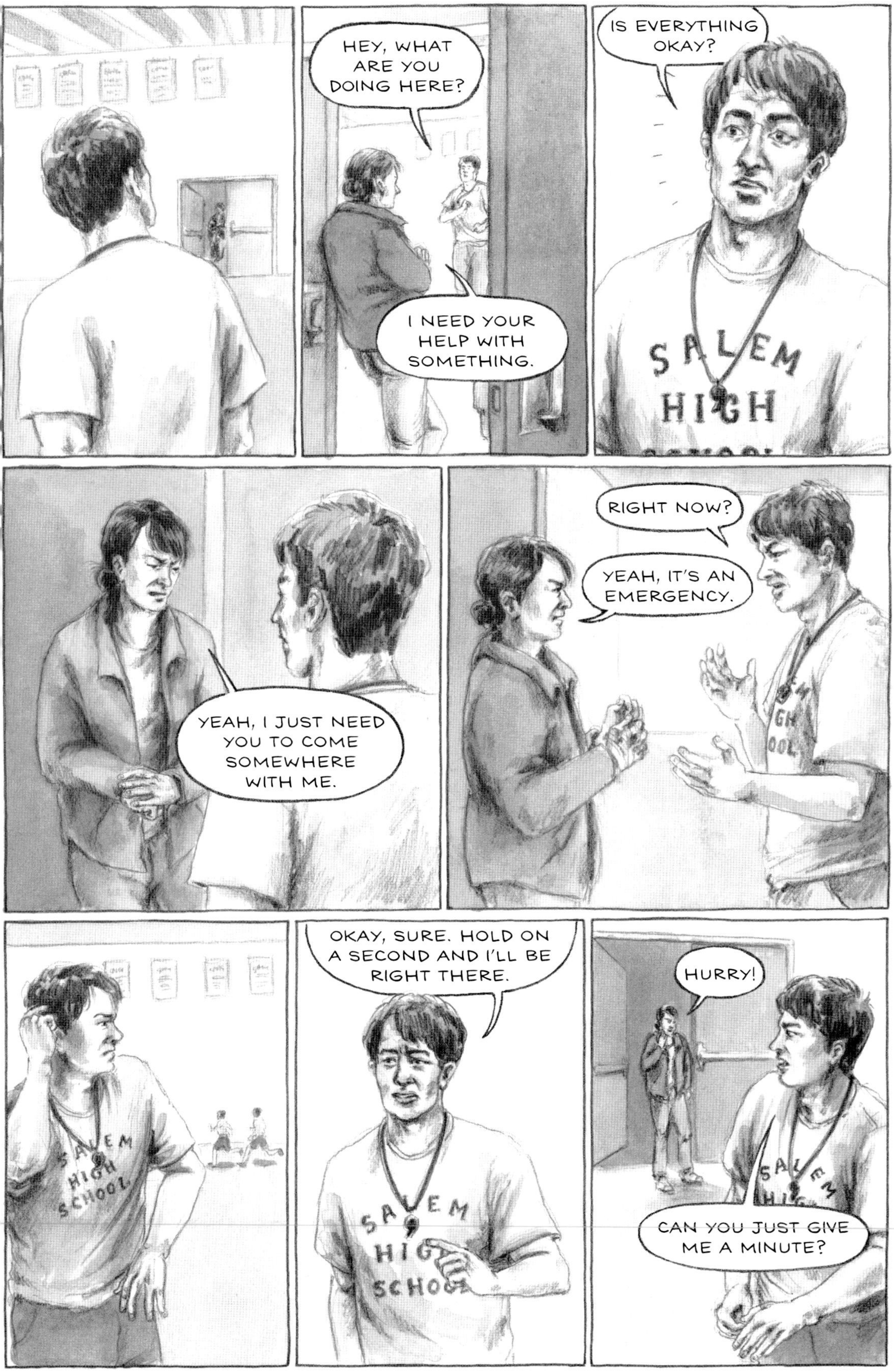
HEY, WHAT ARE YOU DOING HERE?
I NEED YOUR HELP WITH SOMETHING.
IS EVERYTHING OKAY?
SALEM HIGH
YEAH, I JUST NEED YOU TO COME SOMEWHERE WITH ME.
RIGHT NOW?
YEAH, IT'S AN EMERGENCY.
SALEM HIGH SCHOOL
OKAY, SURE. HOLD ON A SECOND AND I'LL BE RIGHT THERE.
HURRY!
CAN YOU JUST GIVE ME A MINUTE?

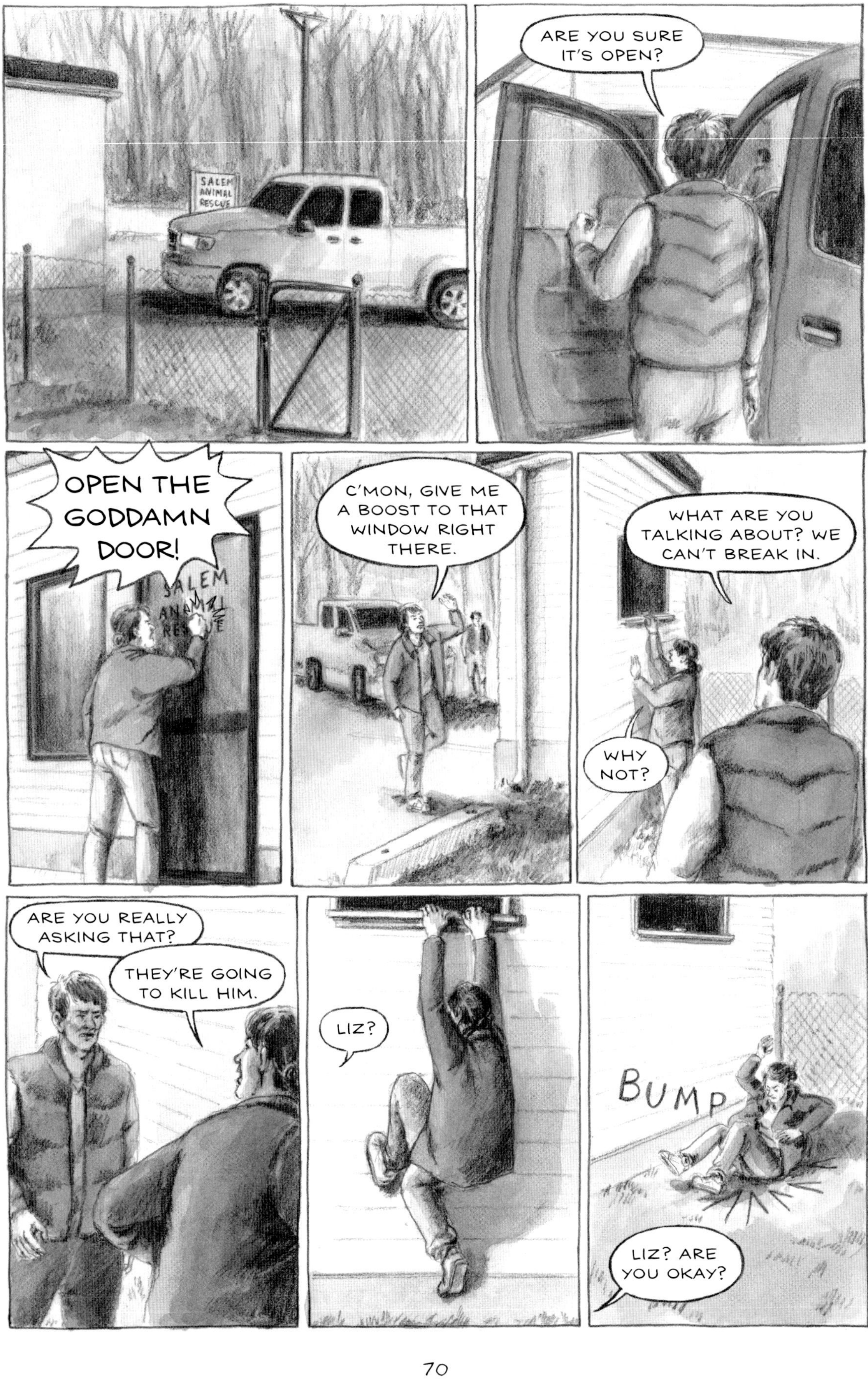
SALEM ANIMAL RESCUE
ARE YOU SURE IT'S OPEN?
OPEN THE GODDAMN DOOR!
C'MON, GIVE ME A BOOST TO THAT WINDOW RIGHT THERE.
WHAT ARE YOU TALKING ABOUT? WE CAN'T BREAK IN.
WHY NOT?
ARE YOU REALLY ASKING THAT?
THEY'RE GOING TO KILL HIM.
LIZ?
BUMP
LIZ? ARE YOU OKAY?

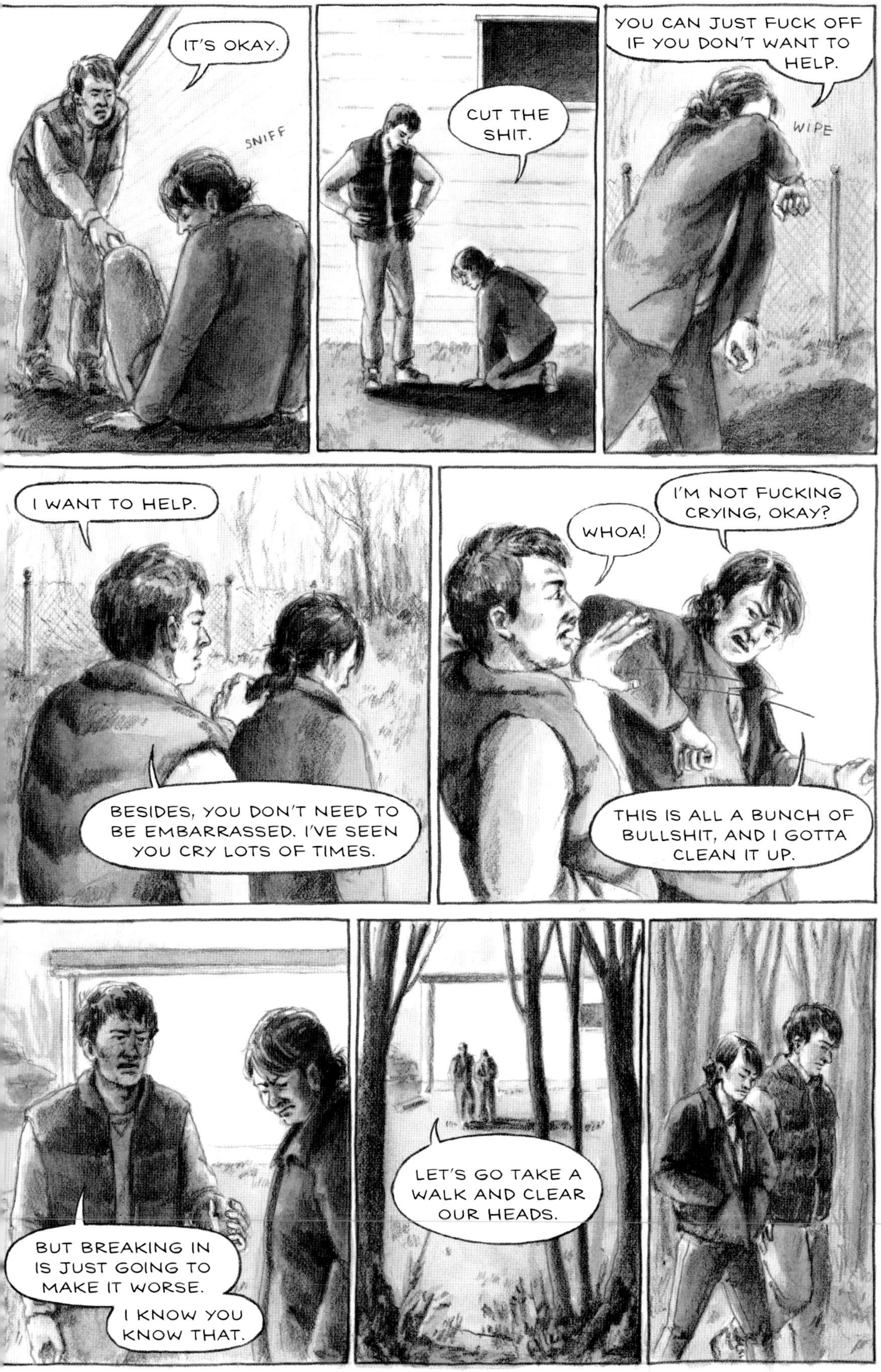
IT'S OKAY.
SNIFF
CUT THE SHIT.
YOU CAN JUST FUCK OFF IF YOU DON'T WANT TO HELP.
WIPE
I WANT TO HELP.
BESIDES, YOU DON'T NEED TO BE EMBARRASSED. I'VE SEEN YOU CRY LOTS OF TIMES.
WHOA!
I'M NOT FUCKING CRYING, OKAY?
THIS IS ALL A BUNCH OF BULLSHIT, AND I GOTTA CLEAN IT UP.
BUT BREAKING IN IS JUST GOING TO MAKE IT WORSE.
I KNOW YOU KNOW THAT.
LET'S GO TAKE A WALK AND CLEAR OUR HEADS.

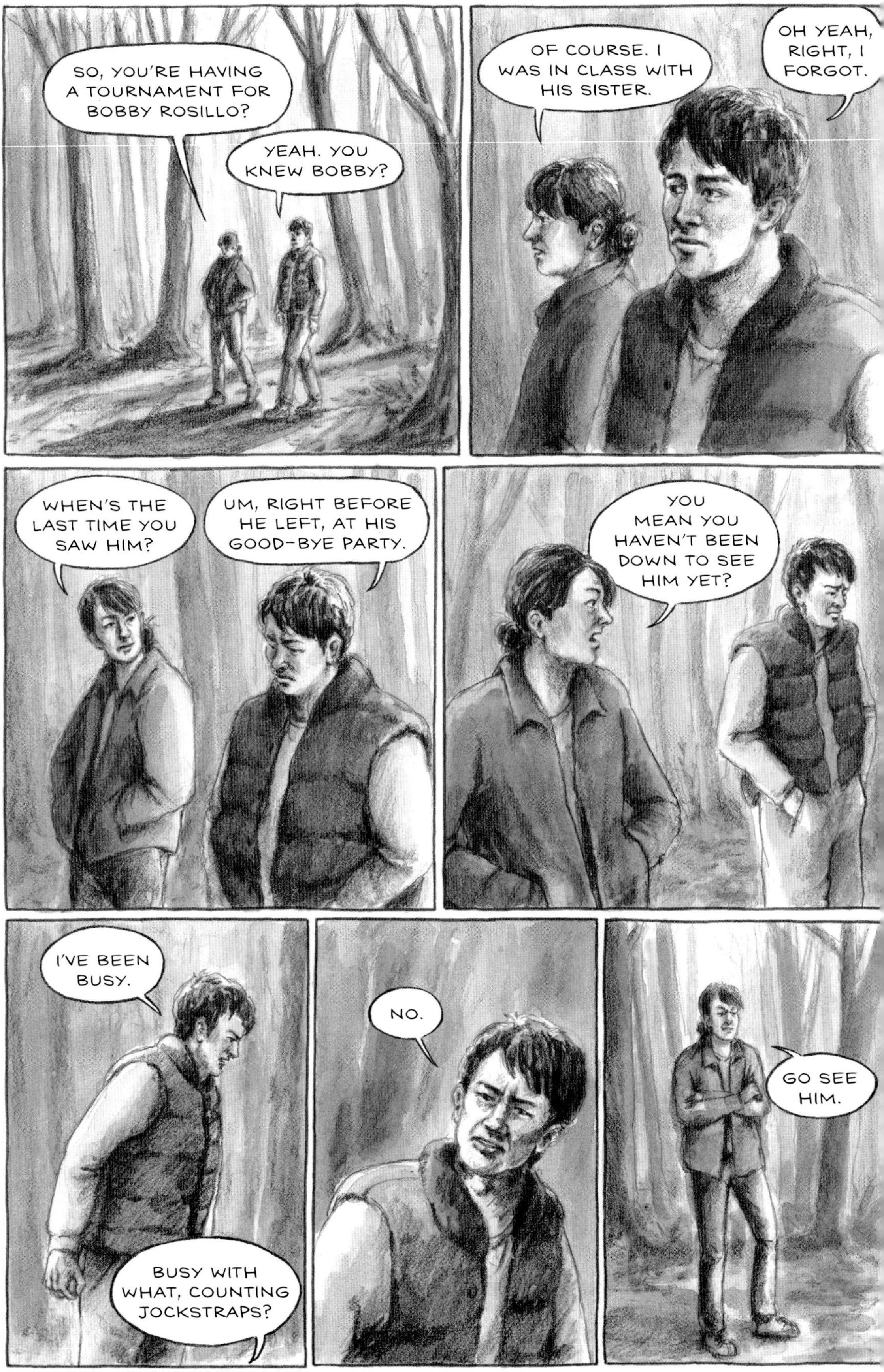
SO, YOU'RE HAVING A TOURNAMENT FOR BOBBY ROSILLO?
YEAH. YOU KNEW BOBBY?
OF COURSE. I WAS IN CLASS WITH HIS SISTER.
OH YEAH, RIGHT, I FORGOT.
WHEN'S THE LAST TIME YOU SAW HIM?
UM, RIGHT BEFORE HE LEFT, AT HIS GOOD-BYE PARTY.
YOU MEAN YOU HAVEN'T BEEN DOWN TO SEE HIM YET?
I'VE BEEN BUSY.
BUSY WITH WHAT, COUNTING JOCKSTRAPS?
NO.
GO SEE HIM.

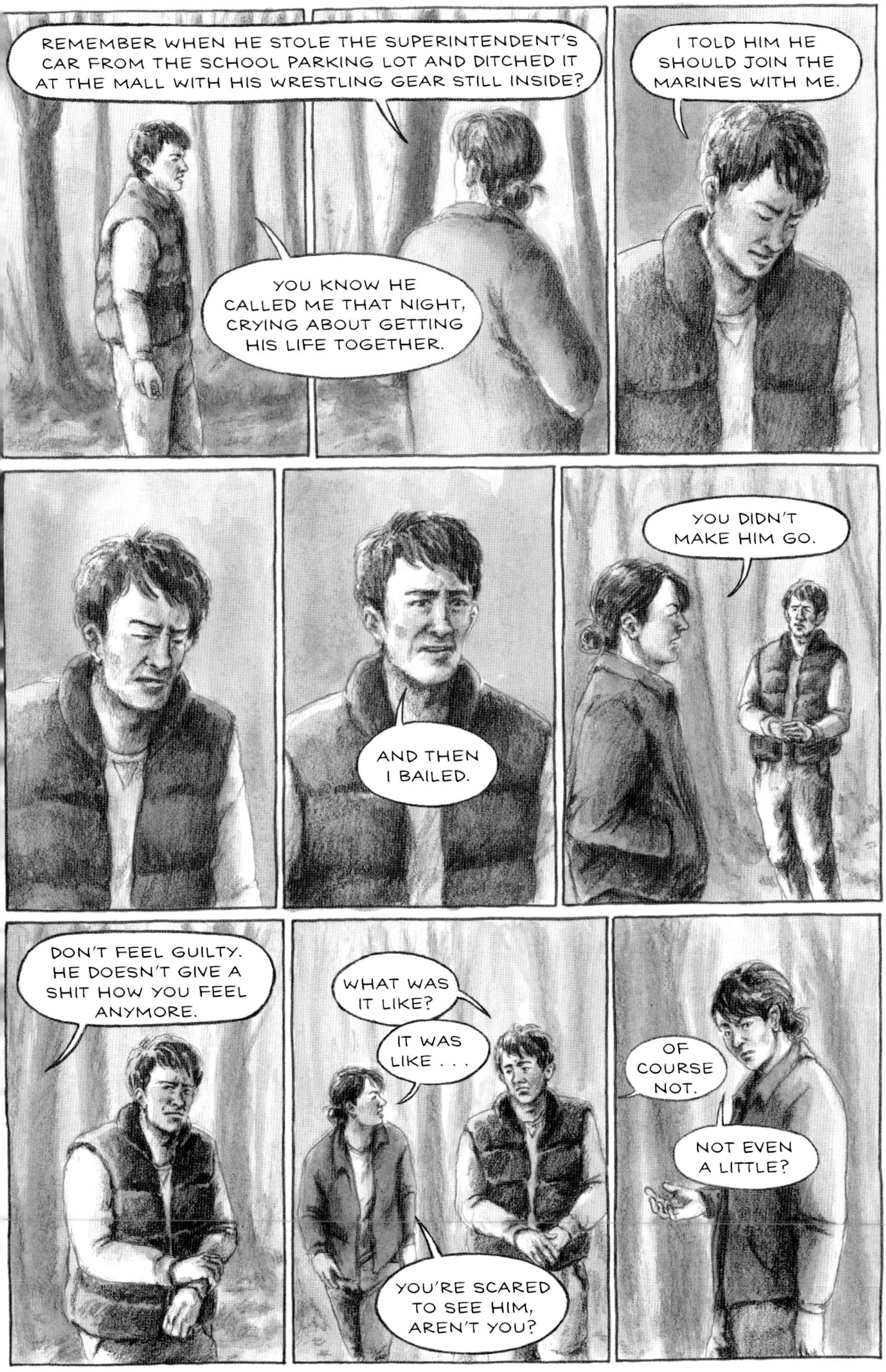
REMEMBER WHEN HE STOLE THE SUPERINTENDENT'S CAR FROM THE SCHOOL PARKING LOT AND DITCHED IT AT THE MALL WITH HIS WRESTLING GEAR STILL INSIDE?
YOU KNOW HE CALLED ME THAT NIGHT, CRYING ABOUT GETTING HIS LIFE TOGETHER.
I TOLD HIM HE SHOULD JOIN THE MARINES WITH ME.
AND THEN I BAILED.
YOU DIDN'T MAKE HIM GO.
DON'T FEEL GUILTY. HE DOESN'T GIVE A SHIT HOW YOU FEEL ANYMORE.
WHAT WAS IT LIKE?
IT WAS LIKE . . .
YOU'RE SCARED TO SEE HIM, AREN'T YOU?
OF COURSE NOT.
NOT EVEN A LITTLE?

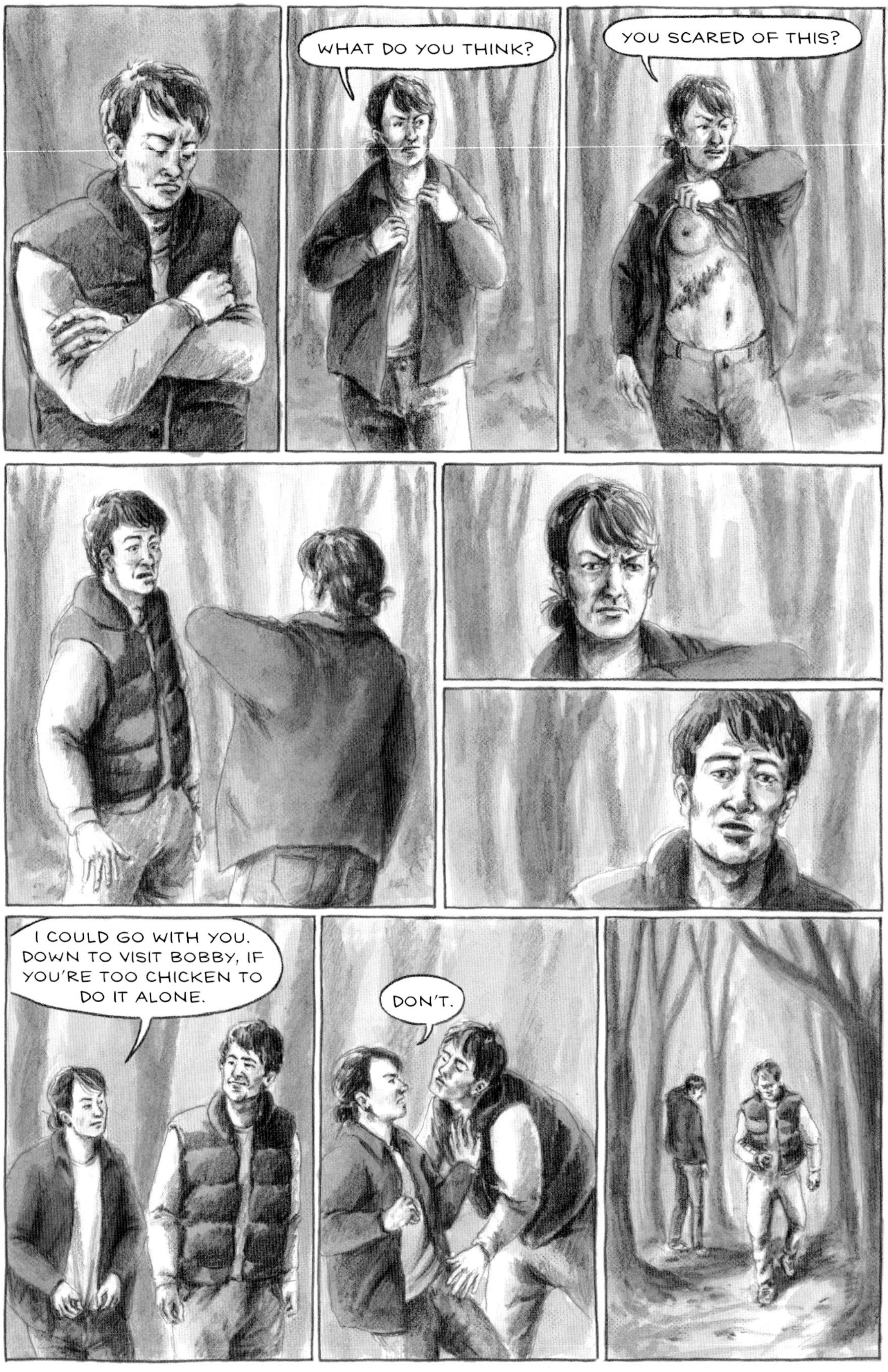
WHAT DO YOU THINK?
YOU SCARED OF THIS?
I COULD GO WITH YOU. DOWN TO VISIT BOBBY, IF YOU'RE TOO CHICKEN TO DO IT ALONE.
DON'T.

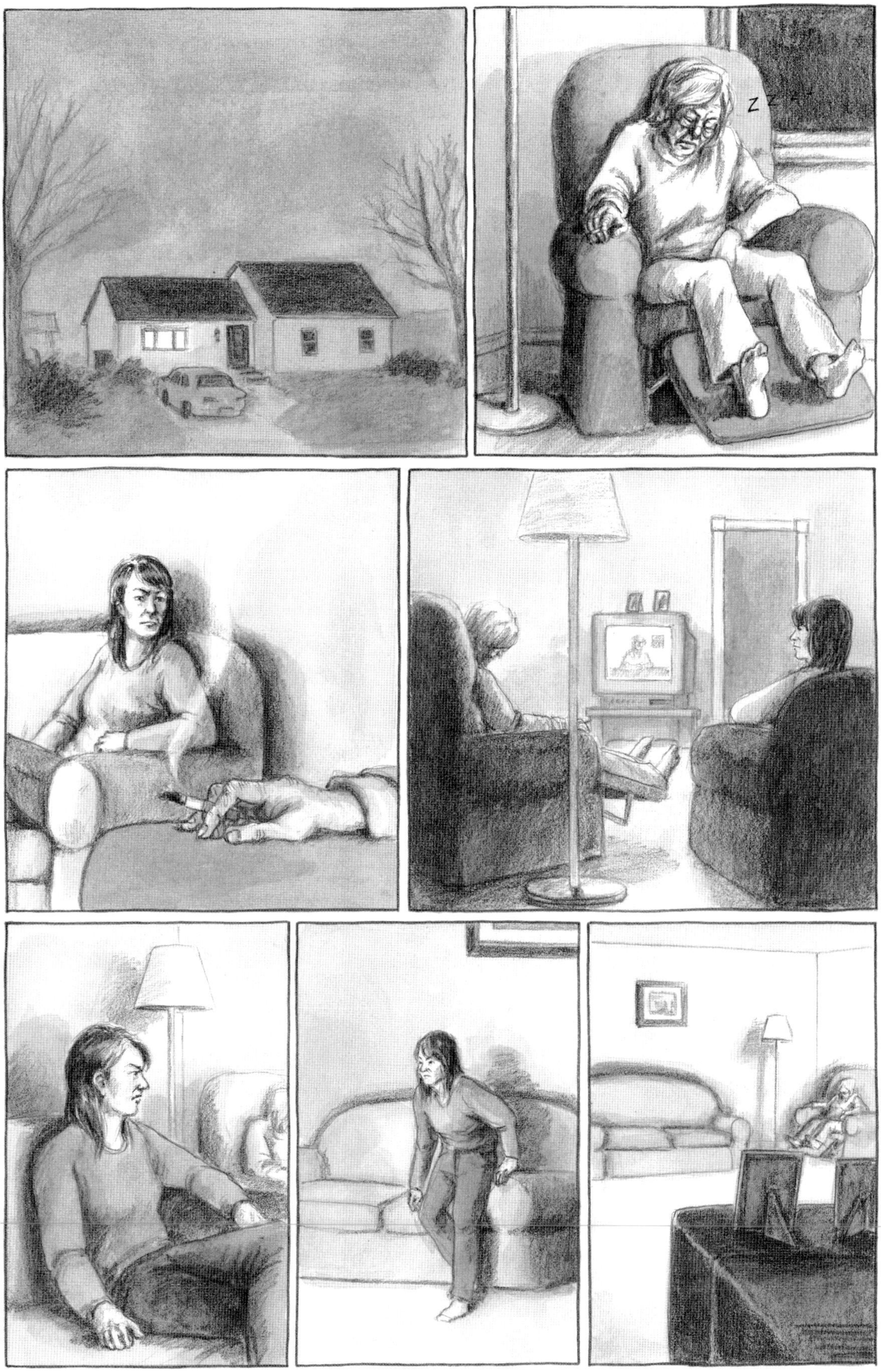
Z Z Z

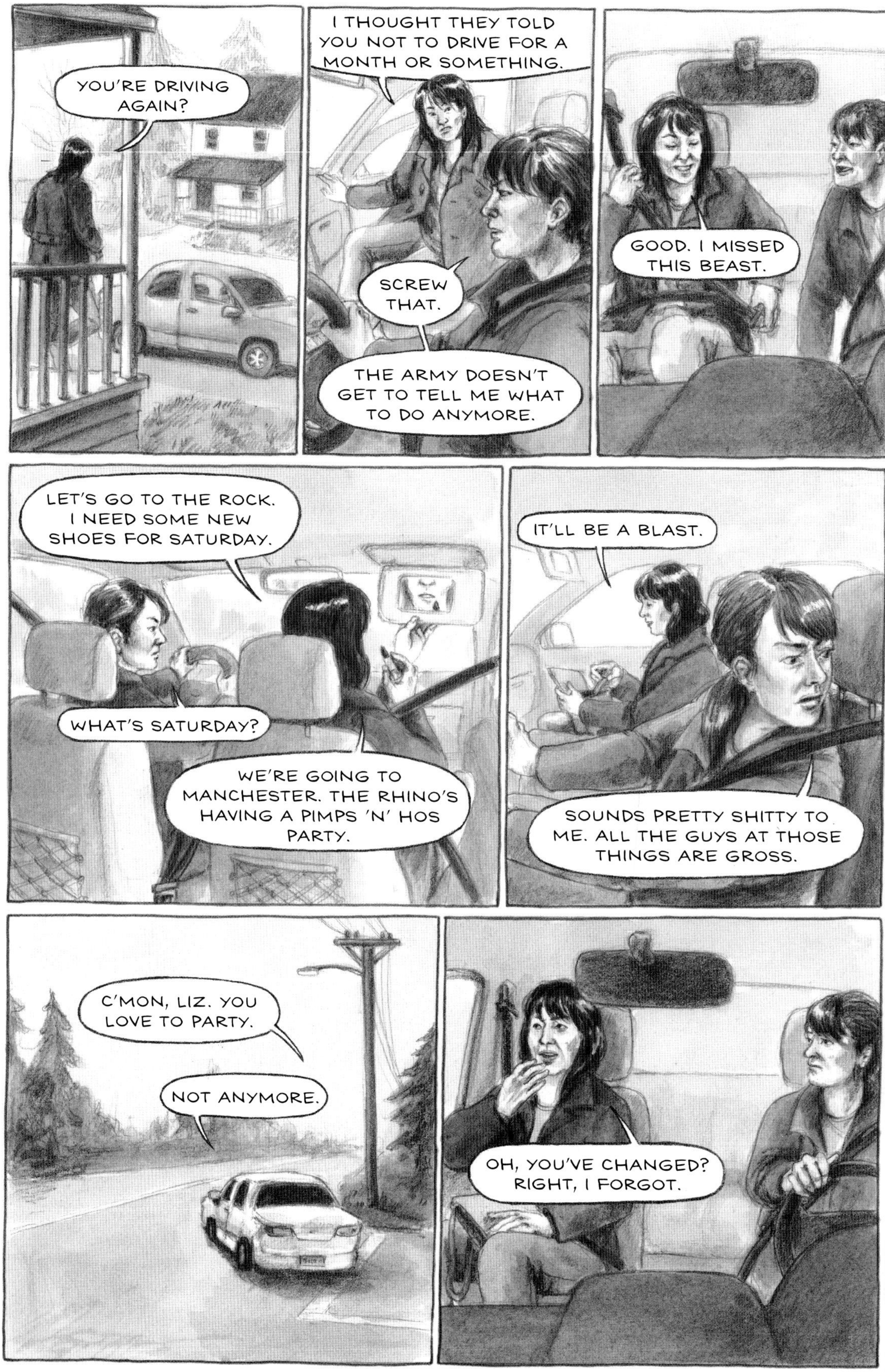
YOU'RE DRIVING AGAIN?
I THOUGHT THEY TOLD YOU NOT TO DRIVE FOR A MONTH OR SOMETHING.
SCREW THAT.
THE ARMY DOESN'T GET TO TELL ME WHAT TO DO ANYMORE.
GOOD. I MISSED THIS BEAST.
LET'S GO TO THE ROCK. I NEED SOME NEW SHOES FOR SATURDAY.
WHAT'S SATURDAY?
WE'RE GOING TO MANCHESTER. THE RHINO'S HAVING A PIMPS 'N' HOS PARTY.
IT'LL BE A BLAST.
SOUNDS PRETTY SHITTY TO ME. ALL THE GUYS AT THOSE THINGS ARE GROSS.
C'MON, LIZ. YOU LOVE TO PARTY.
NOT ANYMORE.
OH, YOU'VE CHANGED? RIGHT, I FORGOT.

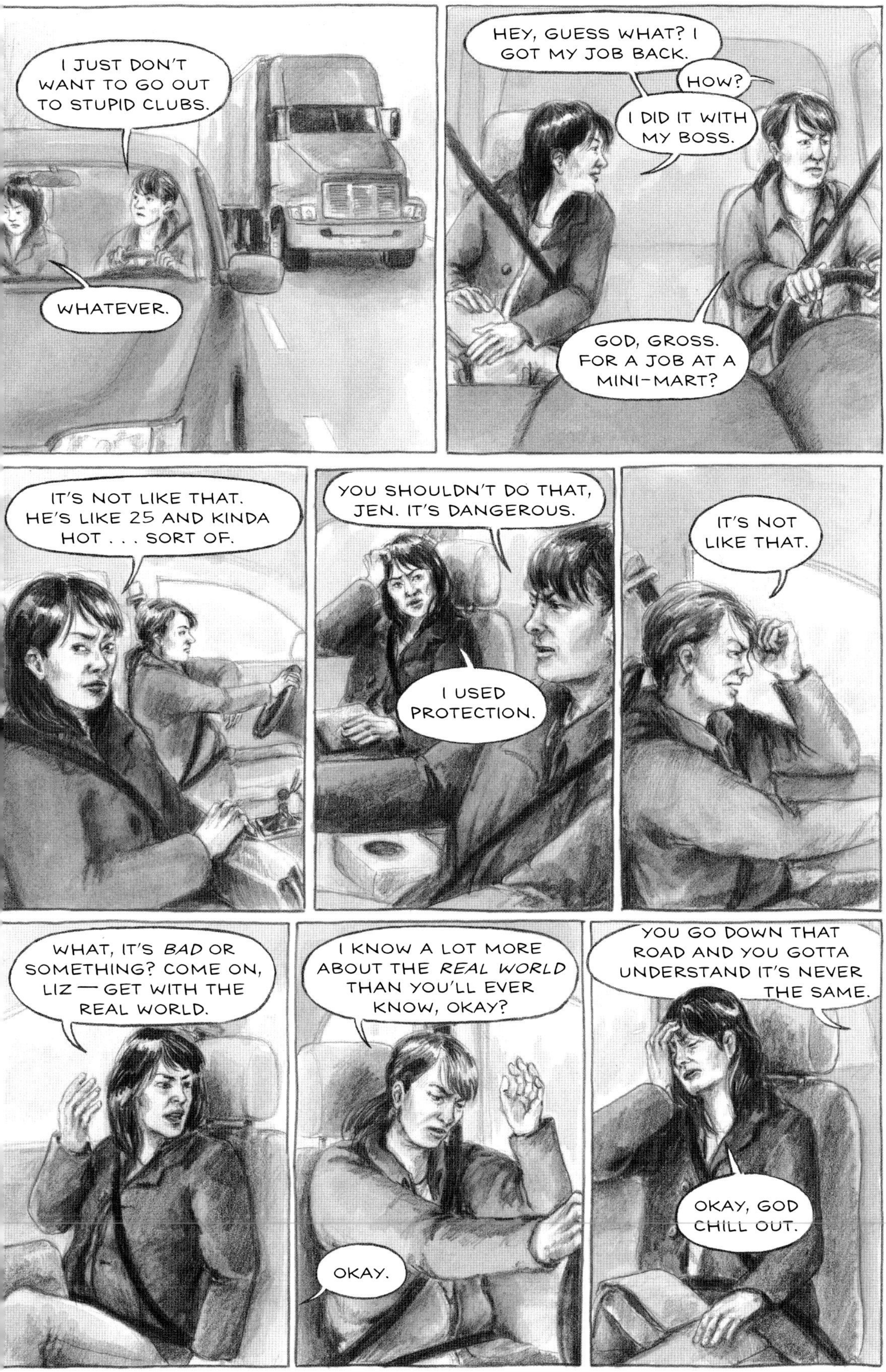
I JUST DON'T WANT TO GO OUT TO STUPID CLUBS.
WHATEVER.
HEY, GUESS WHAT? I GOT MY JOB BACK.
HOW?
I DID IT WITH MY BOSS.
GOD, GROSS. FOR A JOB AT A MINI-MART?
IT'S NOT LIKE THAT. HE'S LIKE 25 AND KINDA HOT . . . SORT OF.
YOU SHOULDN'T DO THAT, JEN. IT'S DANGEROUS.
I USED PROTECTION.
IT'S NOT LIKE THAT.
WHAT, IT'S *BAD* OR SOMETHING? COME ON, LIZ — GET WITH THE REAL WORLD.
I KNOW A LOT MORE ABOUT THE *REAL WORLD* THAN YOU'LL EVER KNOW, OKAY?
OKAY.
YOU GO DOWN THAT ROAD AND YOU GOTTA UNDERSTAND IT'S NEVER THE SAME.
OKAY, GOD CHILL OUT.

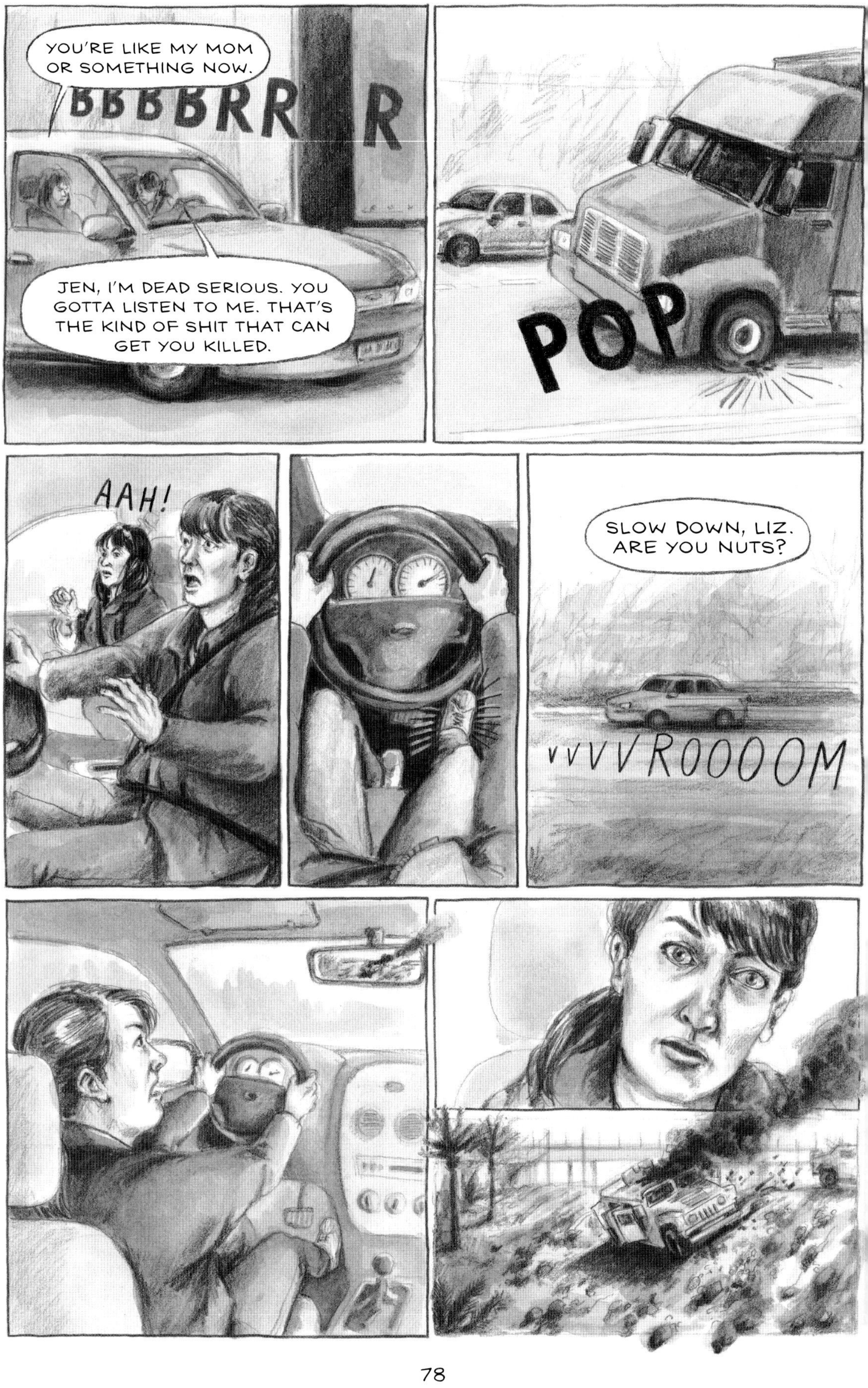
YOU'RE LIKE MY MOM OR SOMETHING NOW.
BBBBRR R
JEN, I'M DEAD SERIOUS. YOU GOTTA LISTEN TO ME. THAT'S THE KIND OF SHIT THAT CAN GET YOU KILLED.
POP
AAH!
SLOW DOWN, LIZ. ARE YOU NUTS?
VVVVROOOOM

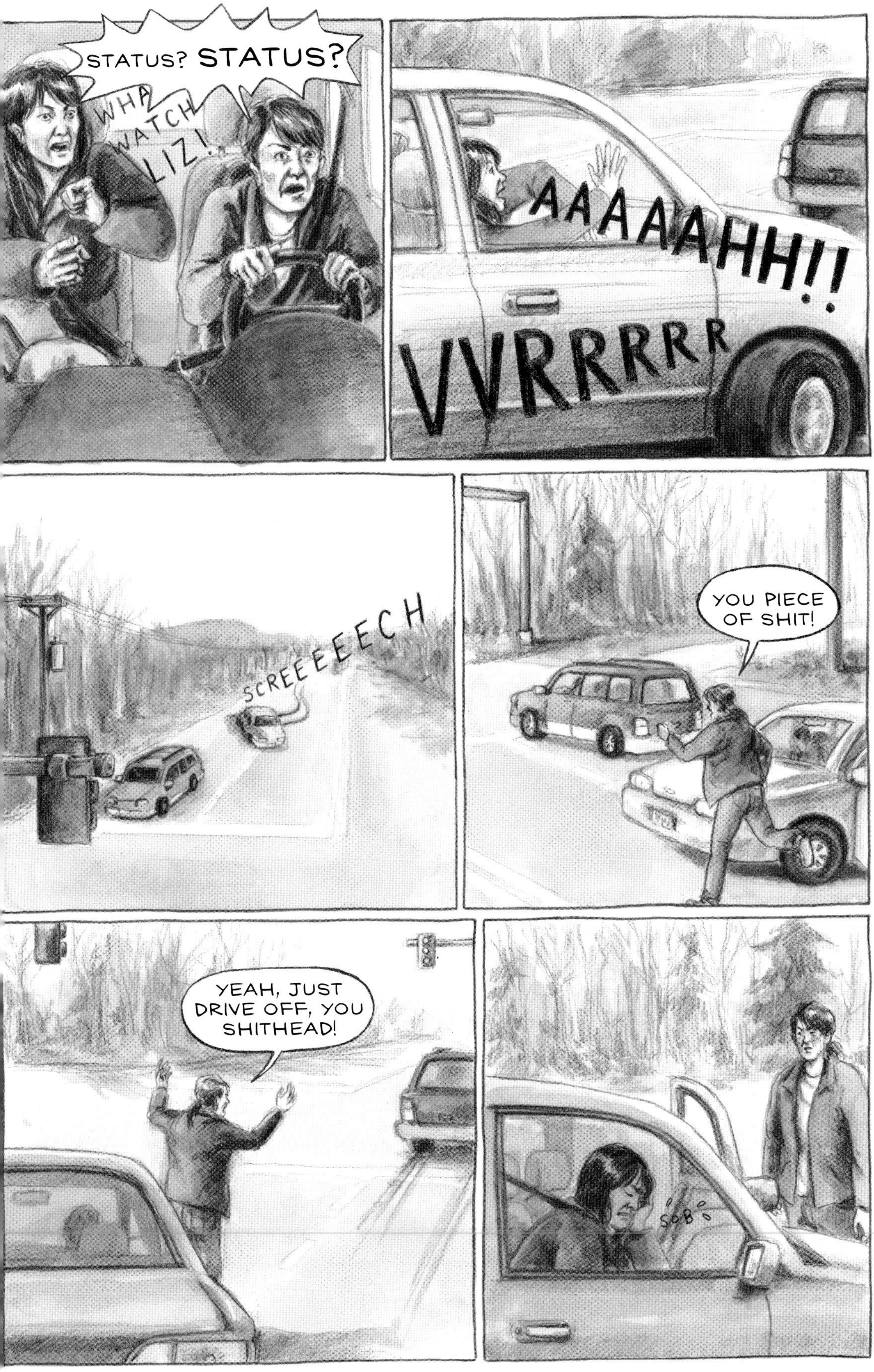
STATUS? STATUS?
WHA
WATCH
LIZ!
AAAAAHH!!
VVRRRRRR
SCREEEEEECH
YOU PIECE OF SHIT!
YEAH, JUST DRIVE OFF, YOU SHITHEAD!
SOB

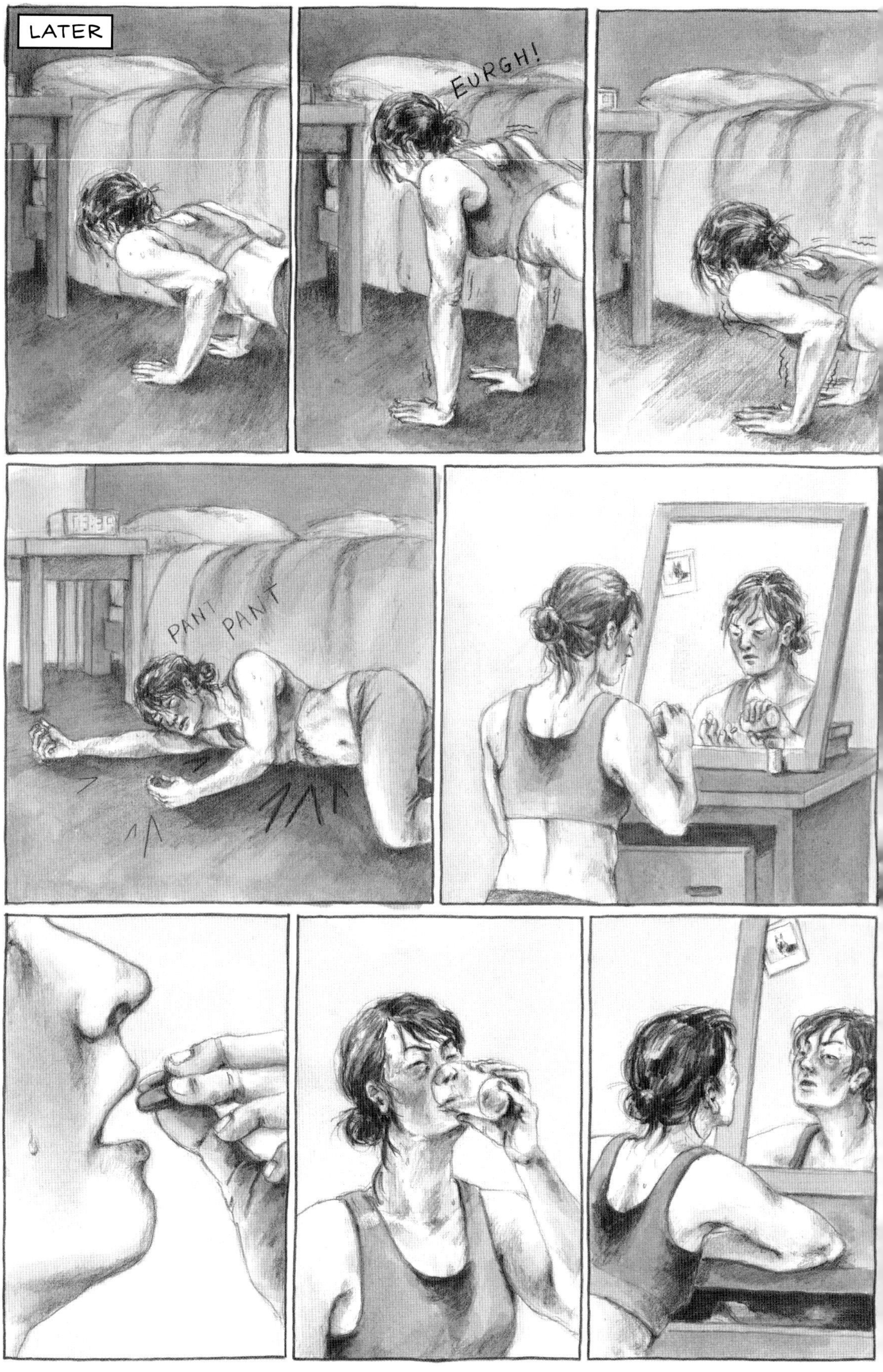
LATER
EURGH!
PANT
PANT

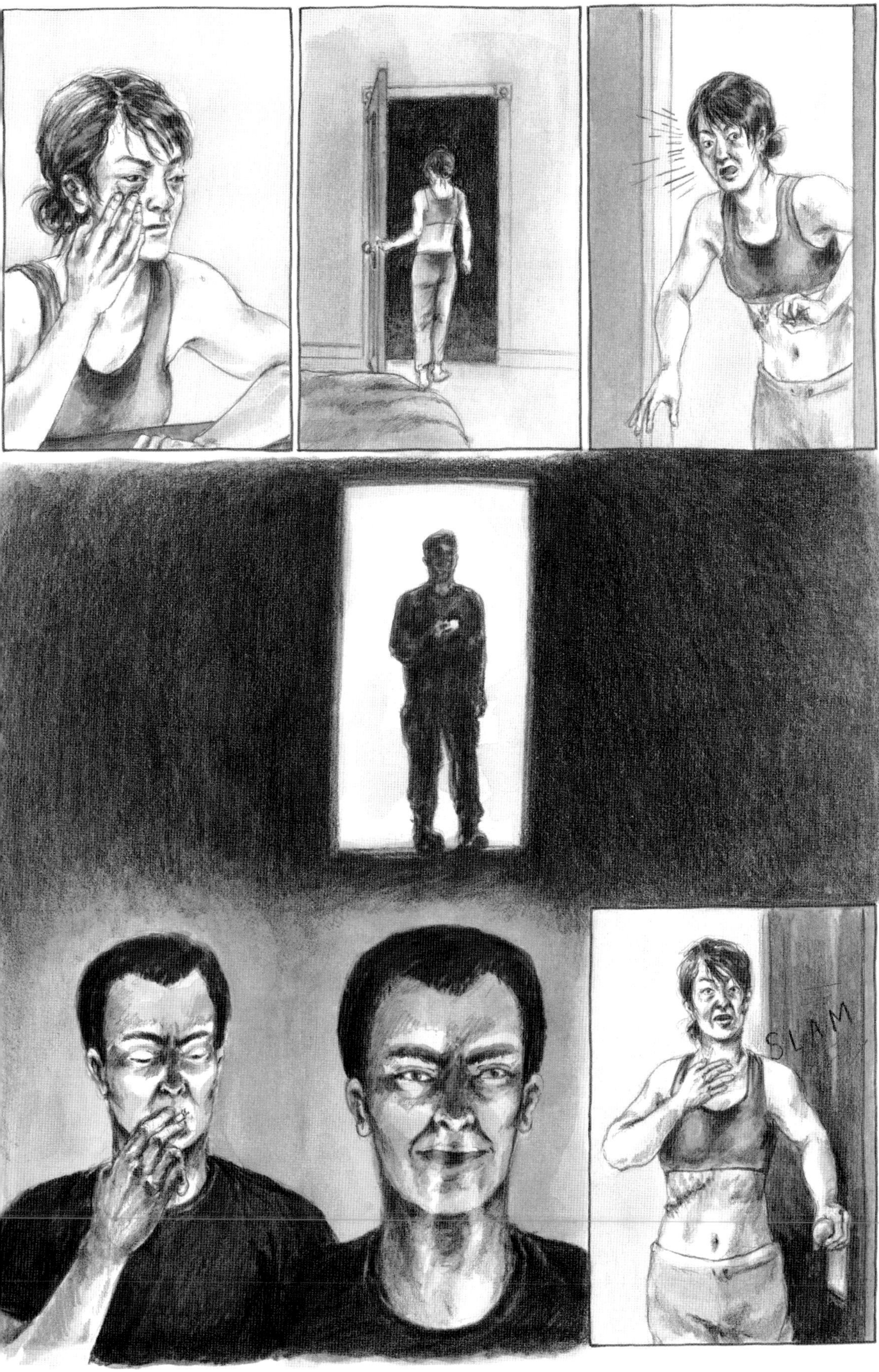
SLAM

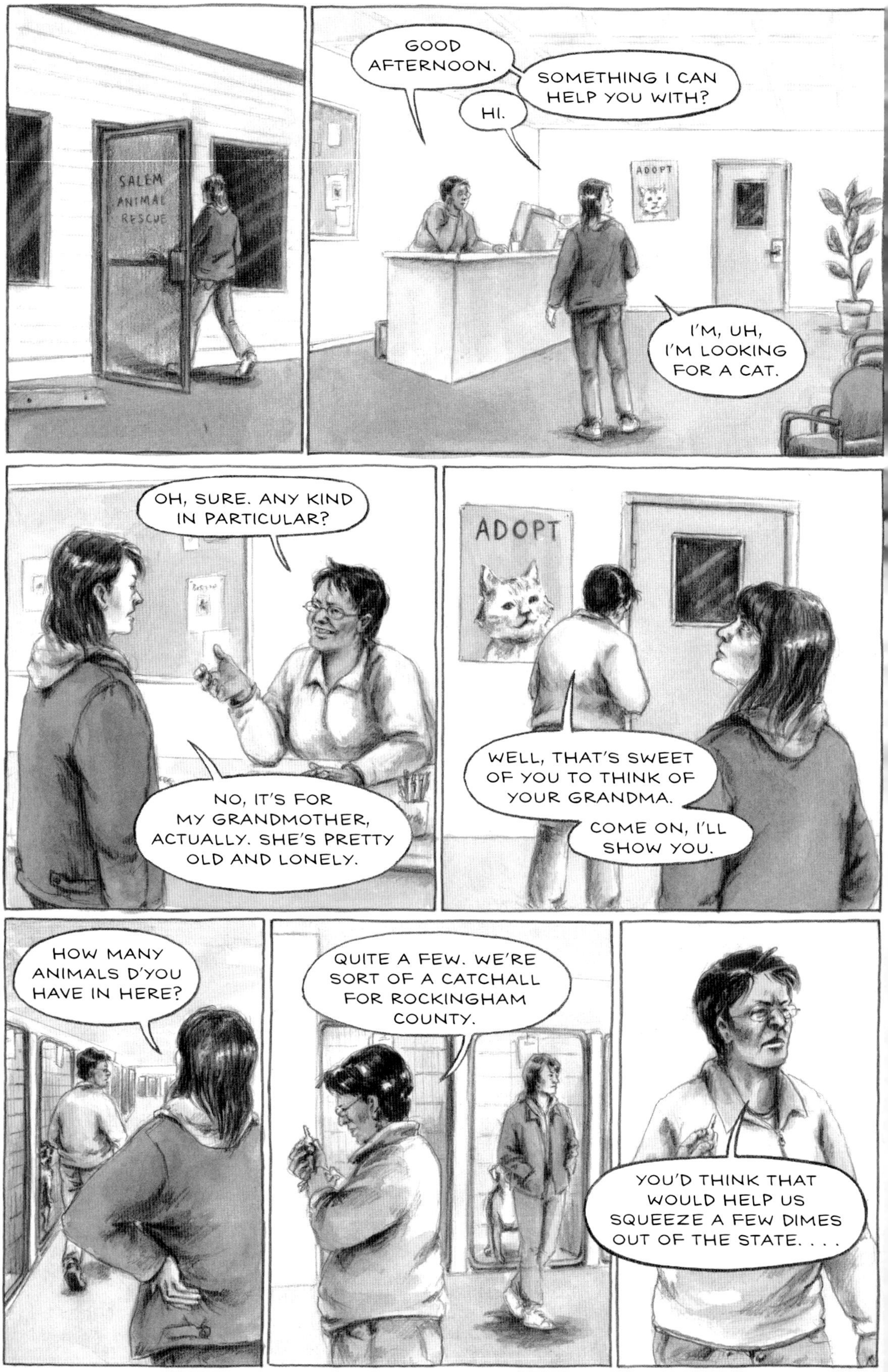
SALEM ANIMAL RESCUE
GOOD AFTERNOON.
SOMETHING I CAN HELP YOU WITH?
HI.
ADOPT
I'M, UH, I'M LOOKING FOR A CAT.
OH, SURE. ANY KIND IN PARTICULAR?
NO, IT'S FOR MY GRANDMOTHER, ACTUALLY. SHE'S PRETTY OLD AND LONELY.
ADOPT
WELL, THAT'S SWEET OF YOU TO THINK OF YOUR GRANDMA.
COME ON, I'LL SHOW YOU.
HOW MANY ANIMALS D'YOU HAVE IN HERE?
QUITE A FEW. WE'RE SORT OF A CATCHALL FOR ROCKINGHAM COUNTY.
YOU'D THINK THAT WOULD HELP US SQUEEZE A FEW DIMES OUT OF THE STATE. . . .

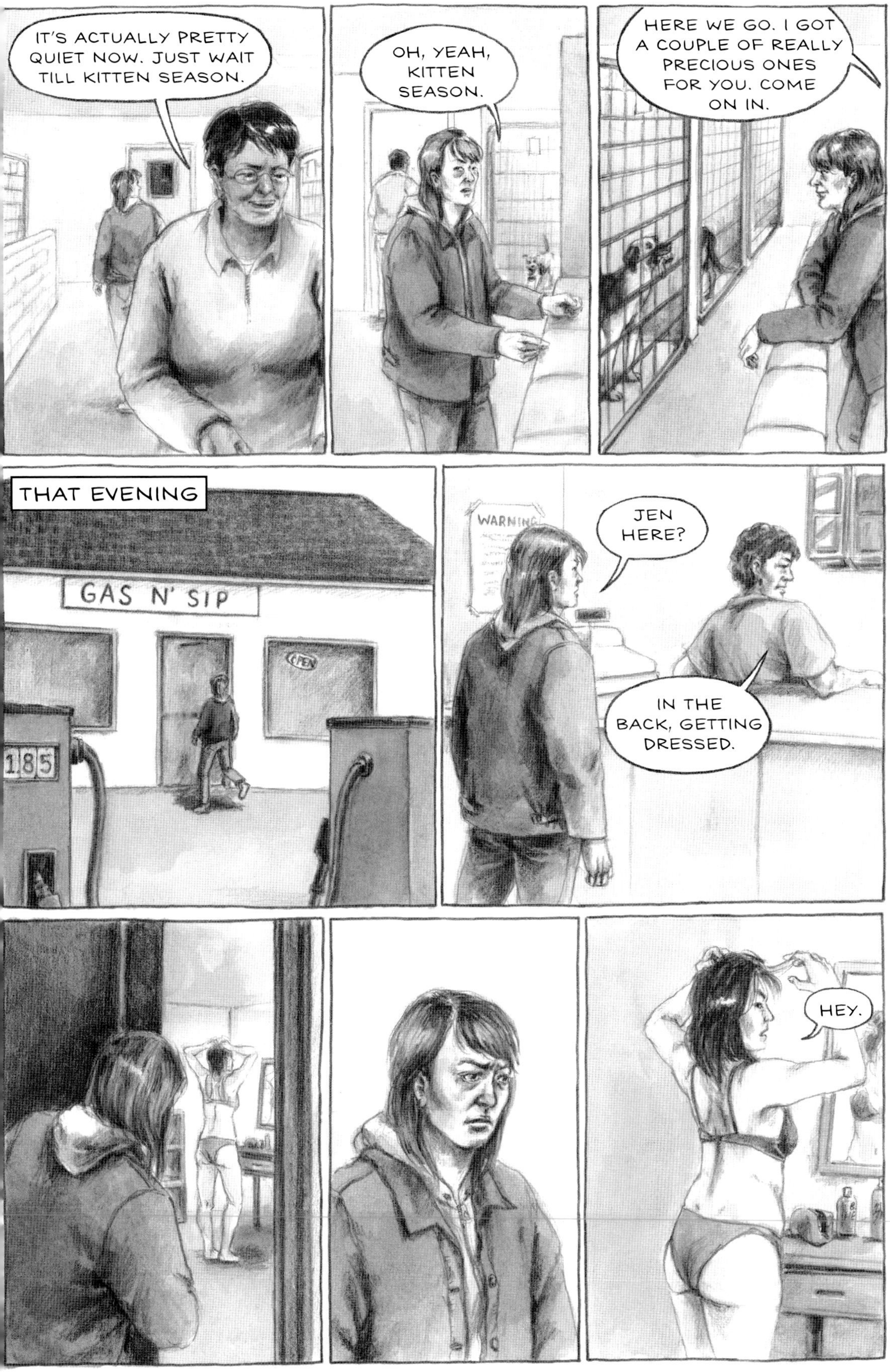
IT'S ACTUALLY PRETTY QUIET NOW. JUST WAIT TILL KITTEN SEASON.
OH, YEAH, KITTEN SEASON.
HERE WE GO. I GOT A COUPLE OF REALLY PRECIOUS ONES FOR YOU. COME ON IN.
THAT EVENING
GAS N' SIP
OPEN
185
WARNING
JEN HERE?
IN THE BACK, GETTING DRESSED.
HEY.

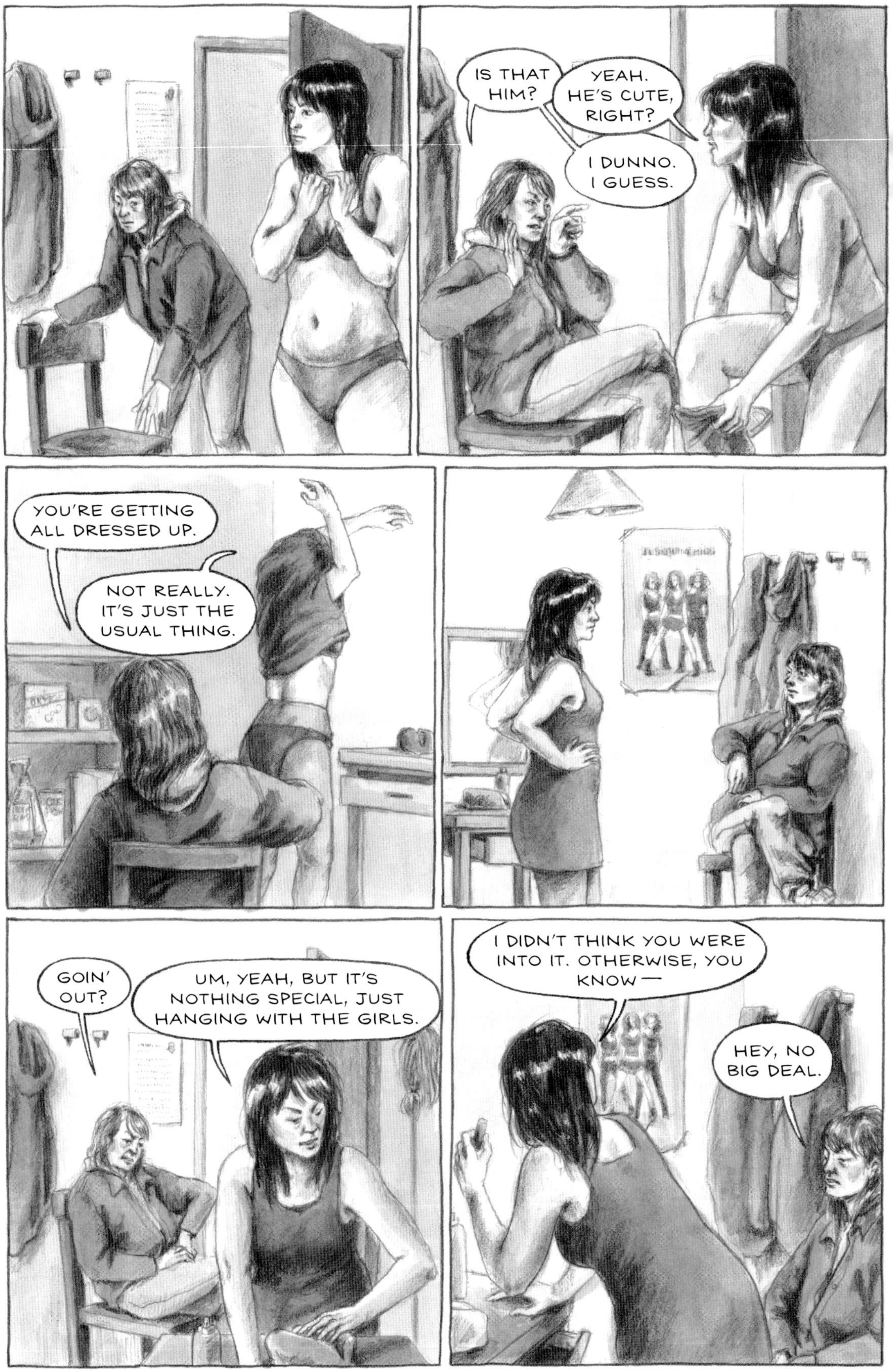
IS THAT HIM?
YEAH. HE'S CUTE, RIGHT?
I DUNNO. I GUESS.
YOU'RE GETTING ALL DRESSED UP.
NOT REALLY. IT'S JUST THE USUAL THING.
GOIN' OUT?
UM, YEAH, BUT IT'S NOTHING SPECIAL, JUST HANGING WITH THE GIRLS.
I DIDN'T THINK YOU WERE INTO IT. OTHERWISE, YOU KNOW—
HEY, NO BIG DEAL.

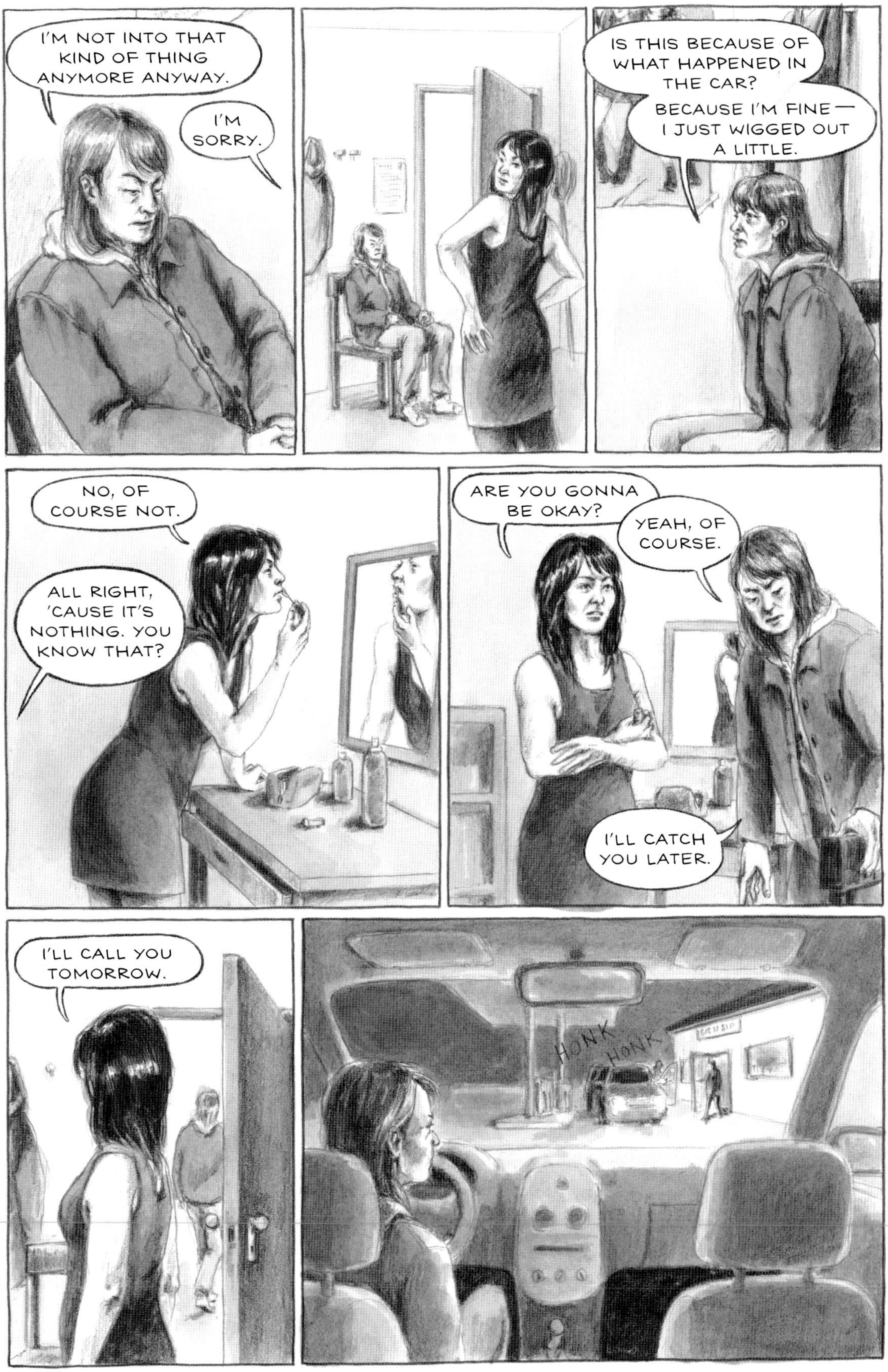
I'M NOT INTO THAT KIND OF THING ANYMORE ANYWAY.
I'M SORRY.
IS THIS BECAUSE OF WHAT HAPPENED IN THE CAR?
BECAUSE I'M FINE— I JUST WIGGED OUT A LITTLE.
NO, OF COURSE NOT.
ALL RIGHT, 'CAUSE IT'S NOTHING. YOU KNOW THAT?
ARE YOU GONNA BE OKAY?
YEAH, OF COURSE.
I'LL CATCH YOU LATER.
I'LL CALL YOU TOMORROW.
HONK
HONK

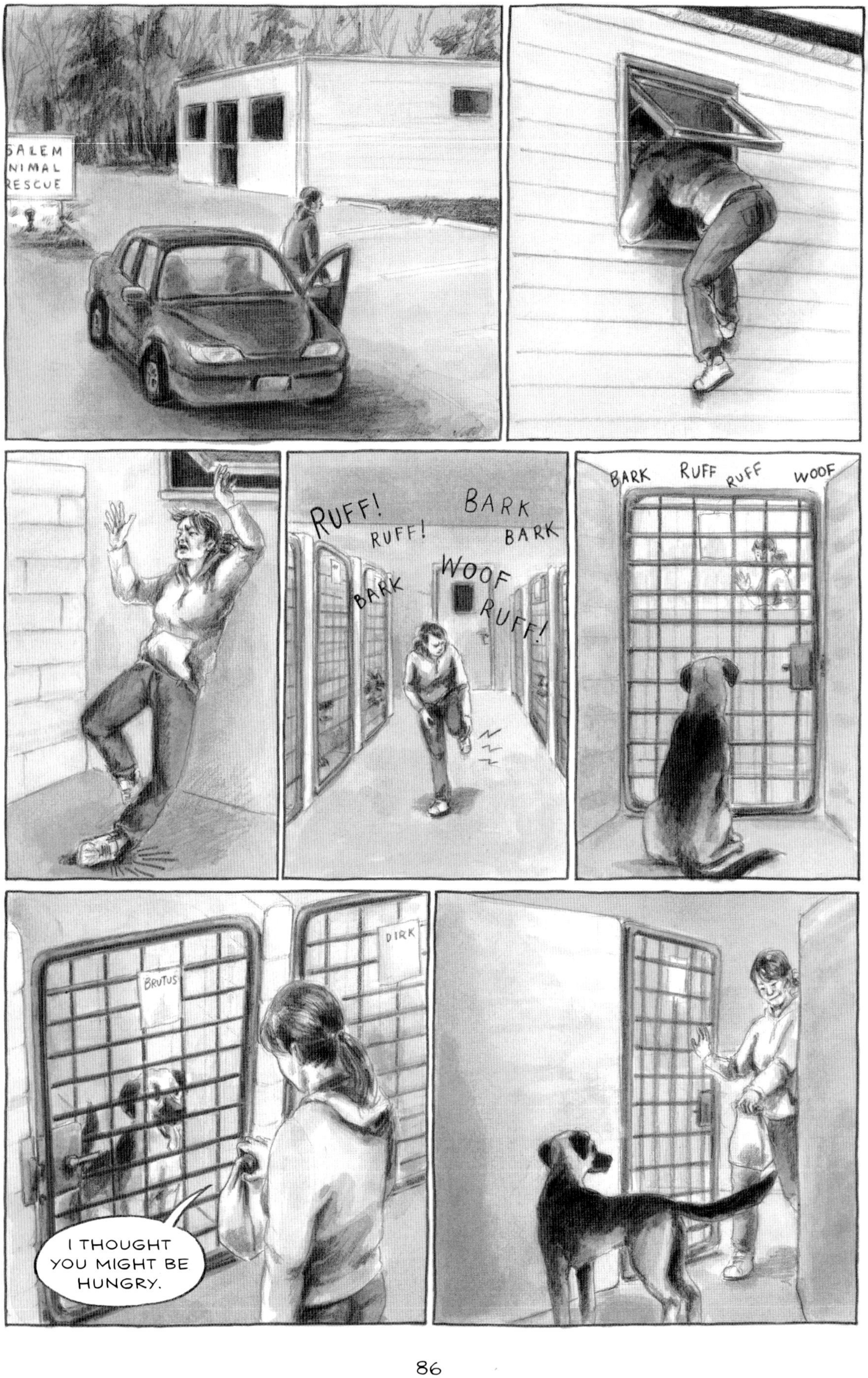
SALEM
NIMAL
RESCUE
RUFF!
RUFF!
BARK
BARK
WOOF
BARK
RUFF!
BARK
RUFF
RUFF
WOOF
BRUTUS
DIRK
I THOUGHT YOU MIGHT BE HUNGRY.

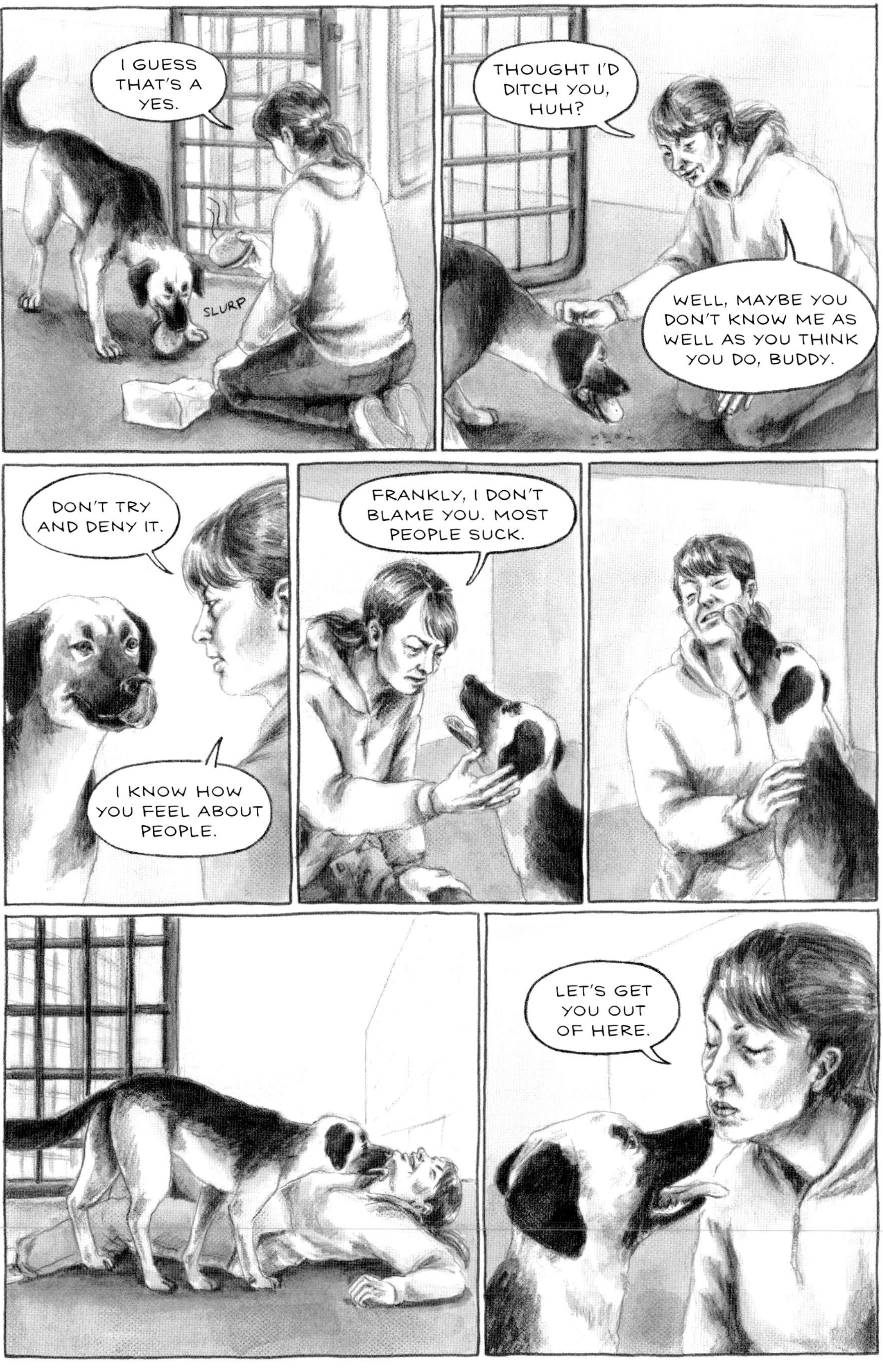
I GUESS THAT'S A YES.
SLURP
THOUGHT I'D DITCH YOU, HUH?
WELL, MAYBE YOU DON'T KNOW ME AS WELL AS YOU THINK YOU DO, BUDDY.
DON'T TRY AND DENY IT.
I KNOW HOW YOU FEEL ABOUT PEOPLE.
FRANKLY, I DON'T BLAME YOU. MOST PEOPLE SUCK.
LET'S GET YOU OUT OF HERE.

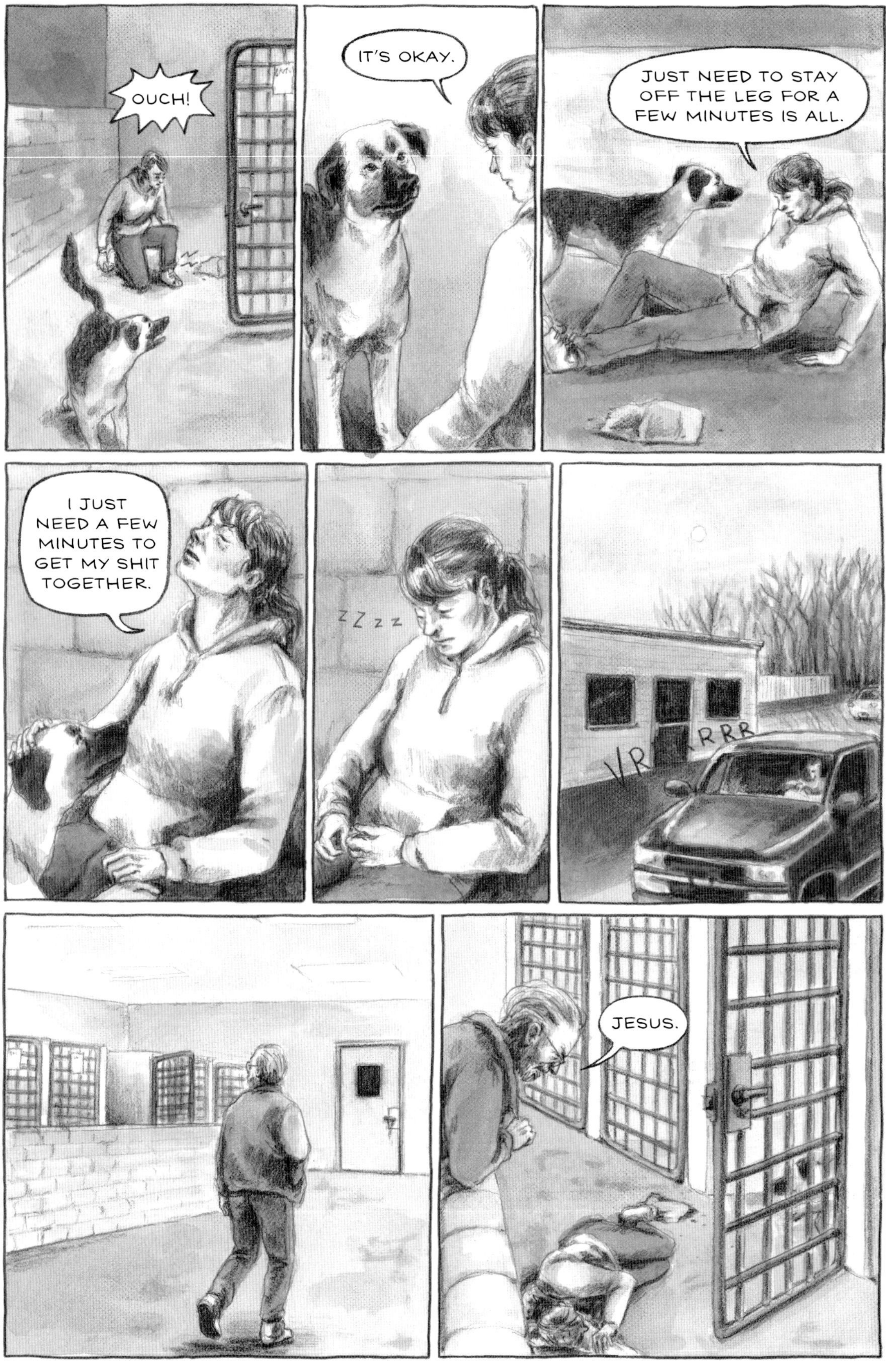
OUCH!
IT'S OKAY.
JUST NEED TO STAY OFF THE LEG FOR A FEW MINUTES IS ALL.
I JUST NEED A FEW MINUTES TO GET MY SHIT TOGETHER.
ZZZZ
VRRRRR
JESUS.

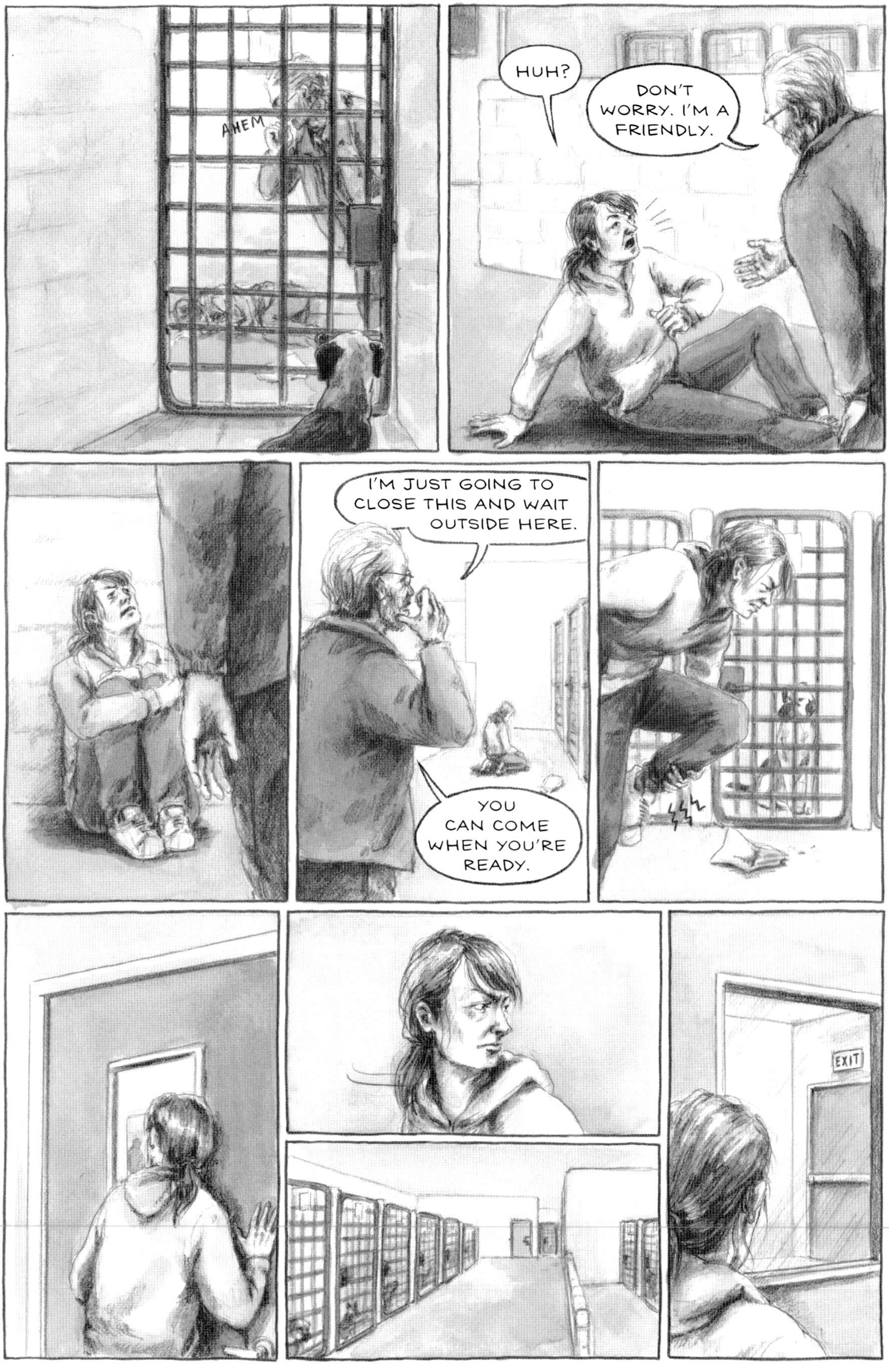
AHEM
HUH?
DON'T WORRY. I'M A FRIENDLY.
I'M JUST GOING TO CLOSE THIS AND WAIT OUTSIDE HERE.
YOU CAN COME WHEN YOU'RE READY.
EXIT

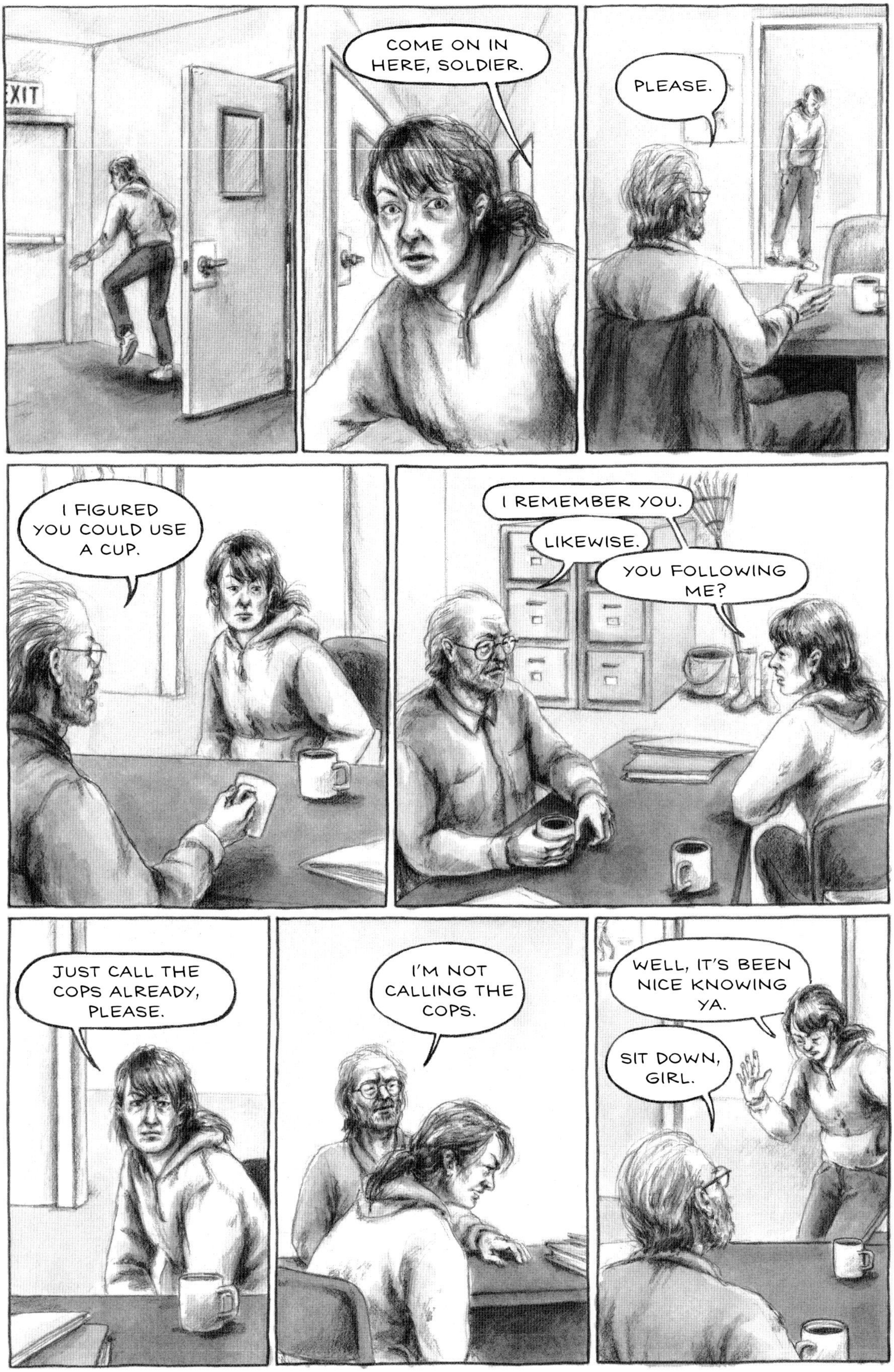
EXIT
COME ON IN HERE, SOLDIER.
PLEASE.
I FIGURED YOU COULD USE A CUP.
I REMEMBER YOU.
LIKEWISE.
YOU FOLLOWING ME?
JUST CALL THE COPS ALREADY, PLEASE.
I'M NOT CALLING THE COPS.
WELL, IT'S BEEN NICE KNOWING YA.
SIT DOWN, GIRL.

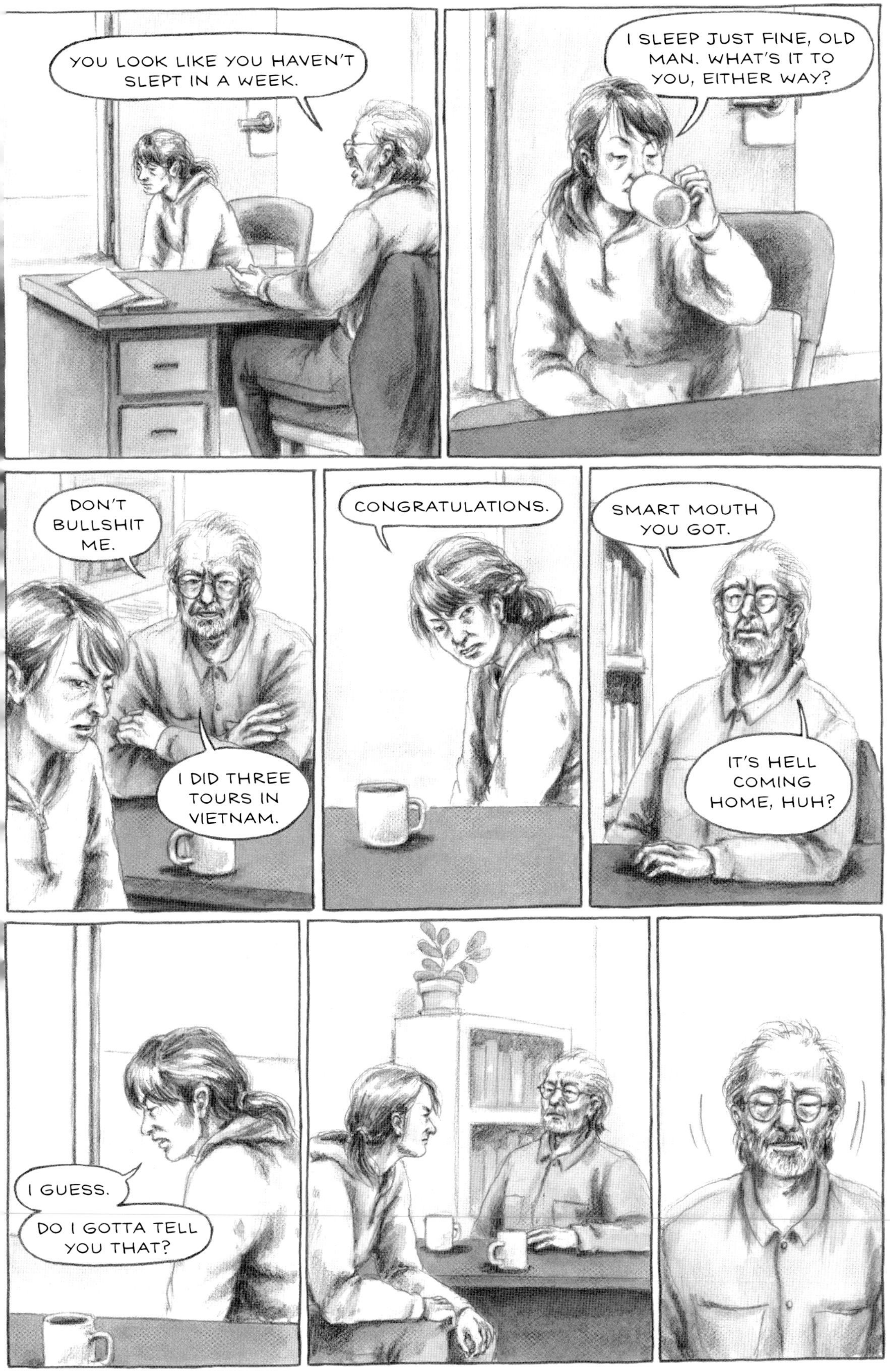
YOU LOOK LIKE YOU HAVEN'T SLEPT IN A WEEK.
I SLEEP JUST FINE, OLD MAN. WHAT'S IT TO YOU, EITHER WAY?
DON'T BULLSHIT ME.
I DID THREE TOURS IN VIETNAM.
CONGRATULATIONS.
SMART MOUTH YOU GOT.
IT'S HELL COMING HOME, HUH?
I GUESS.
DO I GOTTA TELL YOU THAT?

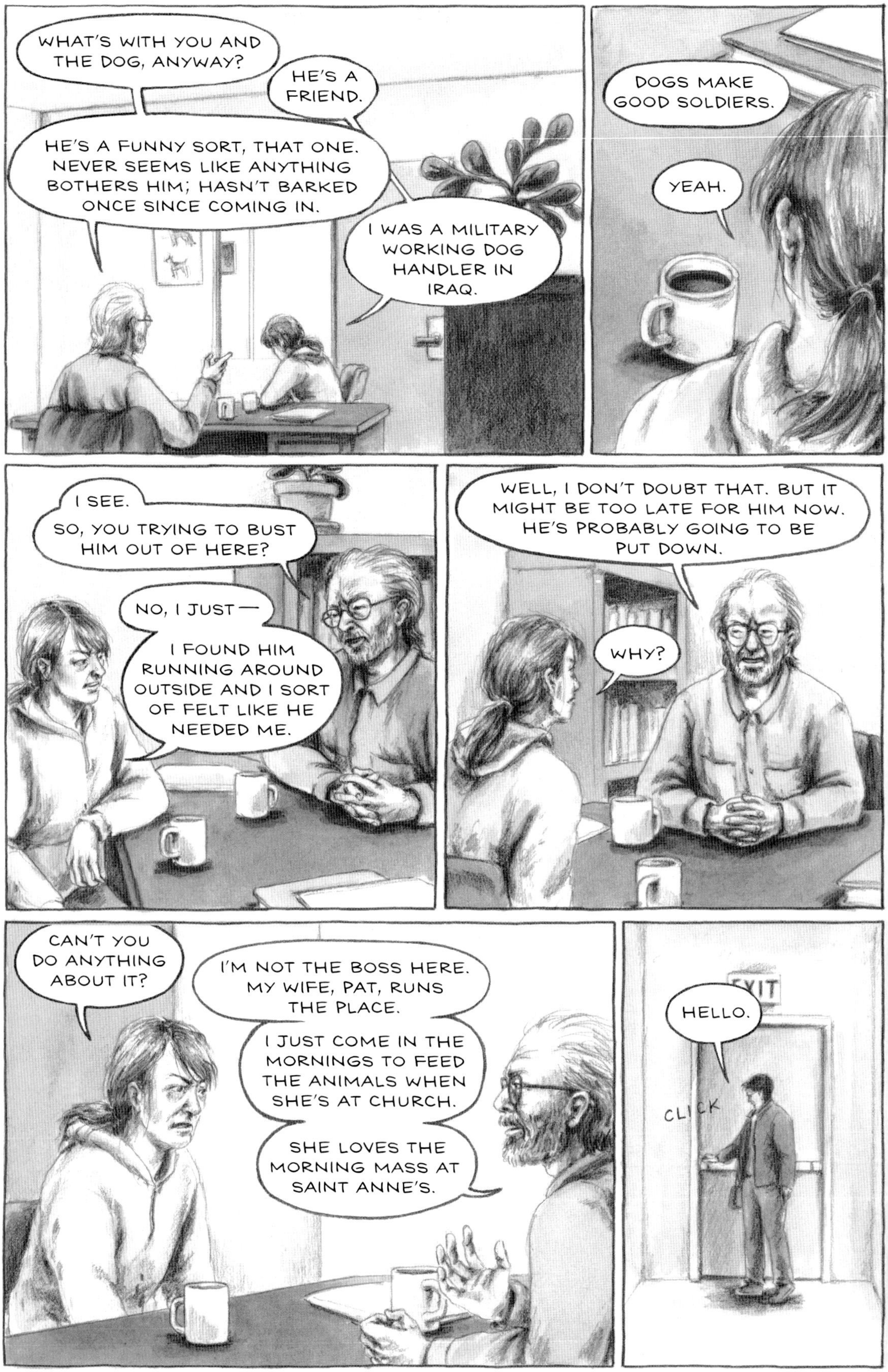
WHAT'S WITH YOU AND THE DOG, ANYWAY?
HE'S A FRIEND.
HE'S A FUNNY SORT, THAT ONE. NEVER SEEMS LIKE ANYTHING BOTHERS HIM; HASN'T BARKED ONCE SINCE COMING IN.
I WAS A MILITARY WORKING DOG HANDLER IN IRAQ.
DOGS MAKE GOOD SOLDIERS.
YEAH.
I SEE.
SO, YOU TRYING TO BUST HIM OUT OF HERE?
NO, I JUST—
I FOUND HIM RUNNING AROUND OUTSIDE AND I SORT OF FELT LIKE HE NEEDED ME.
WELL, I DON'T DOUBT THAT. BUT IT MIGHT BE TOO LATE FOR HIM NOW. HE'S PROBABLY GOING TO BE PUT DOWN.
WHY?
CAN'T YOU DO ANYTHING ABOUT IT?
I'M NOT THE BOSS HERE. MY WIFE, PAT, RUNS THE PLACE.
I JUST COME IN THE MORNINGS TO FEED THE ANIMALS WHEN SHE'S AT CHURCH.
SHE LOVES THE MORNING MASS AT SAINT ANNE'S.
HELLO.
CLICK

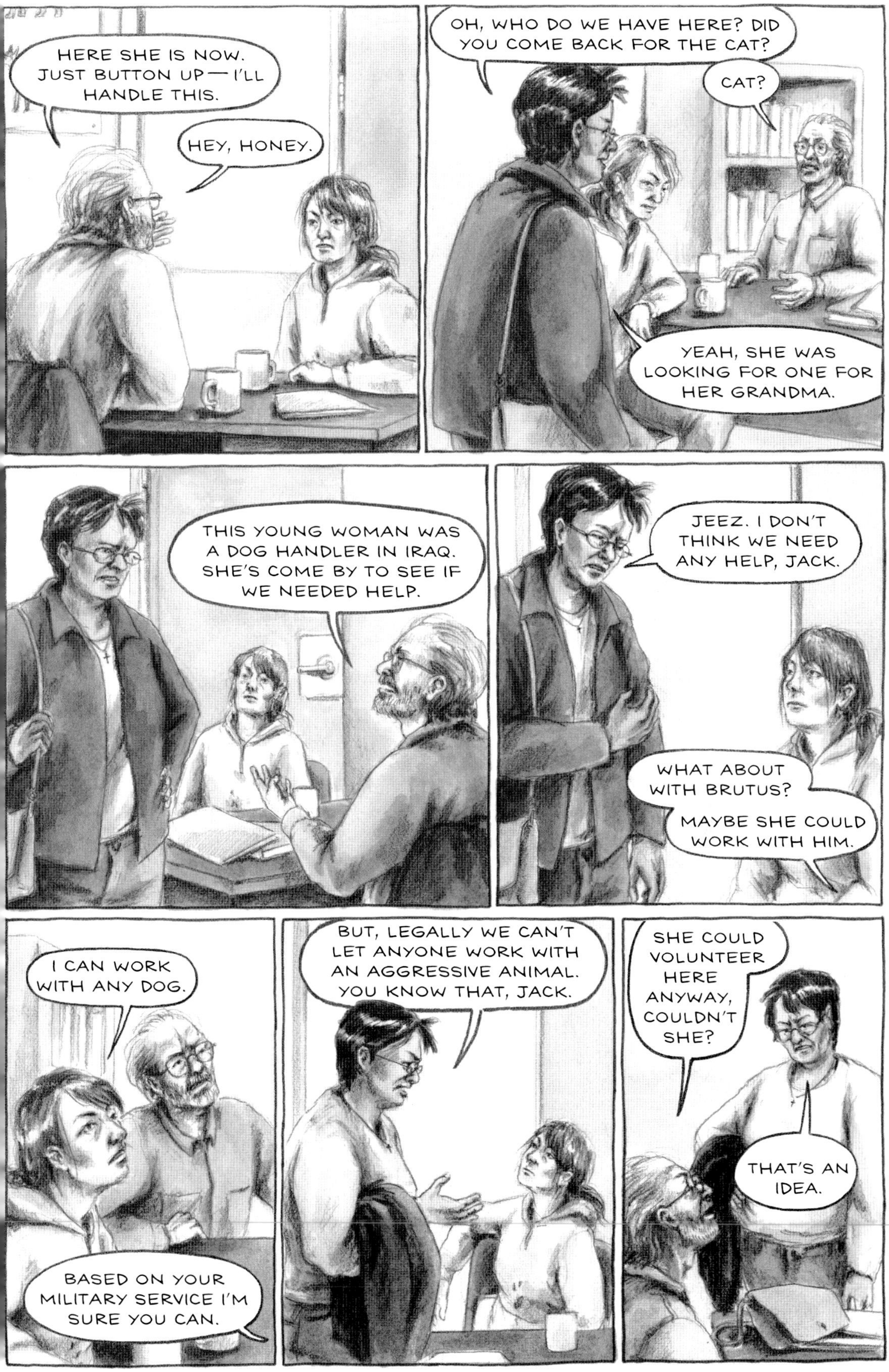
HERE SHE IS NOW. JUST BUTTON UP — I'LL HANDLE THIS.
HEY, HONEY.
OH, WHO DO WE HAVE HERE? DID YOU COME BACK FOR THE CAT?
CAT?
YEAH, SHE WAS LOOKING FOR ONE FOR HER GRANDMA.
THIS YOUNG WOMAN WAS A DOG HANDLER IN IRAQ. SHE'S COME BY TO SEE IF WE NEEDED HELP.
JEEZ. I DON'T THINK WE NEED ANY HELP, JACK.
WHAT ABOUT WITH BRUTUS?
MAYBE SHE COULD WORK WITH HIM.
I CAN WORK WITH ANY DOG.
BASED ON YOUR MILITARY SERVICE I'M SURE YOU CAN.
BUT, LEGALLY WE CAN'T LET ANYONE WORK WITH AN AGGRESSIVE ANIMAL. YOU KNOW THAT, JACK.
SHE COULD VOLUNTEER HERE ANYWAY, COULDN'T SHE?
THAT'S AN IDEA.

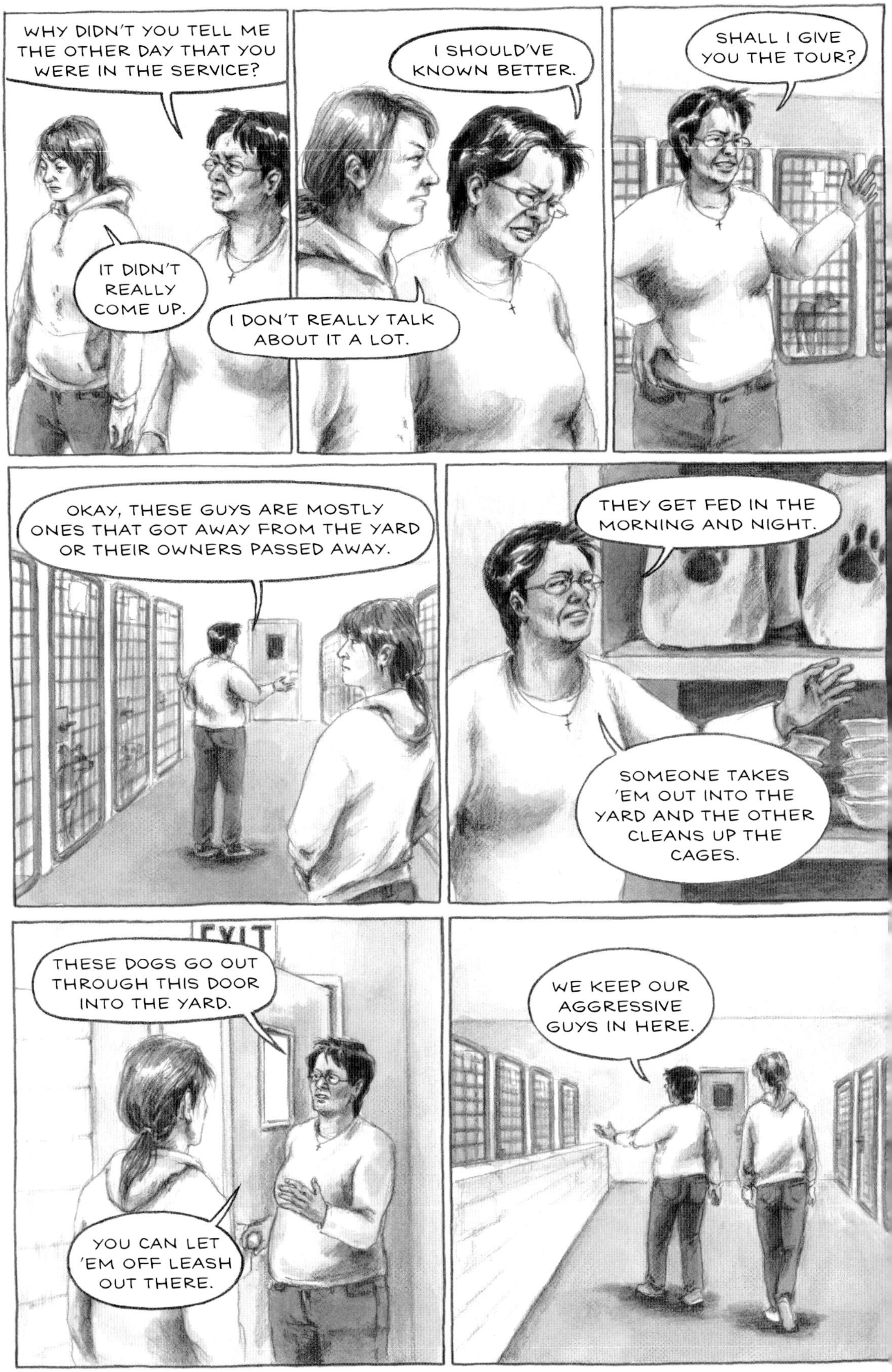
WHY DIDN'T YOU TELL ME THE OTHER DAY THAT YOU WERE IN THE SERVICE?
IT DIDN'T REALLY COME UP.
I SHOULD'VE KNOWN BETTER.
I DON'T REALLY TALK ABOUT IT A LOT.
SHALL I GIVE YOU THE TOUR?
OKAY, THESE GUYS ARE MOSTLY ONES THAT GOT AWAY FROM THE YARD OR THEIR OWNERS PASSED AWAY.
THEY GET FED IN THE MORNING AND NIGHT.
SOMEONE TAKES 'EM OUT INTO THE YARD AND THE OTHER CLEANS UP THE CAGES.
THESE DOGS GO OUT THROUGH THIS DOOR INTO THE YARD.
YOU CAN LET 'EM OFF LEASH OUT THERE.
WE KEEP OUR AGGRESSIVE GUYS IN HERE.

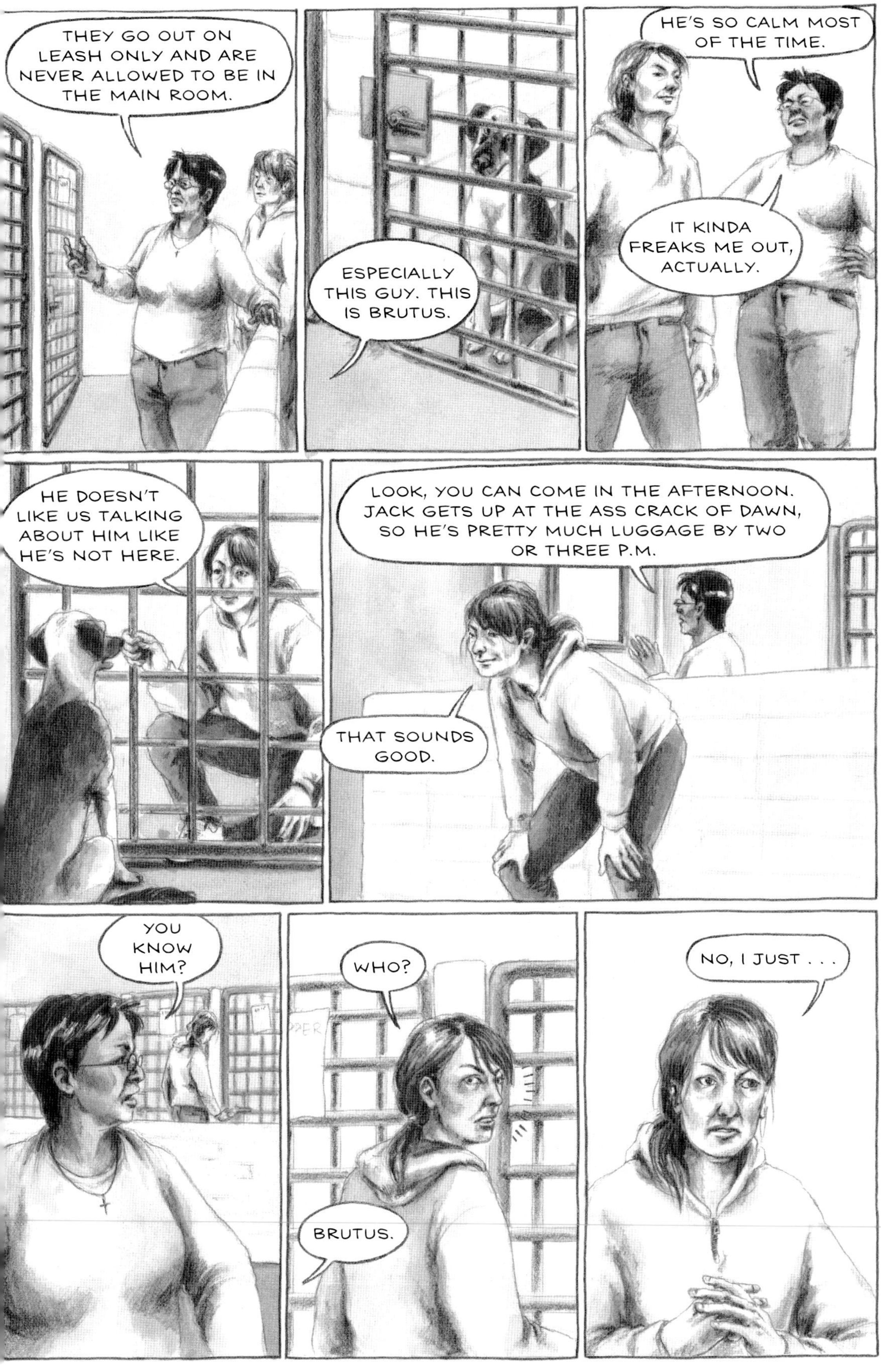
THEY GO OUT ON LEASH ONLY AND ARE NEVER ALLOWED TO BE IN THE MAIN ROOM.
ESPECIALLY THIS GUY. THIS IS BRUTUS.
HE'S SO CALM MOST OF THE TIME.
IT KINDA FREAKS ME OUT, ACTUALLY.
HE DOESN'T LIKE US TALKING ABOUT HIM LIKE HE'S NOT HERE.
LOOK, YOU CAN COME IN THE AFTERNOON. JACK GETS UP AT THE ASS CRACK OF DAWN, SO HE'S PRETTY MUCH LUGGAGE BY TWO OR THREE P.M.
THAT SOUNDS GOOD.
YOU KNOW HIM?
WHO?
BRUTUS.
NO, I JUST . . .

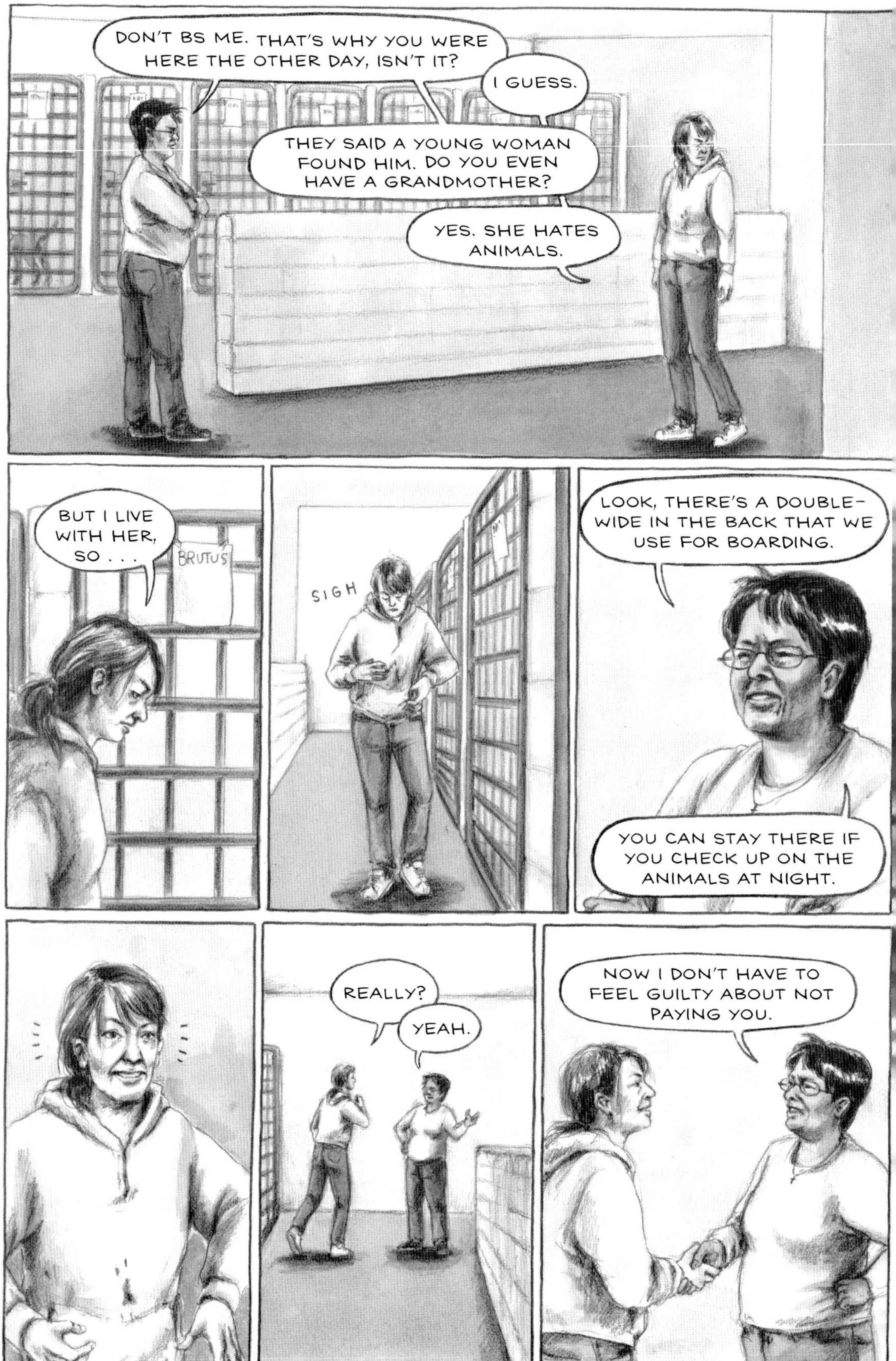
DON'T BS ME. THAT'S WHY YOU WERE HERE THE OTHER DAY, ISN'T IT?
I GUESS.
THEY SAID A YOUNG WOMAN FOUND HIM. DO YOU EVEN HAVE A GRANDMOTHER?
YES. SHE HATES ANIMALS.
BUT I LIVE WITH HER, SO . . .
BRUTUS
SIGH
LOOK, THERE'S A DOUBLE-WIDE IN THE BACK THAT WE USE FOR BOARDING.
YOU CAN STAY THERE IF YOU CHECK UP ON THE ANIMALS AT NIGHT.
REALLY?
YEAH.
NOW I DON'T HAVE TO FEEL GUILTY ABOUT NOT PAYING YOU.

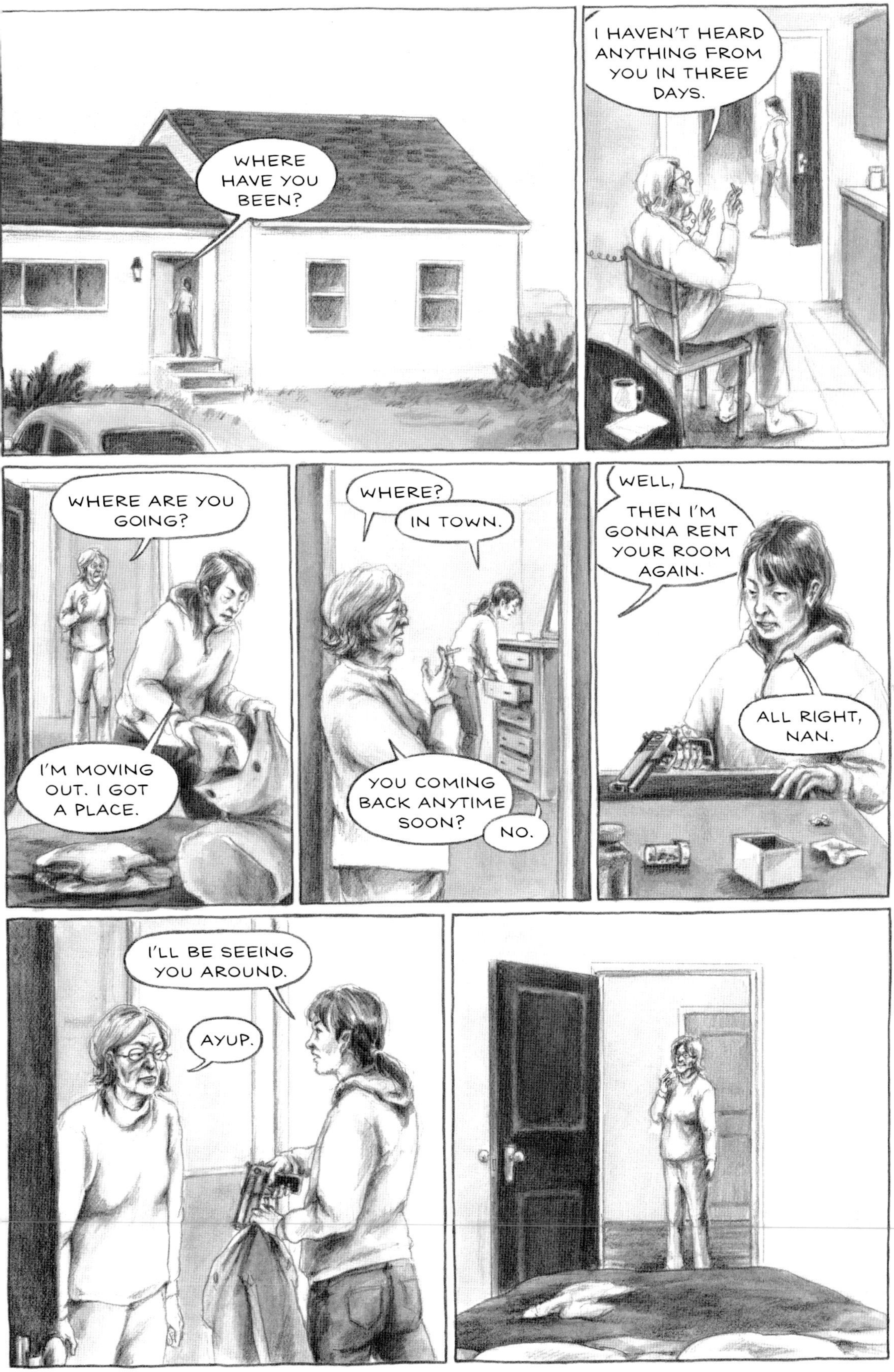
WHERE HAVE YOU BEEN?
I HAVEN'T HEARD ANYTHING FROM YOU IN THREE DAYS.
WHERE ARE YOU GOING?
I'M MOVING OUT. I GOT A PLACE.
WHERE?
IN TOWN.
YOU COMING BACK ANYTIME SOON?
NO.
WELL,
THEN I'M GONNA RENT YOUR ROOM AGAIN.
ALL RIGHT, NAN.
I'LL BE SEEING YOU AROUND.
AYUP.

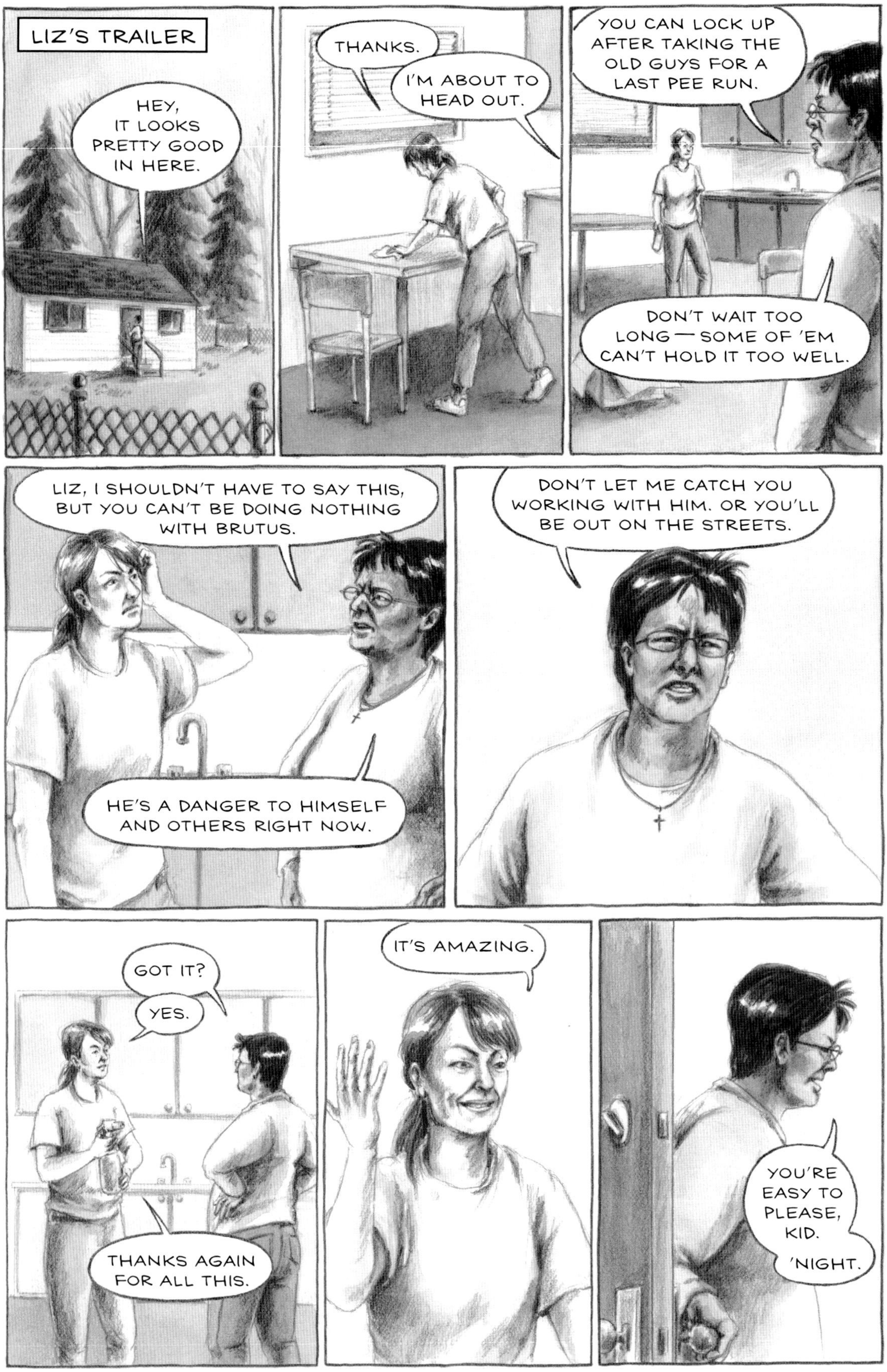
LIZ'S TRAILER
HEY, IT LOOKS PRETTY GOOD IN HERE.
THANKS.
I'M ABOUT TO HEAD OUT.
YOU CAN LOCK UP AFTER TAKING THE OLD GUYS FOR A LAST PEE RUN.
DON'T WAIT TOO LONG—SOME OF 'EM CAN'T HOLD IT TOO WELL.
LIZ, I SHOULDN'T HAVE TO SAY THIS, BUT YOU CAN'T BE DOING NOTHING WITH BRUTUS.
HE'S A DANGER TO HIMSELF AND OTHERS RIGHT NOW.
DON'T LET ME CATCH YOU WORKING WITH HIM. OR YOU'LL BE OUT ON THE STREETS.
GOT IT?
YES.
THANKS AGAIN FOR ALL THIS.
IT'S AMAZING.
YOU'RE EASY TO PLEASE, KID.
'NIGHT.

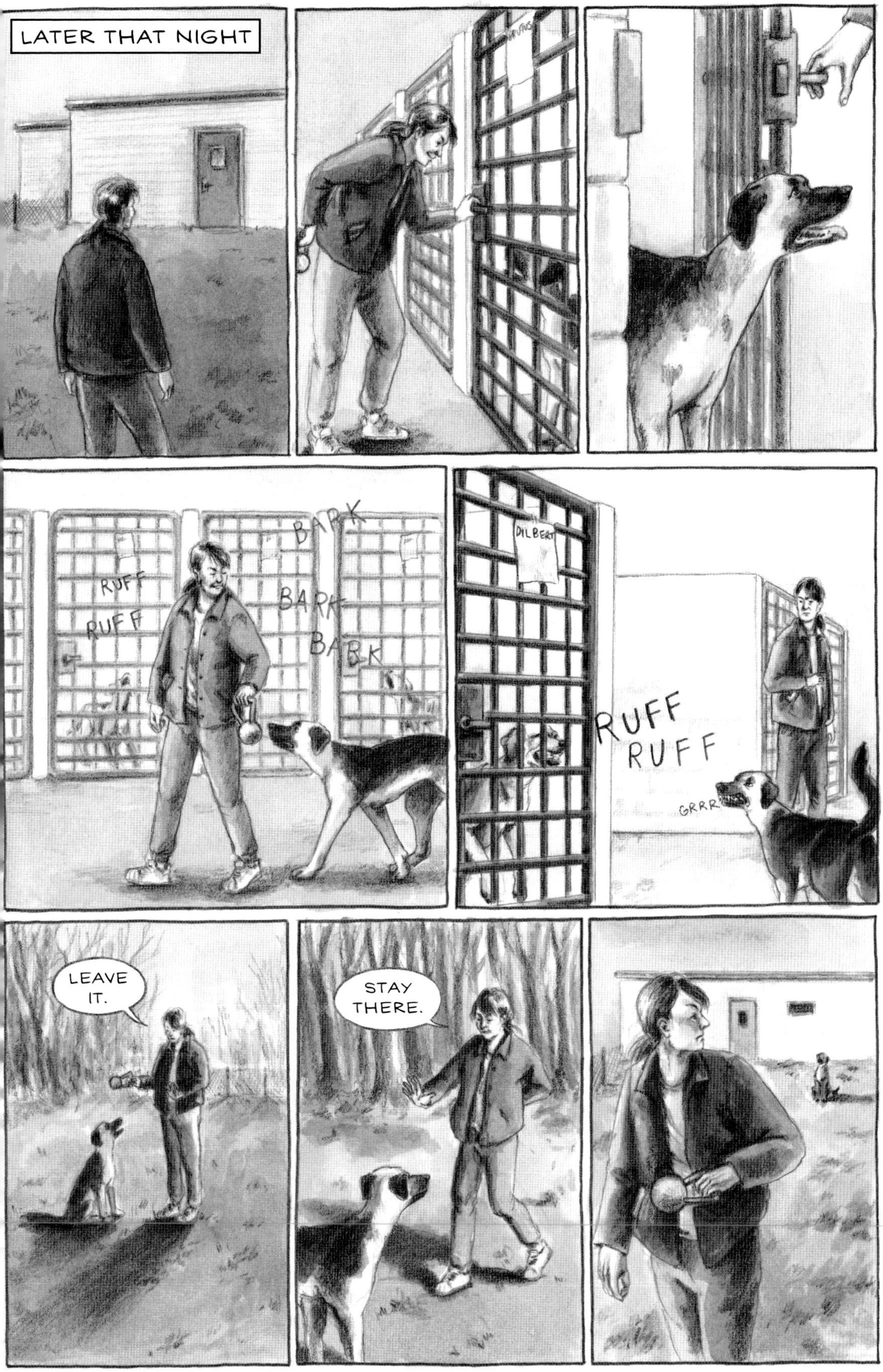
LATER THAT NIGHT
BARK
RUFF
RUFF
BARK
BARK
DILBERT
RUFF
RUFF
GRRR
LEAVE IT.
STAY THERE.

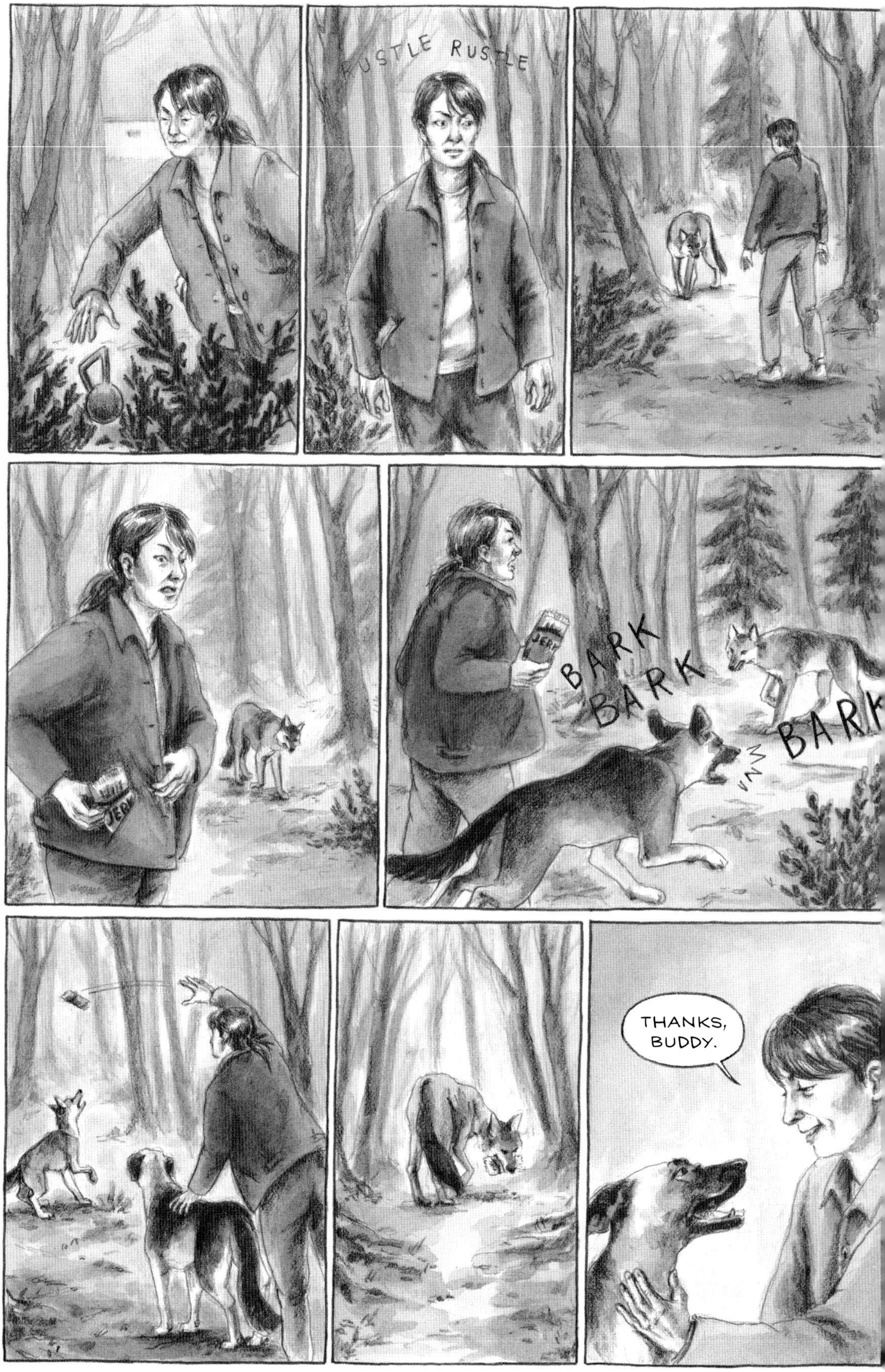
RUSTLE RUSTLE
JERK
BARK
BARK
BARK
THANKS, BUDDY.

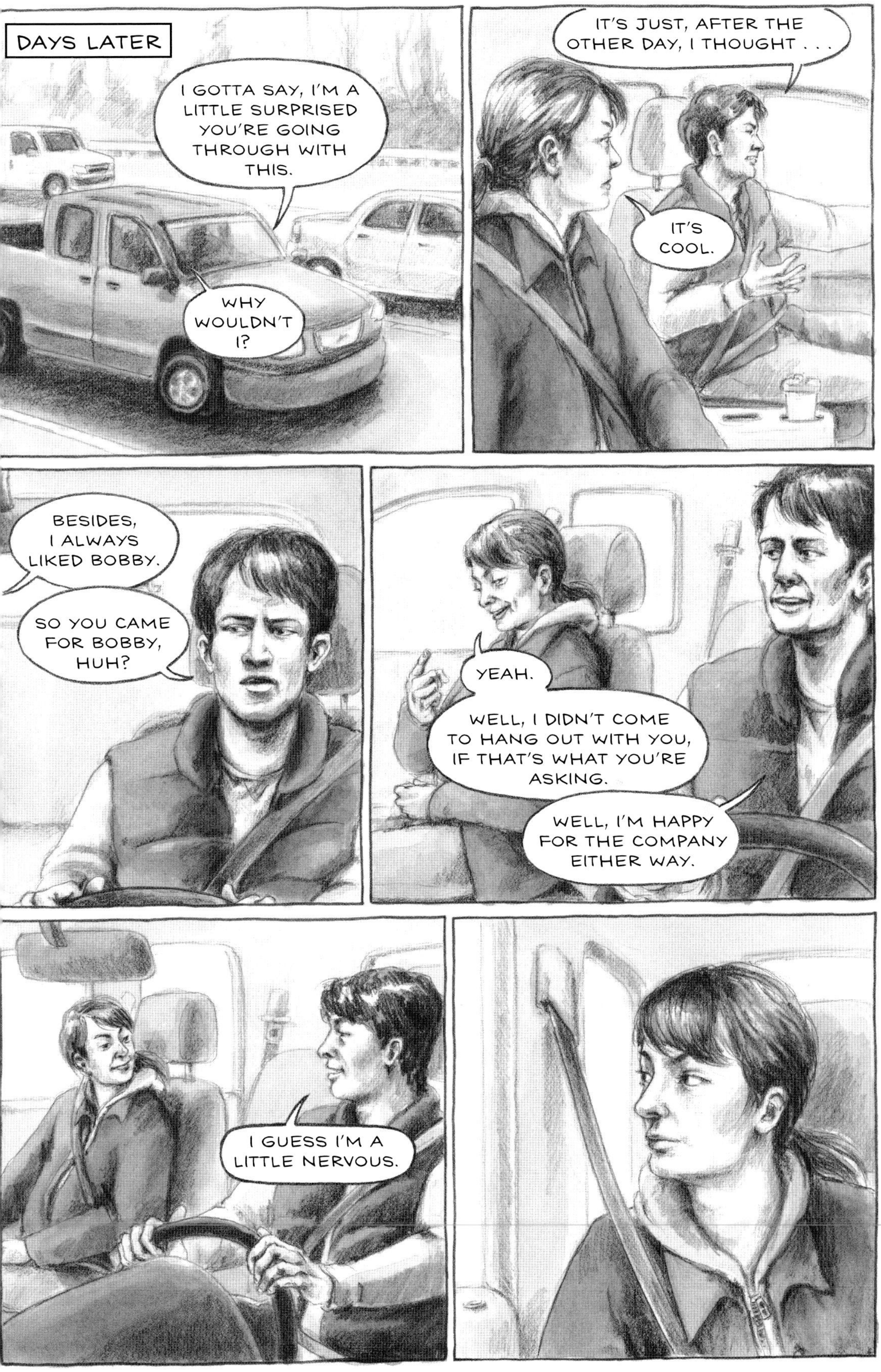
DAYS LATER
I GOTTA SAY, I'M A LITTLE SURPRISED YOU'RE GOING THROUGH WITH THIS.
WHY WOULDN'T I?
IT'S JUST, AFTER THE OTHER DAY, I THOUGHT . . .
IT'S COOL.
BESIDES, I ALWAYS LIKED BOBBY.
SO YOU CAME FOR BOBBY, HUH?
YEAH.
WELL, I DIDN'T COME TO HANG OUT WITH YOU, IF THAT'S WHAT YOU'RE ASKING.
WELL, I'M HAPPY FOR THE COMPANY EITHER WAY.
I GUESS I'M A LITTLE NERVOUS.

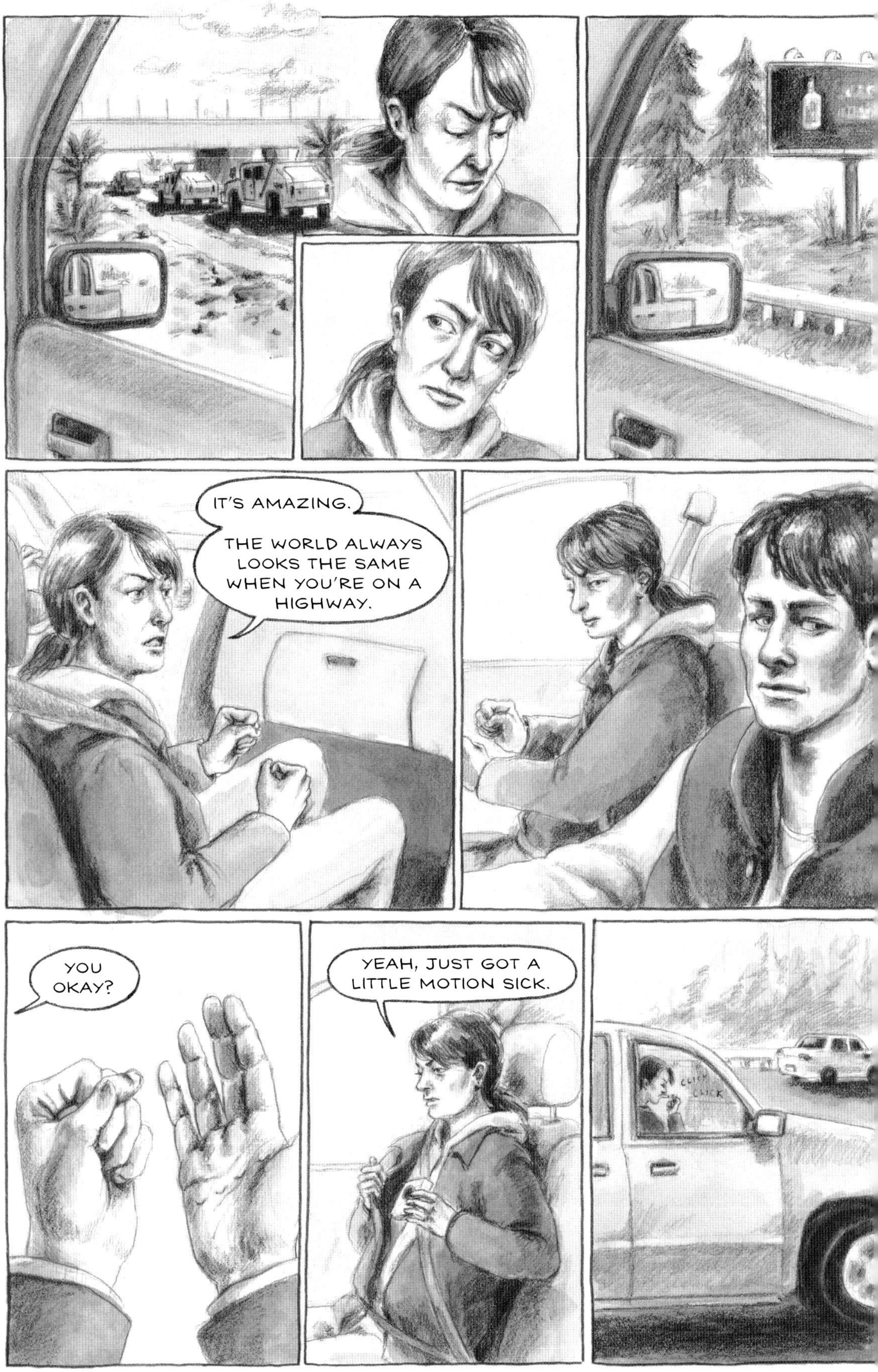
IT'S AMAZING.
THE WORLD ALWAYS LOOKS THE SAME WHEN YOU'RE ON A HIGHWAY.
YOU OKAY?
YEAH, JUST GOT A LITTLE MOTION SICK.
CLICK
CLICK

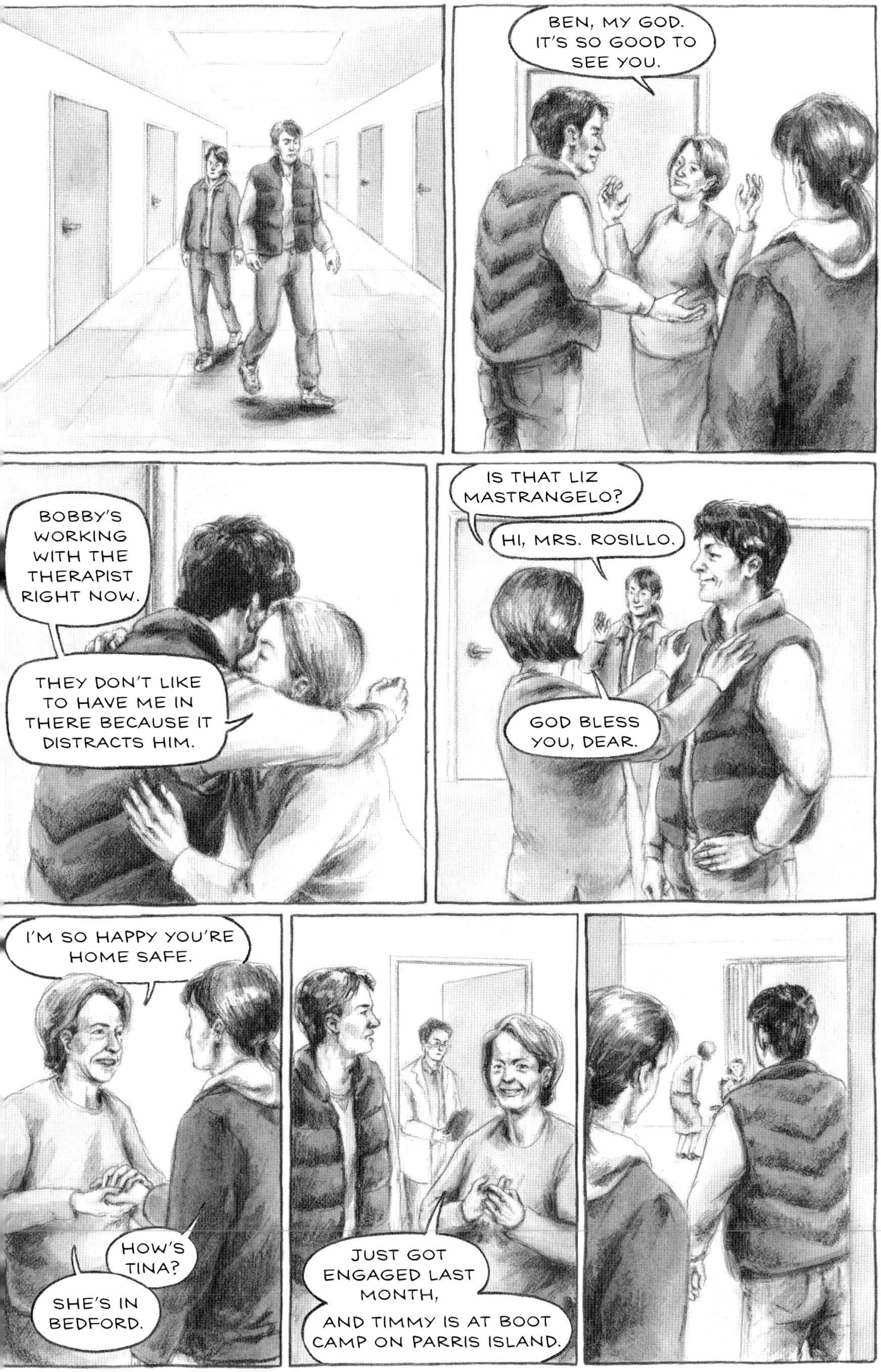
BEN, MY GOD. IT'S SO GOOD TO SEE YOU.
BOBBY'S WORKING WITH THE THERAPIST RIGHT NOW.
THEY DON'T LIKE TO HAVE ME IN THERE BECAUSE IT DISTRACTS HIM.
IS THAT LIZ MASTRANGELO?
HI, MRS. ROSILLO.
GOD BLESS YOU, DEAR.
I'M SO HAPPY YOU'RE HOME SAFE.
HOW'S TINA?
SHE'S IN BEDFORD.
JUST GOT ENGAGED LAST MONTH,
AND TIMMY IS AT BOOT CAMP ON PARRIS ISLAND.

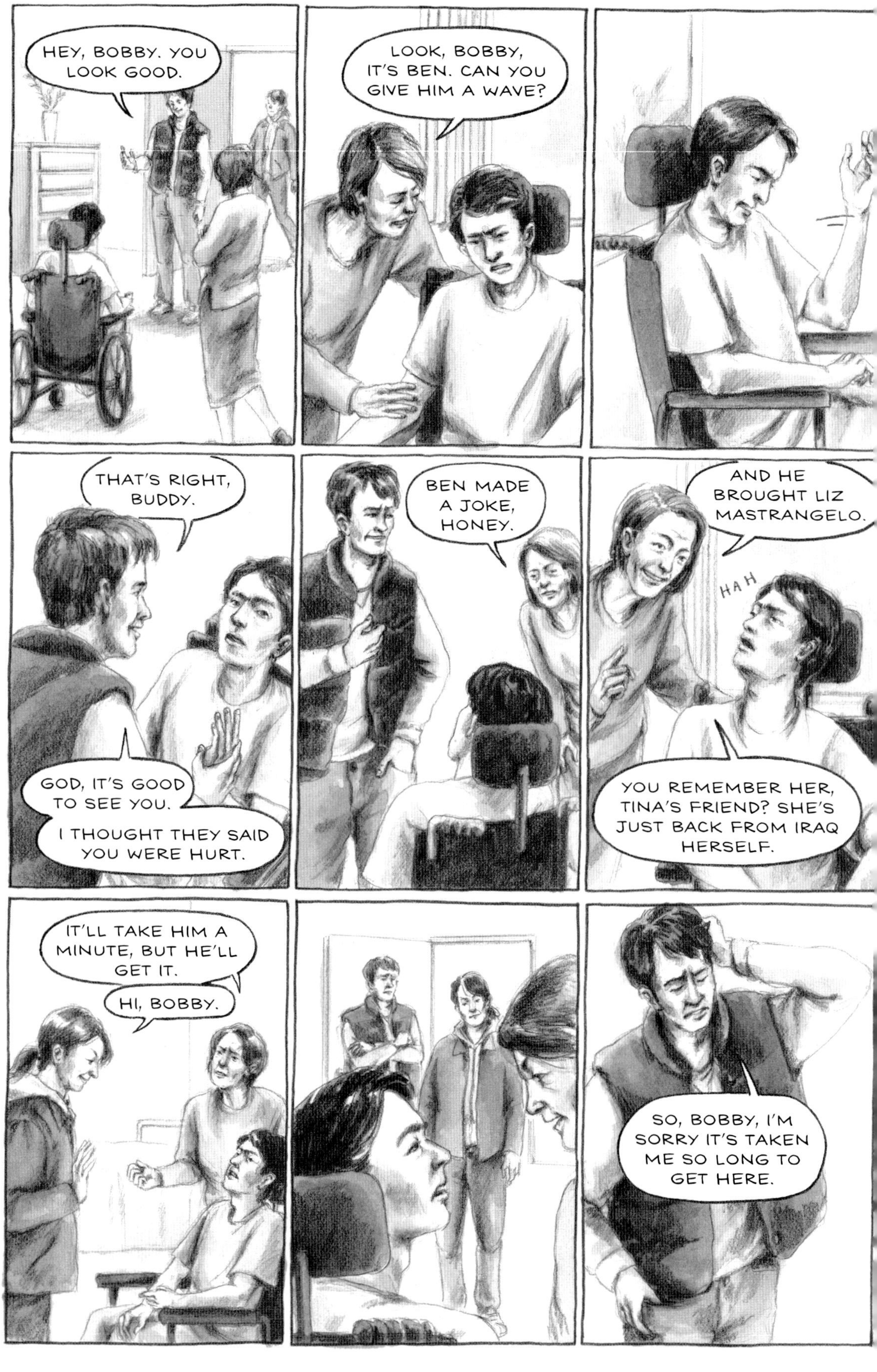
HEY, BOBBY. YOU LOOK GOOD.
LOOK, BOBBY, IT'S BEN. CAN YOU GIVE HIM A WAVE?
THAT'S RIGHT, BUDDY.
GOD, IT'S GOOD TO SEE YOU.
I THOUGHT THEY SAID YOU WERE HURT.
BEN MADE A JOKE, HONEY.
AND HE BROUGHT LIZ MASTRANGELO.
HAH
YOU REMEMBER HER, TINA'S FRIEND? SHE'S JUST BACK FROM IRAQ HERSELF.
IT'LL TAKE HIM A MINUTE, BUT HE'LL GET IT.
HI, BOBBY.
SO, BOBBY, I'M SORRY IT'S TAKEN ME SO LONG TO GET HERE.

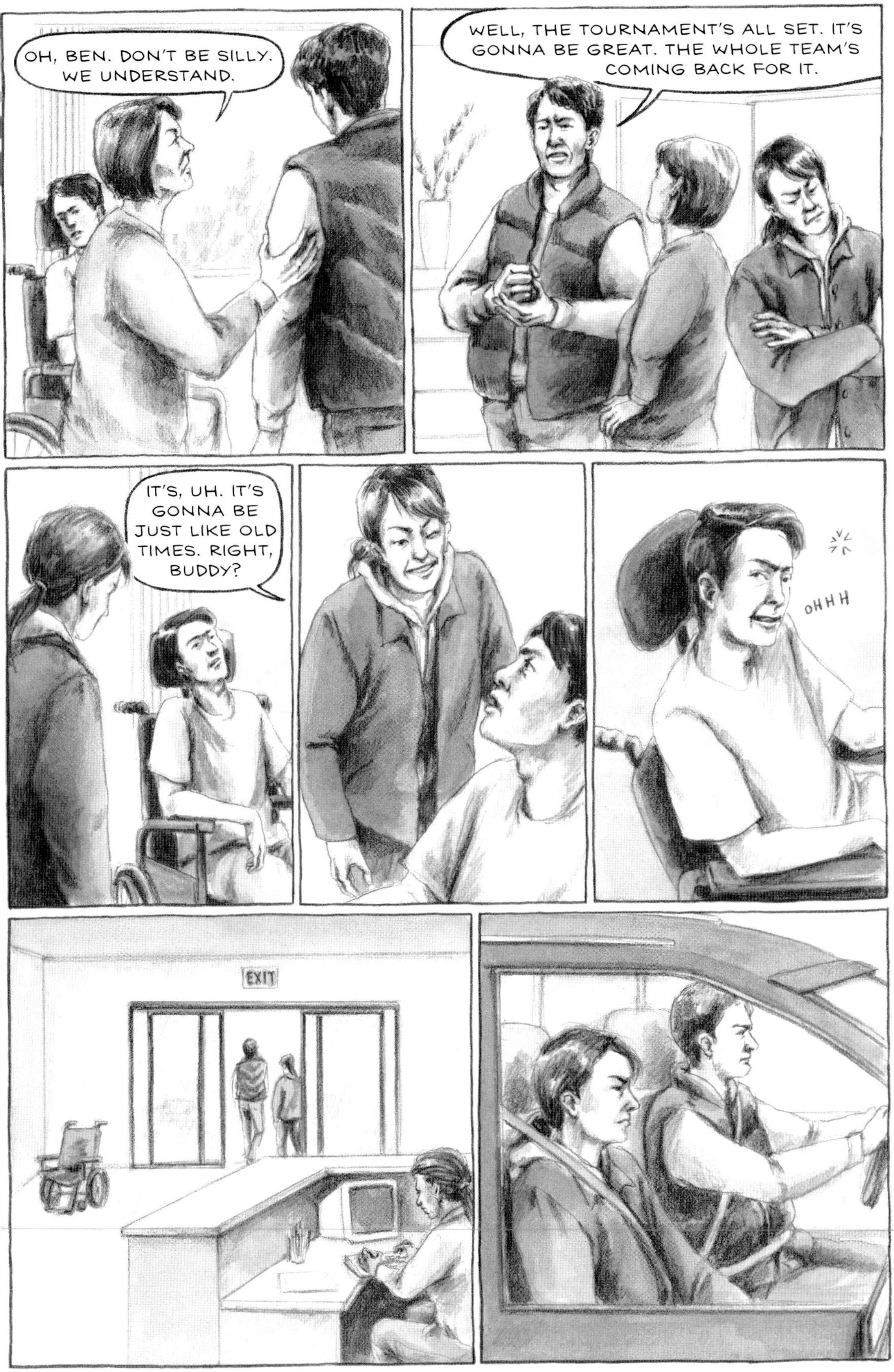
OH, BEN. DON'T BE SILLY. WE UNDERSTAND.
WELL, THE TOURNAMENT'S ALL SET. IT'S GONNA BE GREAT. THE WHOLE TEAM'S COMING BACK FOR IT.
IT'S, UH. IT'S GONNA BE JUST LIKE OLD TIMES. RIGHT, BUDDY?
OHHH
EXIT

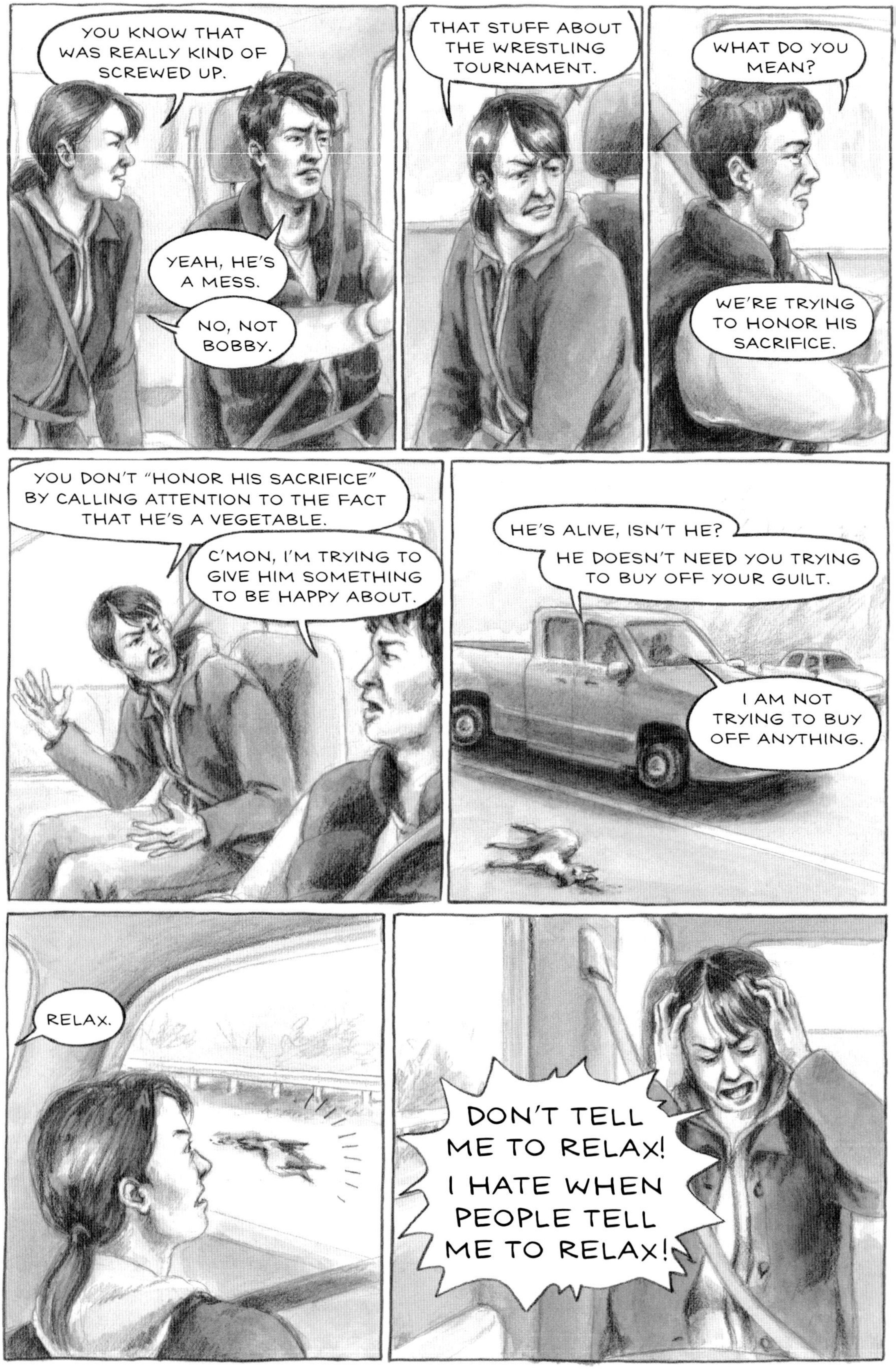
YOU KNOW THAT WAS REALLY KIND OF SCREWED UP.
YEAH, HE'S A MESS.
NO, NOT BOBBY.
THAT STUFF ABOUT THE WRESTLING TOURNAMENT.
WHAT DO YOU MEAN?
WE'RE TRYING TO HONOR HIS SACRIFICE.
YOU DON'T "HONOR HIS SACRIFICE" BY CALLING ATTENTION TO THE FACT THAT HE'S A VEGETABLE.
C'MON, I'M TRYING TO GIVE HIM SOMETHING TO BE HAPPY ABOUT.
HE'S ALIVE, ISN'T HE?
HE DOESN'T NEED YOU TRYING TO BUY OFF YOUR GUILT.
I AM NOT TRYING TO BUY OFF ANYTHING.
RELAX.
DON'T TELL ME TO RELAX!
I HATE WHEN PEOPLE TELL ME TO RELAX!

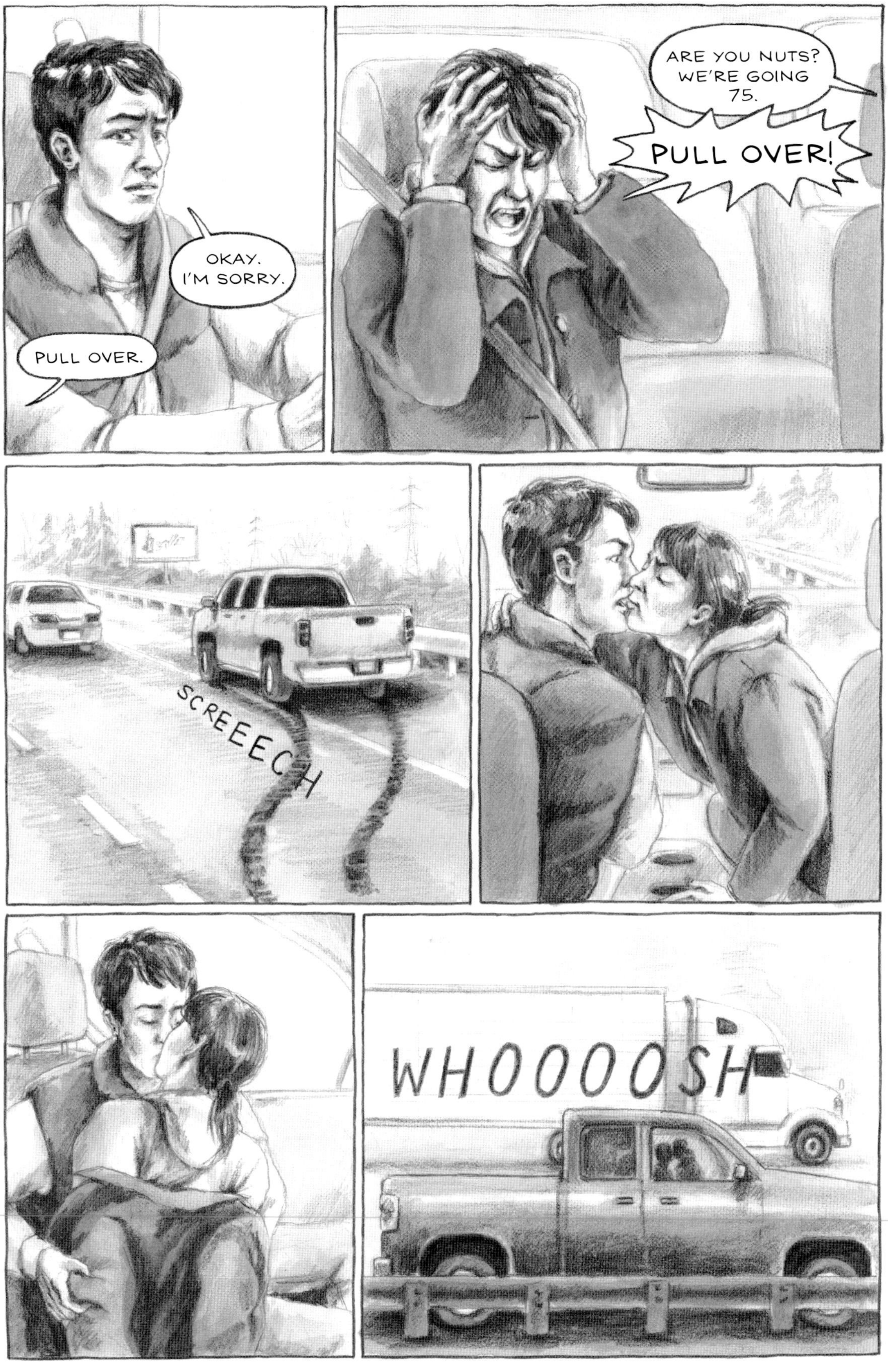
PULL OVER.
OKAY.
I'M SORRY.
ARE YOU NUTS?
WE'RE GOING
75.
PULL OVER!
SCREEECH
WHOOOOSH

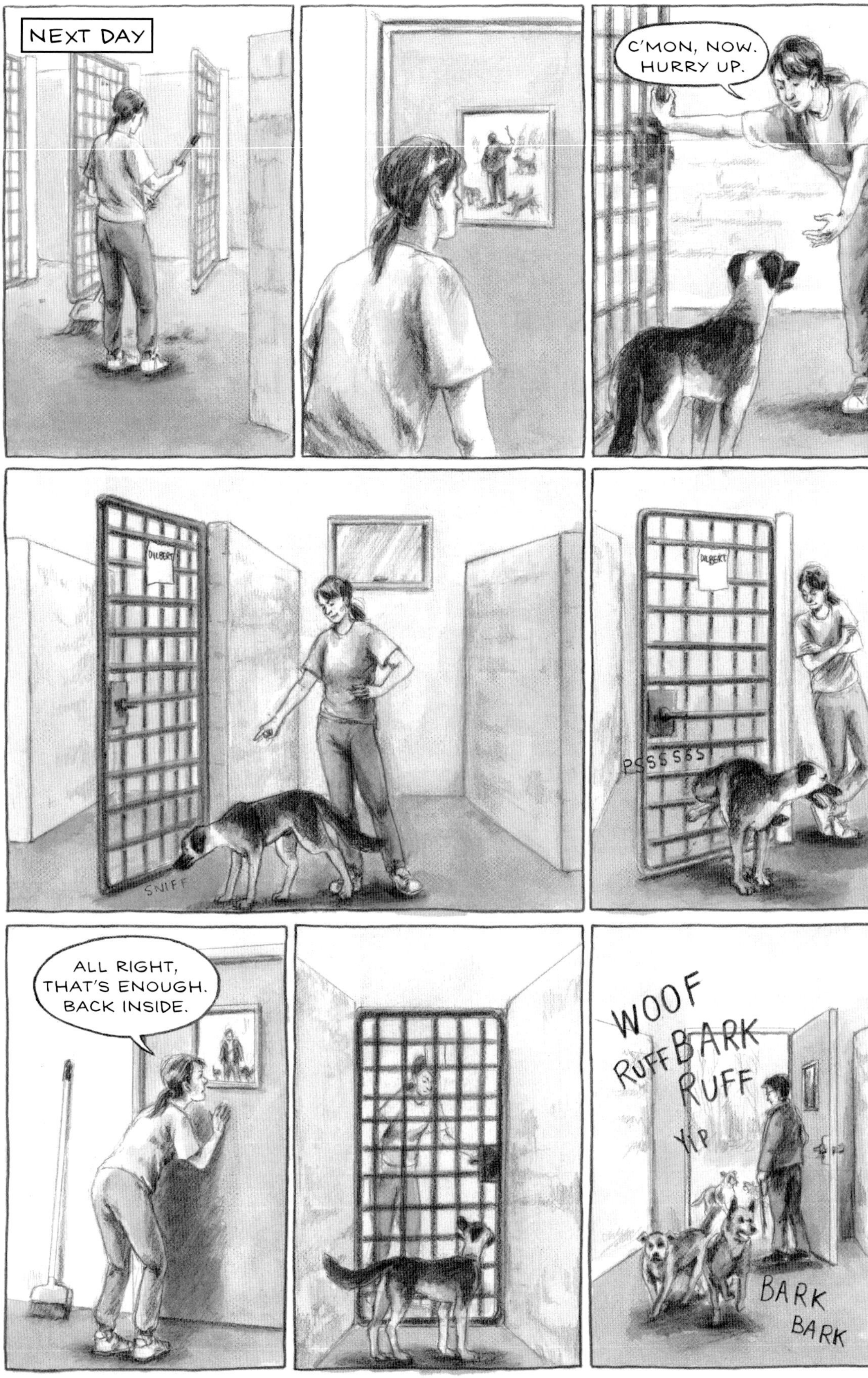

NEXT DAY
C'MON, NOW. HURRY UP.
DILBERT
SNIFF
DILBERT
PSSSSSS
ALL RIGHT, THAT'S ENOUGH. BACK INSIDE.
WOOF
RUFF BARK
RUFF
YIP
BARK
BARK

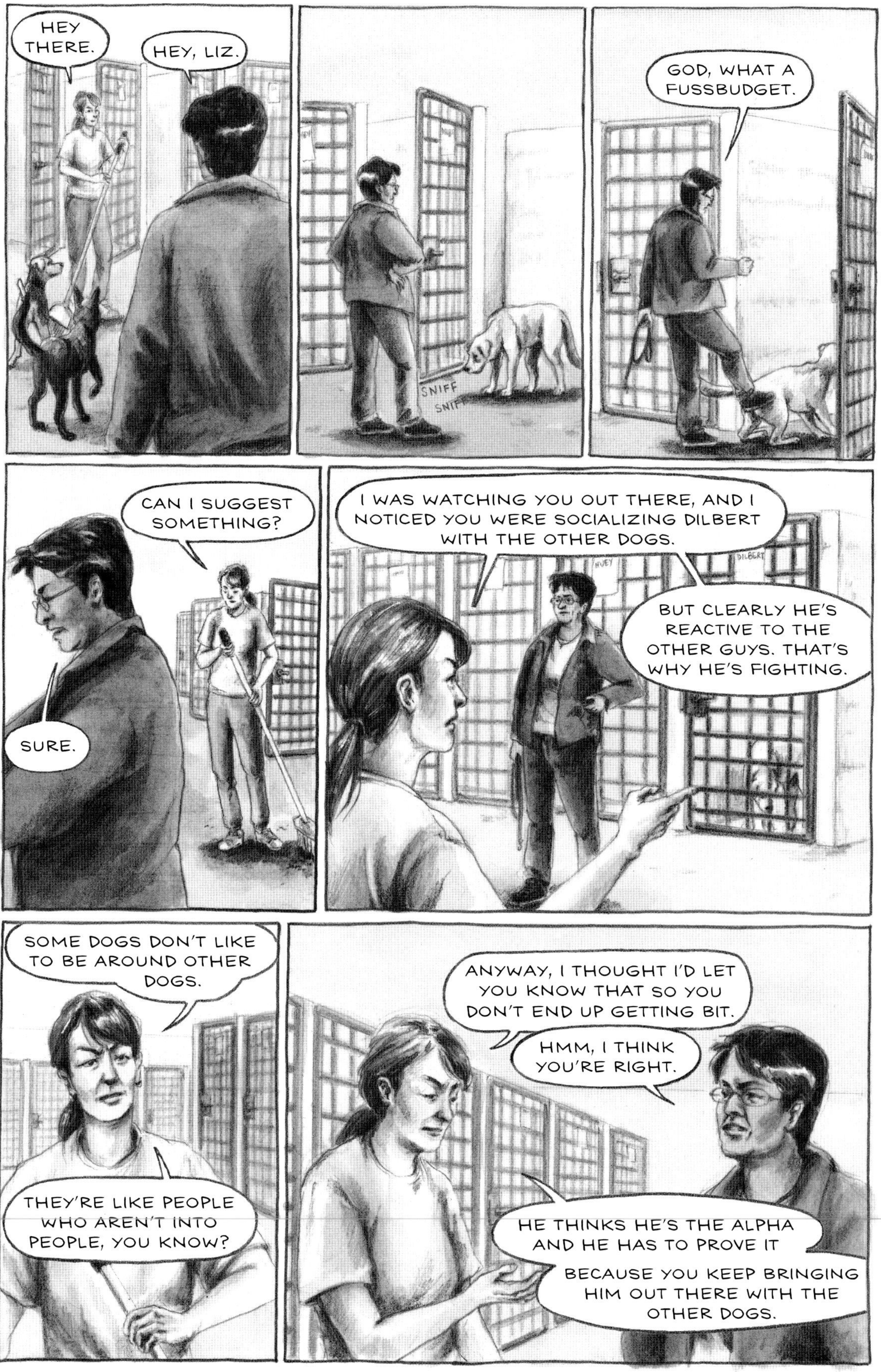
HEY THERE.
HEY, LIZ.
SNIFF SNIFF
GOD, WHAT A FUSSBUDGET.
CAN I SUGGEST SOMETHING?
SURE.
I WAS WATCHING YOU OUT THERE, AND I NOTICED YOU WERE SOCIALIZING DILBERT WITH THE OTHER DOGS.
BUT CLEARLY HE'S REACTIVE TO THE OTHER GUYS. THAT'S WHY HE'S FIGHTING.
SOME DOGS DON'T LIKE TO BE AROUND OTHER DOGS.
THEY'RE LIKE PEOPLE WHO AREN'T INTO PEOPLE, YOU KNOW?
ANYWAY, I THOUGHT I'D LET YOU KNOW THAT SO YOU DON'T END UP GETTING BIT.
HMM, I THINK YOU'RE RIGHT.
HE THINKS HE'S THE ALPHA AND HE HAS TO PROVE IT
BECAUSE YOU KEEP BRINGING HIM OUT THERE WITH THE OTHER DOGS.

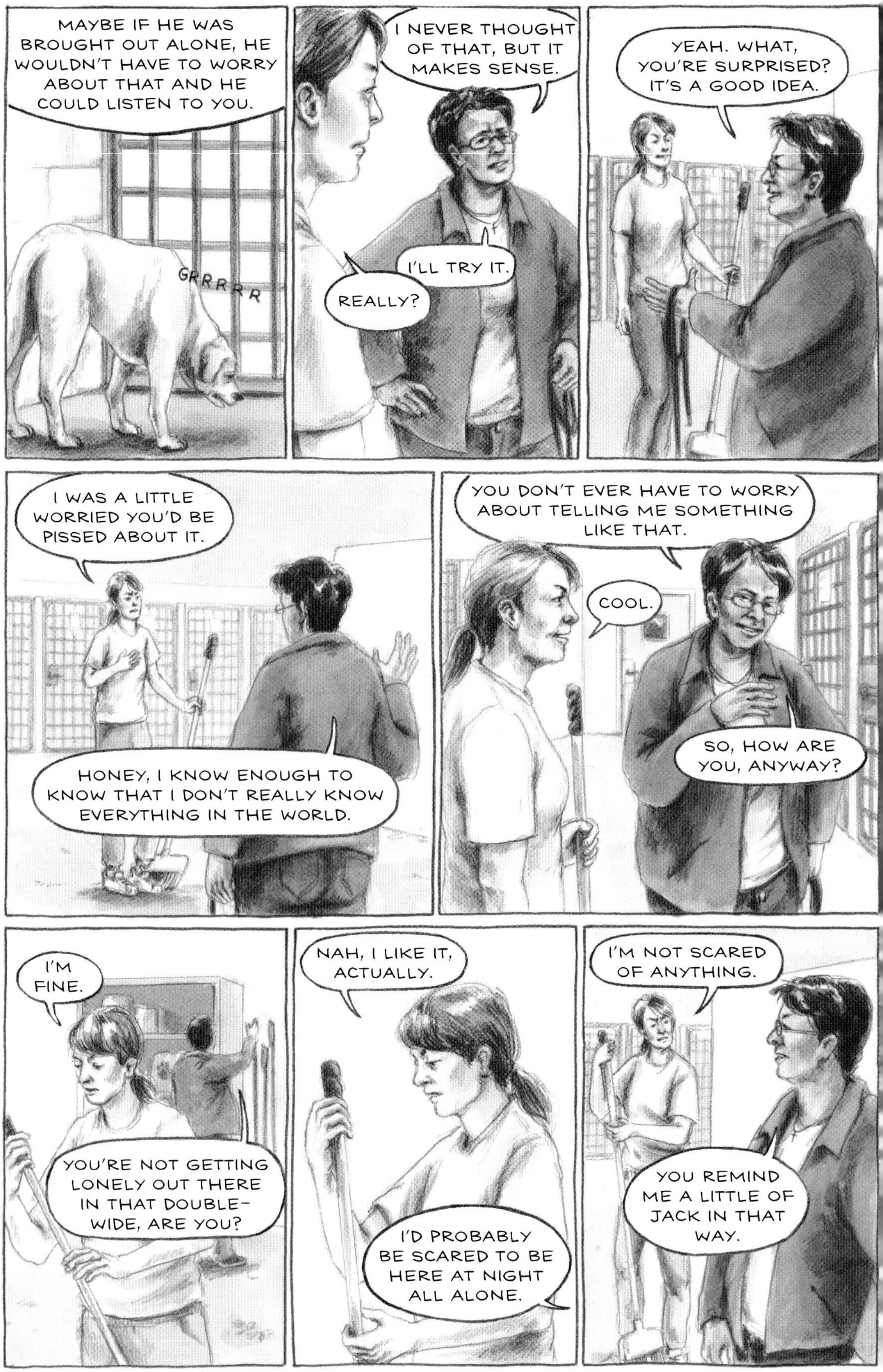
MAYBE IF HE WAS BROUGHT OUT ALONE, HE WOULDN'T HAVE TO WORRY ABOUT THAT AND HE COULD LISTEN TO YOU.
GRRRRRR
I NEVER THOUGHT OF THAT, BUT IT MAKES SENSE.
I'LL TRY IT.
REALLY?
YEAH. WHAT, YOU'RE SURPRISED? IT'S A GOOD IDEA.
I WAS A LITTLE WORRIED YOU'D BE PISSED ABOUT IT.
HONEY, I KNOW ENOUGH TO KNOW THAT I DON'T REALLY KNOW EVERYTHING IN THE WORLD.
YOU DON'T EVER HAVE TO WORRY ABOUT TELLING ME SOMETHING LIKE THAT.
COOL.
SO, HOW ARE YOU, ANYWAY?
I'M FINE.
YOU'RE NOT GETTING LONELY OUT THERE IN THAT DOUBLE-WIDE, ARE YOU?
NAH, I LIKE IT, ACTUALLY.
I'D PROBABLY BE SCARED TO BE HERE AT NIGHT ALL ALONE.
I'M NOT SCARED OF ANYTHING.
YOU REMIND ME A LITTLE OF JACK IN THAT WAY.

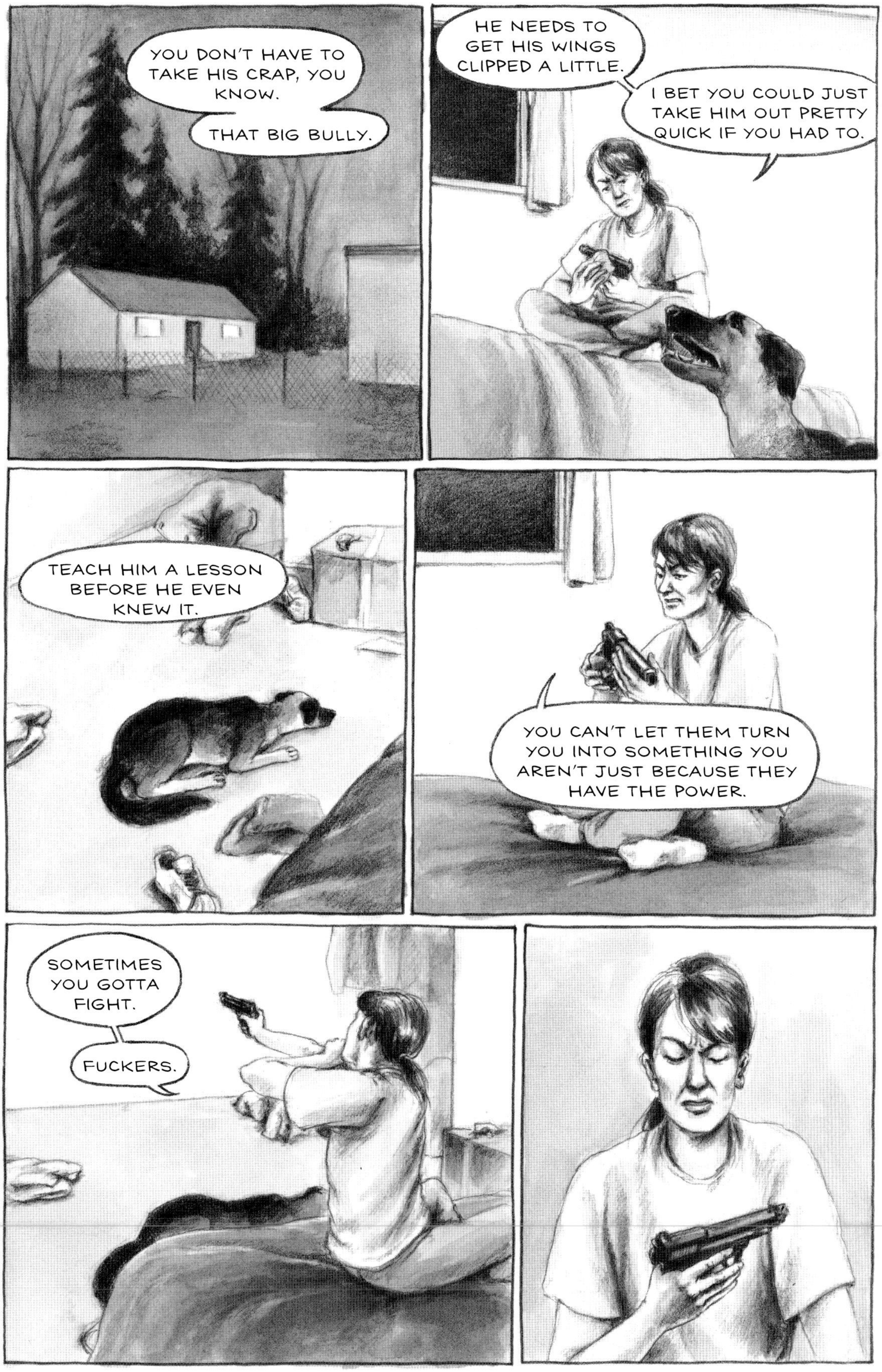
YOU DON'T HAVE TO TAKE HIS CRAP, YOU KNOW.
THAT BIG BULLY.
HE NEEDS TO GET HIS WINGS CLIPPED A LITTLE.
I BET YOU COULD JUST TAKE HIM OUT PRETTY QUICK IF YOU HAD TO.
TEACH HIM A LESSON BEFORE HE EVEN KNEW IT.
YOU CAN'T LET THEM TURN YOU INTO SOMETHING YOU AREN'T JUST BECAUSE THEY HAVE THE POWER.
SOMETIMES YOU GOTTA FIGHT.
FUCKERS.

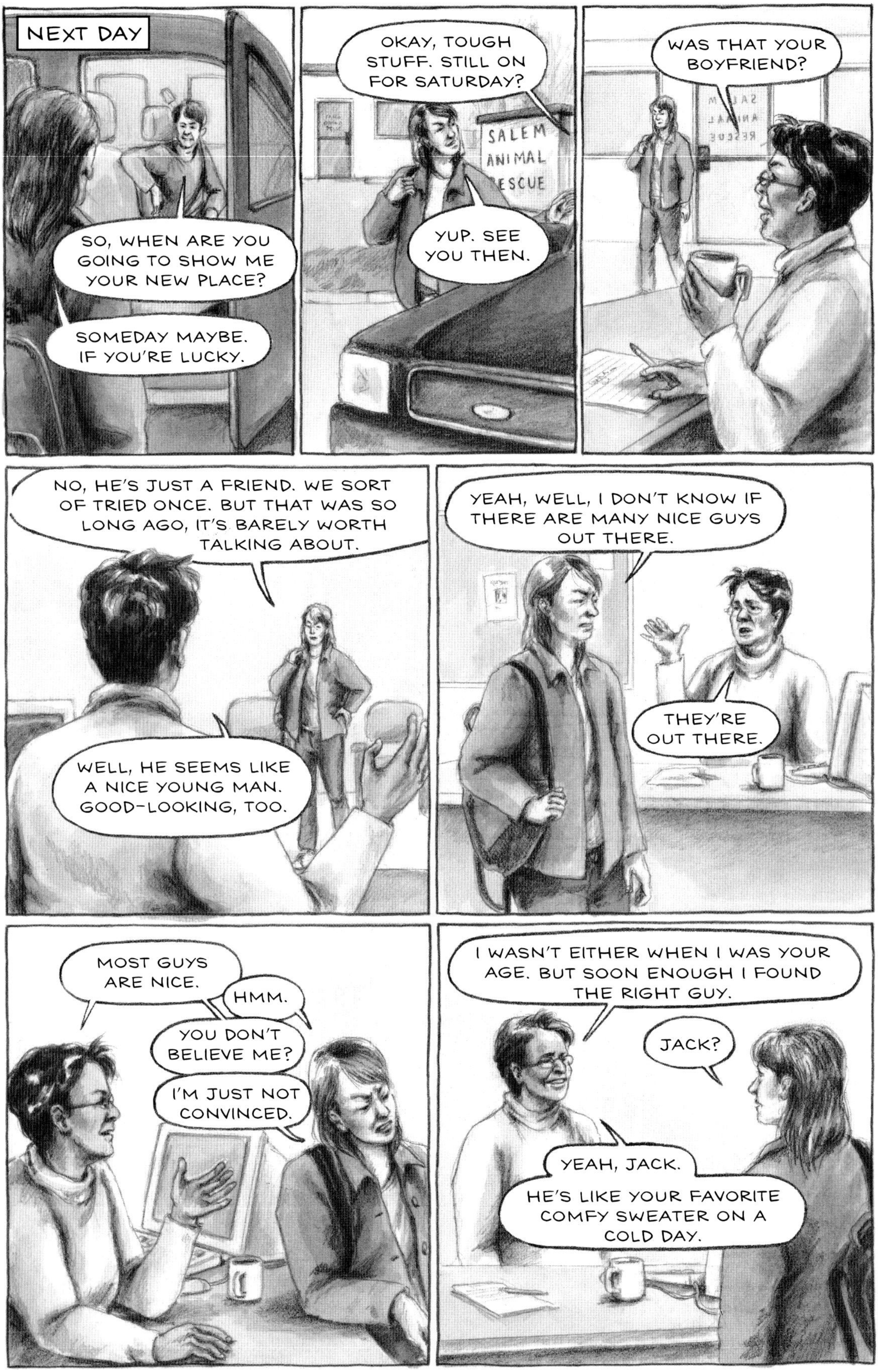
NEXT DAY
SO, WHEN ARE YOU GOING TO SHOW ME YOUR NEW PLACE?
SOMEDAY MAYBE. IF YOU'RE LUCKY.
OKAY, TOUGH STUFF. STILL ON FOR SATURDAY?
SALEM ANIMAL RESCUE
YUP. SEE YOU THEN.
WAS THAT YOUR BOYFRIEND?
NO, HE'S JUST A FRIEND. WE SORT OF TRIED ONCE. BUT THAT WAS SO LONG AGO, IT'S BARELY WORTH TALKING ABOUT.
WELL, HE SEEMS LIKE A NICE YOUNG MAN. GOOD-LOOKING, TOO.
YEAH, WELL, I DON'T KNOW IF THERE ARE MANY NICE GUYS OUT THERE.
THEY'RE OUT THERE.
MOST GUYS ARE NICE.
HMM.
YOU DON'T BELIEVE ME?
I'M JUST NOT CONVINCED.
I WASN'T EITHER WHEN I WAS YOUR AGE. BUT SOON ENOUGH I FOUND THE RIGHT GUY.
JACK?
YEAH, JACK.
HE'S LIKE YOUR FAVORITE COMFY SWEATER ON A COLD DAY.

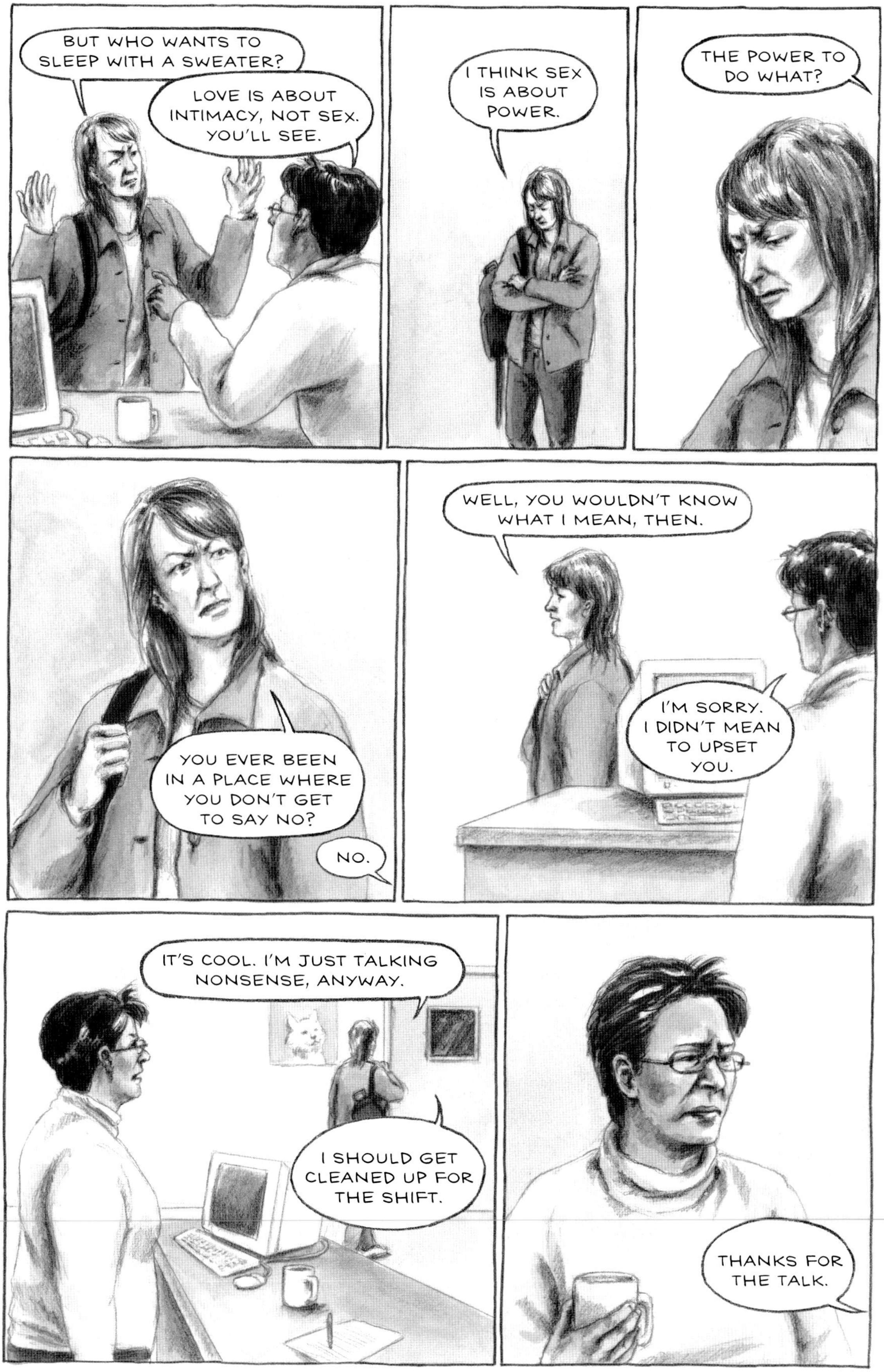
BUT WHO WANTS TO SLEEP WITH A SWEATER?
LOVE IS ABOUT INTIMACY, NOT SEX. YOU'LL SEE.
I THINK SEX IS ABOUT POWER.
THE POWER TO DO WHAT?
YOU EVER BEEN IN A PLACE WHERE YOU DON'T GET TO SAY NO?
NO.
WELL, YOU WOULDN'T KNOW WHAT I MEAN, THEN.
I'M SORRY. I DIDN'T MEAN TO UPSET YOU.
IT'S COOL. I'M JUST TALKING NONSENSE, ANYWAY.
I SHOULD GET CLEANED UP FOR THE SHIFT.
THANKS FOR THE TALK.

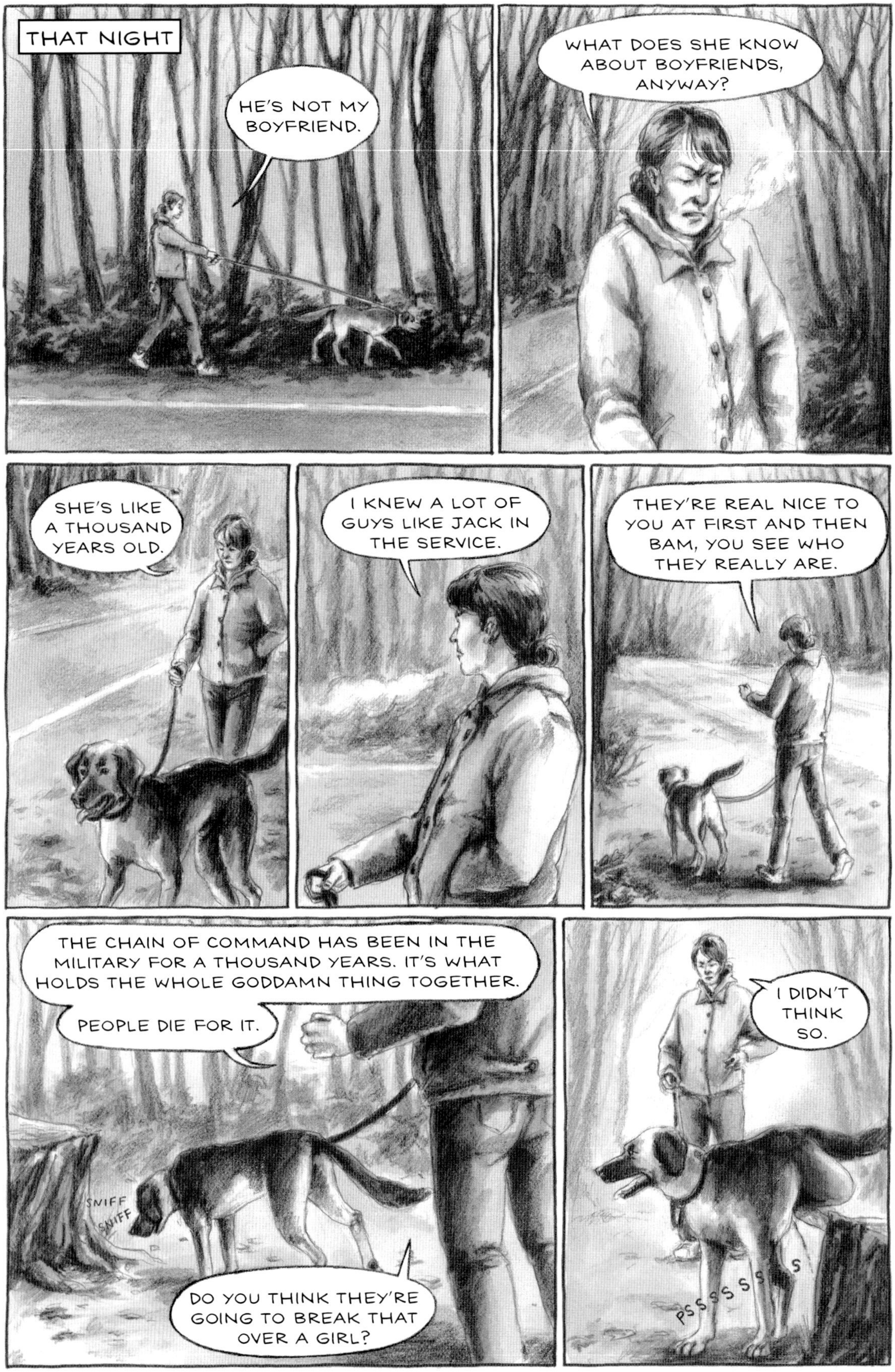
THAT NIGHT
HE'S NOT MY BOYFRIEND.
WHAT DOES SHE KNOW ABOUT BOYFRIENDS, ANYWAY?
SHE'S LIKE A THOUSAND YEARS OLD.
I KNEW A LOT OF GUYS LIKE JACK IN THE SERVICE.
THEY'RE REAL NICE TO YOU AT FIRST AND THEN BAM, YOU SEE WHO THEY REALLY ARE.
THE CHAIN OF COMMAND HAS BEEN IN THE MILITARY FOR A THOUSAND YEARS. IT'S WHAT HOLDS THE WHOLE GODDAMN THING TOGETHER.
PEOPLE DIE FOR IT.
SNIFF SNIFF
DO YOU THINK THEY'RE GOING TO BREAK THAT OVER A GIRL?
I DIDN'T THINK SO.
PSSSSSSS

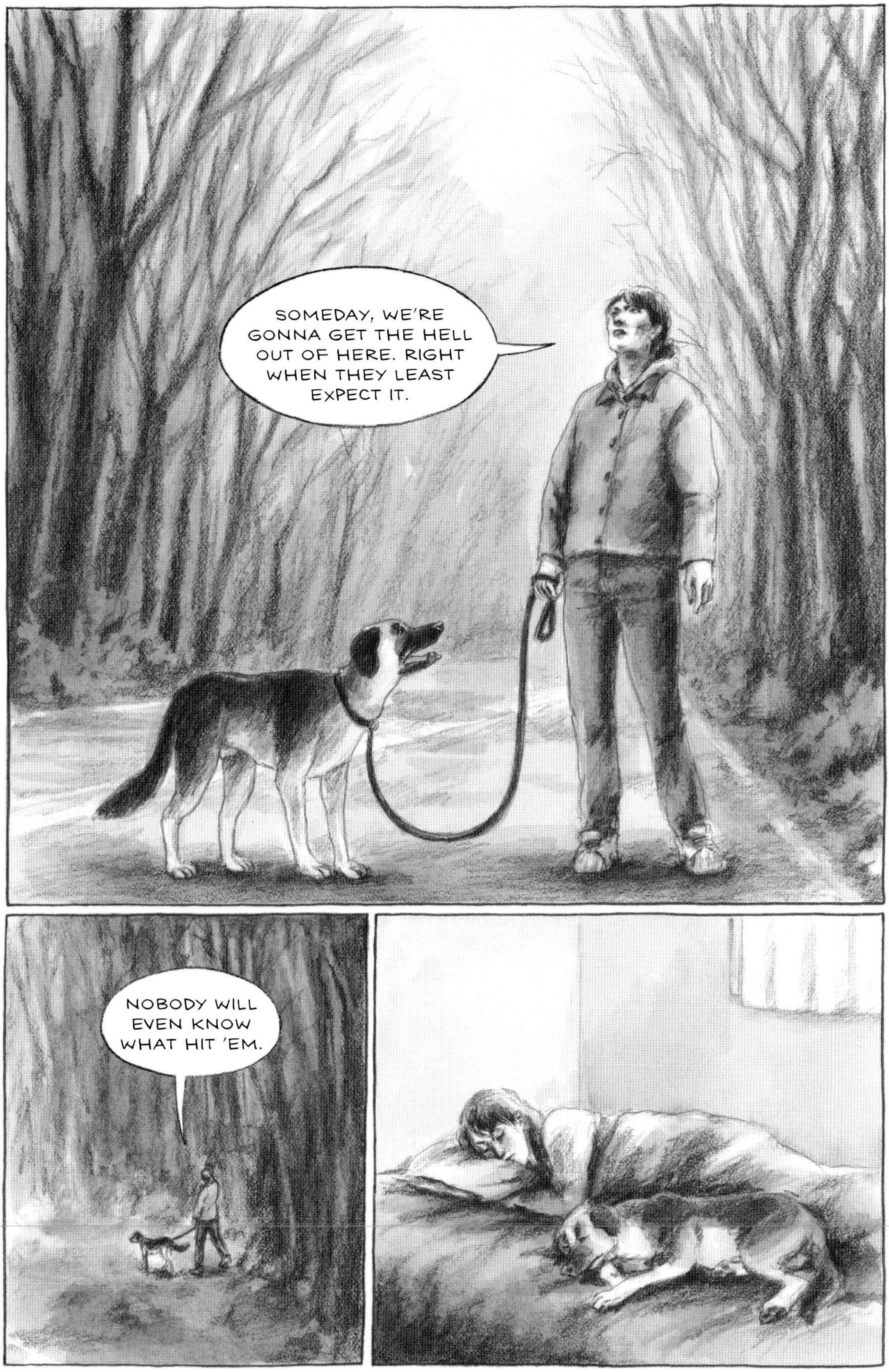
SOMEDAY, WE'RE GONNA GET THE HELL OUT OF HERE. RIGHT WHEN THEY LEAST EXPECT IT.
NOBODY WILL EVEN KNOW WHAT HIT 'EM.

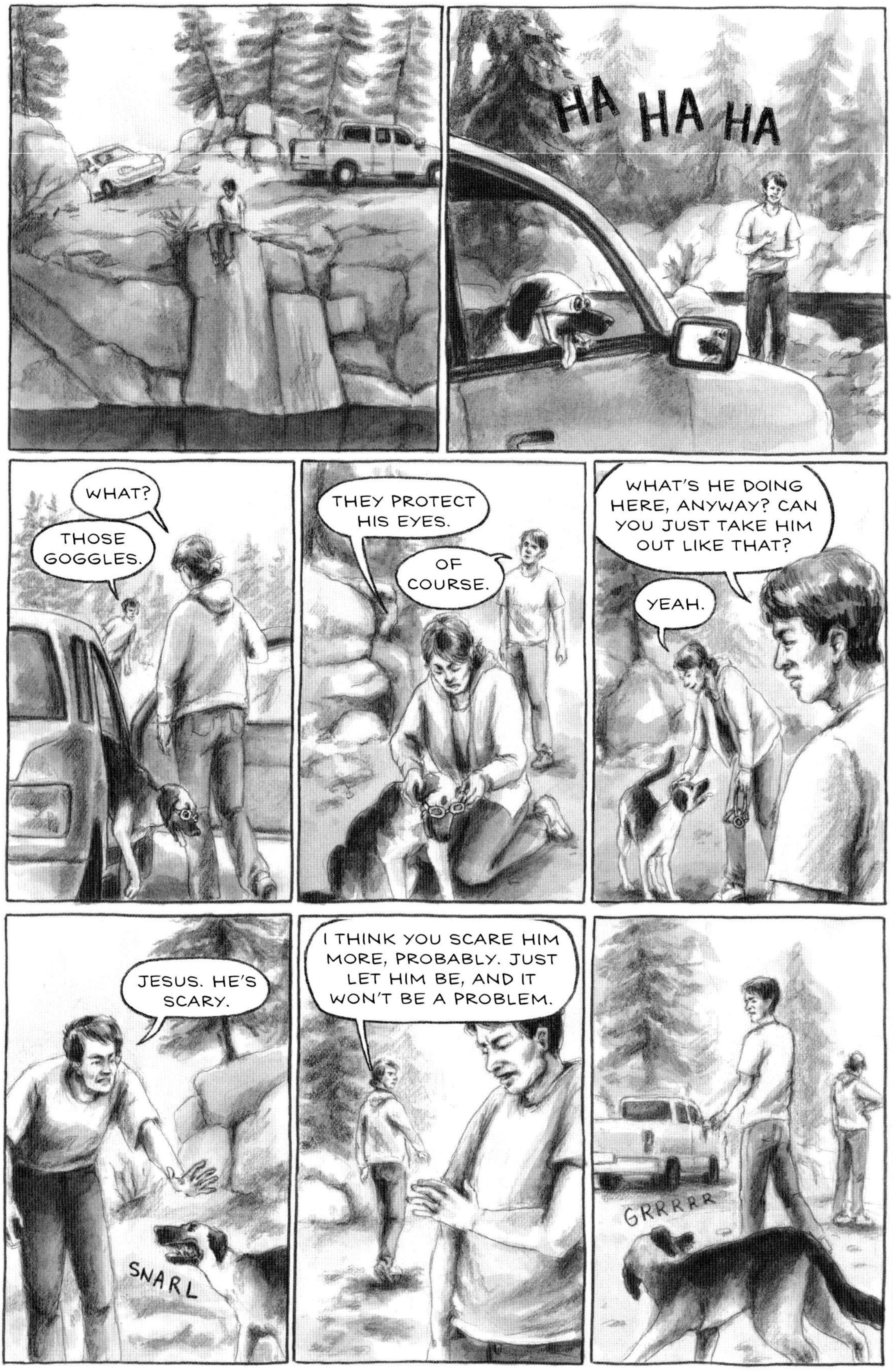
HA HA HA
WHAT?
THOSE GOGGLES.
THEY PROTECT HIS EYES.
OF COURSE.
WHAT'S HE DOING HERE, ANYWAY? CAN YOU JUST TAKE HIM OUT LIKE THAT?
YEAH.
JESUS. HE'S SCARY.
SNARL
I THINK YOU SCARE HIM MORE, PROBABLY. JUST LET HIM BE, AND IT WON'T BE A PROBLEM.
GRRRRR

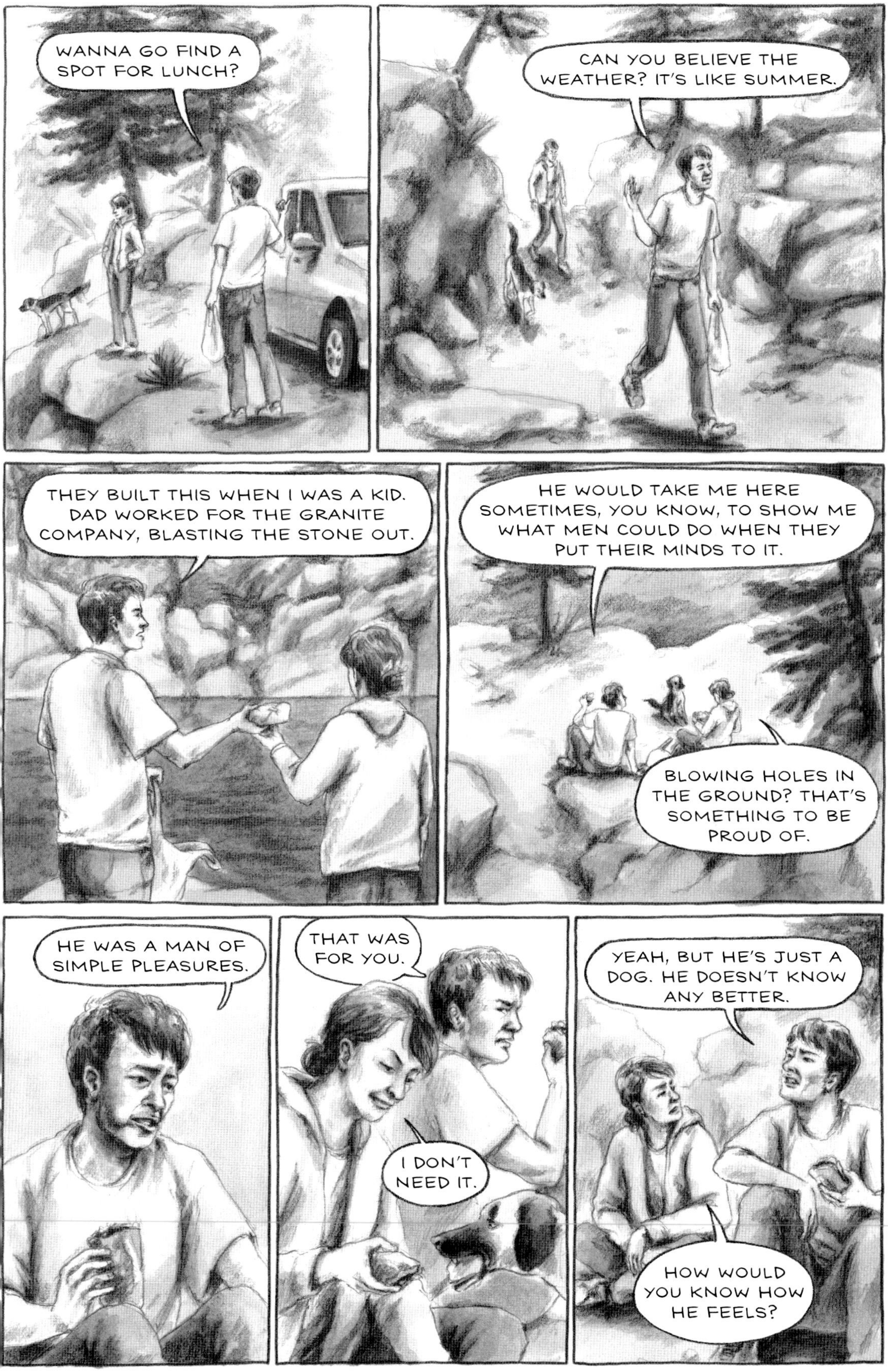
WANNA GO FIND A SPOT FOR LUNCH?
CAN YOU BELIEVE THE WEATHER? IT'S LIKE SUMMER.
THEY BUILT THIS WHEN I WAS A KID. DAD WORKED FOR THE GRANITE COMPANY, BLASTING THE STONE OUT.
HE WOULD TAKE ME HERE SOMETIMES, YOU KNOW, TO SHOW ME WHAT MEN COULD DO WHEN THEY PUT THEIR MINDS TO IT.
BLOWING HOLES IN THE GROUND? THAT'S SOMETHING TO BE PROUD OF.
HE WAS A MAN OF SIMPLE PLEASURES.
THAT WAS FOR YOU.
I DON'T NEED IT.
YEAH, BUT HE'S JUST A DOG. HE DOESN'T KNOW ANY BETTER.
HOW WOULD YOU KNOW HOW HE FEELS?

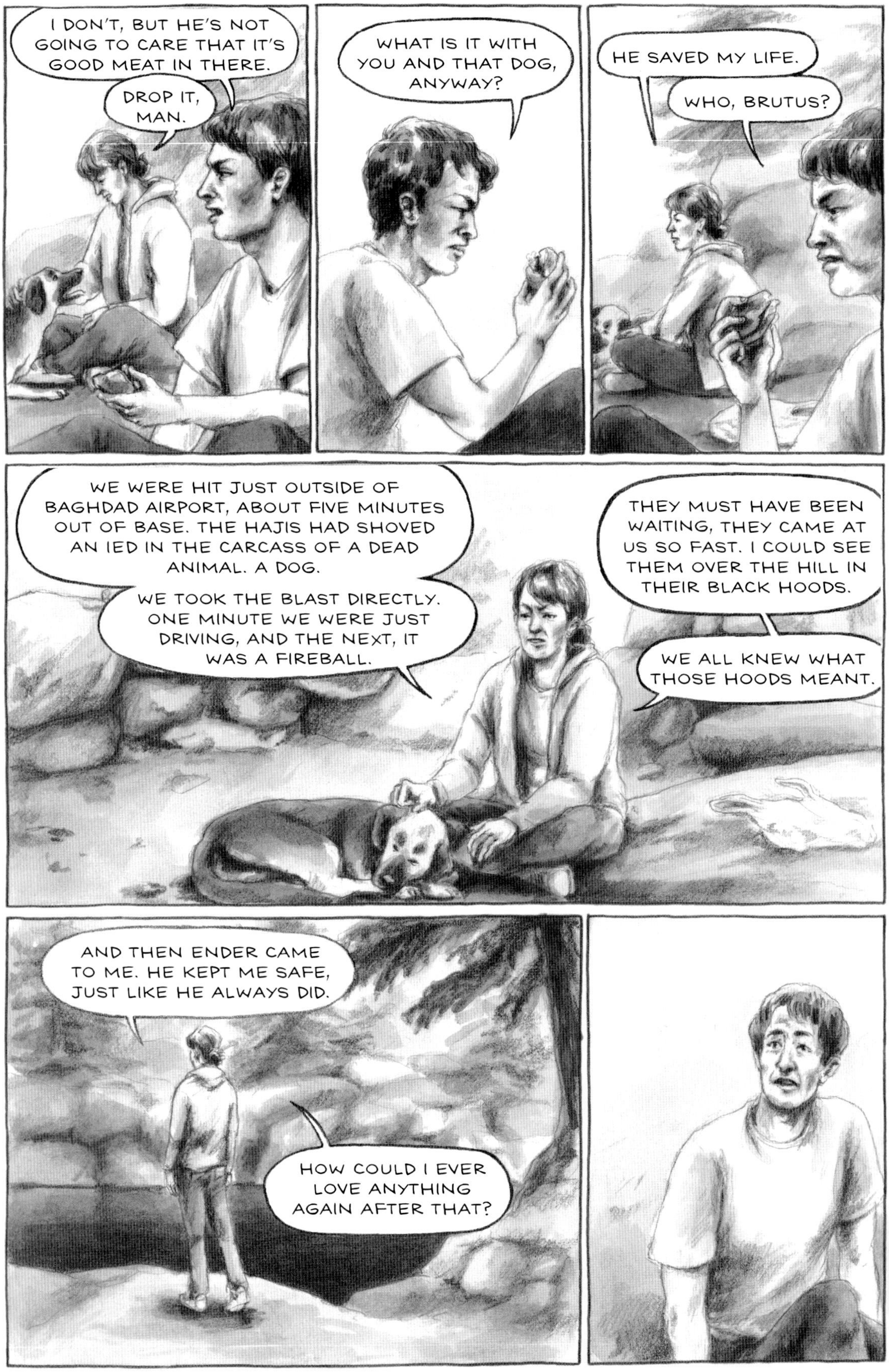
I DON'T, BUT HE'S NOT GOING TO CARE THAT IT'S GOOD MEAT IN THERE.
DROP IT, MAN.
WHAT IS IT WITH YOU AND THAT DOG, ANYWAY?
HE SAVED MY LIFE.
WHO, BRUTUS?
WE WERE HIT JUST OUTSIDE OF BAGHDAD AIRPORT, ABOUT FIVE MINUTES OUT OF BASE. THE HAJIS HAD SHOVED AN IED IN THE CARCASS OF A DEAD ANIMAL. A DOG.
WE TOOK THE BLAST DIRECTLY. ONE MINUTE WE WERE JUST DRIVING, AND THE NEXT, IT WAS A FIREBALL.
THEY MUST HAVE BEEN WAITING, THEY CAME AT US SO FAST. I COULD SEE THEM OVER THE HILL IN THEIR BLACK HOODS.
WE ALL KNEW WHAT THOSE HOODS MEANT.
AND THEN ENDER CAME TO ME. HE KEPT ME SAFE, JUST LIKE HE ALWAYS DID.
HOW COULD I EVER LOVE ANYTHING AGAIN AFTER THAT?

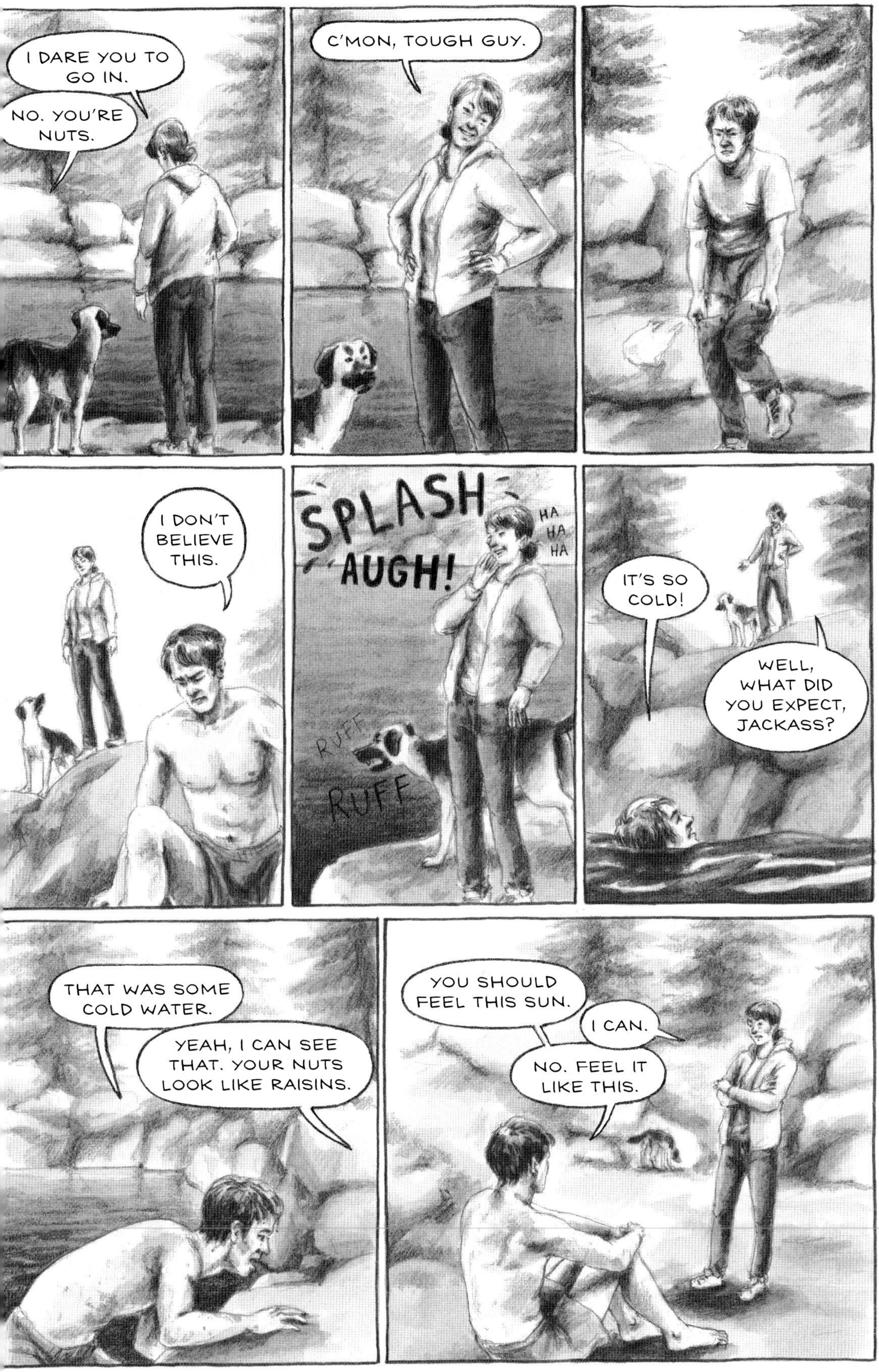
I DARE YOU TO GO IN.
NO. YOU'RE NUTS.
C'MON, TOUGH GUY.
I DON'T BELIEVE THIS.
SPLASH
AUGH!
HA HA HA
RUFF
RUFF
IT'S SO COLD!
WELL, WHAT DID YOU EXPECT, JACKASS?
THAT WAS SOME COLD WATER.
YEAH, I CAN SEE THAT. YOUR NUTS LOOK LIKE RAISINS.
YOU SHOULD FEEL THIS SUN.
I CAN.
NO. FEEL IT LIKE THIS.

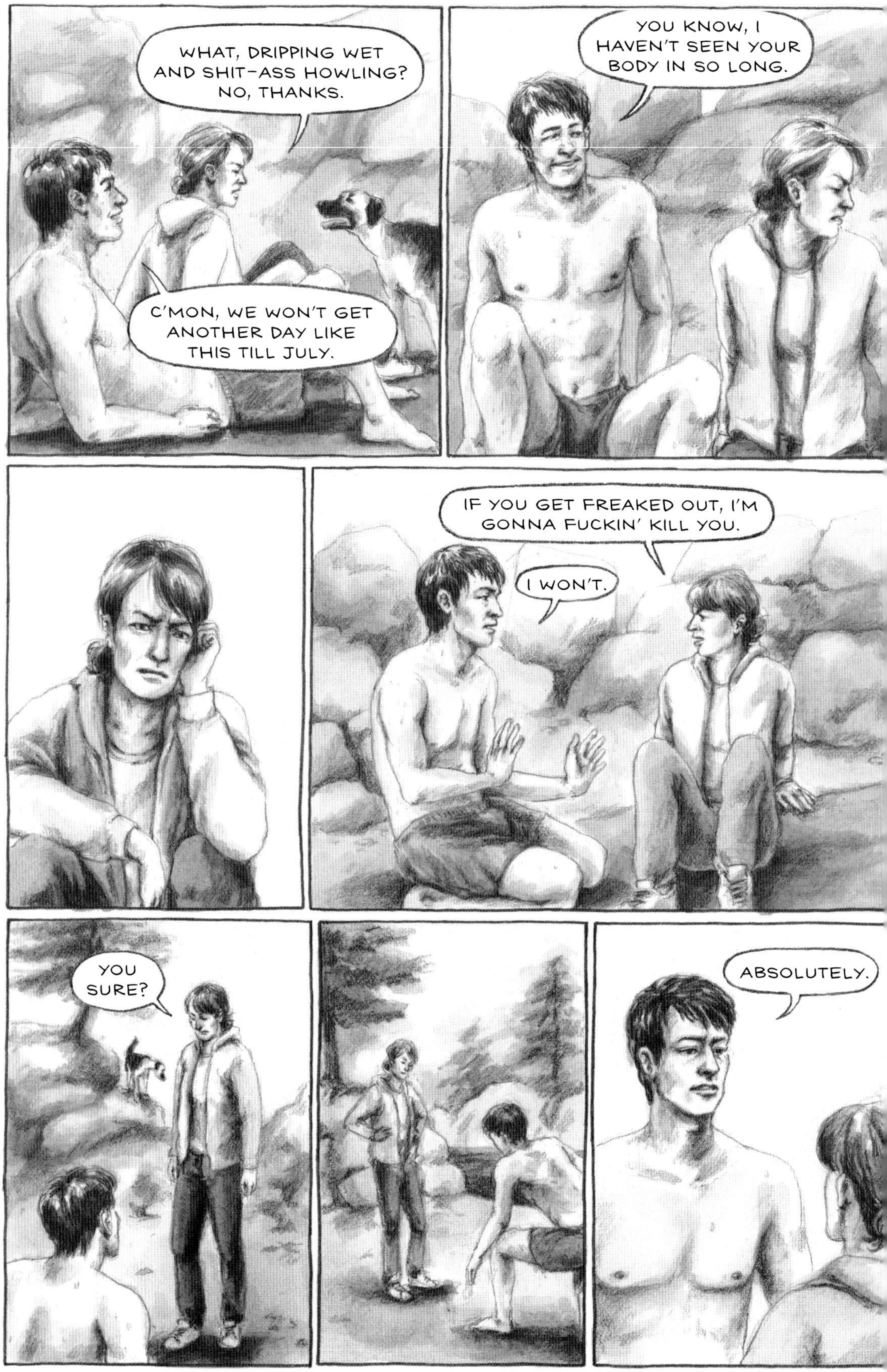
WHAT, DRIPPING WET AND SHIT-ASS HOWLING? NO, THANKS.
C'MON, WE WON'T GET ANOTHER DAY LIKE THIS TILL JULY.
YOU KNOW, I HAVEN'T SEEN YOUR BODY IN SO LONG.
IF YOU GET FREAKED OUT, I'M GONNA FUCKIN' KILL YOU.
I WON'T.
YOU SURE?
ABSOLUTELY.

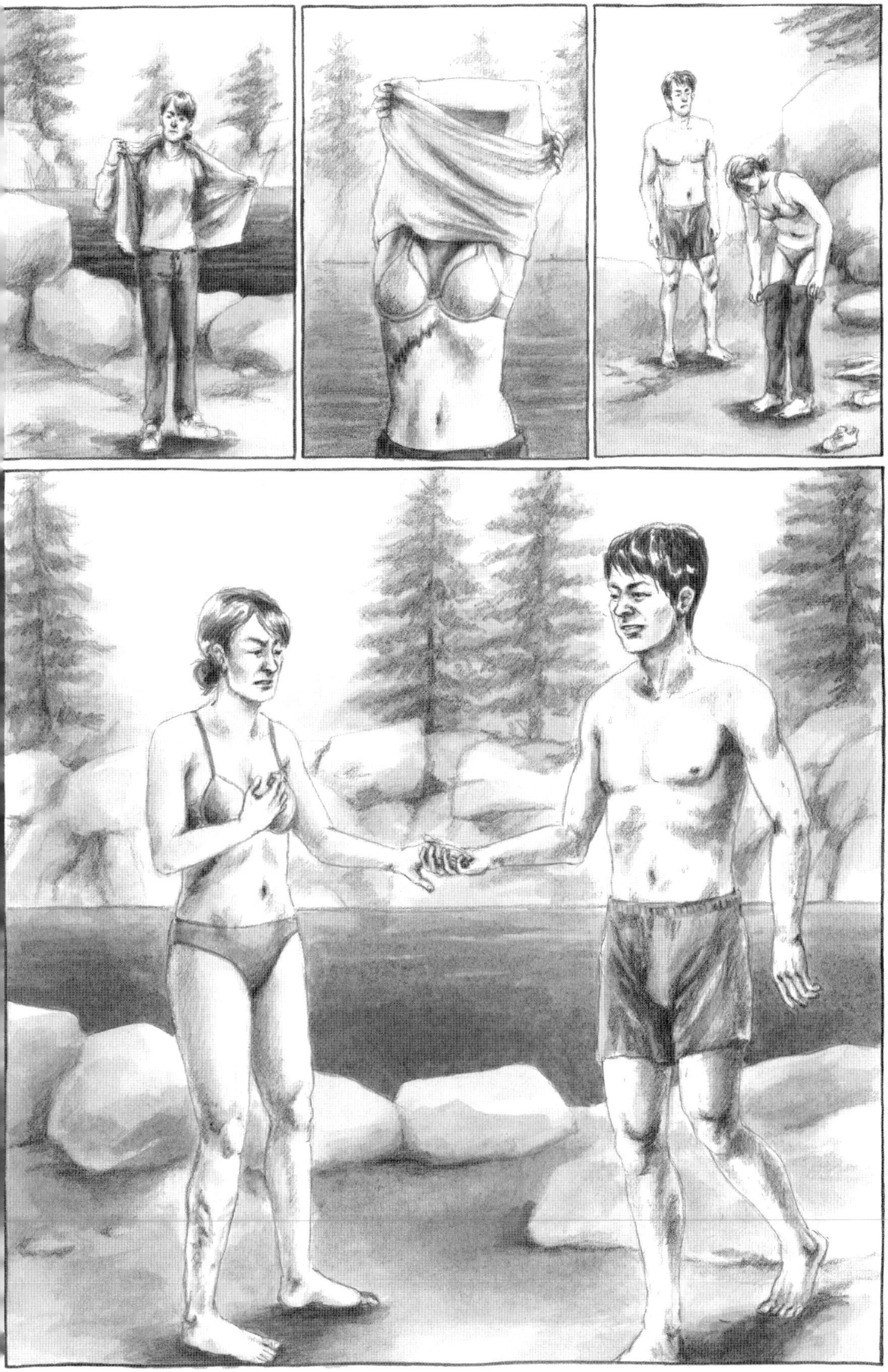

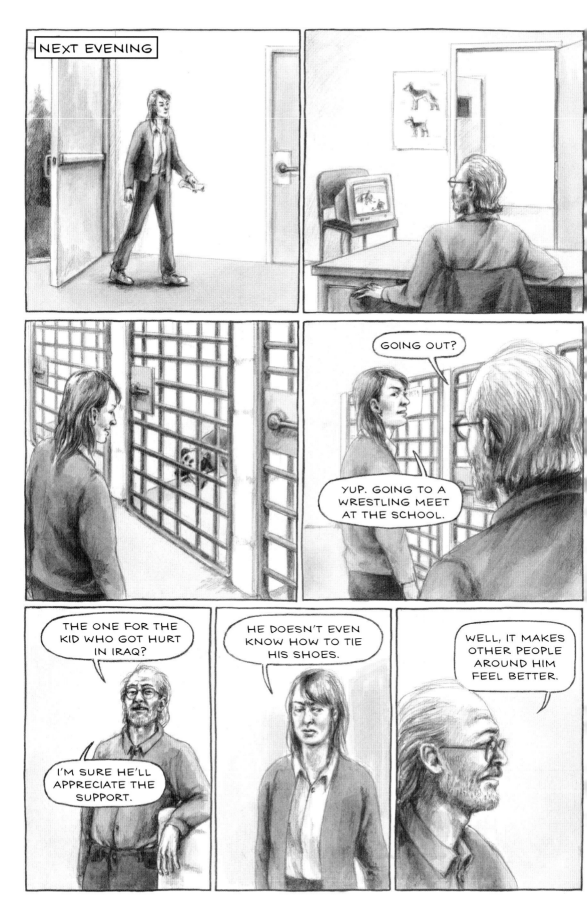

NEXT EVENING

GOING OUT?

YUP. GOING TO A WRESTLING MEET AT THE SCHOOL.

THE ONE FOR THE KID WHO GOT HURT IN IRAQ?

I'M SURE HE'LL APPRECIATE THE SUPPORT.

HE DOESN'T EVEN KNOW HOW TO TIE HIS SHOES.

WELL, IT MAKES OTHER PEOPLE AROUND HIM FEEL BETTER.

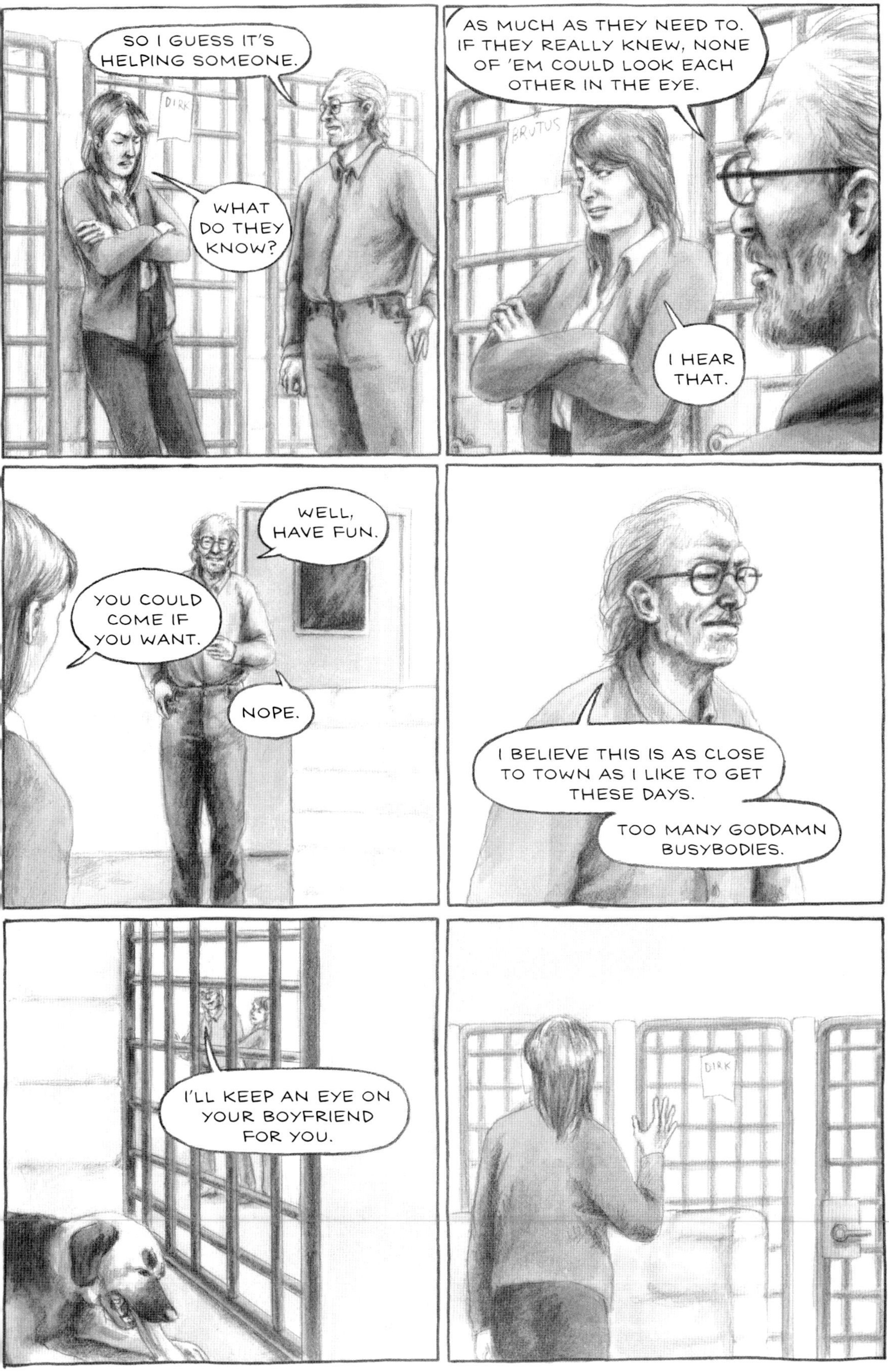
SO I GUESS IT'S HELPING SOMEONE.
DIRK
WHAT DO THEY KNOW?
AS MUCH AS THEY NEED TO. IF THEY REALLY KNEW, NONE OF 'EM COULD LOOK EACH OTHER IN THE EYE.
BRUTUS
I HEAR THAT.
WELL, HAVE FUN.
YOU COULD COME IF YOU WANT.
NOPE.
I BELIEVE THIS IS AS CLOSE TO TOWN AS I LIKE TO GET THESE DAYS.
TOO MANY GODDAMN BUSYBODIES.
I'LL KEEP AN EYE ON YOUR BOYFRIEND FOR YOU.
DIRK

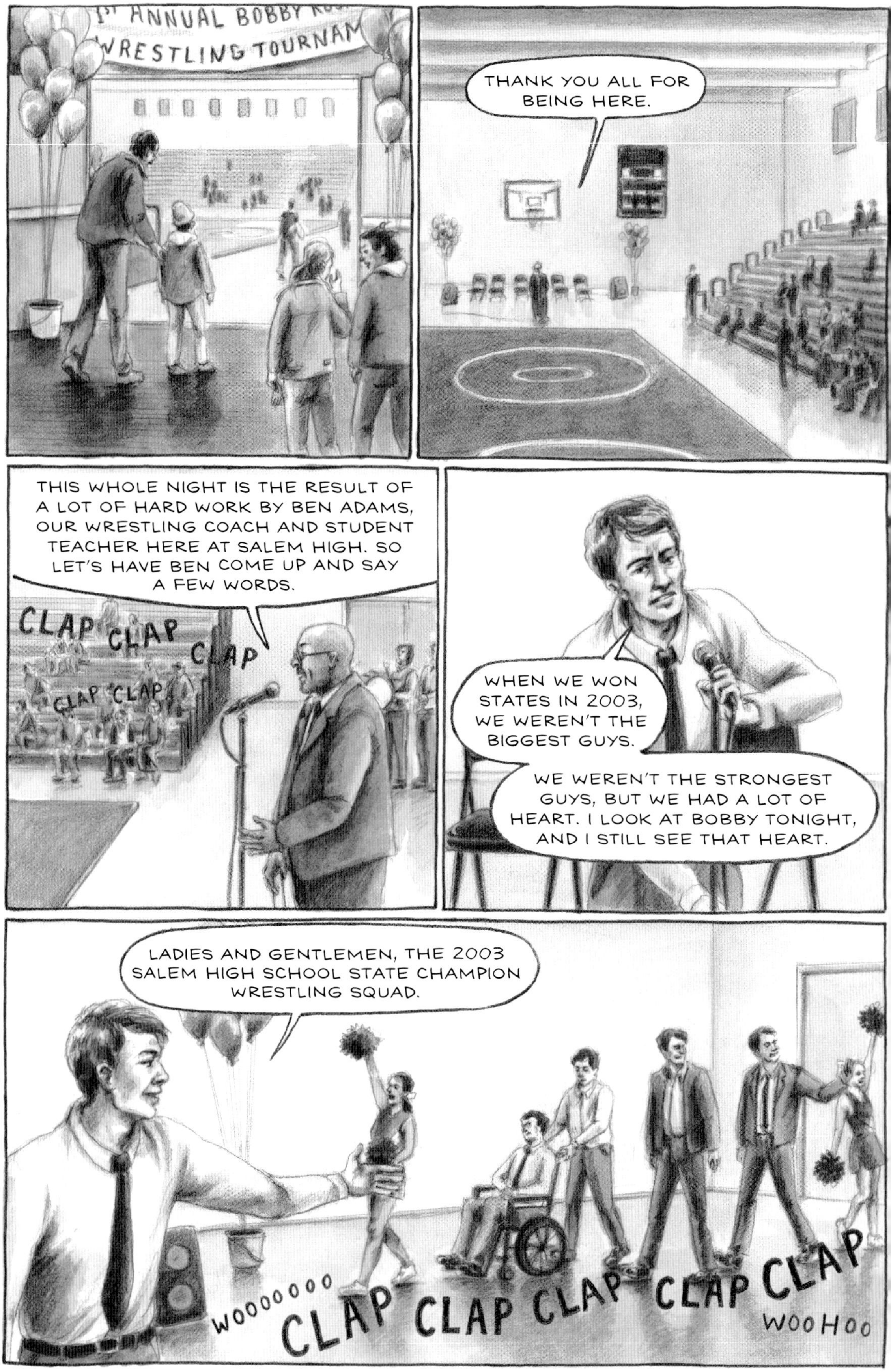
1st ANNUAL BOBBY RO
WRESTLING TOURNAM
THANK YOU ALL FOR BEING HERE.
THIS WHOLE NIGHT IS THE RESULT OF A LOT OF HARD WORK BY BEN ADAMS, OUR WRESTLING COACH AND STUDENT TEACHER HERE AT SALEM HIGH. SO LET'S HAVE BEN COME UP AND SAY A FEW WORDS.
CLAP CLAP CLAP
CLAP CLAP
WHEN WE WON STATES IN 2003, WE WEREN'T THE BIGGEST GUYS.
WE WEREN'T THE STRONGEST GUYS, BUT WE HAD A LOT OF HEART. I LOOK AT BOBBY TONIGHT, AND I STILL SEE THAT HEART.
LADIES AND GENTLEMEN, THE 2003 SALEM HIGH SCHOOL STATE CHAMPION WRESTLING SQUAD.
WOOOOOOO
CLAP CLAP CLAP CLAP CLAP
WOOHOO

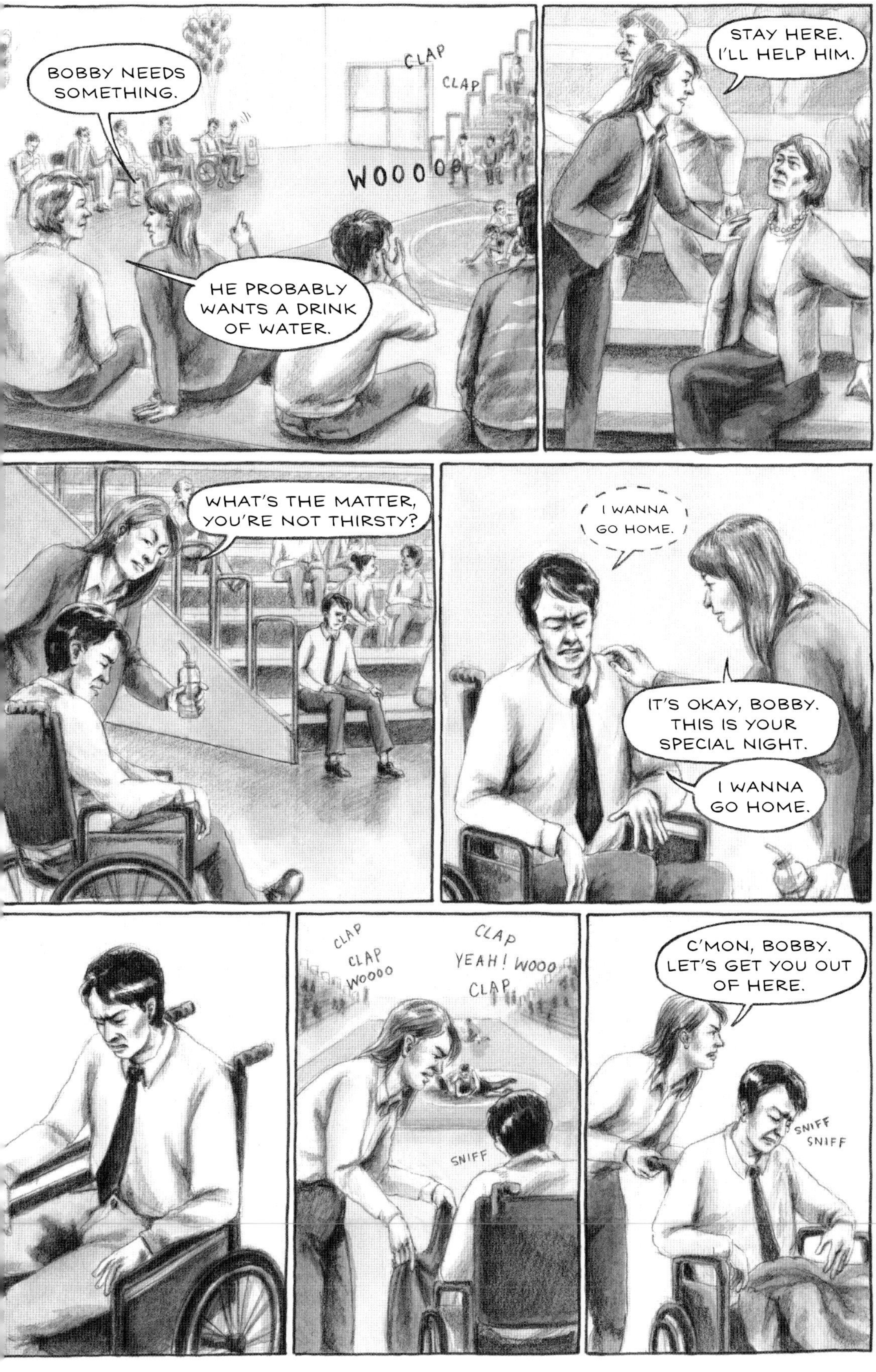
BOBBY NEEDS SOMETHING.
CLAP
CLAP
WOOOOP
HE PROBABLY WANTS A DRINK OF WATER.
STAY HERE. I'LL HELP HIM.
WHAT'S THE MATTER, YOU'RE NOT THIRSTY?
I WANNA GO HOME.
IT'S OKAY, BOBBY. THIS IS YOUR SPECIAL NIGHT.
I WANNA GO HOME.
CLAP
CLAP
WOOOO
CLAP
YEAH! WOOO
CLAP
SNIFF
C'MON, BOBBY. LET'S GET YOU OUT OF HERE.
SNIFF
SNIFF

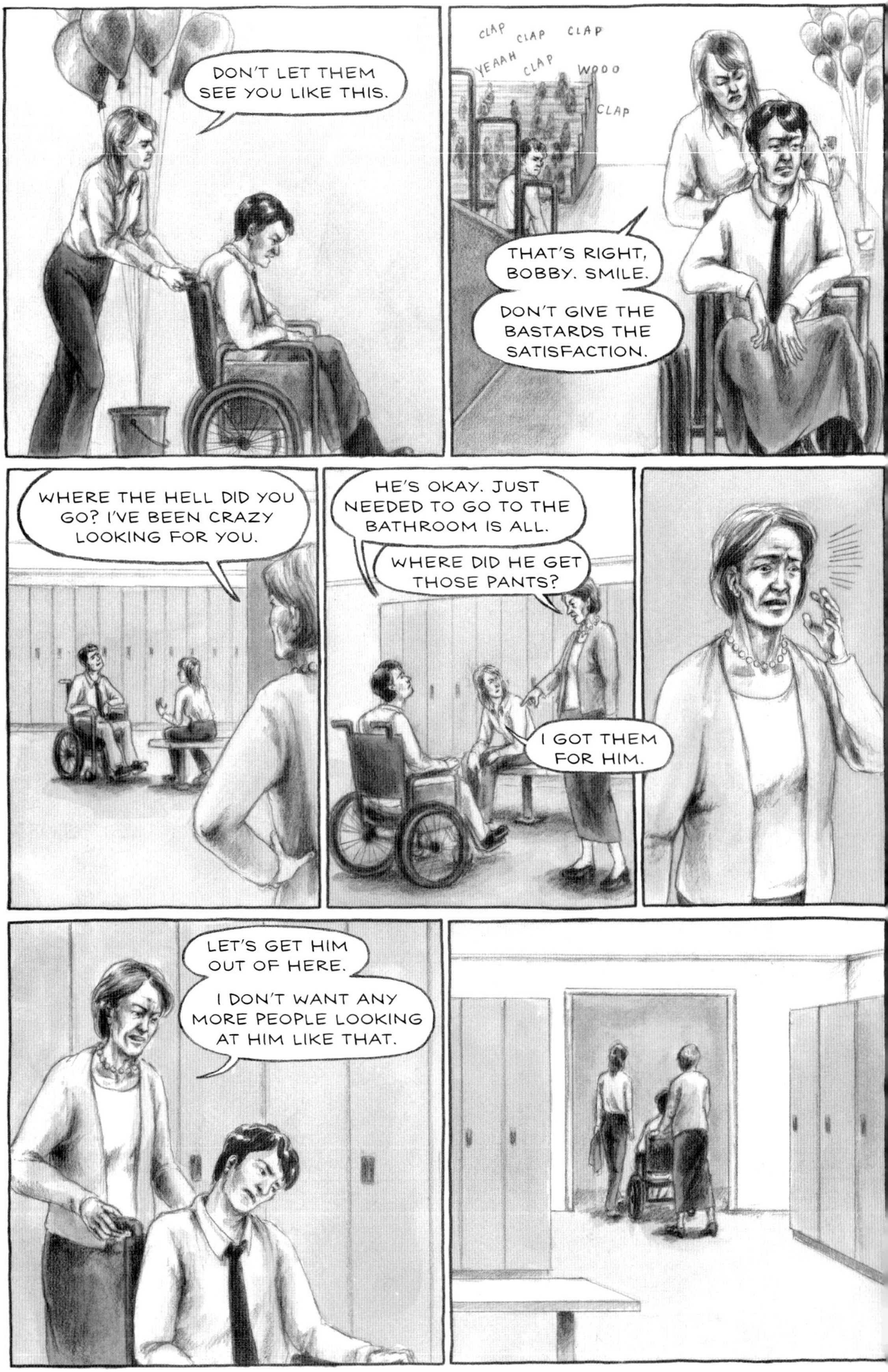
DON'T LET THEM SEE YOU LIKE THIS.
CLAP CLAP CLAP YEAAH CLAP WOOO CLAP
THAT'S RIGHT, BOBBY. SMILE.
DON'T GIVE THE BASTARDS THE SATISFACTION.
WHERE THE HELL DID YOU GO? I'VE BEEN CRAZY LOOKING FOR YOU.
HE'S OKAY. JUST NEEDED TO GO TO THE BATHROOM IS ALL.
WHERE DID HE GET THOSE PANTS?
I GOT THEM FOR HIM.
LET'S GET HIM OUT OF HERE.
I DON'T WANT ANY MORE PEOPLE LOOKING AT HIM LIKE THAT.

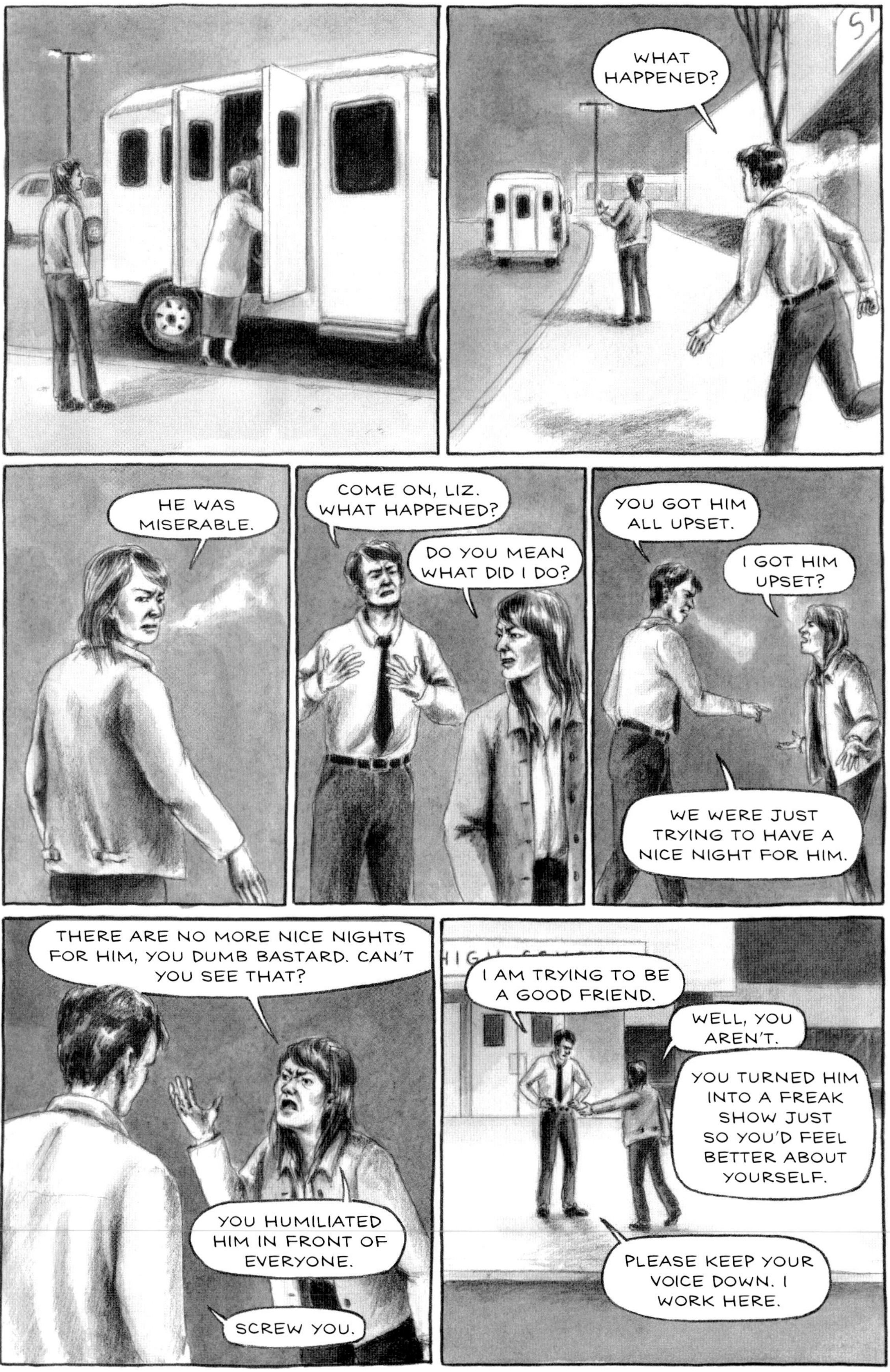

WHAT HAPPENED?
HE WAS MISERABLE.
COME ON, LIZ. WHAT HAPPENED?
DO YOU MEAN WHAT DID I DO?
YOU GOT HIM ALL UPSET.
I GOT HIM UPSET?
WE WERE JUST TRYING TO HAVE A NICE NIGHT FOR HIM.
THERE ARE NO MORE NICE NIGHTS FOR HIM, YOU DUMB BASTARD. CAN'T YOU SEE THAT?
YOU HUMILIATED HIM IN FRONT OF EVERYONE.
SCREW YOU.
I AM TRYING TO BE A GOOD FRIEND.
WELL, YOU AREN'T.
YOU TURNED HIM INTO A FREAK SHOW JUST SO YOU'D FEEL BETTER ABOUT YOURSELF.
PLEASE KEEP YOUR VOICE DOWN. I WORK HERE.

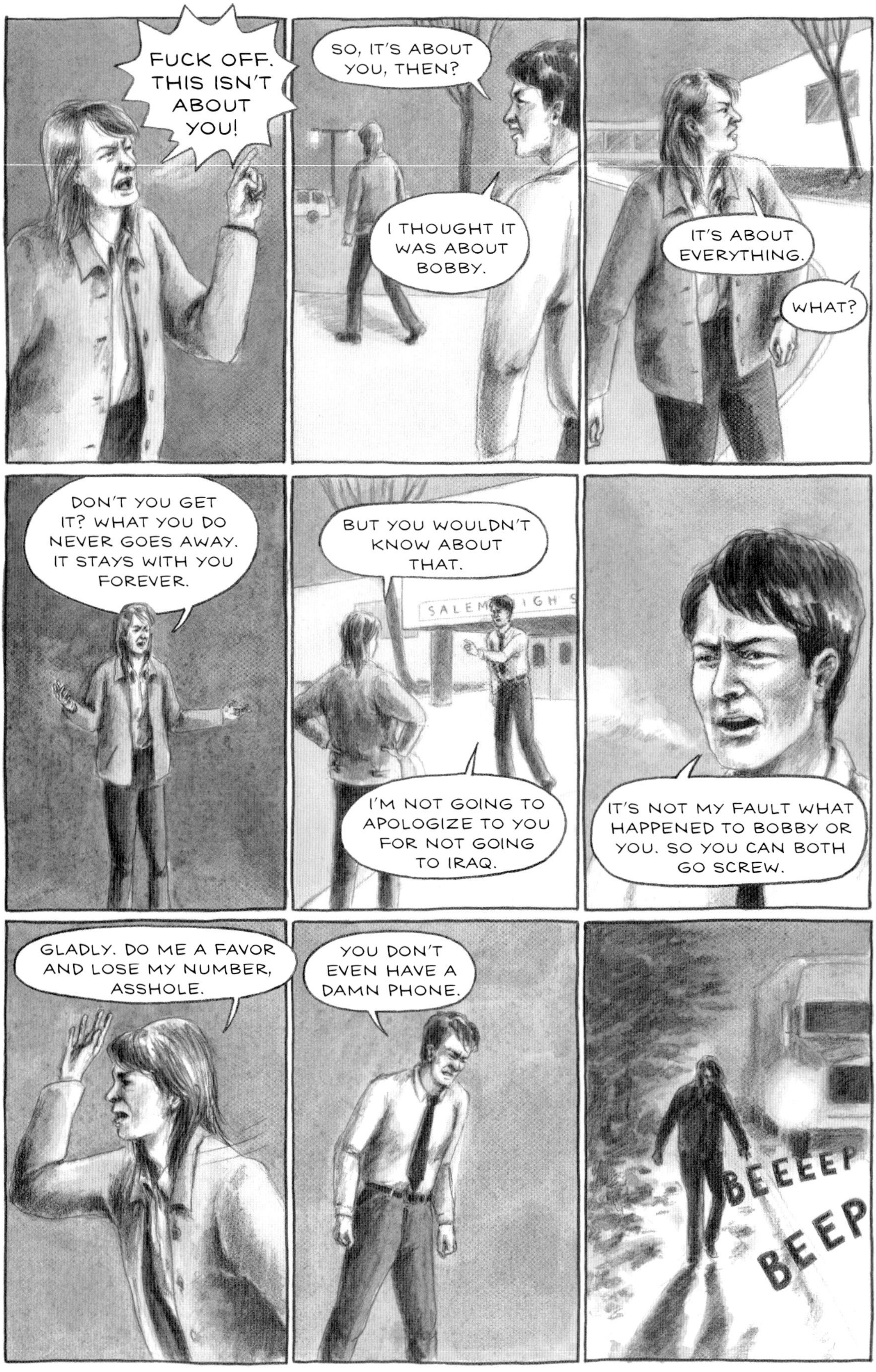
FUCK OFF. THIS ISN'T ABOUT YOU!
SO, IT'S ABOUT YOU, THEN?
I THOUGHT IT WAS ABOUT BOBBY.
IT'S ABOUT EVERYTHING.
WHAT?
DON'T YOU GET IT? WHAT YOU DO NEVER GOES AWAY. IT STAYS WITH YOU FOREVER.
BUT YOU WOULDN'T KNOW ABOUT THAT.
I'M NOT GOING TO APOLOGIZE TO YOU FOR NOT GOING TO IRAQ.
IT'S NOT MY FAULT WHAT HAPPENED TO BOBBY OR YOU. SO YOU CAN BOTH GO SCREW.
GLADLY. DO ME A FAVOR AND LOSE MY NUMBER, ASSHOLE.
YOU DON'T EVEN HAVE A DAMN PHONE.
BEEEEP
BEEP

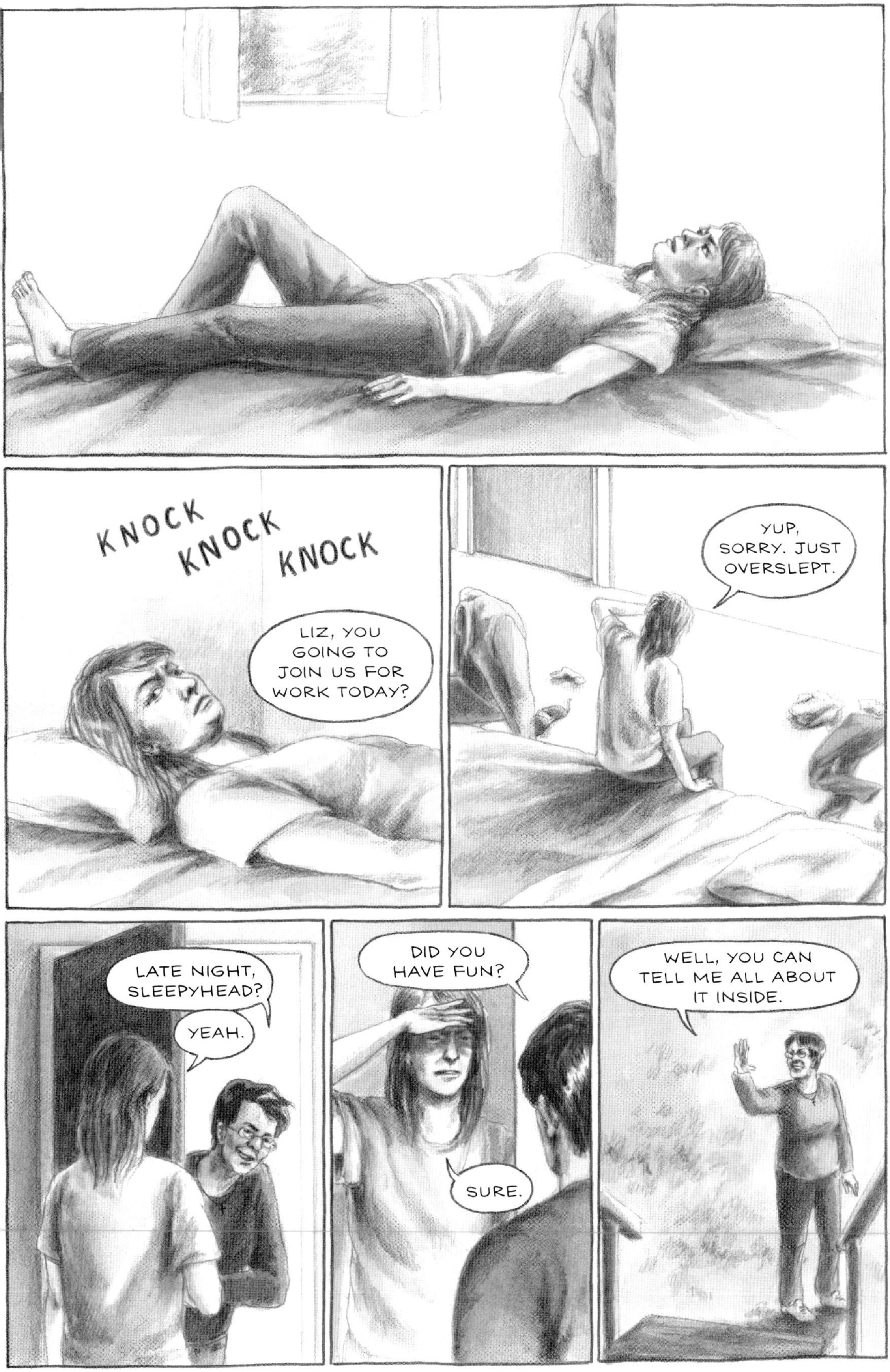
KNOCK KNOCK KNOCK
LIZ, YOU GOING TO JOIN US FOR WORK TODAY?
YUP, SORRY. JUST OVERSLEPT.
LATE NIGHT, SLEEPYHEAD?
YEAH.
DID YOU HAVE FUN?
SURE.
WELL, YOU CAN TELL ME ALL ABOUT IT INSIDE.

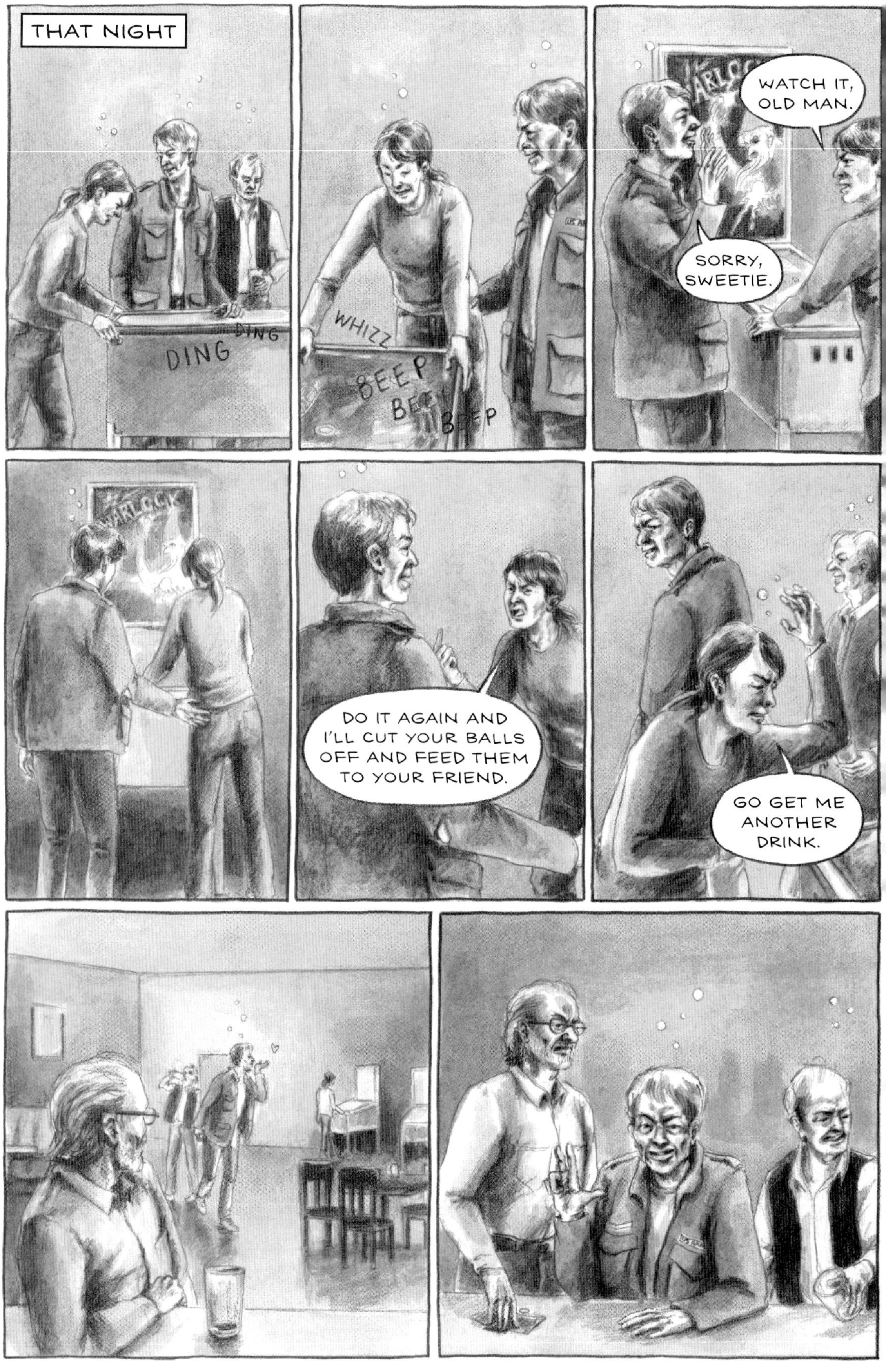
THAT NIGHT
DING
DING
WHIZZ
BEEP
BEEP
BEEP
WATCH IT, OLD MAN.
SORRY, SWEETIE.
DO IT AGAIN AND I'LL CUT YOUR BALLS OFF AND FEED THEM TO YOUR FRIEND.
GO GET ME ANOTHER DRINK.

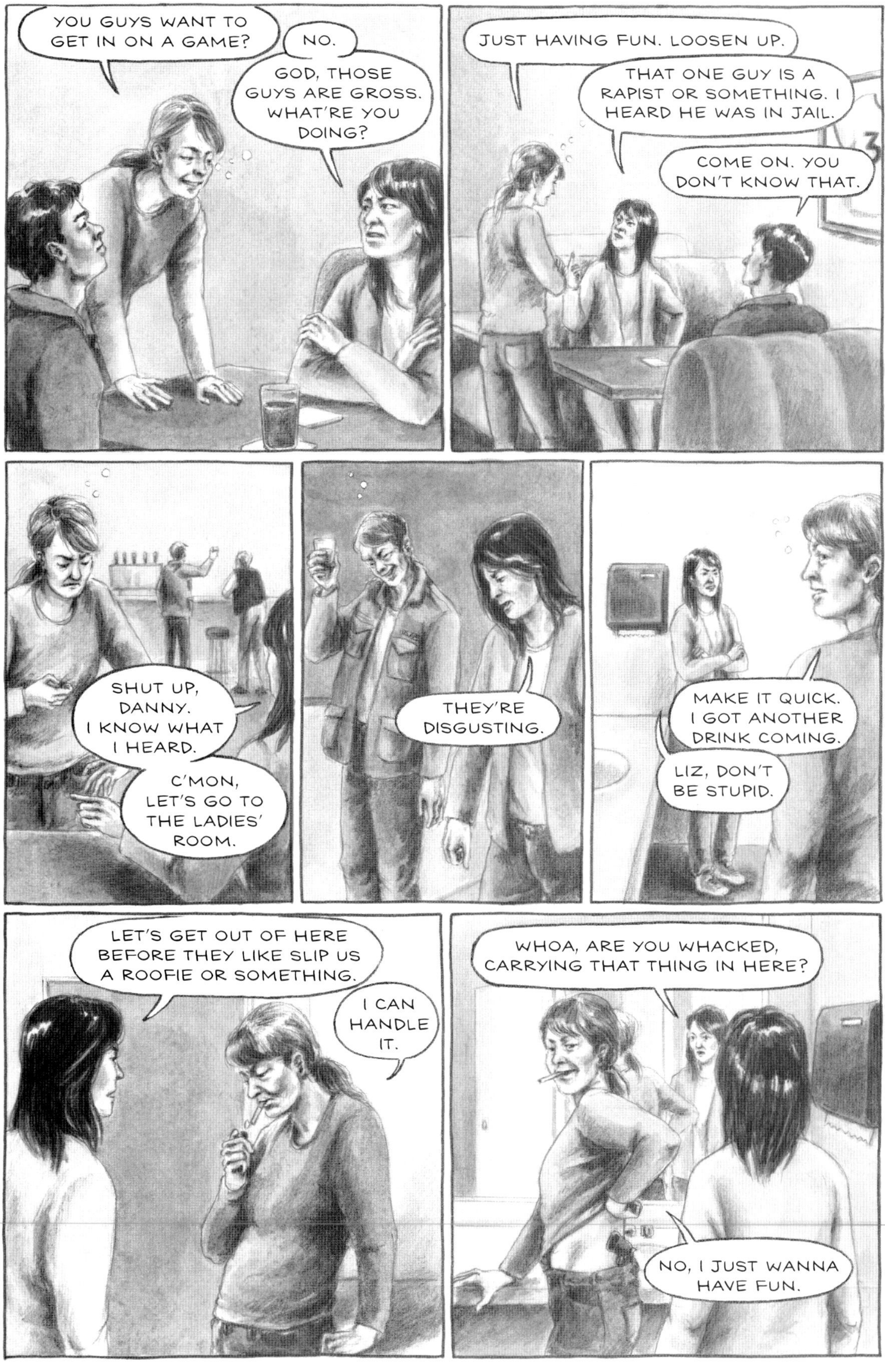
YOU GUYS WANT TO GET IN ON A GAME?
NO.
GOD, THOSE GUYS ARE GROSS. WHAT'RE YOU DOING?
JUST HAVING FUN. LOOSEN UP.
THAT ONE GUY IS A RAPIST OR SOMETHING. I HEARD HE WAS IN JAIL.
COME ON. YOU DON'T KNOW THAT.
SHUT UP, DANNY. I KNOW WHAT I HEARD.
C'MON, LET'S GO TO THE LADIES' ROOM.
THEY'RE DISGUSTING.
MAKE IT QUICK. I GOT ANOTHER DRINK COMING.
LIZ, DON'T BE STUPID.
LET'S GET OUT OF HERE BEFORE THEY LIKE SLIP US A ROOFIE OR SOMETHING.
I CAN HANDLE IT.
WHOA, ARE YOU WHACKED, CARRYING THAT THING IN HERE?
NO, I JUST WANNA HAVE FUN.

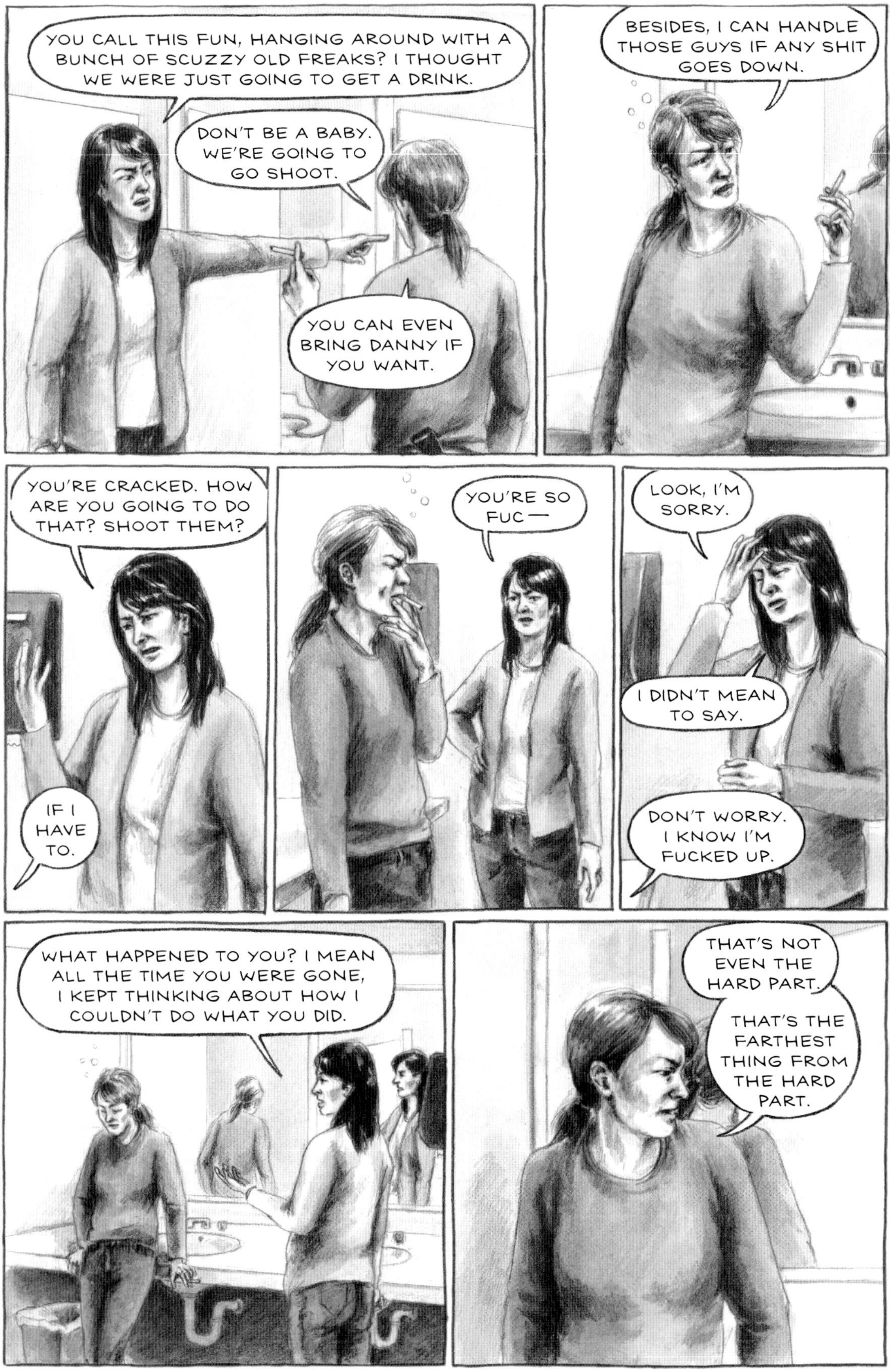
YOU CALL THIS FUN, HANGING AROUND WITH A BUNCH OF SCUZZY OLD FREAKS? I THOUGHT WE WERE JUST GOING TO GET A DRINK.
DON'T BE A BABY. WE'RE GOING TO GO SHOOT.
YOU CAN EVEN BRING DANNY IF YOU WANT.
BESIDES, I CAN HANDLE THOSE GUYS IF ANY SHIT GOES DOWN.
YOU'RE CRACKED. HOW ARE YOU GOING TO DO THAT? SHOOT THEM?
IF I HAVE TO.
YOU'RE SO FUC—
LOOK, I'M SORRY.
I DIDN'T MEAN TO SAY.
DON'T WORRY. I KNOW I'M FUCKED UP.
WHAT HAPPENED TO YOU? I MEAN ALL THE TIME YOU WERE GONE, I KEPT THINKING ABOUT HOW I COULDN'T DO WHAT YOU DID.
THAT'S NOT EVEN THE HARD PART.
THAT'S THE FARTHEST THING FROM THE HARD PART.

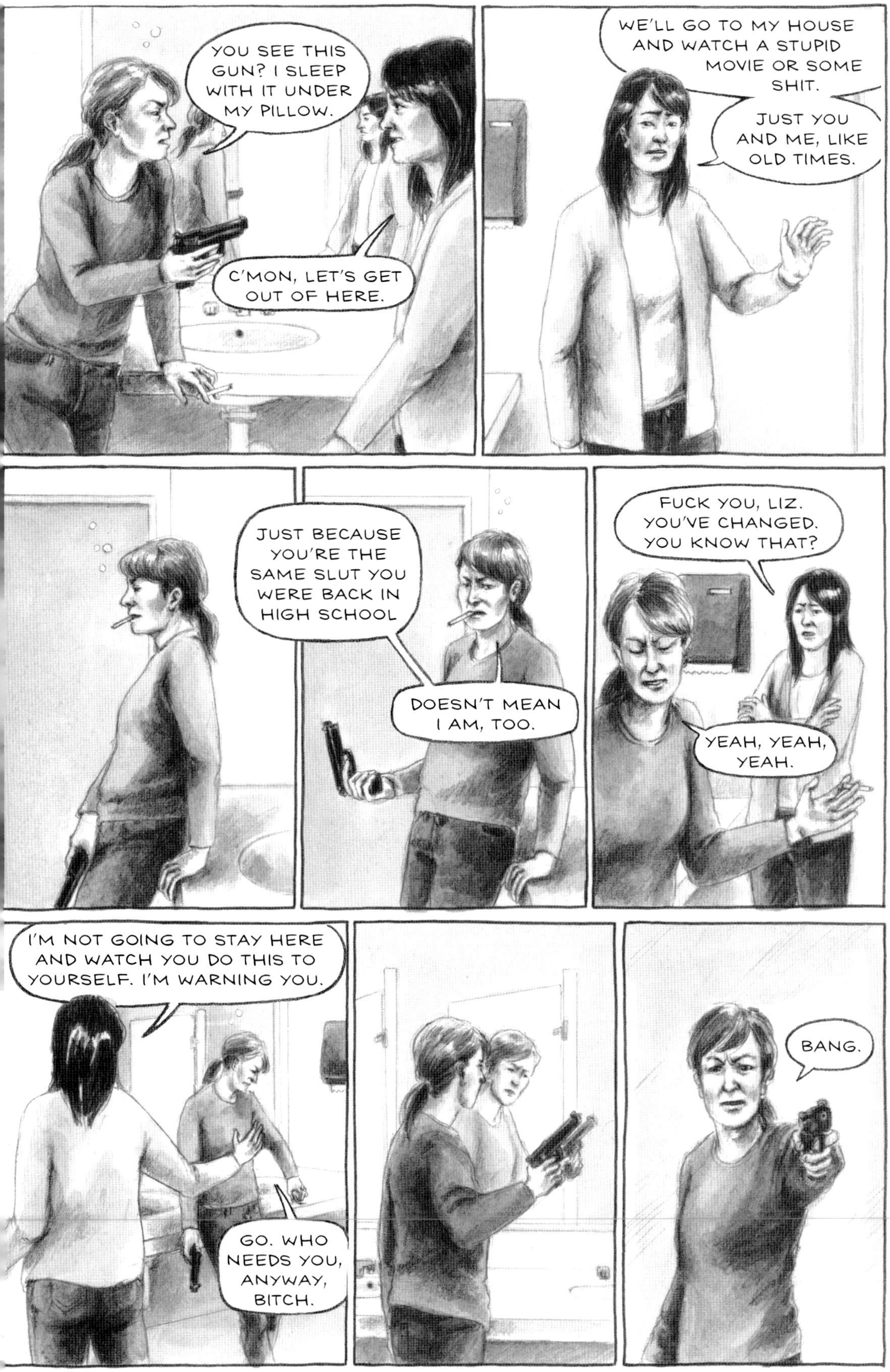
YOU SEE THIS GUN? I SLEEP WITH IT UNDER MY PILLOW.
C'MON, LET'S GET OUT OF HERE.
WE'LL GO TO MY HOUSE AND WATCH A STUPID MOVIE OR SOME SHIT.
JUST YOU AND ME, LIKE OLD TIMES.
JUST BECAUSE YOU'RE THE SAME SLUT YOU WERE BACK IN HIGH SCHOOL
DOESN'T MEAN I AM, TOO.
FUCK YOU, LIZ. YOU'VE CHANGED. YOU KNOW THAT?
YEAH, YEAH, YEAH.
I'M NOT GOING TO STAY HERE AND WATCH YOU DO THIS TO YOURSELF. I'M WARNING YOU.
GO. WHO NEEDS YOU, ANYWAY, BITCH.
BANG.

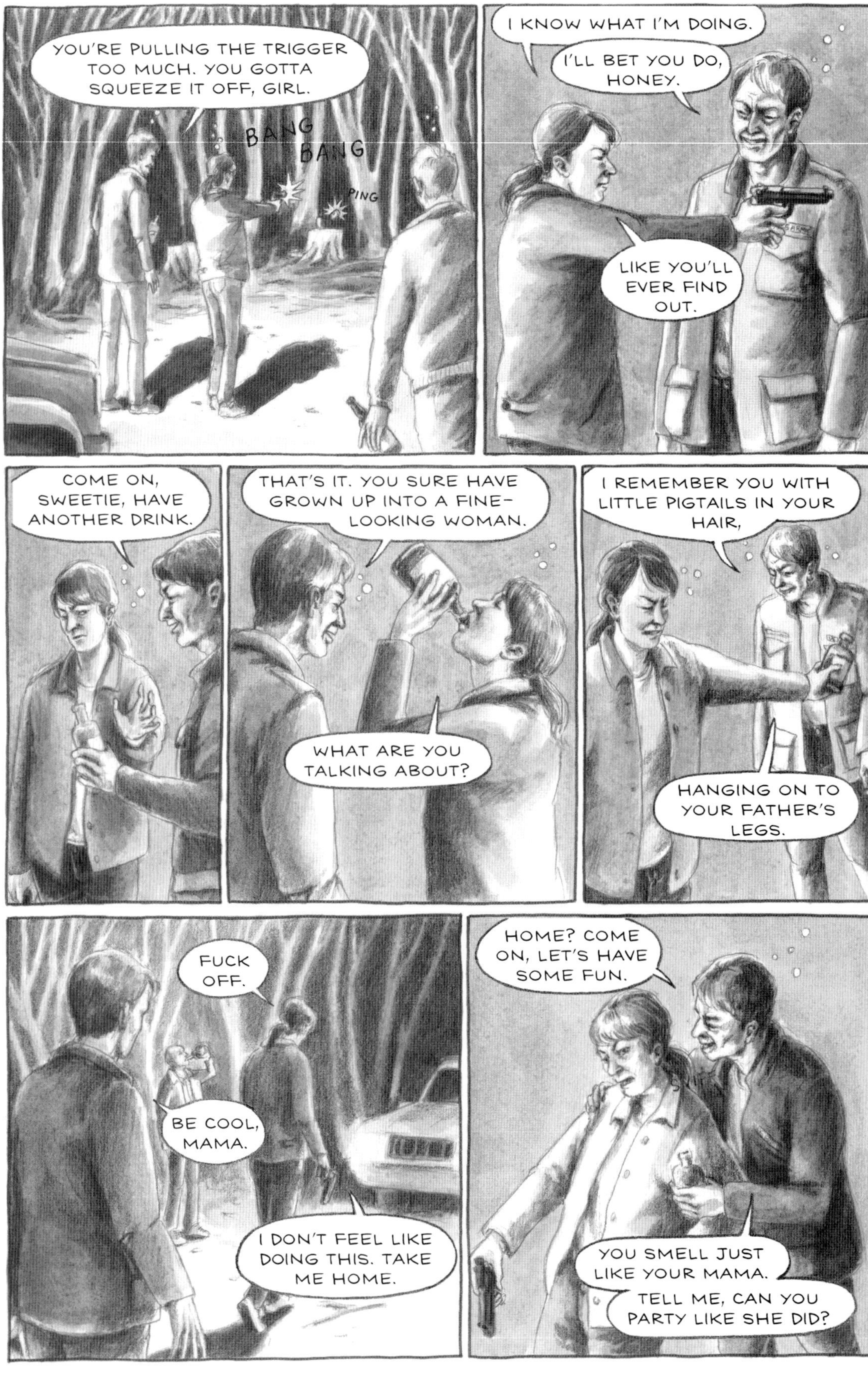
YOU'RE PULLING THE TRIGGER TOO MUCH. YOU GOTTA SQUEEZE IT OFF, GIRL.
BANG
BANG
PING
I KNOW WHAT I'M DOING.
I'LL BET YOU DO, HONEY.
LIKE YOU'LL EVER FIND OUT.
COME ON, SWEETIE, HAVE ANOTHER DRINK.
THAT'S IT. YOU SURE HAVE GROWN UP INTO A FINE-LOOKING WOMAN.
WHAT ARE YOU TALKING ABOUT?
I REMEMBER YOU WITH LITTLE PIGTAILS IN YOUR HAIR,
HANGING ON TO YOUR FATHER'S LEGS.
FUCK OFF.
BE COOL, MAMA.
I DON'T FEEL LIKE DOING THIS. TAKE ME HOME.
HOME? COME ON, LET'S HAVE SOME FUN.
YOU SMELL JUST LIKE YOUR MAMA.
TELL ME, CAN YOU PARTY LIKE SHE DID?

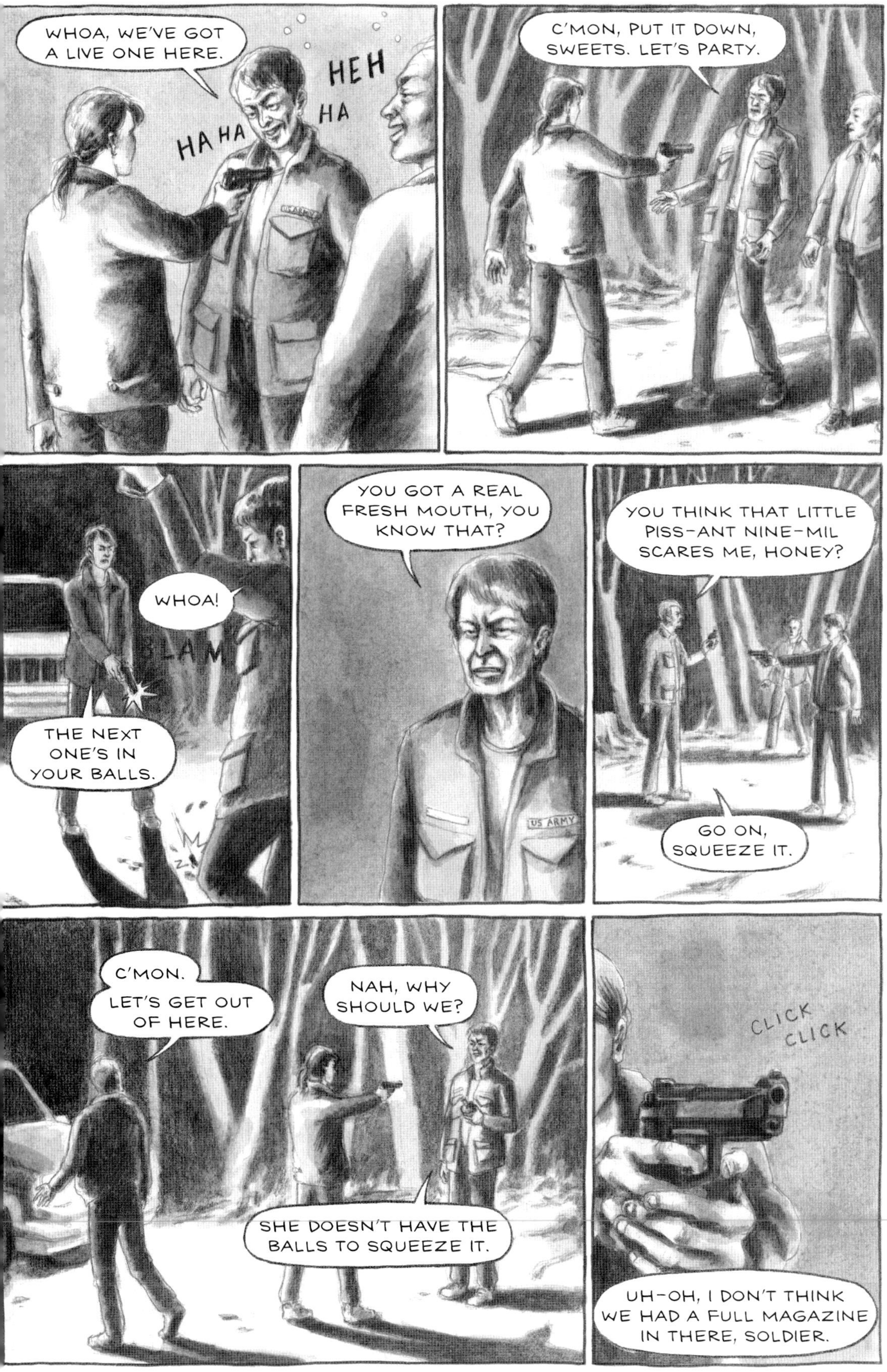
WHOA, WE'VE GOT A LIVE ONE HERE.
HEH
HA
HA HA
C'MON, PUT IT DOWN, SWEETS. LET'S PARTY.
WHOA!
BLAM
THE NEXT ONE'S IN YOUR BALLS.
YOU GOT A REAL FRESH MOUTH, YOU KNOW THAT?
US ARMY
YOU THINK THAT LITTLE PISS-ANT NINE-MIL SCARES ME, HONEY?
GO ON, SQUEEZE IT.
C'MON. LET'S GET OUT OF HERE.
NAH, WHY SHOULD WE?
SHE DOESN'T HAVE THE BALLS TO SQUEEZE IT.
CLICK
CLICK
UH-OH, I DON'T THINK WE HAD A FULL MAGAZINE IN THERE, SOLDIER.

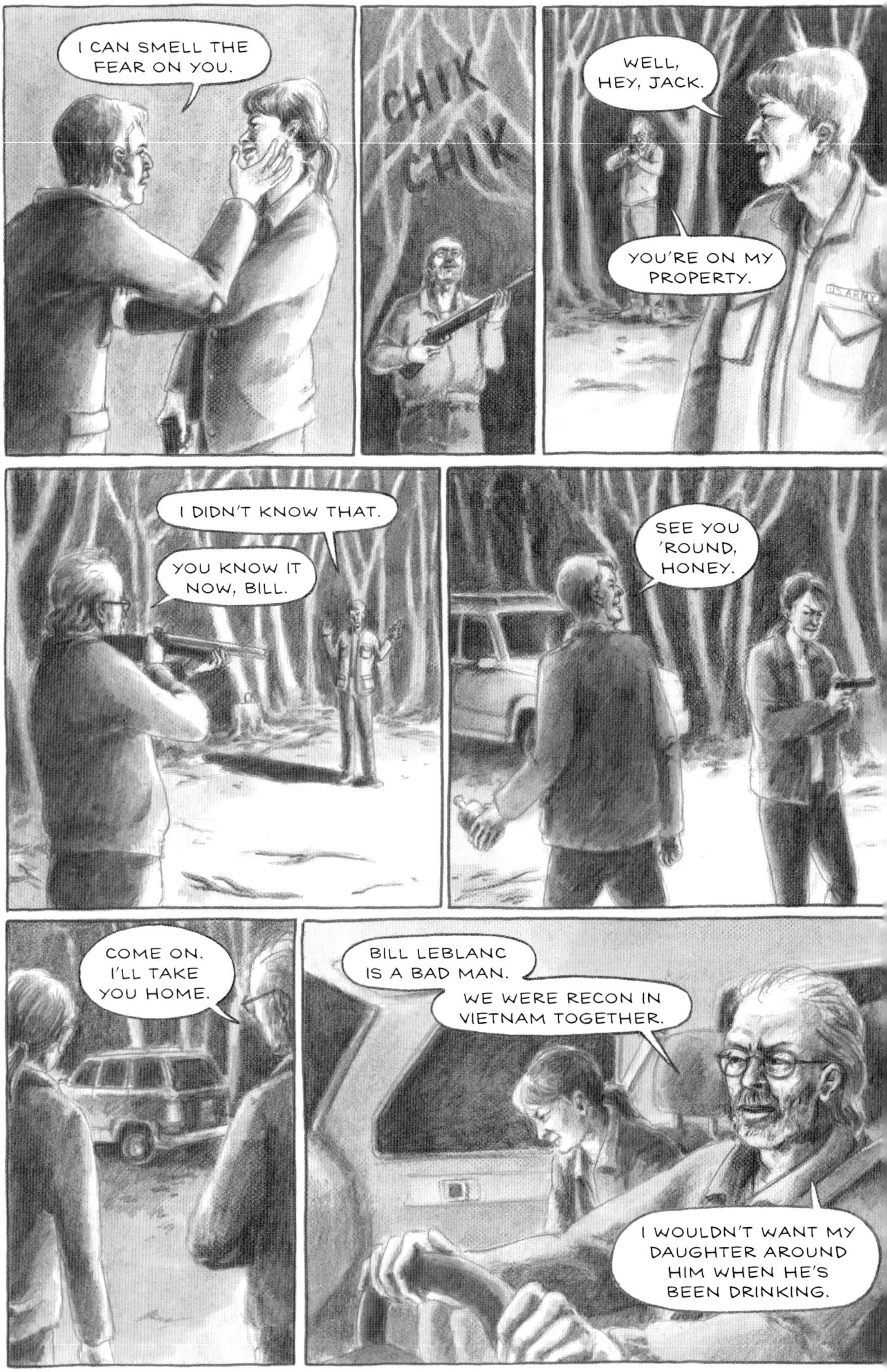

I CAN SMELL THE FEAR ON YOU.
CHIK CHIK
WELL, HEY, JACK.
YOU'RE ON MY PROPERTY.
I DIDN'T KNOW THAT.
YOU KNOW IT NOW, BILL.
SEE YOU 'ROUND, HONEY.
COME ON. I'LL TAKE YOU HOME.
BILL LEBLANC IS A BAD MAN.
WE WERE RECON IN VIETNAM TOGETHER.
I WOULDN'T WANT MY DAUGHTER AROUND HIM WHEN HE'S BEEN DRINKING.

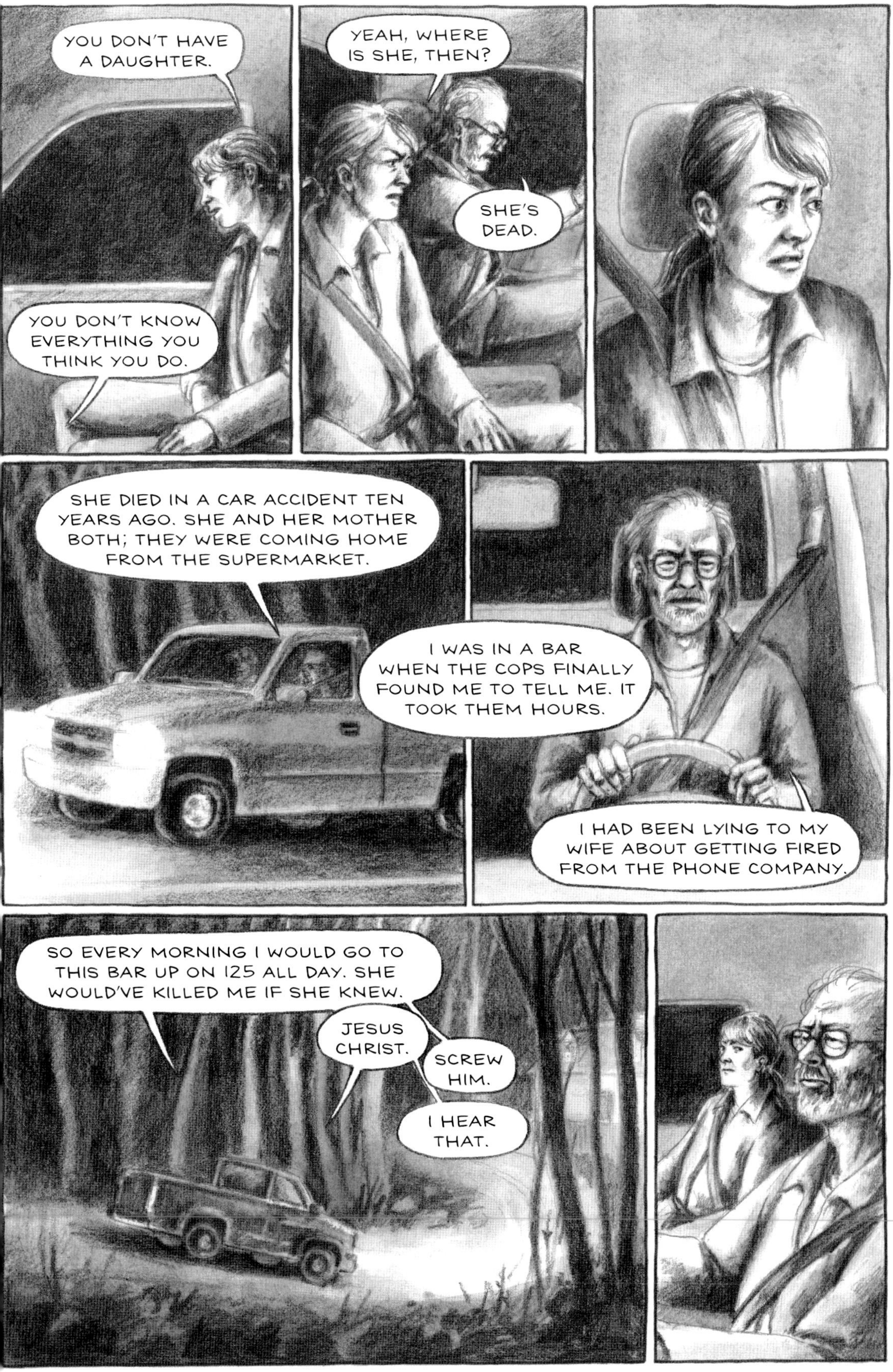
YOU DON'T HAVE A DAUGHTER.
YOU DON'T KNOW EVERYTHING YOU THINK YOU DO.
YEAH, WHERE IS SHE, THEN?
SHE'S DEAD.
SHE DIED IN A CAR ACCIDENT TEN YEARS AGO. SHE AND HER MOTHER BOTH; THEY WERE COMING HOME FROM THE SUPERMARKET.
I WAS IN A BAR WHEN THE COPS FINALLY FOUND ME TO TELL ME. IT TOOK THEM HOURS.
I HAD BEEN LYING TO MY WIFE ABOUT GETTING FIRED FROM THE PHONE COMPANY.
SO EVERY MORNING I WOULD GO TO THIS BAR UP ON 125 ALL DAY. SHE WOULD'VE KILLED ME IF SHE KNEW.
JESUS CHRIST.
SCREW HIM.
I HEAR THAT.

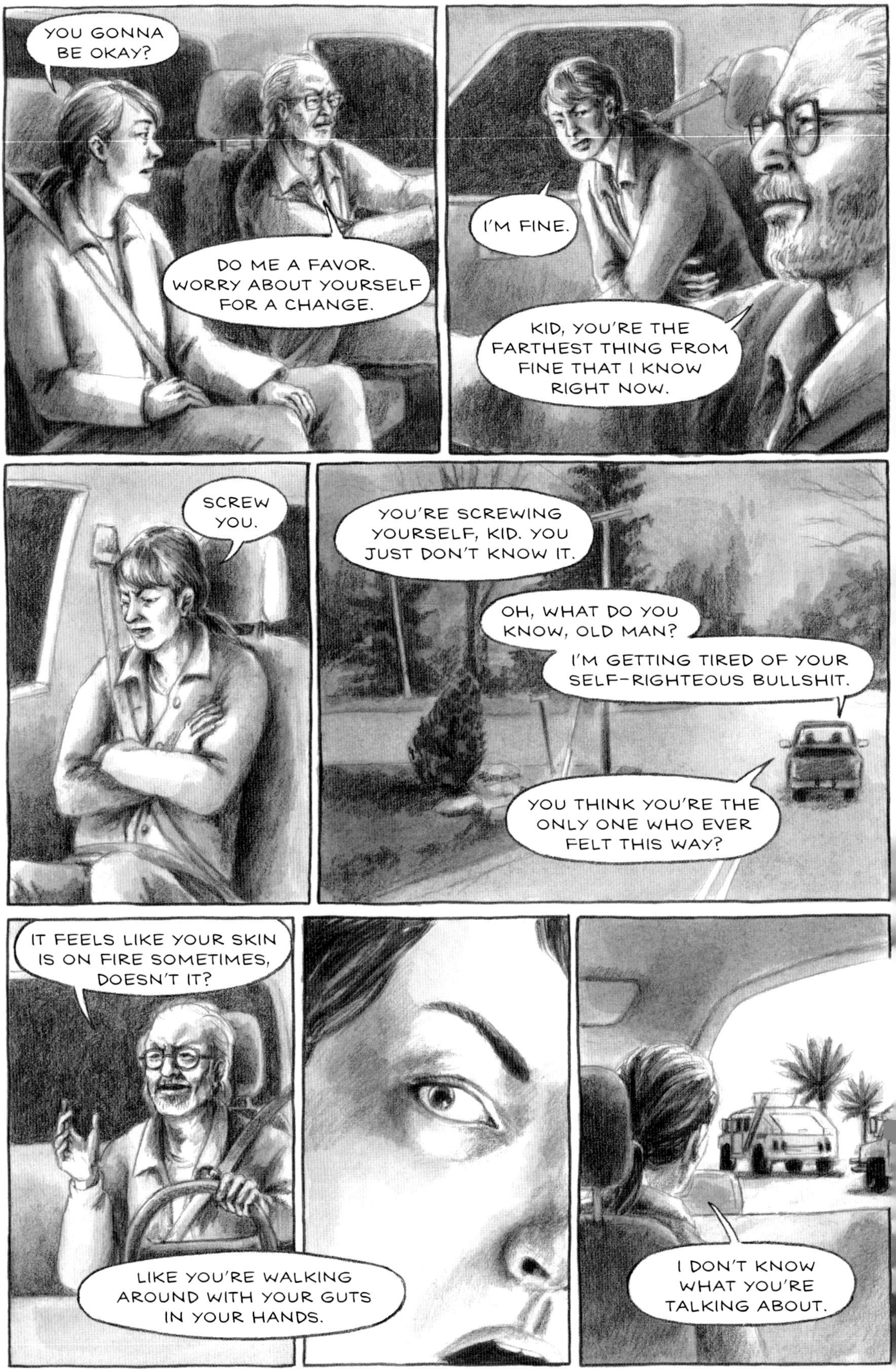
YOU GONNA BE OKAY?
DO ME A FAVOR. WORRY ABOUT YOURSELF FOR A CHANGE.
I'M FINE.
KID, YOU'RE THE FARTHEST THING FROM FINE THAT I KNOW RIGHT NOW.
SCREW YOU.
YOU'RE SCREWING YOURSELF, KID. YOU JUST DON'T KNOW IT.
OH, WHAT DO YOU KNOW, OLD MAN?
I'M GETTING TIRED OF YOUR SELF-RIGHTEOUS BULLSHIT.
YOU THINK YOU'RE THE ONLY ONE WHO EVER FELT THIS WAY?
IT FEELS LIKE YOUR SKIN IS ON FIRE SOMETIMES, DOESN'T IT?
LIKE YOU'RE WALKING AROUND WITH YOUR GUTS IN YOUR HANDS.
I DON'T KNOW WHAT YOU'RE TALKING ABOUT.

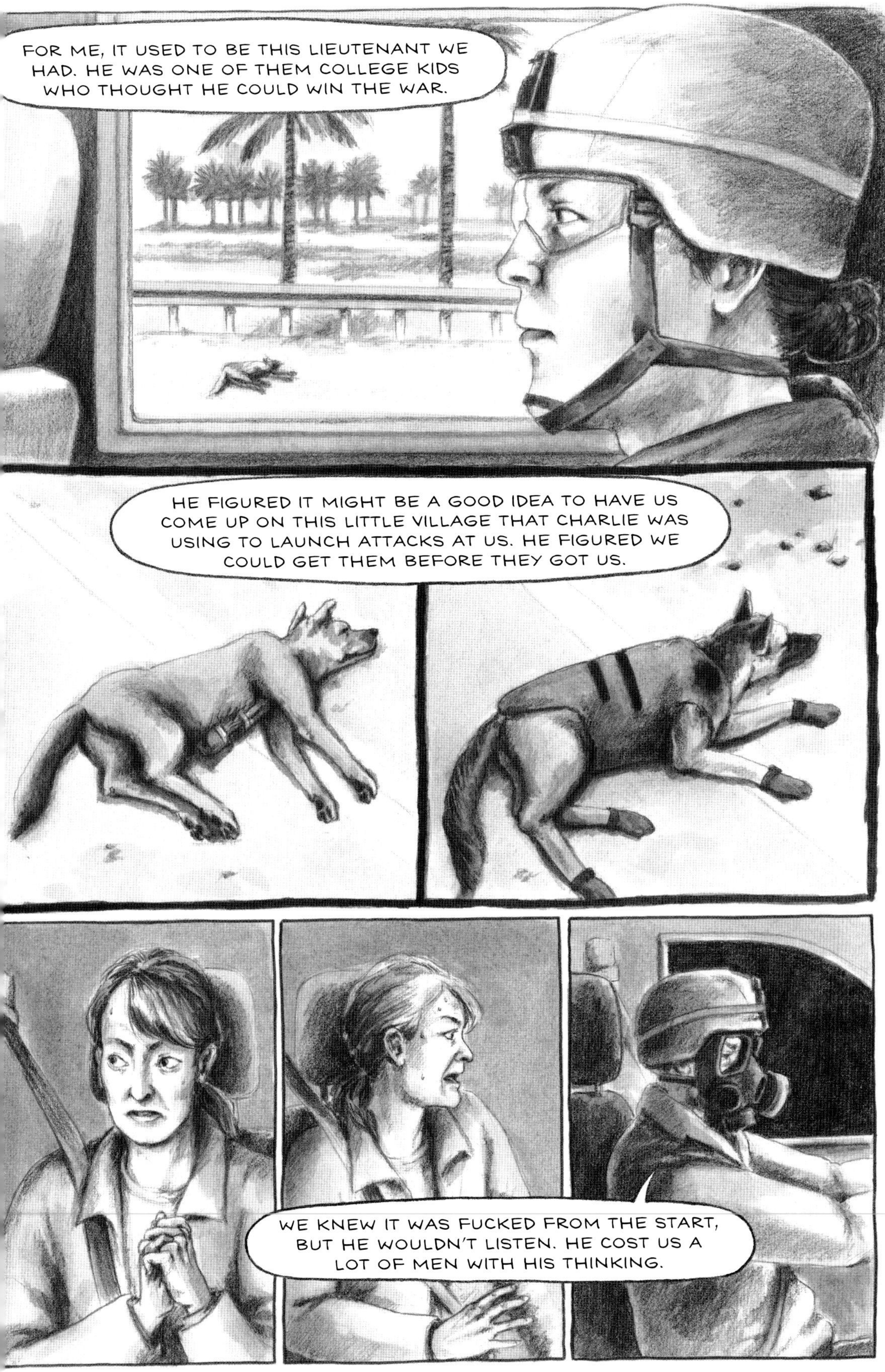
FOR ME, IT USED TO BE THIS LIEUTENANT WE HAD. HE WAS ONE OF THEM COLLEGE KIDS WHO THOUGHT HE COULD WIN THE WAR.
HE FIGURED IT MIGHT BE A GOOD IDEA TO HAVE US COME UP ON THIS LITTLE VILLAGE THAT CHARLIE WAS USING TO LAUNCH ATTACKS AT US. HE FIGURED WE COULD GET THEM BEFORE THEY GOT US.
WE KNEW IT WAS FUCKED FROM THE START, BUT HE WOULDN'T LISTEN. HE COST US A LOT OF MEN WITH HIS THINKING.

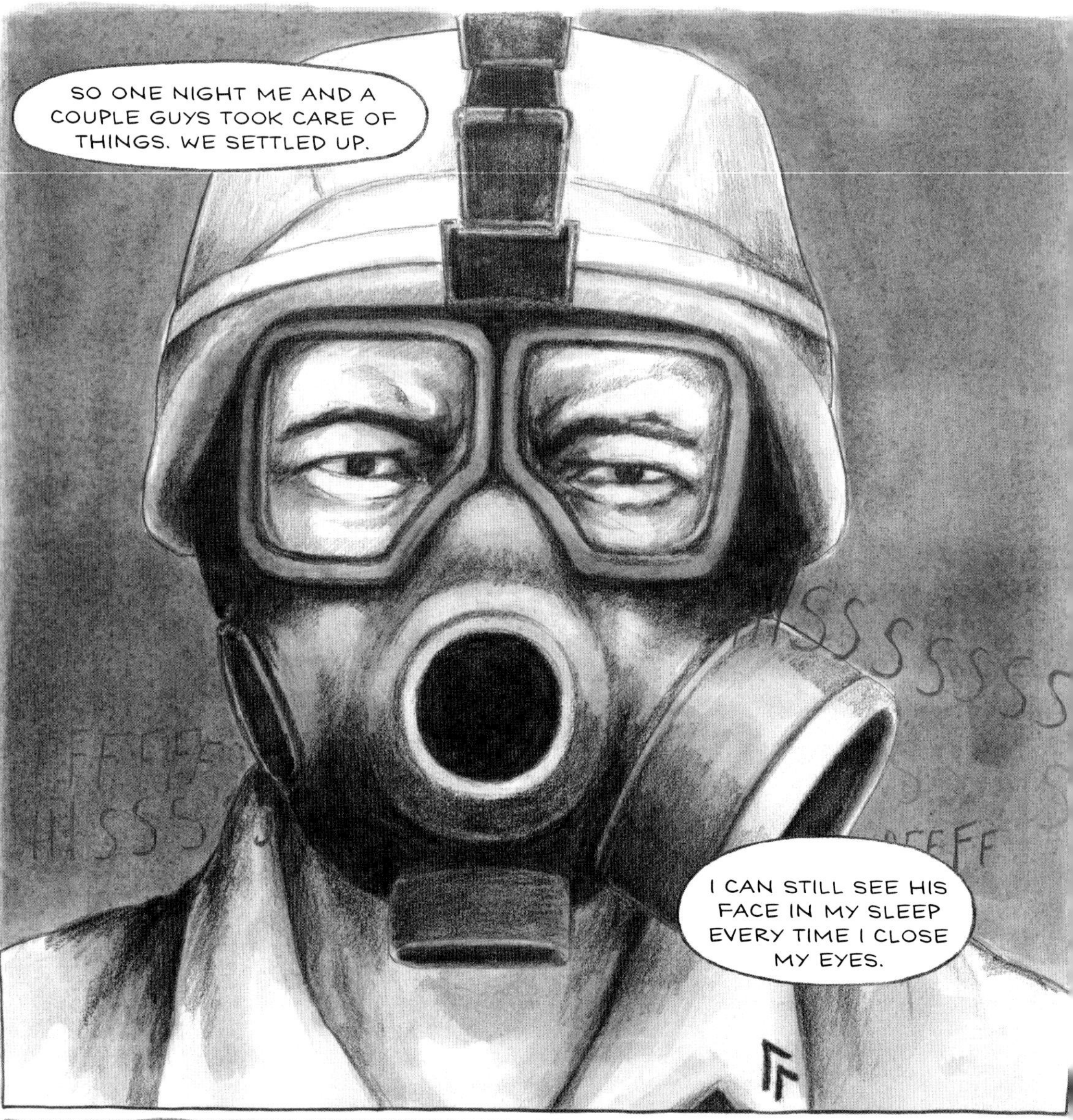
SO ONE NIGHT ME AND A COUPLE GUYS TOOK CARE OF THINGS. WE SETTLED UP.
I CAN STILL SEE HIS FACE IN MY SLEEP EVERY TIME I CLOSE MY EYES.

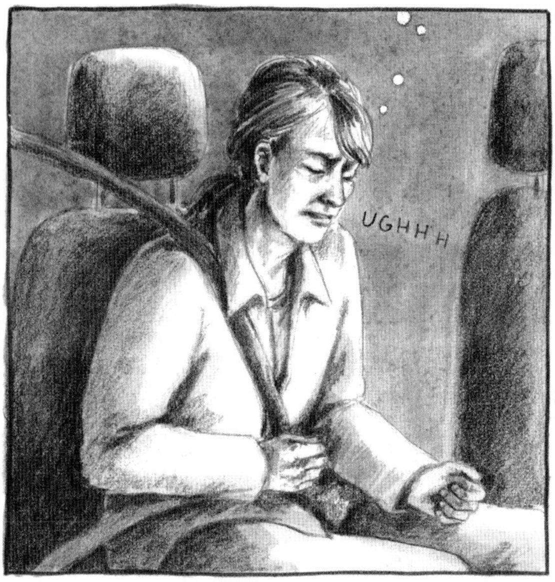
UGHHH

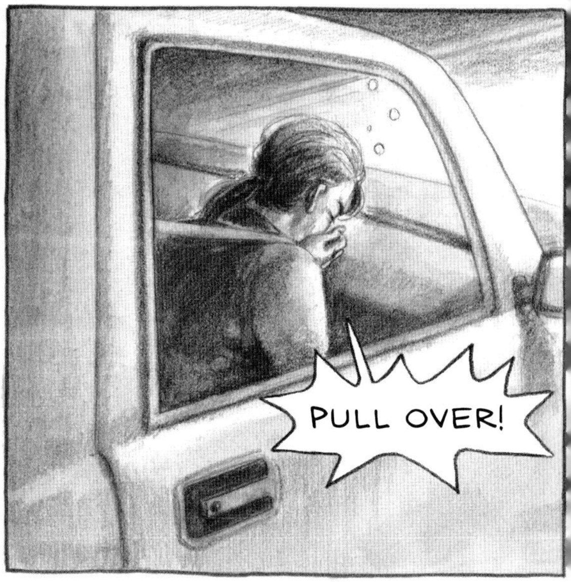
PULL OVER!

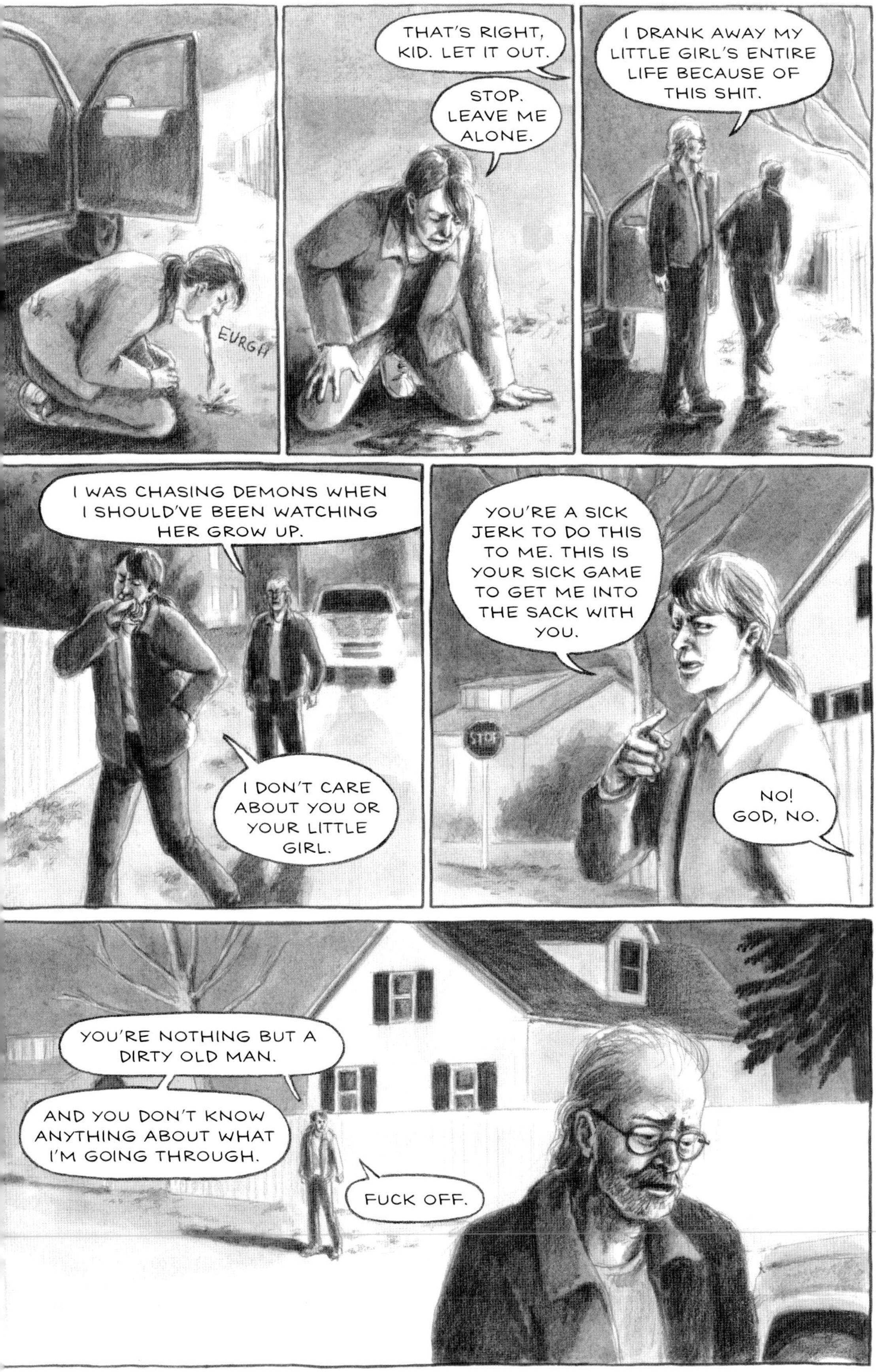
EURGH
THAT'S RIGHT, KID. LET IT OUT.
STOP. LEAVE ME ALONE.
I DRANK AWAY MY LITTLE GIRL'S ENTIRE LIFE BECAUSE OF THIS SHIT.
I WAS CHASING DEMONS WHEN I SHOULD'VE BEEN WATCHING HER GROW UP.
I DON'T CARE ABOUT YOU OR YOUR LITTLE GIRL.
YOU'RE A SICK JERK TO DO THIS TO ME. THIS IS YOUR SICK GAME TO GET ME INTO THE SACK WITH YOU.
NO! GOD, NO.
STOP
YOU'RE NOTHING BUT A DIRTY OLD MAN.
AND YOU DON'T KNOW ANYTHING ABOUT WHAT I'M GOING THROUGH.
FUCK OFF.

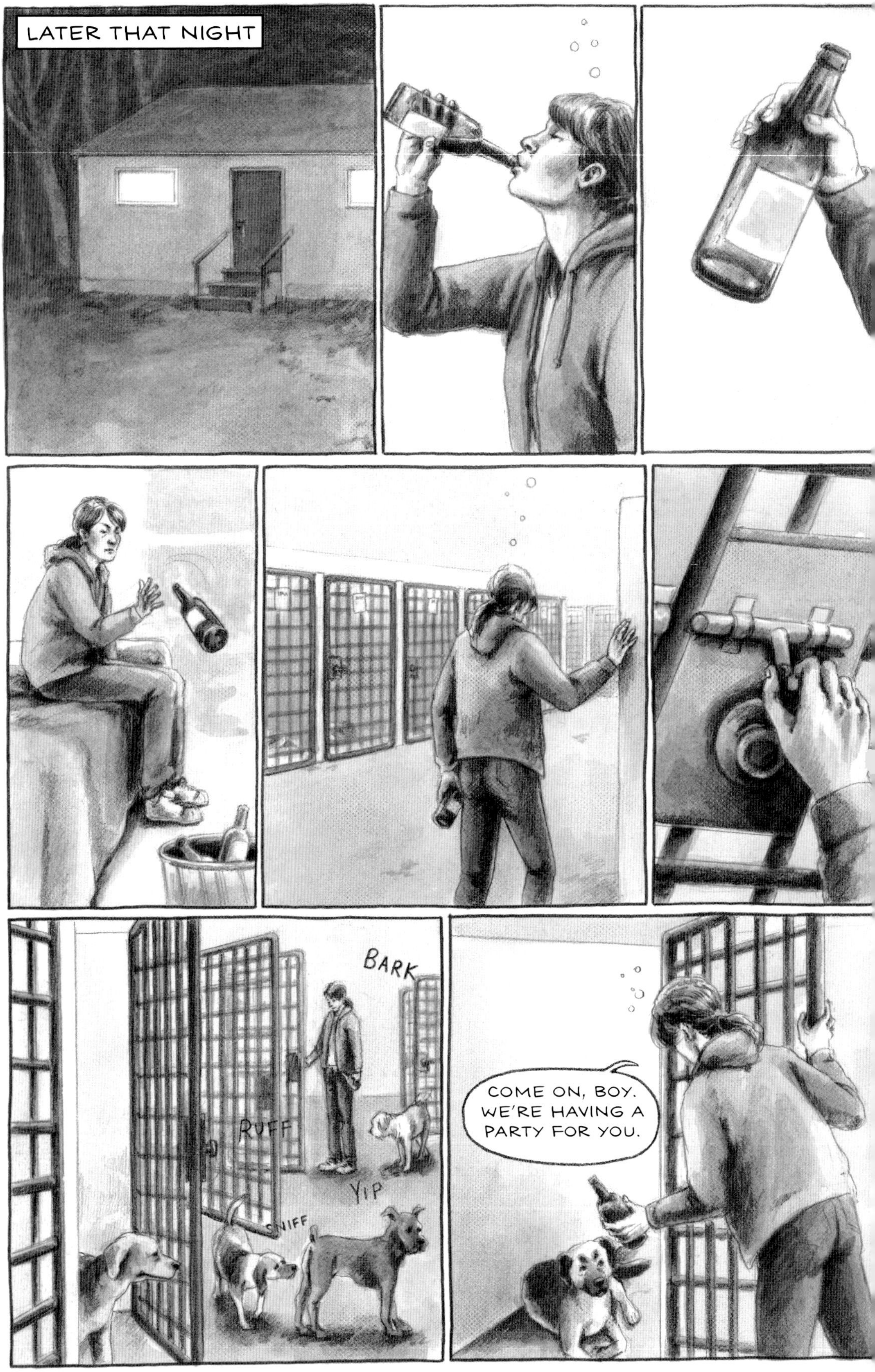
LATER THAT NIGHT
BARK
RUFF
YIP
SNIFF
COME ON, BOY. WE'RE HAVING A PARTY FOR YOU.

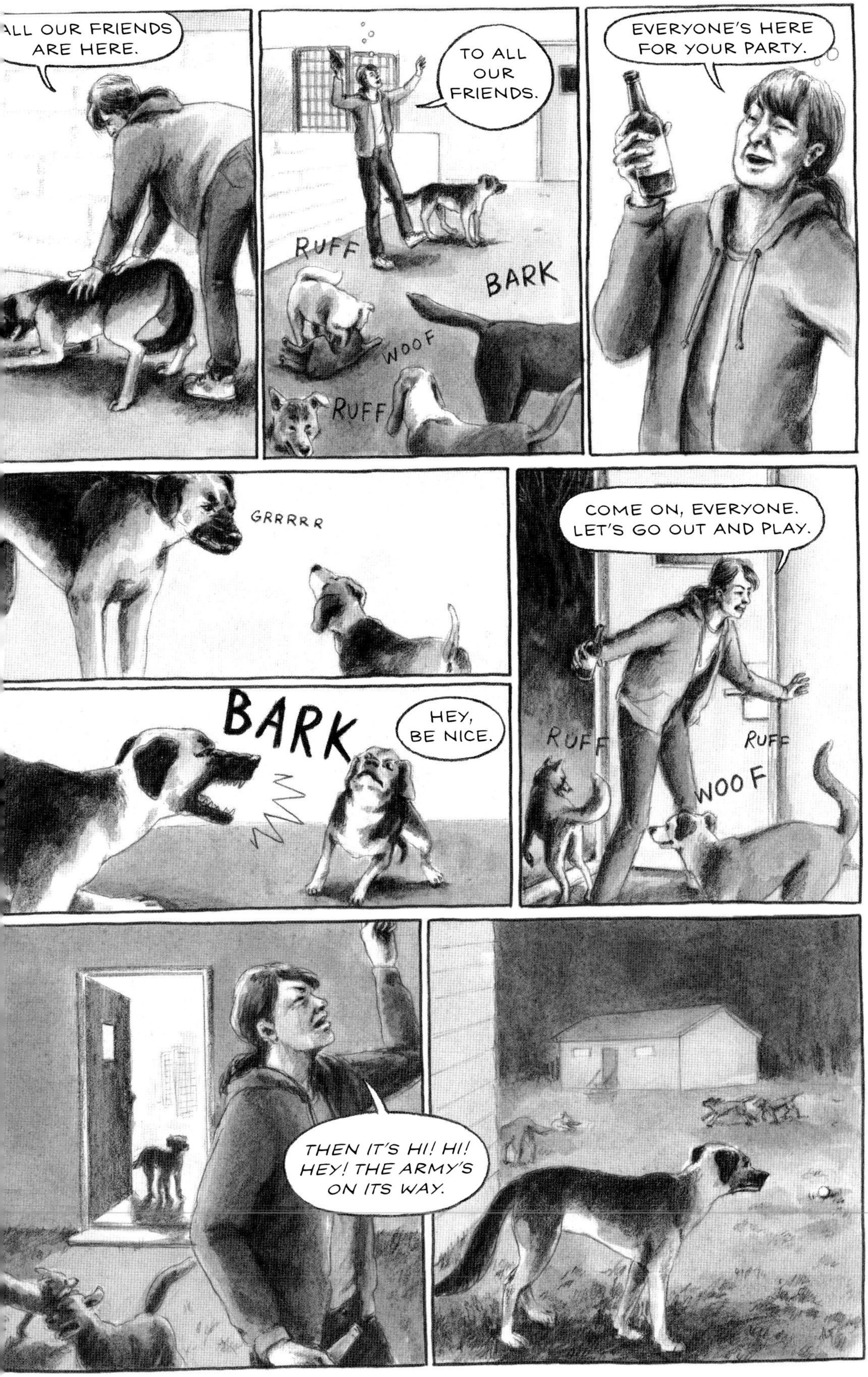
ALL OUR FRIENDS ARE HERE.
TO ALL OUR FRIENDS.
RUFF
BARK
WOOF
RUFF
EVERYONE'S HERE FOR YOUR PARTY.
GRRRRR
COME ON, EVERYONE. LET'S GO OUT AND PLAY.
BARK
HEY, BE NICE.
RUFF
RUFF
WOOF
THEN IT'S HI! HI! HEY! THE ARMY'S ON ITS WAY.

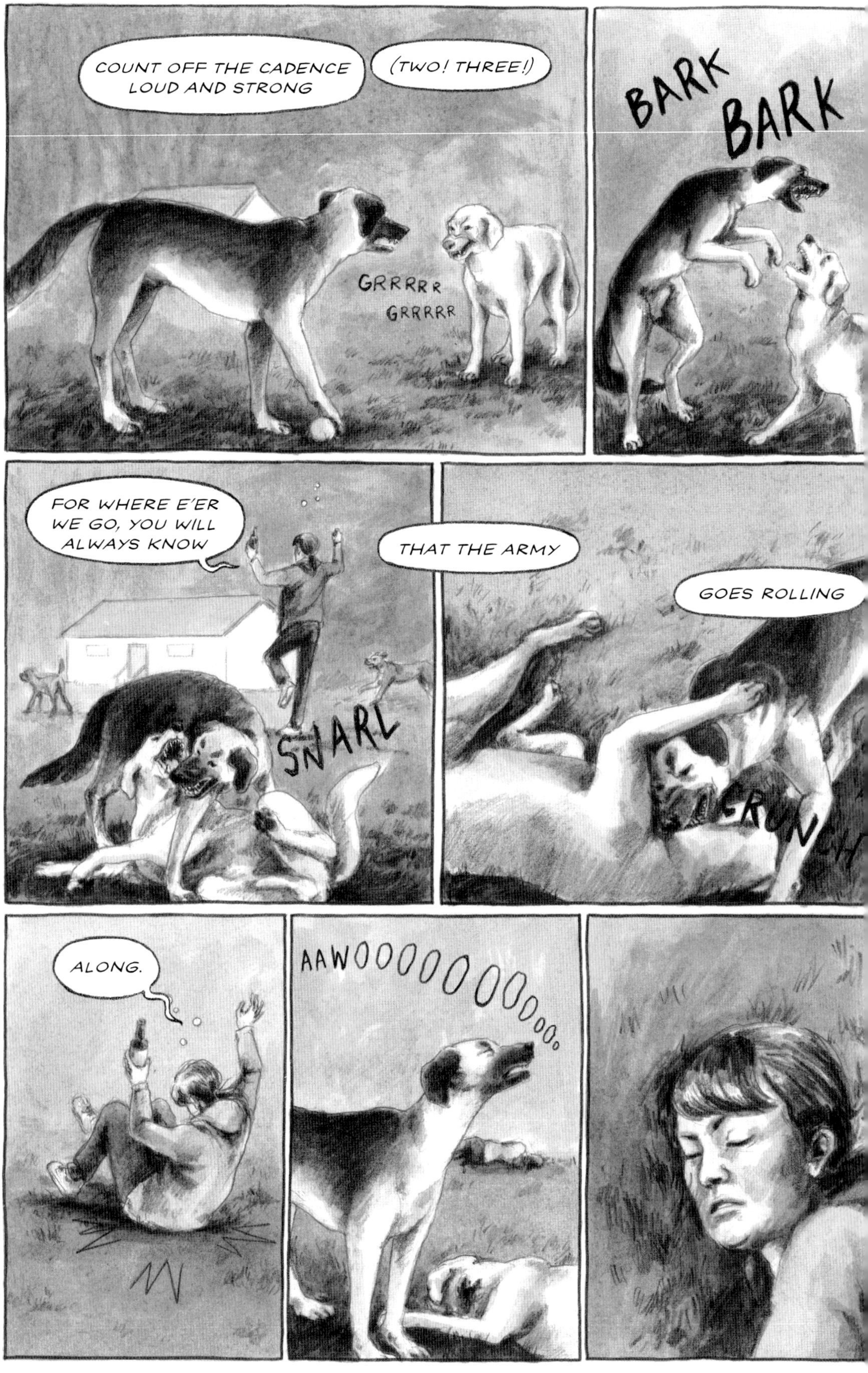
COUNT OFF THE CADENCE LOUD AND STRONG
(TWO! THREE!)
GRRRRR
GRRRRR
BARK
BARK
FOR WHERE E'ER WE GO, YOU WILL ALWAYS KNOW
SNARL
THAT THE ARMY
GOES ROLLING
CRUNCH
ALONG.
AAWOOOOOOOOOOooo

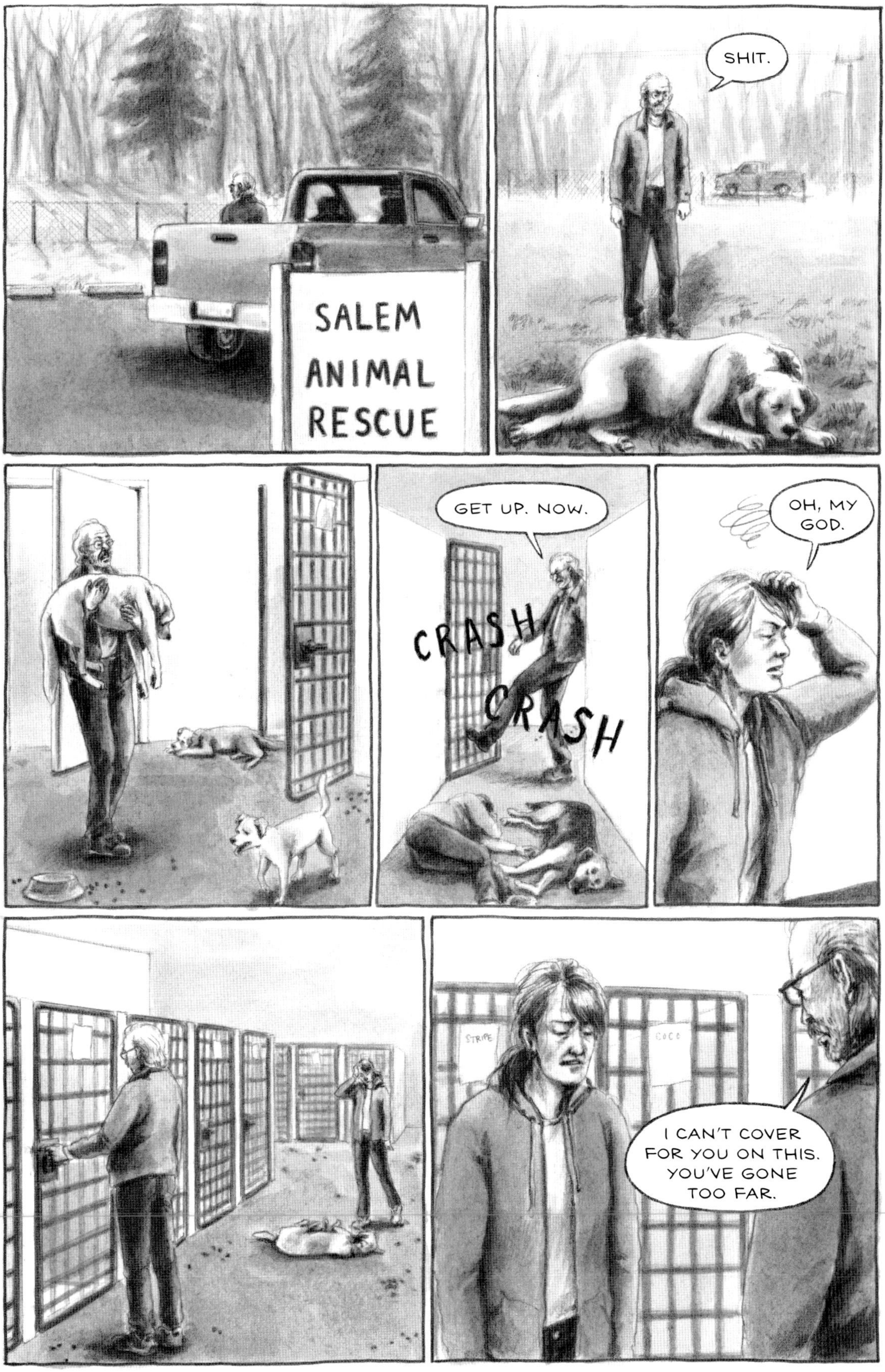
SALEM
ANIMAL
RESCUE
SHIT.
GET UP. NOW.
CRASH
CRASH
OH, MY GOD.
STRIPE
COCO
I CAN'T COVER FOR YOU ON THIS. YOU'VE GONE TOO FAR.

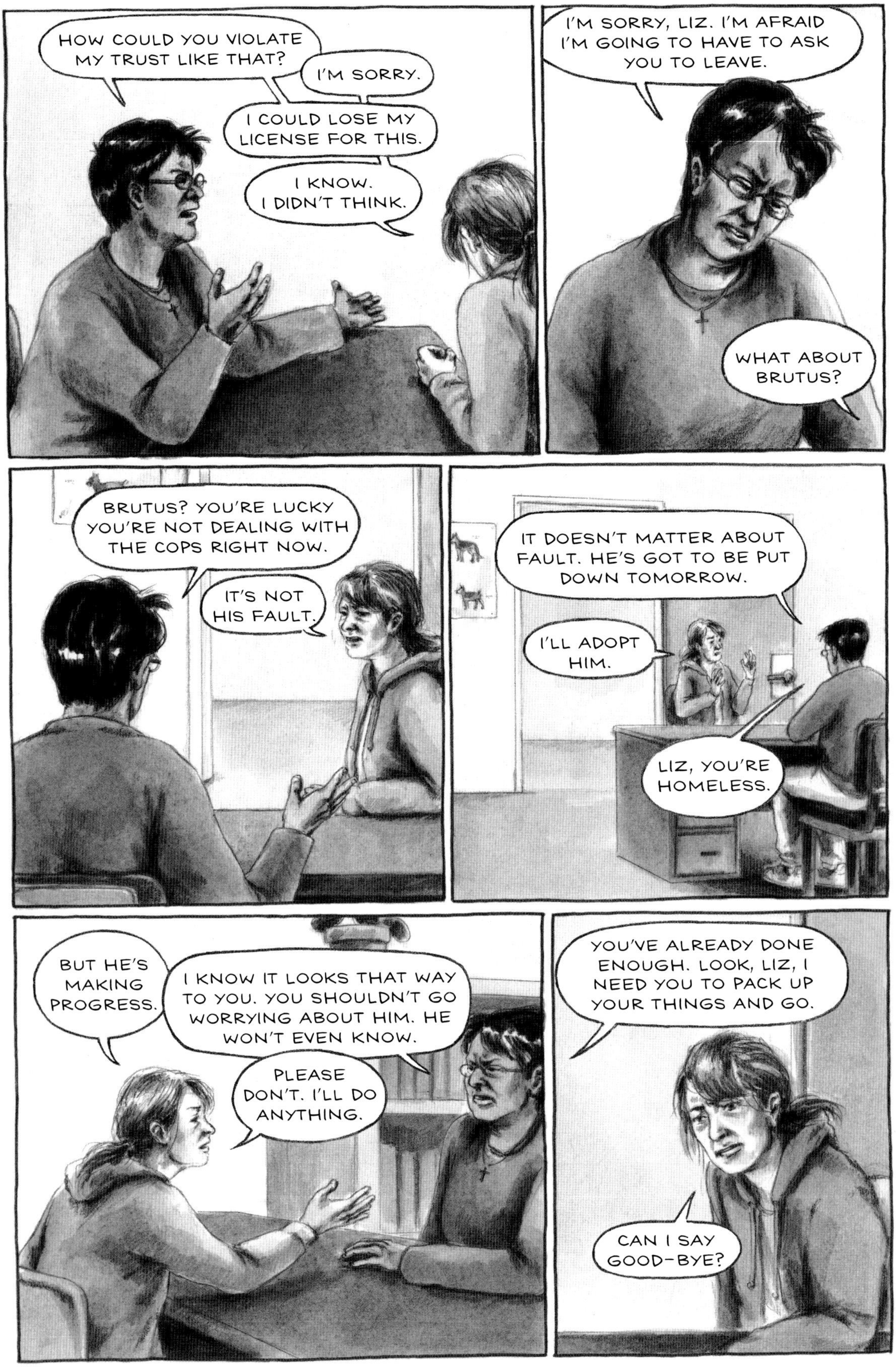
HOW COULD YOU VIOLATE MY TRUST LIKE THAT?
I'M SORRY.
I COULD LOSE MY LICENSE FOR THIS.
I KNOW. I DIDN'T THINK.
I'M SORRY, LIZ. I'M AFRAID I'M GOING TO HAVE TO ASK YOU TO LEAVE.
WHAT ABOUT BRUTUS?
BRUTUS? YOU'RE LUCKY YOU'RE NOT DEALING WITH THE COPS RIGHT NOW.
IT'S NOT HIS FAULT.
IT DOESN'T MATTER ABOUT FAULT. HE'S GOT TO BE PUT DOWN TOMORROW.
I'LL ADOPT HIM.
LIZ, YOU'RE HOMELESS.
BUT HE'S MAKING PROGRESS.
I KNOW IT LOOKS THAT WAY TO YOU. YOU SHOULDN'T GO WORRYING ABOUT HIM. HE WON'T EVEN KNOW.
PLEASE DON'T. I'LL DO ANYTHING.
YOU'VE ALREADY DONE ENOUGH. LOOK, LIZ, I NEED YOU TO PACK UP YOUR THINGS AND GO.
CAN I SAY GOOD-BYE?

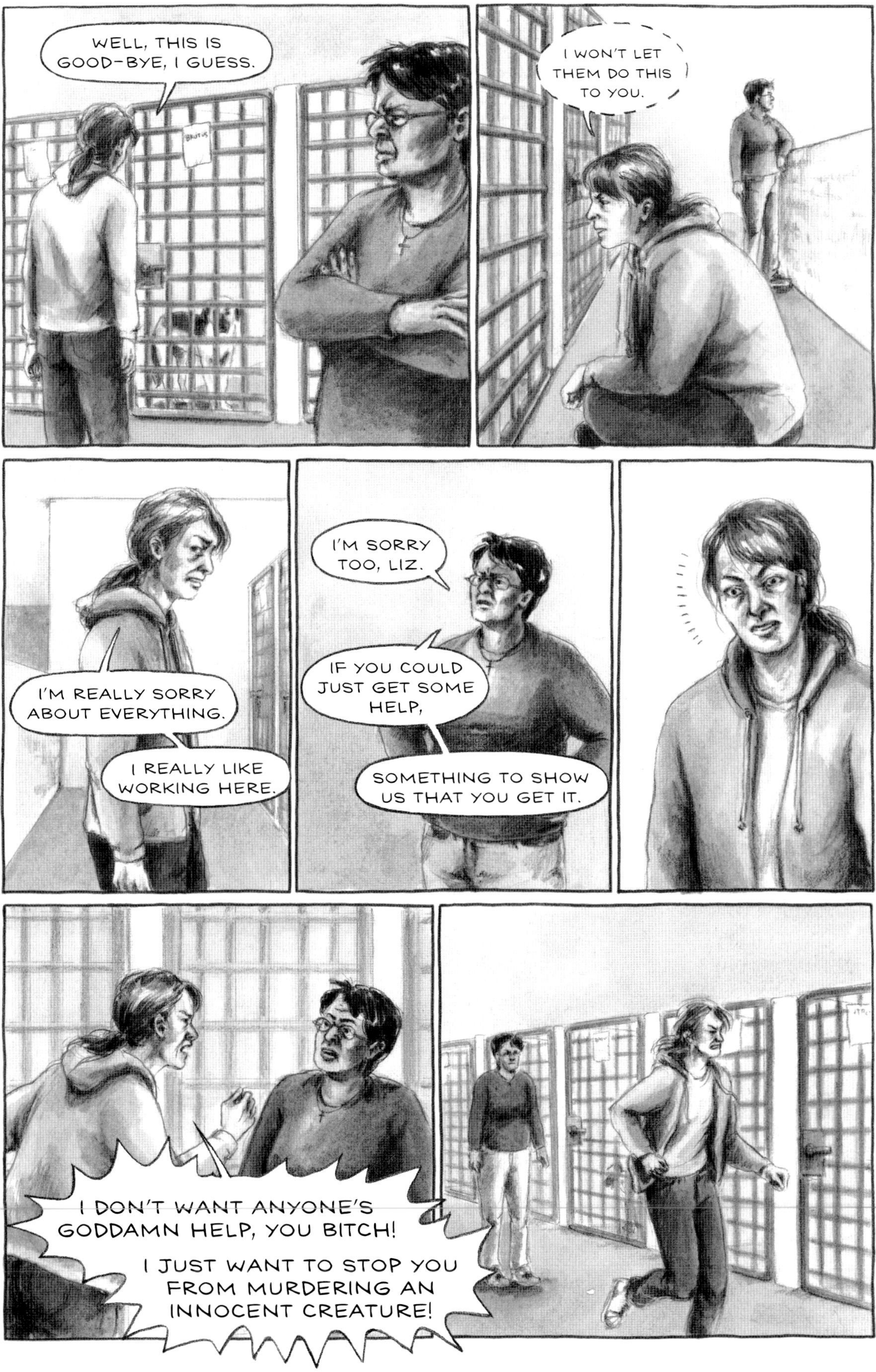
WELL, THIS IS GOOD-BYE, I GUESS.
I WON'T LET THEM DO THIS TO YOU.
I'M REALLY SORRY ABOUT EVERYTHING.
I REALLY LIKE WORKING HERE.
I'M SORRY TOO, LIZ.
IF YOU COULD JUST GET SOME HELP,
SOMETHING TO SHOW US THAT YOU GET IT.
I DON'T WANT ANYONE'S GODDAMN HELP, YOU BITCH!
I JUST WANT TO STOP YOU FROM MURDERING AN INNOCENT CREATURE!

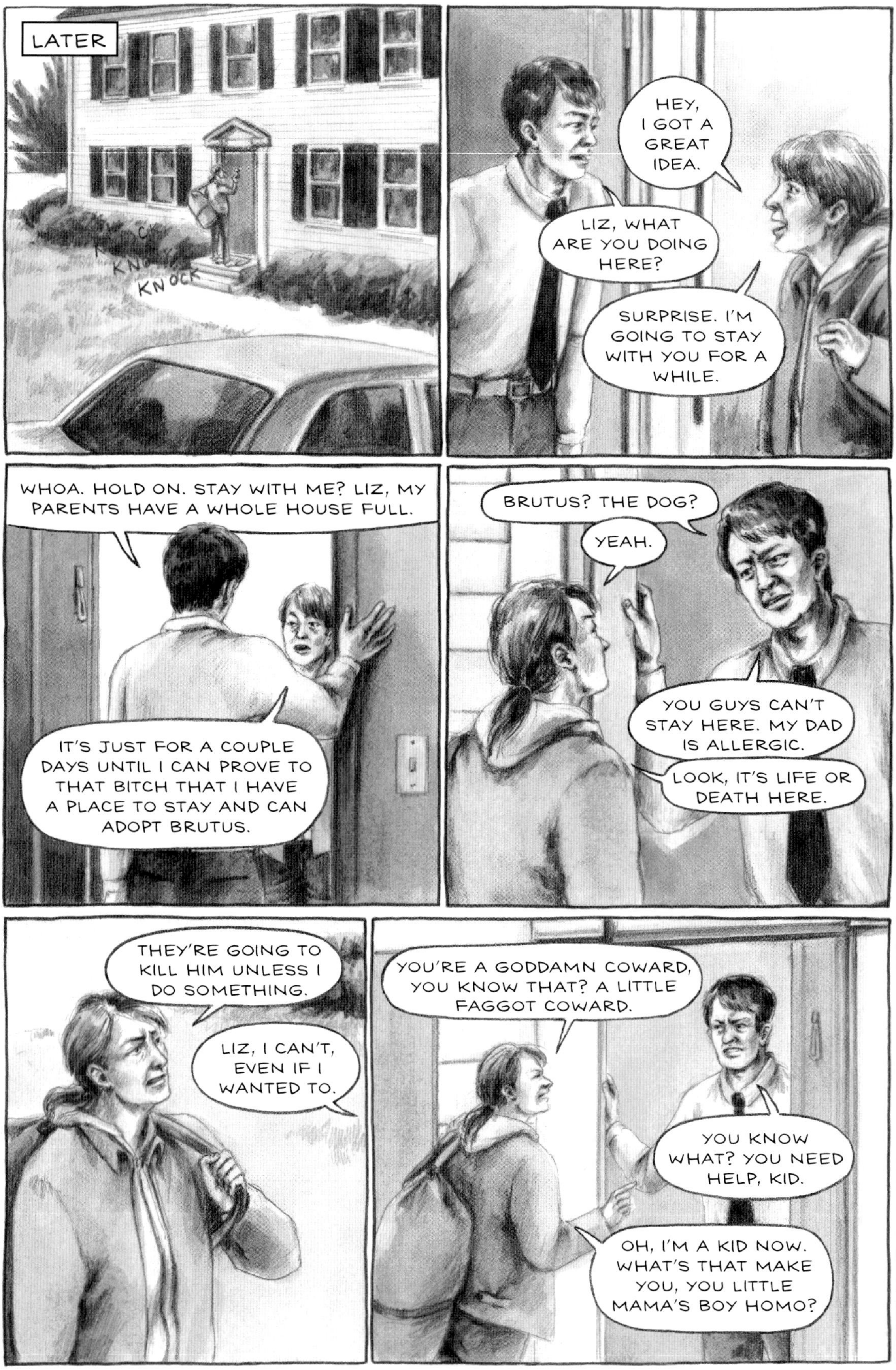
LATER
KNOCK
KNOCK
KNOCK
HEY, I GOT A GREAT IDEA.
LIZ, WHAT ARE YOU DOING HERE?
SURPRISE. I'M GOING TO STAY WITH YOU FOR A WHILE.
WHOA. HOLD ON. STAY WITH ME? LIZ, MY PARENTS HAVE A WHOLE HOUSE FULL.
IT'S JUST FOR A COUPLE DAYS UNTIL I CAN PROVE TO THAT BITCH THAT I HAVE A PLACE TO STAY AND CAN ADOPT BRUTUS.
BRUTUS? THE DOG?
YEAH.
YOU GUYS CAN'T STAY HERE. MY DAD IS ALLERGIC.
LOOK, IT'S LIFE OR DEATH HERE.
THEY'RE GOING TO KILL HIM UNLESS I DO SOMETHING.
LIZ, I CAN'T, EVEN IF I WANTED TO.
YOU'RE A GODDAMN COWARD, YOU KNOW THAT? A LITTLE FAGGOT COWARD.
YOU KNOW WHAT? YOU NEED HELP, KID.
OH, I'M A KID NOW. WHAT'S THAT MAKE YOU, YOU LITTLE MAMA'S BOY HOMO?

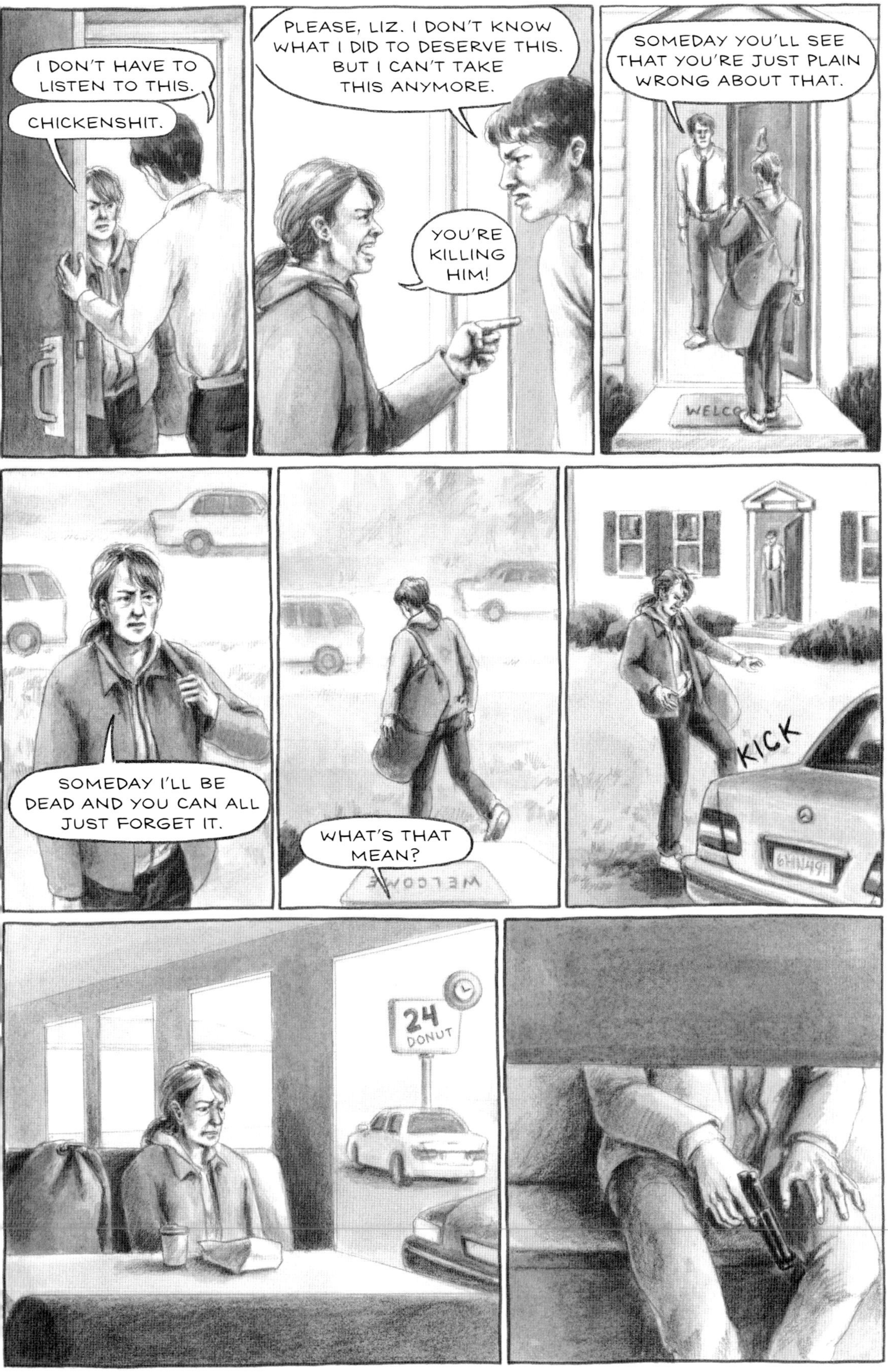
I DON'T HAVE TO LISTEN TO THIS.
CHICKENSHIT.
PLEASE, LIZ. I DON'T KNOW WHAT I DID TO DESERVE THIS. BUT I CAN'T TAKE THIS ANYMORE.
YOU'RE KILLING HIM!
SOMEDAY YOU'LL SEE THAT YOU'RE JUST PLAIN WRONG ABOUT THAT.
SOMEDAY I'LL BE DEAD AND YOU CAN ALL JUST FORGET IT.
WHAT'S THAT MEAN?
KICK
24 DONUT

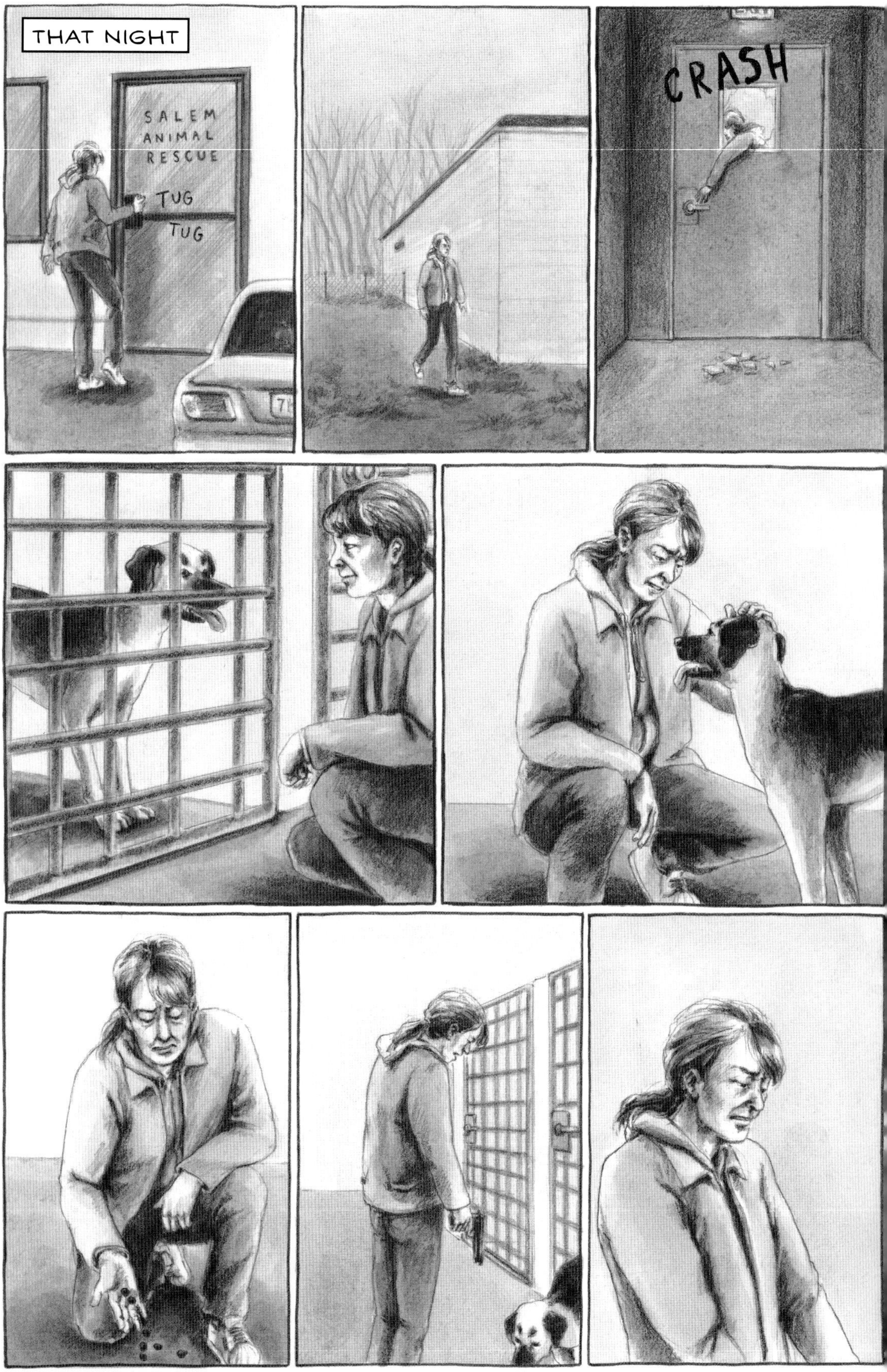
THAT NIGHT
SALEM ANIMAL RESCUE
TUG
TUG
CRASH

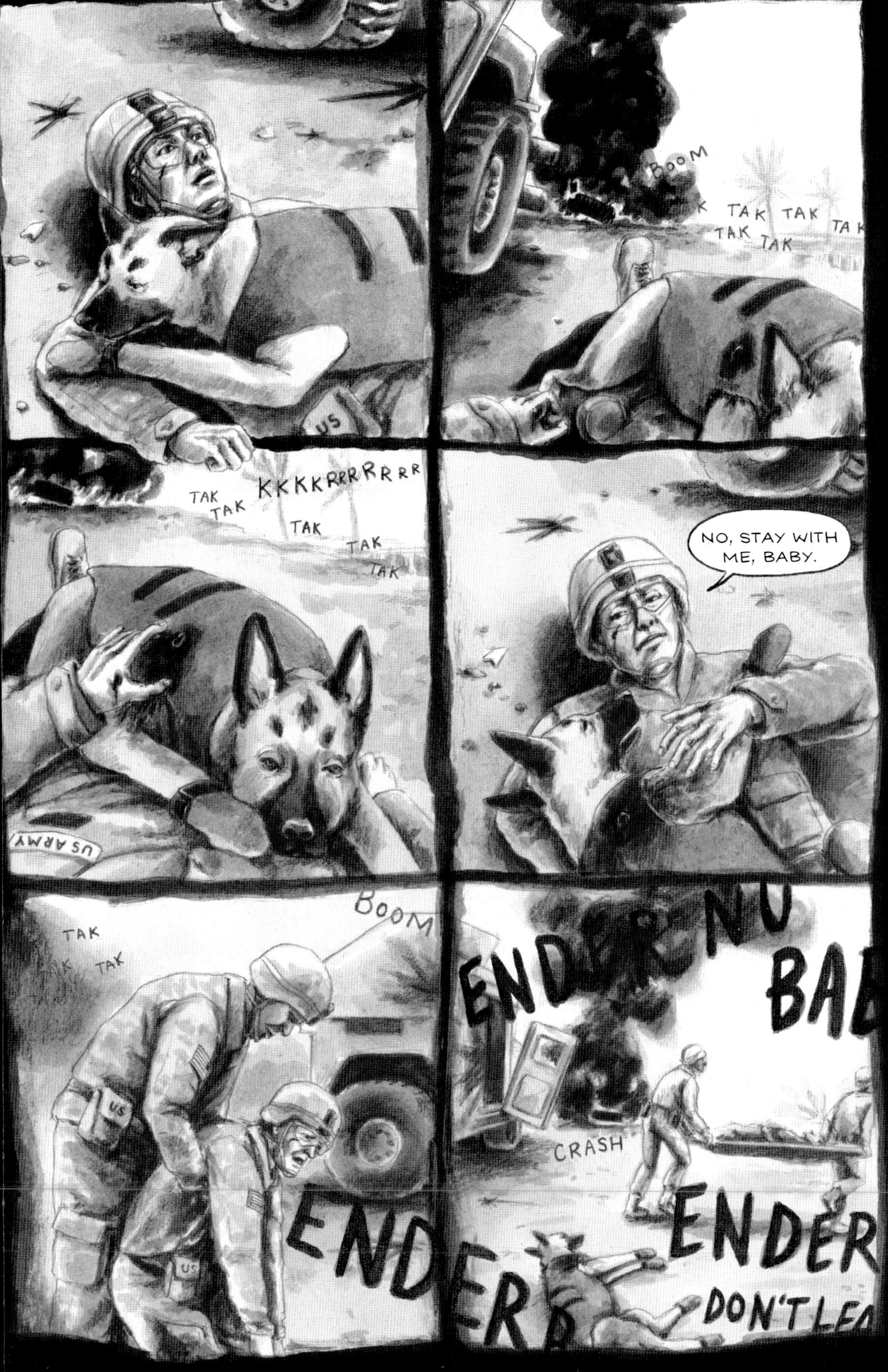
US
BOOM
TAK TAK TAK
TAK TAK
TAK TAK KKKKRRRRRRRR
TAK
TAK
TAK
NO, STAY WITH ME, BABY.
US ARMY
BOOM
TAK
TAK
US
US
ENDER
BAB
CRASH
ENDER
DON'T LEA

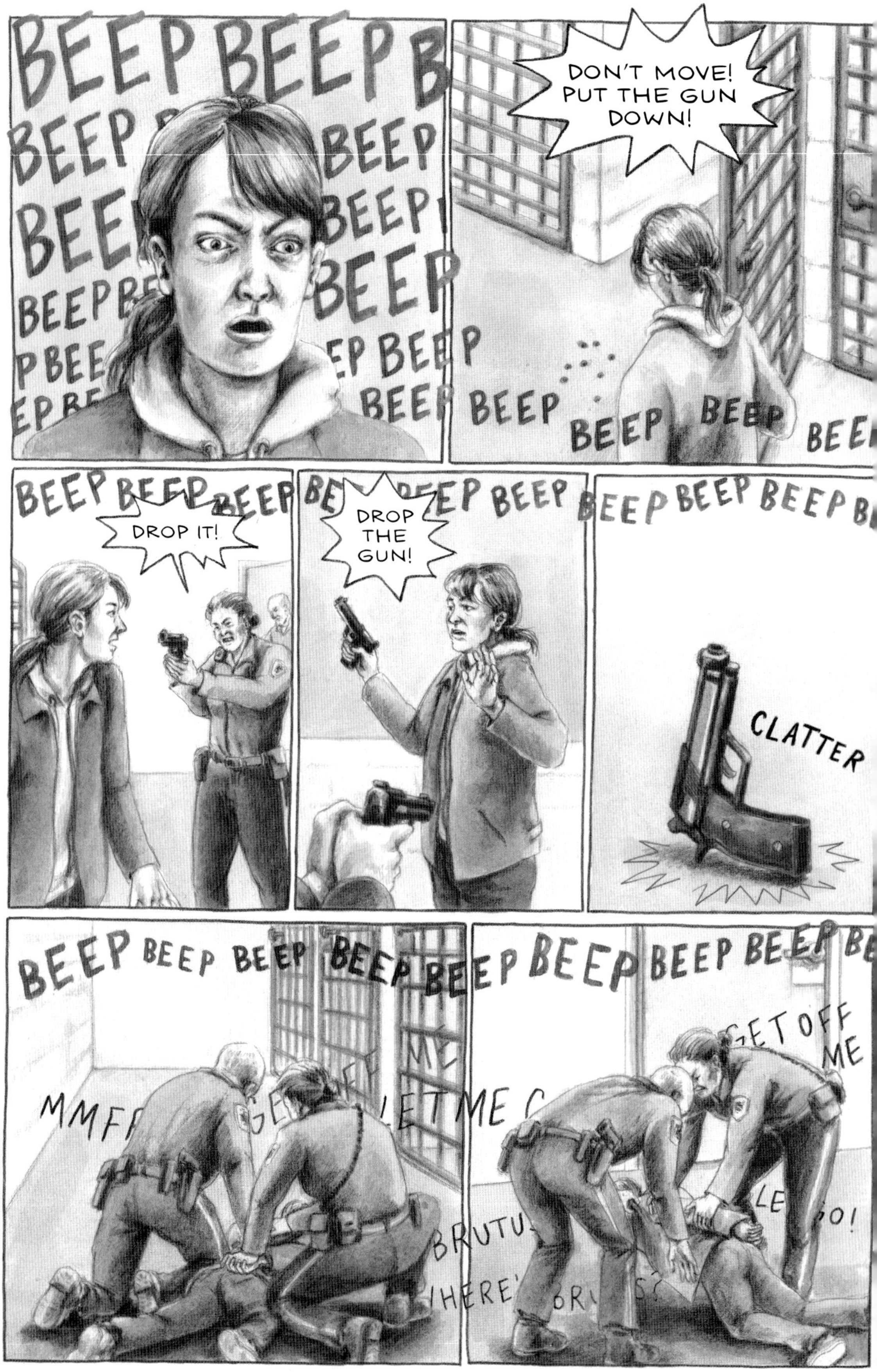
BEEP BEEP
DON'T MOVE! PUT THE GUN DOWN!
BEEP BEEP BEEP
DROP IT!
DROP THE GUN!
CLATTER
BEEP BEEP BEEP
GET OFF ME

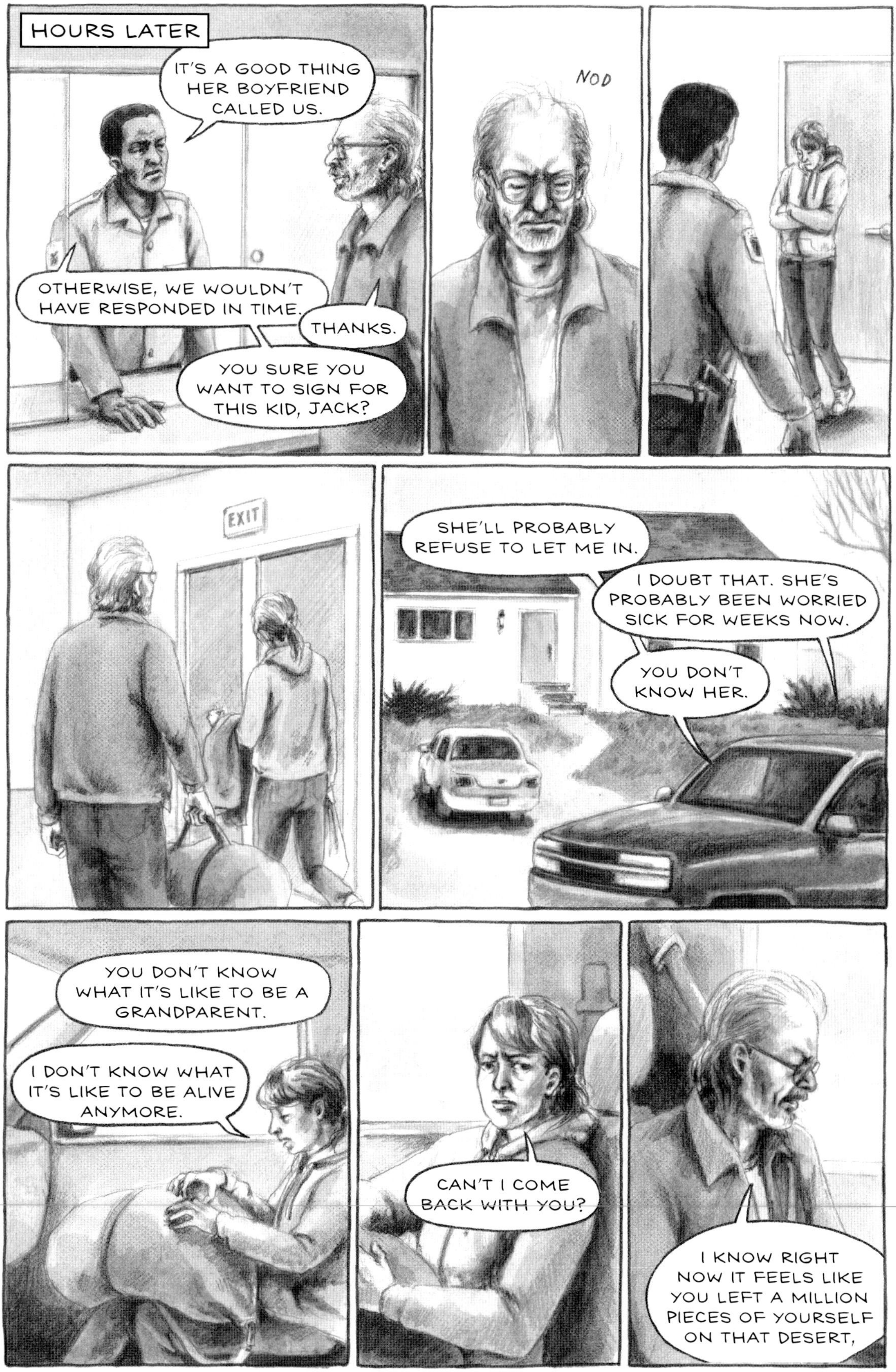
HOURS LATER
IT'S A GOOD THING HER BOYFRIEND CALLED US.
OTHERWISE, WE WOULDN'T HAVE RESPONDED IN TIME.
THANKS.
YOU SURE YOU WANT TO SIGN FOR THIS KID, JACK?
NOD
EXIT
SHE'LL PROBABLY REFUSE TO LET ME IN.
I DOUBT THAT. SHE'S PROBABLY BEEN WORRIED SICK FOR WEEKS NOW.
YOU DON'T KNOW HER.
YOU DON'T KNOW WHAT IT'S LIKE TO BE A GRANDPARENT.
I DON'T KNOW WHAT IT'S LIKE TO BE ALIVE ANYMORE.
CAN'T I COME BACK WITH YOU?
I KNOW RIGHT NOW IT FEELS LIKE YOU LEFT A MILLION PIECES OF YOURSELF ON THAT DESERT,

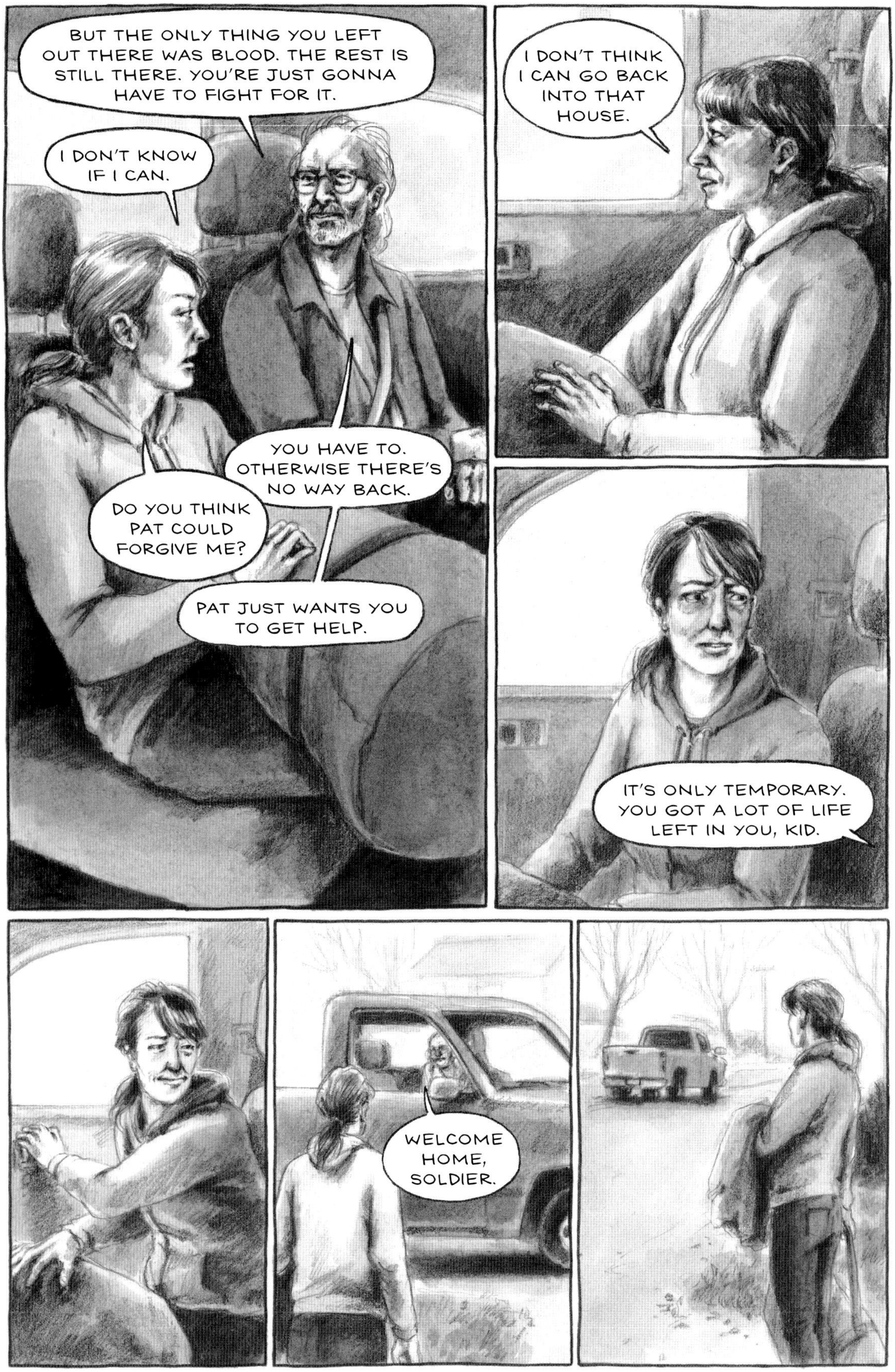
BUT THE ONLY THING YOU LEFT OUT THERE WAS BLOOD. THE REST IS STILL THERE. YOU'RE JUST GONNA HAVE TO FIGHT FOR IT.
I DON'T KNOW IF I CAN.
YOU HAVE TO. OTHERWISE THERE'S NO WAY BACK.
DO YOU THINK PAT COULD FORGIVE ME?
PAT JUST WANTS YOU TO GET HELP.
I DON'T THINK I CAN GO BACK INTO THAT HOUSE.
IT'S ONLY TEMPORARY. YOU GOT A LOT OF LIFE LEFT IN YOU, KID.
WELCOME HOME, SOLDIER.

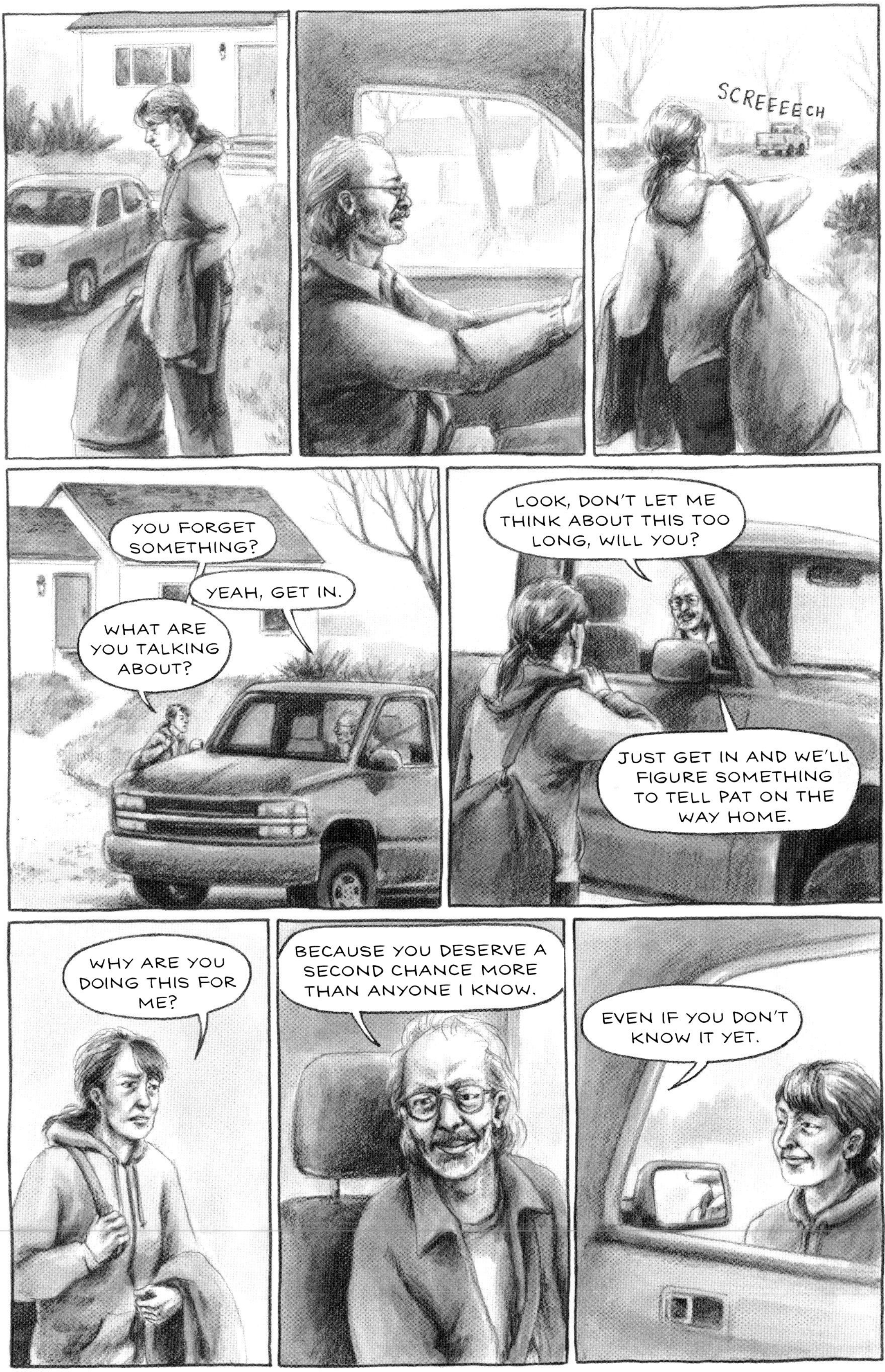
SCREEEECH
YOU FORGET SOMETHING?
YEAH, GET IN.
WHAT ARE YOU TALKING ABOUT?
LOOK, DON'T LET ME THINK ABOUT THIS TOO LONG, WILL YOU?
JUST GET IN AND WE'LL FIGURE SOMETHING TO TELL PAT ON THE WAY HOME.
WHY ARE YOU DOING THIS FOR ME?
BECAUSE YOU DESERVE A SECOND CHANCE MORE THAN ANYONE I KNOW.
EVEN IF YOU DON'T KNOW IT YET.

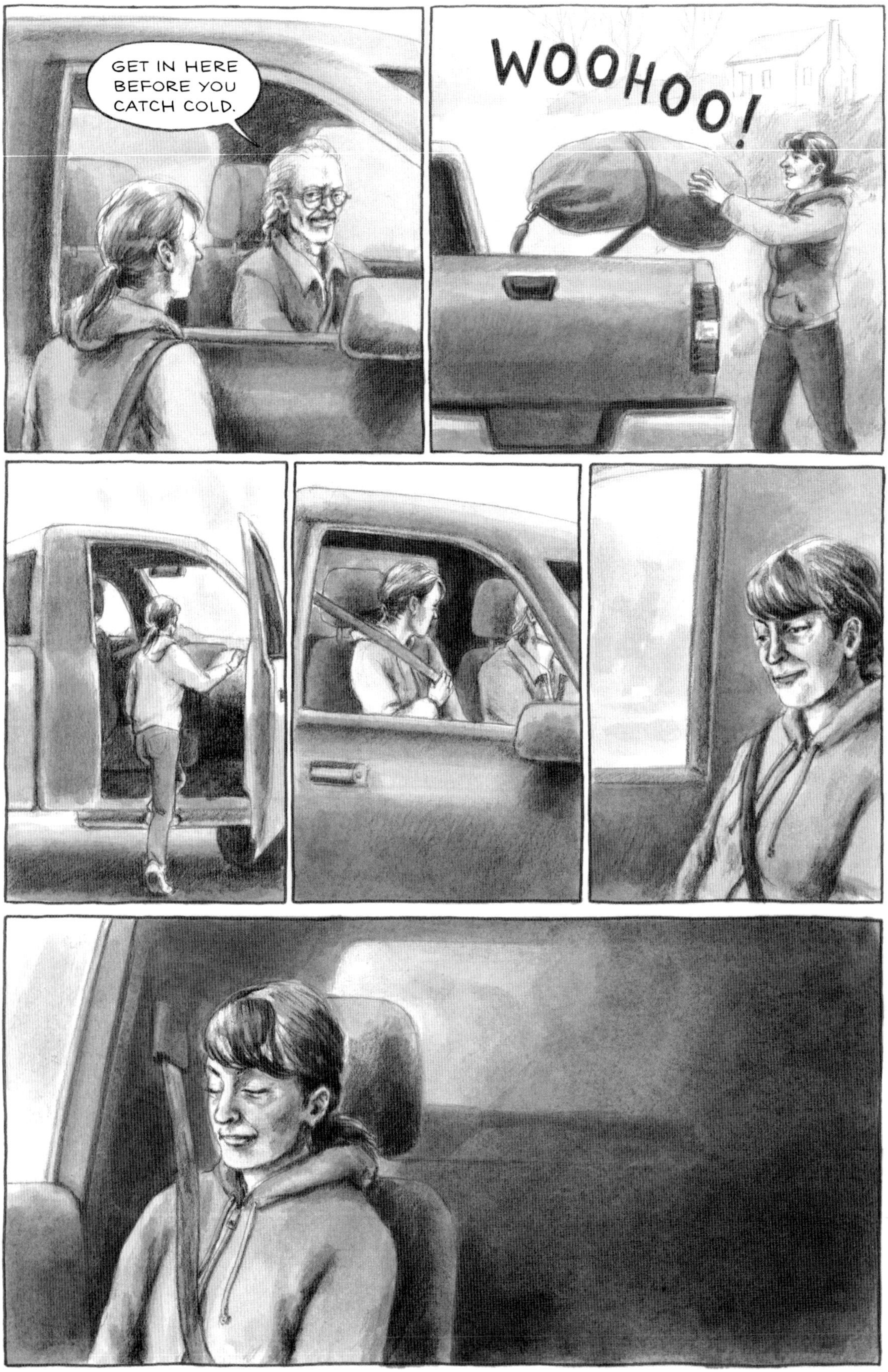
GET IN HERE BEFORE YOU CATCH COLD.
WOOHOO!

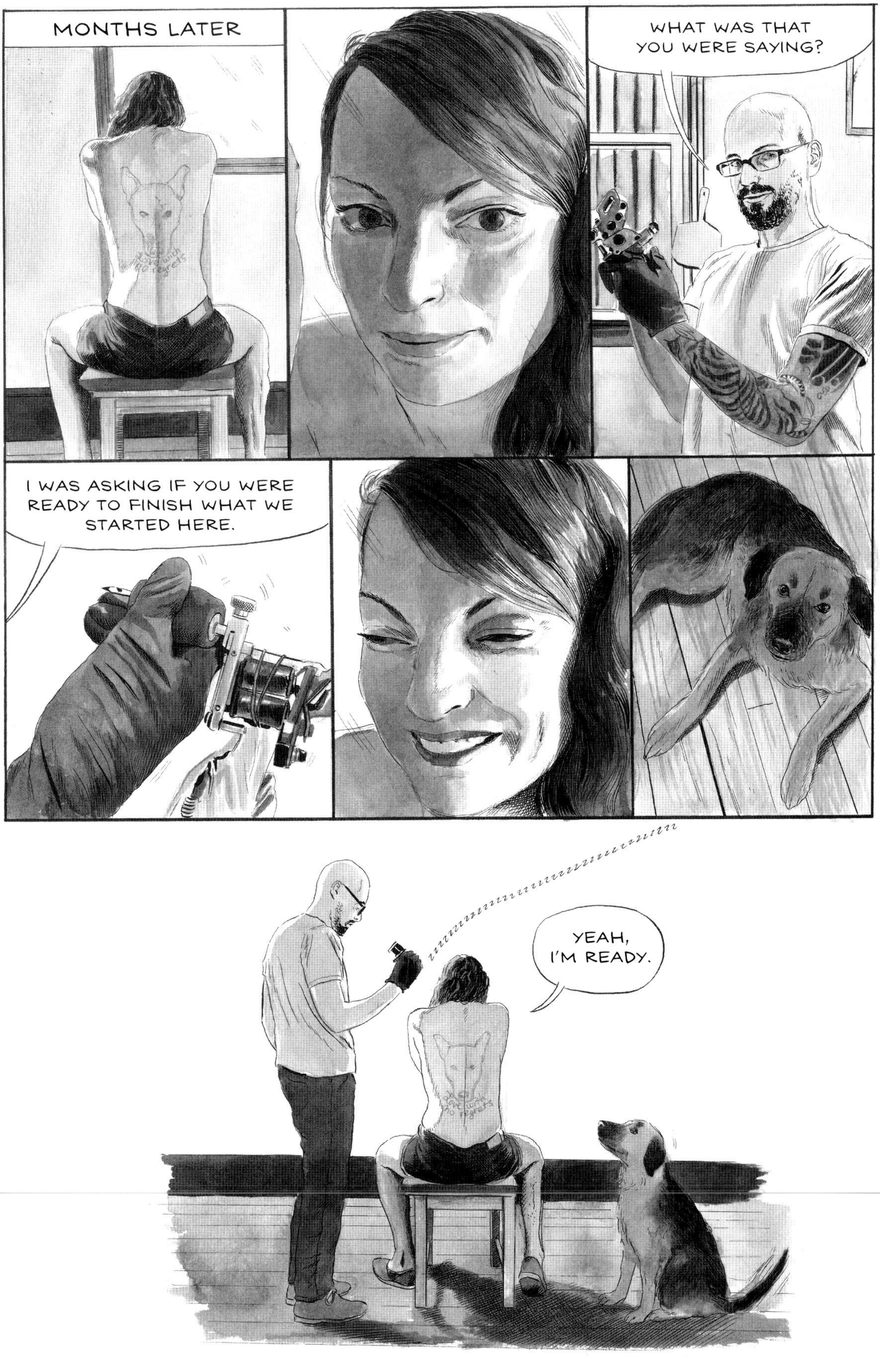
MONTHS LATER
WHAT WAS THAT YOU WERE SAYING?
I WAS ASKING IF YOU WERE READY TO FINISH WHAT WE STARTED HERE.
YEAH, I'M READY.

Acknowledgments

When Jan Egleson first discussed this project with me, my son, Max, was just a few weeks old. As of publication, we are approaching his tenth birthday. A decade of blood, sweat, and tears went into this book.

So much has changed since we started writing this book. For example, when we started, women served in the military but were not allowed to fight in combat. Today, men and women fight side by side on the battlefield. Also, "Don't Ask, Don't Tell"—the military's policy of trying to pretend gay and lesbian soldiers didn't exist—is referred to in this book. That policy was repealed in 2010. In fact, much of the world we wrote about has changed since 2007, with the sad exception of the war we wrote about, which is still going on.

In 2007, I was obsessed with the war in Iraq. When I was an editorial assistant for the Associated Press in 2004, my friend Tony Castaneda had told me that he was going to cover the war and that I should come with him. I didn't go with him but I worried that I had missed the story of a lifetime. Tony went on to become a correspondent, covering the front lines of a war that I believe we will look back on as a turning point in our country's history.

I stayed home, working as a reporter for a local newspaper in northern Massachusetts. One day, the war came home to me when a local marine was killed outside Fallujah, just six weeks after he'd arrived in Iraq. The conversation I had with his sister moments after finding out that her brother was incinerated by an IED still affects me, and a picture of her holding her brother's photo (which we ran on the front page) still sits in my living room. The sadness on her face was my inspiration for Liz. Many of the stories I heard during that week of covering this young man's death made their way, in some form or other, into *MWD*.

Sadly, that would not be the last soldier's funeral I would attend. In 2013, my wife's step-nephew Lance Corporal William Taylor Wild IV was killed in a military training accident that also took the lives of six other young marines in Nevada. This book is lovingly dedicated to his memory, as well as to all the other women and men who risk their lives for a war we too often forget.

My secret weapons with *MWD* were my sisters-in-law, Laura Kleinman and Shade Whitesel.

Laura is a social worker who has counseled female veterans with PTSD. She made me aware of the unique complications women face in serving their country, the complex (and sometimes deadly) sexual politics they must navigate and the scars they can bear as a result.

My sister-in-law Shade was another guardian angel. She trains German shepherds in the Schutzhund school of dog training. Not only was watching her training videos essential to this book, but her dog Ender served as the inspiration for our dog in the book.

MWD started off as a movie script. By the time we finished our first true draft, Jan and I had wandered so far afield from our original concept that the story looked more like *Born on the Fourth of July* than a meditative treatise on PTSD. As we tried to find a path to get the film made, we experimented with so many ideas that I lost track of the manuscript's many incarnations.

Throughout the process, Jan kept me on track and continuing to improve the story. We fought a lot over the years, but his dedication to keeping this project alive is a lesson in persistence. He fought for the characters as if they were his own children. He pushed me out of my comfort zone and was never afraid to propose an idea that might have at first seemed implausible but would eventually turn into something great.

It's important to note that our editors at Candlewick, Deborah Noyes and Katie Cunningham, were instrumental in this process. They saw through the big, bulky screenplay we gave them and helped us strip it away to its barest of bones. Once we tore the original story down to the studs, what we found was simple, elegant, and more poignant than I could have ever imagined.

Finally, I want to thank my family. My wife, Bess, is a constant source of strength, and our children — Max, who is my inspiration to be a better man, and our daughter, Frankie — make my life worth living. Thanks to my mom, Pam Rossi, and my stepfather, Chris Tsouros, who fostered my writing from childhood, and my brothers and sister, who always have my back. A special thanks to my brother Eric, an illustrator, who often counseled me during freakouts over the book.

Brian David Johnson

I am grateful to have had the opportunity to illustrate Liz's story and introduce readers to this young woman's experience of physical, psychological, and sexual trauma and her missteps along the journey to healing. It is imperative to share a narrative like this, fictional though it is, to strengthen our acceptance of women's real-life experiences and incorporate them into our judgments of how to improve the world around us.

Thank you to everyone who helped me along the way, and especially thank you to Jason.

Laila Milevski

I would like to thank my models, Alex, Angela, Shea, Brent, Josh, and Jamie, for their wonderful patience and support.

Karl Stevens

For Bess, Max, and Frankie
B. D. J.

For Jason
L. M.

For Alex
K. S.

Text copyright © 2017 by Brian David Johnson and Jan Egleson
Illustrations on pages 32–156 copyright © 2017 by Laila Milevski
Illustrations on pages 2–31, 157 copyright © 2017 by Karl Stevens

First edition 2017

Library of Congress Catalog Card Number 2013955956
ISBN 978-0-7636-5706-2

16 17 18 19 20 21 TLF 10 9 8 7 6 5 4 3 2 1

Printed in Dongguan, Guangdong, China

This book was typeset in WPGKarlStevens.
Laila Milevski's illustrations were done in ink wash and graphite.
Karl Stevens's illustrations were done in pen and ink with watercolor washes.

Candlewick Press
99 Dover Street
Somerville, Massachusetts 02144

visit us at www.candlewick.com